My plan to fulfill #3 on my To-Do list, Go on a Date:

> **PRODIGY SEEKS GENIUS**—SWF, 19, very smart, seeks nonsmoking, nondrug-doing very very smart SM 18-25 to talk about philosophy and life. No hypocrites, religious freaks, macho men or psychos.

I can't wait to see the responses I get.

* * *

Carrie Pilby

Caren Lissner

HARLEQUIN®
TEEN

HARLEQUIN®
TEEN

ISBN-13: 978-0-373-21010-7

CARRIE PILBY

Copyright © 2010 by Caren Lissner.

Originally published June 2003 by Red Dress Ink.

Excerpt from *Infinite Jest*, by David Foster Wallace, reprinted with
permission of Little, Brown and Company. Copyright © 1996.

Dictionary definitions from *Webster's II New Riverside University
Dictionary*. Copyright © 1994 by Houghton Mifflin Company. Adapted and
reproduced by permission.

HAPPY MOTORING, PUT A TIGER IN YOUR TANK and ESSOLENE are
trademarks of Exxon Mobil Corporation.

This is a work of fiction. Names, characters, places and incidents are
either the product of the author's imagination or are used fictitiously,
and any resemblance to actual persons, living or dead, business
establishments, events or locales is entirely coincidental.

This edition published by arrangement with Harlequin Books S.A.

For questions and comments about the quality of this book
please contact us at Customer_eCare@Harlequin.ca.

www.HarlequinTEEN.com

Printed in U.S.A.

Chapter One

Grocery stores always give me a bag when I don't need one, when I've bought just a pack of gum or a banana or some potato chips that are in a bag already, and then I feel guilty about their wasting the plastic, but the bag is on before I've noticed them reaching for it so I don't say anything. But in the video store, on the other hand, they always ask if I want a bag, and even though, theoretically, I should be able to carry my DVD without a bag, and the bag is another waste of plastic, I always need a bag at the video store because, for reasons that will soon be understood, I believe all DVDs should be sheathed.

The camouflage doesn't work today. I'm only half a block out of the store when I see Ronald, the rice-haired Milquetoast who works at the coffee shop around the corner, approaching. "Hey, Carrie," he says, looking down at my DVD. "What'd you get?"

Uh-oh. I have to give this speech again.

"I can't tell you," I say, "and there's a reason I can't. Someday, I might want to rent something embarrassing, and I don't necessarily mean porn. It could be a movie that's considered too childish for my age or something violent or maybe Nazi propaganda—for research purposes, of course—and even though the movie I have in my hand is considered a classic, and nothing to be ashamed of, if I show it to you this time but next time I can't, then you'll know for sure that I'm hiding something next time. But if I never tell you what I've rented, it puts enough doubt in your mind that I'm hiding something, so I can feel free to rent porn or cartoons or fascist propaganda or whatever I want without fear of having to reveal what I've rented. The same goes for what I'm reading. I want to be able to pick a mindless novel, as well as Dostoyevsky. And I also want to be able to choose something no one's heard of. Most of the time, people say, 'What are you reading?' and if I tell them the name of the book and it's not Moby Dick, they've never heard of it so I have to give an explanation, and if the book's any good it's not something I can explain in two seconds, so I'm stuck giving a twenty-five-page dissertation and by the time I'm done I have no time to finish reading. So books I read and movies I rent are off-limits for discussion. It's nothing personal."

Ronald stands there blinking for a second, then leaves.

My rules make perfect sense to me, but people find them strange. Still, I need them to survive. This world isn't one I understand completely, and it doesn't understand me completely, either. People think I'm odd for a nineteen-year-old girl—or woman, if you're technical—that I neither act excessively young nor excessively "girlish."

In truth, I feel asexual a lot of the time, like a walking brain with glasses and long dark hair and a mouth in good working order. If we were to talk about sex as in sex, as opposed to gender—as everyone seems to want to these days—I would say that my mind's not on sex that much, and I was never boy-crazy when I was younger. Which makes me different from just about everyone. I did have crushes on two of my professors in college, one of which actually turned into something, but that's a story for later on. That whole saga only confused me in the end. So much of the world is sex-obsessed that it takes someone practically asexual to realize just how extreme and pervasive it is. It's the main motivator of people's activities, the pith of their jokes and the driving force behind their art, and if you don't have the same level of drive, you almost question whether you should exist. If it's sex that makes the world go around, should the world stop for those of us who are asexual?

I graduated from college a year ago, three years ahead of my peers, and now I spend most of my time inside my apartment in the city. My father pays my rent. I could leave the house more, and I could even get a job, but I don't have much motivation to. My father would like me to work, but he has no right to complain. I remind him that it was his idea to skip me three grades in grammar school, forever putting me at the top of my class academically, in the bottom fifth heightwise, and in the bottom twenty-second socially.

My father is also the one who told me what I refer to as the Big Lie. But that, like all the business with my professor, is a story for later on.

When I get back to my apartment building, Bobby, the superintendent, asks how I'm doing, then takes the opportunity to stare at my rear end. I ignore him and climb the front steps. Bobby's always staring at my rear end. He is also too old to be named Bobby. There are some names that a person should retire after age twelve. Sally, for example. If Sally is your name, you should have it changed upon reaching puberty. Grown men should not be called Joey, Bobby, Billy, Jamie or Jimmy. They can be Harry until the age of ten and after fifty, but not between. They can be Mike, Joe and Jim all their lives. They cannot be Bob during their teenage years. They can be Stuart, Stefan or Jonathan if they're gay. Christian is not acceptable for Jews. Moishe is not acceptable for Christians. Herbert is not acceptable for anyone. Buddy is good for a beagle. Matt is good for a flat piece of rubber. Fox is good for a fox. Dylan is too trendy.

I get in through the front door and the stairwell door and the apartment door. When I am finally inside, I experience tremendous afterglow. They make the apartments in New York as hard to get into as Tylenol bottles and almost as big.

I see a therapist, Dr. Petrov, once a week. He and my father grew up in London together. I don't really need to see him, but I go each week because I might as well get my father's money's worth.

The morning after I rent the DVD, I leave my apartment to see Petrov. It's drizzling softly outside. The air, a soupy mess, scrubs my cheeks, and the few remaining leaves on the trees bend under the weight of raindrops and dive to their deaths. A pothole in front of my building catches them, emitting a soggy symphony.

There's something I love about visiting Petrov: His building is on one of those quaint little blocks that almost make you forget how seedy other parts of New York can be. Both sides are lined with stately brownstones whose bright painted shutters flank lively flower boxes, the tendrils dripping down and hooking around wires and trellises. The signs on the sidewalk are extremely polite: Please Curb Your Dog; $500 Fine For Noise Here. It's idyllic and lovely. But the only people who get to live here are the folks who inherited these rent-controlled apartments from their rich old grandmas who wore tons of jewelry and played tennis with Robert Moses.

Petrov's waiting room is like a cozy living room, with a gold-colored trodden carpet and regal-footed chairs. One wall is lined with classic novels, a pointless feature since one does not have the time to read Ulysses while waiting for a doctor's appointment. A person would have to make more than 300 visits to Petrov in order to finish the book, which just proves that someone would have to be crazy to read all of Ulysses. But a waiting room is not the proper place or situation to read any book. All books have a time and a place. Anything by Henry Miller, for instance, should be read where no one can see you. Carson McCullers should be read in your window on a hot summer night. Sylvia Plath should be read if you're ready to commit suicide or want people to think you're really close.

On Petrov's coffee table, there's more literature: the L.L. Bean catalogue, Psychology Today, the Eddie Bauer catalogue, the Pfizer annual stockholders' report. I admire Petrov's ability to incorporate his junk mail into his profession.

The door to Petrov's office opens, and a short guy walks out, lowering his eyes as he hurries past me. No one I've ever passed coming into this office has made eye contact with me, as if it's embarrassing to be caught coming from a therapy appointment by someone who is about to do exactly the same thing.

Petrov stands in his doorway. "How are you doing today, Carrie?" he asks, waving me inside. There are books piled high on his desk and diplomas on the wall. Petrov sits down in a red chair and balances a yellow legal pad on his knee. I sink into the reclining chair opposite him.

"I'm fine."

"Did you make any new friends this week?"

I think my father put this theme into his head. I don't have many friends, but there's a good reason for this, which I'll explain in the near future.

"It rained this week," I tell him, "so mostly I stayed inside."

Petrov's hand flutters across the page. What could he be writing? It did rain all week.

"So you haven't been outside your apartment much. What about this coming week? Do you have any social plans?"

"I have a job interview today," I say. "Right after this appointment."

"That's wonderful!" he says. "What kind of job?"

"I don't know," I say. "The interview's with some guy my dad knows. I'm sure it'll be mindless and pointless."

"Perhaps by going in thinking that, you'll cause it to be so."

"If you're trying to say it could become a self-fulfilling prophecy, that's psychobabble," I say. "If I tell you that the job might turn out to be mindless, then it might, or it might not. The outcome really has no relationship to whether I've said it."

"It might," Petrov says. "You put the suggestion out there." He leans back in his chair. "I think you often thwart yourself. Let's look at how you do it with friendships. Whenever you have met someone, you then tell me that the person was unintelligent or a hypocrite. Perhaps you have too narrow a definition of smart or too wide a one for hypocrite. There are some people who are very street-smart."

"You can't have an intelligent discussion with street smarts," I say. "And even if I could find other people who are smart, they'd probably still be hypocritical and dishonest."

It's true. I went to college with a lot of supposedly smart people, and they'd rationalize the stupid, dangerous or hypocritical things they did all the time: getting drunk, having sex with lots of different people, trying drugs. Nobody did any of that in the beginning of school, but once the temptation started, my classmates got sucked in, then began making excuses for it. Even the self-possessed religious kids came up with ridiculous rationalizations. If they want to believe in certain things, fine, and if they don't want to, that's fine, too, but they shouldn't lie to themselves about their reasons for changing their minds. The hypocrisy isn't any better out of school, especially in the city.

"I want you to tell me something positive right now," Petrov says. "About anything. Tell me something you love. As in, 'I love a sunset.' 'I love Miami Beach.'"

"I love it when people sound like Hallmark cards."

Petrov sighs. "Try harder."

"Okay." I think about it a bit. "I love peace and quiet."

He looks at me. "Go on."

"I guess you missed the point."

He sighs again. "Give me another example."

"I love…when I can just stretch out in my bed, hearing no horns, no chatter, no TV, nothing but the buzz of the electrical wiring in the wall. But sometimes I like the sounds from the street."

"I like that," Petrov says. "Now, tell me something that makes you sad. Something besides hypocrites and people who aren't smart. Tell me about a time recently when you cried."

I think. "I haven't cried in a long time."

"I know."

I hate when Petrov thinks he knows things about me without my telling him. "How do you know?"

"Because you're guarded. Because you were put into college at fifteen, when everyone was three to seven years older than you, and at fifteen, you weren't socially advanced or sexually aware. All kinds of behavior goes on at college, people drinking, losing their virginity right and left, experimenting with who knows what. Some people respond by trying to fit in, but you chose to opt out of the system completely. Which was understandable. But now, you've been out of college a year and you're still not experienced in adjusting to social changes. Being smart doesn't mean being skilled at social interaction. No one ever said being a genius was easy."

I hear it start to rain harder outside. Petrov gets up, shuts the window and sits back down.

"You've mentioned your father's Big Lie a few times," he says. "I think we should talk about that sometime."

"Yes—"

"But not today. I have an assignment for you."

I look at the rug. It's full of tiny ropes and filaments.

"I want you to, just for a little while, be a little more social. Just to see the other side of it, to determine if there is such thing as a comfortable middle ground. I don't want you to do anything dangerous or immoral, but I want you to do things like go to a party, join an organization or club. After you do some of these things, I want you to tell me how you felt doing them. You don't have to start right away. You can wait a bit until you feel comfortable."

"Okay. How about next year?"

Petrov smiles. "That's not a bad idea," he says. "New Year's Eve would be a good night for you to spend time with friends. You could go to a New Year's Eve party."

"Maybe I should just vomit on Times Square," I say. "Then I'd be fitting in."

Petrov shakes his head. "You know I'm not suggesting you do anything dangerous. But I do want you to learn to socialize better. What you should do is work up to spending New Year's Eve with people. We'll start small first. A five-point plan."

Petrov grabs a memo cube that has Zoloft embossed at the top. Some people will take anything if it's free.

"First," he says, "I want you to write a list for me of ten things you love. The street sounds were a good start, but I want ten of them. Secondly, I want you to join at least one organization or

club. That way, you might meet some people with similar interests, maybe even people you think are smart." He's writing this
down. "Third, go on a date…"

"Okay…"

"Fourth, I want you to tell someone you really care about
him or her. It can't be sarcastic."

"Sarcastic? Me?"

Petrov tears off a piece of paper and hands it to me.

ZOLOFT®

1. List 10 things you love
2. Join an org./club
3. Go on date
4. Tell someone you care
5. Celebrate New Yr's

"The point's to help you adjust," he says. "Not to teach you
to do anything bad. But to help you see that there could be positive aspects of social interaction."

"I wouldn't have such trouble adjusting to the world," I say,
"if the world made sense. Which it doesn't. I've seen that time
and time again. Maybe the world should adjust to me."

"Just try," he pleads. "When you meet someone new, for
instance, don't…"

"What?"

"Don't pontificate." He scratches his goatee. "Don't feel the
need to show off everything you know at the same time, or
make every argument that's in your head."

"If I'm not comfortable saying what I'm thinking, then isn't
the person wrong for me? And if they don't like me, isn't it better I find out sooner? Besides, if I say what I believe, this way
we find out right away if we're compatible."

He blinks for a minute. "It's good to meet compatible people,
but you don't have to hit them with tests all at once."

I shrug. "I'll think about it."

He nods. "Just try."

When I get outside, I pull my coat over my head to ward off the pouring rain, and I run to the subway. I am dying to get home, slide under the sheets and doze off. But I can't. I have a job interview.

As I get close to the subway, a guy in a raincoat seethes at me, "Smile!"

This makes me feel worse. I was lost in thought, minding my own business, and someone felt he had the right to disturb me anyway. Doesn't he realize that by making me feel like I was doing something wrong, he only made me feel less like smiling? It actually had the reverse effect he intended. It's like striking a bawling kid to stop him from crying, and we've all seen that done.

I don't see what it had to do with him anyway. I never go around demanding that people change their facial expressions. How come everyone tells me what to do, but they would never let me do a tenth of the same back to them?

The café where I am to meet Brad Nickerson is two stops up. When I arrive, he's already seated at a table. He's got slicked-back blond hair and a nondescript face. He's also younger than I expected, and I'm not so sure this isn't secretly a blind date rather than a business meeting.

He stands and smiles.

"It's good to meet you," he says.

"Likewise."

We both sit down. He lets one of his legs hang over the other—he has long legs—and he briefly asks me how my trip up there went. Then he turns his attention to a clipboard. "I'm just going to ask you a few questions about your qualifications."

"All right."

"Your father says you type," he says.

"I have."

"Which computers do you use?"

"In school I used Macs, Dells, Gateways, HP's, most of the off-brand PC's, and all of the Mac and Windows operating systems. I wish they were more compatible. If Europe accepted the Euro, why can't our computers be a little more compatible?"

His eyes narrow. "How old did you say you were?" he asks.

"I'm nineteen."

"You seem awfully serious for a nineteen-year-old."

I don't know what to say to that. Now I feel bad, just like I felt when the guy yelled "Smile." As if I was doing something wrong simply by existing.

Brad doesn't say anything either, only stares at me and waits. And waits. When they send people to do job interviews, they should at least make sure they're half as competent as the people they're interviewing.

"You could tell me what the job's about," I say.

"Oh!" he says. "Well, it would be, at first, sort of an administrative assistant to the boss, typing things when need be, helping with office work. But eventually it could lead to greater responsibilities." He picks up his coffee cup. "How does that sound?"

I don't suppose he really wants a truthful answer. "Ducky," I say.

"Mmm-hmm." He sips his coffee. "Mmm." He thinks for a second. "Well, why don't you tell me your strengths and weaknesses?"

A relevant question, at last! I say, "I try to figure out what's right and wrong, and then I stick by it. I don't engage in activities that are dangerous to others or myself. I try not to make judgments about people."

"I wasn't making a judgment about you," he says, apropos of nothing.

"I didn't say you were."

We're stuck in a stalemate again. He reverts to common ground.

"How fast do you type?"

"Sixty to sixty-five words a minute," I say.

He doesn't add anything.

I ask, "Would you like that in metric?"

He shrugs. "Sure."

"Sixty to sixty-five words a minute."

I smile, but apparently, this doesn't pass muster as a satisfactory attempt to prove I'm not so serious. He finishes his coffee. "Well," he says, standing and smiling, "it really was nice to meet you. We'll probably give you a call."

"Great," I say, but I'm really complimenting his discretion in bringing the matter to a close.

When I'm finally home, I'm incredibly relieved. Thank God I'm out of there.

I close my bedroom door, drop my purse to the ground and strip off my moist clothes. My pants leave a red elastic mark all the way around my waist. I rub it to obliterate it. Then I drape my clothes over a chair and walk to my bed.

Now I can engage in my favorite activity in the world.

Sleeping.

My bed is a vast ocean with three fat, starchy pillows. Slowly I slide under the covers, naked. I feel the cool sheets around me. The cotton caresses my back. I close my eyes and let each notch of my spine relax.

My mind is blank now. Every part of my body is sinking and empty. I don't have to think about anything, hear anything, say anything, feel anything, worry about anything. Everything is distilled until it is completely clear.

The roof may rain down and shower me with concrete. The forked crack in my wall may creep all the way to the ceiling. Still, I can lie here forever if I choose. There is no one to stop me.

In my bed, there are no psychologists, no job interviewers, no hypocrites. I do not have to make up lists of ways to socialize. I do not have to smile. I do not have to justify my beliefs. I don't have to wear dress shoes. I don't have to pledge allegiance to the flag. I don't have to use a number two pencil. I don't have to read the fine print. I don't have to sell fifty boxes of mint cookies. I don't have to be over five foot four to ride.

It is true that lying in bed is not an intellectual activity. It is true that it is nonproductive.

But when ninety-five percent of out-of-bed activities hold the possibility of pain, to be pain-free is simply the most delicious feeling in the world.

I lie there for an hour, listening to the rain type a soggy message on my windows. When the storm has subsided a bit, I lift my head.

A hint of a cherry scent curls under my nose. I don't know where it's coming from—maybe through the window. The scent reminds me of cherry soda, something I haven't had in years. I think about its virulent fizz, the way it bubbles deep in one's gut.

I picture a giant glass, dark plumes of liquid bouncing off the sides. I recall a New Year's party my father threw when I was young, how black cherry soda was what we kids were allowed to have while the adults downed highballs. There was a kid named Ted there, and he dropped M&M's and corn chips and peanuts into his cherry soda to make us cringe. He got so much attention from the threat of drinking it that I don't think he actually had to do the deed.

I grab a notebook from on top of my stereo and start writing my "things I love" list for Dr. Petrov. Soon, I actually have managed to come up with a few.

1. Cherry soda
2. Street sounds
3. My bed

The best bed I ever had was one with a powder-blue canopy when I was eight. My room was great back then. It had a black shag rug, Parcheesi, a giant periodic table of the elements, a diagram of Hegel's dialectic, a model solar system, a couple of abstract paintings, and a sextant.

4. The green-blue hue of an indoor pool
5. Starfish
6. The Victorians
7. Rainbow sprinkles
8. Rain during the day (makes it easier to sleep)

I think a little more. I'm out of ideas.
If I could write a hate list, I could fill three notebooks.
That would be fun. A list of things I hate.
I could start with the couple across the street.
The couple across the street are in their late twenties or early thirties. They're tall and fairly professional-looking. I see them in their kitchen window more than I do outside. They always mess around in front of the oven, pinching and poking each other, and before you know it, there's a little free-love show going on,

and finally, they repair to a different room. You'd think they'd have enough respect for their neighbors to keep us out of their delirious debauchery. But that's not the reason I hate them.

The reason I hate them is that whenever they pass me on the street, they never say hi to me. They must know I'm their neighbor. I've lived here for almost a year.

Then again, I never say hi to them.

I try for a little while longer, but I can't come up with nine and ten for my list. I put the notebook down and lie in bed on my side, my hands crossed over each other like the paws of a Great Dane.

I think about Petrov's five-point plan. Join an organization. Go on a date. Petrov must think that I'm incapable of these things. It's not at all that I can't do them. It's that I choose not to.

Sure, being alone can get boring, but why should I have to force myself to go out and meet all the people who have lowered their moral, ethical and intellectual standards in order to fit in with all of the other people with low moral, ethical and intellectual standards? That's all I would find if I went out there.

I could prove to Petrov that he's wrong. I could show him that the problem is not with me, but with everyone else. I could do it just to prove how ridiculous it is.

Going on a date, or joining a club, will push me right into the thick of the social situations that people get into every day. I'm sure it can't be that hard. And even if Petrov believes there is the .0001 percent chance that I'll meet one person who understands me, more likely, I will simply be able to say that I tried.

It will be a pain, but it shouldn't be that difficult. I will be a spy in the house of socializers. And then I will be able to prove once again to myself, as well as to Petrov, that even when I'm alone, it's much better than going outside.

★ ★ ★

That evening the phone rings. It could be bad news. It could be my father calling to say I didn't get the job. Or worse, it could be my father calling to say I got the job. But it also could be the MacArthur Committee calling to tell me I've won the Genius Grant. I jump up and catch it on the third ring.

It's my father.

"I spoke with Brad," he says. "He seemed to think you weren't that interested in the job."

"Oh, now I remember," I say. "The vapid, immature guy."

"I got the feeling you weren't very nice to him."

"I didn't ask for the interview."

"You have to tell me how, at some point, you are going to support yourself."

"Right now I'm using a Sealy Posturepedic."

"Carrie."

"I saw Dr. Petrov this morning."

This seems to cheer him up. "Okay. And what did he say?"

"He wants me to do some kind of socialization experiment. Go on a date. Join a club."

"And what did you say?"

"I said I'll try."

"That's what I like to hear."

"You know, you owe me," I say.

"Why?"

"You know why."

Silence.

He knows I mean the Big Lie.

"I know," he says.

"Good."

"Well, if there was a job you might be interested in, what would it be?"

"Something where I can use my intelligence," I say. "Something where the hours aren't ridiculous. Something where I can sleep while others are awake and be awake while others are asleep. Something where people aren't condescending...."

"Yes...."

"Something I don't hate."

Chapter Two

"You ever been here before?"

"No."

The woman behind the desk peers at me through small round glasses. I don't know what her problem is. Everyone in this office has, at some point, never been there before.

She gives me three forms to fill out, including a W-4 and a confidentiality pledge, and this wastes twenty minutes. If only the rest of the job is like this.

She hands me two hulking toothpaste-white stacks of paper. "The lawyers need you to compare them word for word," she says. "A full read. It could take a few hours."

Dad has gotten me work legal proofreading, which he says pays well and can be sporadic. I can work night or day. I'm smarter than ninety-nine percent of lawyers, so it should be easy.

I reach my cubicle, which has a drawerless desk. This is even lower in the office furniture hierarchy than a drafting table. Behind me, an old guy in squarish glasses is reading two documents, his eyes swinging from one to the other.

He looks a little too old for me to consider him for a possible date. But who knows? He's bald and unthreatening-looking. Maybe I can figure out how to flirt with him enough to lure him to dinner, and then I'll be satisfying Petrov's requirement. That would leave me with three requirements to go.

I look over my desk. It's rife with supplies. Someone has taken a long piece of yellow legal paper and colored in every other stripe with a red Flair pen, and then completely filled in the remaining stripes with Wite-Out. And that person has also drawn a box in the left-hand corner with blue ink. It's some sort of flag. It must have taken a good half hour to do.

A supervisor comes in to further explain my task. The first document I have to look at is an original. The second document is a version they got by scanning in the first one and printing it out. But sometimes, when they scan documents in, the new copies that they print out accidentally have extra commas or extra letters in them, due to dirt on the scanner, marks on the original document, or something else.

So my job is to compare the original and the printout word for word, making sure they're exactly the same. I am supposed to do this for 210 pages.

It seems like there must be a faster way to do this sort of labor in this era of technological advances. No wonder lawyers charge $400 an hour. They're paying proofreaders to sit and play Concentration.

I lean back in the hard chair and close my eyes. Within a minute, I have my answer. But I can't use my easier system until Oldie behind me goes to get coffee. Which, I soon find out, he does every ten minutes. And it takes him ten minutes to do it. My father thinks I don't want to work, but the truth is, no one else is really working. It's all a big sham. No one says anything about it because they're doing it, too. If all of the BS-ing was automatically extracted from the American workday, the American workday would last three hours. There are still tons of secrets in the world to which I am only just becoming privy.

While Oldie is gone, I take the top page of my original, put it in front of the top page of the new copy, and hold them both up to the light. They match exactly: not a line, word or dot out of place. So these pages are fine. I put them both down and move on to the next pair. I hold them up to the light, and there's not a stray line, streak or speck. This probably takes two percent of the time it would take to read the whole thing.

When I finish, I leave the document a third of the way open on my desk so it looks like I'm in the process.

I use my extra time to think about a lot of things.

I think about why, if the highest speed limit anywhere in the U.S. is seventy-five, they sell cars that can go up to one hundred fifty.

I think about whether the liquid inside a coconut should be called "milk" or "juice."

I think about why there are Penn Stations in New York and Maryland but not in Pennsylvania.

I think about Michel Foucault's views of the panoptic modality of power, and whether they're comprehensive enough and ever could be.

Behind me, Oldie picks up the phone and taps at the buttons. He asks for someone named Edna. On the one percent chance this won't be completely boring, I eavesdrop.

"Oh, I know what I wanted to tell you," he says. "I called Jackie this morning, but she wasn't there, but Raymond was. So Raymond tells me he's home because he has all this sick leave saved up, you know, because teachers are allowed to accumulate their sick days, and so this is the third Friday in a row he's taken off from school, and he was getting ready to go over to the

Poconos to ski. He was practically bragging about it. And I say to him, 'Raymond, that's lying. Sick days are if you're sick.' Yeah, he's cheating the kids. I know. I know. So he backs off and says, 'Well, I only do it once in a while.' And I say, 'Raymond, excuse me, but you just said you did it three Fridays in a row, so don't back off now.' Do you know why our daughter married someone like that? He's amazing, bragging like that. Amazing. I know. I said to him, 'Work ethics like yours are why America's going to pot. Because everyone tries to get away with everything.'"

Eventually, the guy hangs up.

I have to turn around.

"Excuse me," I say. "I couldn't help overhearing. You're annoyed because your son-in-law was goofing off. But you were just having a personal conversation on the phone for twenty minutes when you were supposed to be doing your proofreading. Isn't this a little hypocritical?"

There is nothing more fulfilling than watching people get caught in the thick, coarse gossamer of their own hypocrisy.

Oldie is stunned. "We're entitled to breaks," he says, but his voice is quavering.

"I'll take that as a yes."

Oldie sniffs, "I don't see why it's any of your business," and returns to his assignment.

There are no new assignments, so I rest my eyes and sit back in my chair. I hear a fax machine whirr behind me, and the choppy sounds of someone's discordant clock radio. Soon a young guy with dark, tufty hair pokes his head into the room. He looks around but apparently doesn't see whom he had hoped to. He's ready to retreat, but then he notices me. "Oh," he says. "Hi. You a student?"

"No," I say. "I graduated. I'm a temp." I'm barely able to hide my elation at the diversion. Oldie gives us both a sneer.

"You just in for tonight?"

"Far as I know."

He extends his hand. "Douglas P. Winters. Front desk dude." He sniffs and wipes his nose with his arm. There's something appealing about ending your sentences with a snort. I also get the feeling he's smart and slumming. I can spot an underemployed lazy intellectual anywhere.

"Carrie Pilby," I say.

"You here till morning?"

"I guess so."

"So you said you graduated. Where'd you go to school?"

This is always a dilemma. Everyone who went to Harvard has it. The problem is, if you say Harvard, it either sounds like you're bragging, or conversely, people think you're making a joke. A lot of Harvard graduates say "Boston," and then when the other person asks where specifically, they say, "Cambridge," and finally, if pressed again, they admit where they went.

I decide to get it over with. "Harvard."

"For real?"

I nod.

"Say something smart."

This is another disincentive. It's like finding out someone's part Puerto Rican and saying, "Say something in Spanish." Just because I went to a top college doesn't mean I have a complex mathematical axiom on the tip of my tongue. I mean, I do, but it's not because of where I went to college.

But I decide to play along. "I think that the influence of Kierkegaard on Camus is underestimated. I believe Hobbes is just Rousseau in a dark mirror. I believe, with Hegel, that transcendence is absorption."

Doug stands there for a second. "Wow."

I don't tell him that I stole the whole thing from David Foster

Wallace's Infinite Jest, which I read one day when I had three hours to kill.

Oldie looks back at both of us. "You two gonna do any work tonight?"

"Why don't you call 60 Minutes and rat out your son-in-law?" I ask. He sniffs and goes back to his work.

"Come outside," Doug says. "I'm out front."

I assume this means that if I get in trouble, I can blame him. I follow him through the glass doors into the waiting room, which has plush chairs and golden letters on the walls bearing the name of the firm. Fancy-schmancy. Doug motions to an armchair next to the security desk, and I sit by his side. "Are you looking for a regular job?"

"Someday." This conversation has gone on long enough without my knowing what's important. "Where did you go to school?"

"Hempstead State," he says. Oh well. I guess he's not so smart after all. Then again, maybe I'm judging too quickly. At least, Petrov thinks I do. "I didn't feel like going to Harvard," he adds, opening a bag of pistachios and pouring a few onto the table.

"Right."

"You got a boyfriend?"

I wonder if he's asking because he likes me, or he's just making fun of me because he knows no one would want to be my boyfriend. "No," I say.

He cracks a pistachio on the table, then opens it like a tulip. "You just kind of play the field?"

"Mostly, I sleep."

Doug laughs. "If I could, I would. Any time in bed is time well spent."

We're silent for a minute while he swallows his pistachio nut. Then he cracks another against the desk. "Did you know that pistachio nuts are like orgasms?"

That is so disgusting! I turn away and look at the paintings on the wall. I think they're Edward Hopper.

Doug pinches the green meat from inside the shell and pops it into his mouth. He chews, swallows and posits: "One nut will taste all salty, but the next one will taste almost buttery. The third one will be shriveled and brown with a weird kind of tartness. They're like sexual climaxes. Each one is completely different in its own way, but they're all great."

"Fascinating." I look away.

"Did I embarrass yew?" He laughs. "Here, I'm sorry. Have one."

I put my hand out.

"No. An orgasm."

I look up.

"Just kidding. Here." He hands me a nut. I can't believe he talks about something so intimate like it's as routine as brushing your teeth. I mumble a thank-you and return to my seat.

I spend the rest of the night reading Black's Law Dictionary until I can barely see straight. Now at least I can pepper my conversations with ex aequo et bono and de minimus non curat lex.

The shift ends when the first rays of dawn filter through the office's tinted windows, which I imagine were created to remove the only joy of working there—the view. There is a commotion as a group of workers leaves and another arrives. With all the gossiping, peeking at the newspaper headlines and getting coffee, this takes a half hour. I may have underestimated the amount of fakery that goes on in the workplace.

When one has been up all night, one gets a filmy taste in one's mouth and a bleariness in one's eyes. I wipe my lips and stand straight up, stretching. My bones ache.

I throw my backpack across my shoulder and head out into

the carpeted lobby. Doug and I shake hands, and I stretch some more. I guess I'll see him again if I return to the firm.

In the elevator, there's a guy holding a metal cart bursting with donuts. They smell delicious. Some are topped with a thick cairn of chocolate cream, some are glazed, some are powdered and jelly-filled, and some have a slab of strawberry frosting and sprinkles. Eating one would get rid of this taste in my mouth. But the donut guy gets off on the third floor. I continue to the bottom and step out into the sunshine.

It looks like today will be nicer than the last few. In the park, homeless people are emerging from boxes pushed together like trains. Cardboard condos. I wend my way past intricate metal stairways and under mélanges of scaffolding and torn advertisements for magazines, and sunlight bounces off glistening marble statues and embeds itself in glass doors. Hordes of commuters flood the streets in their gray and navy-blue uniforms, all of them walking—as is often the case—in the opposite direction of me.

On a corner, a balding, timid-looking guy is handing out something and yelling. Everyone brushes past him. He keeps trying to give them a yellow flyer, and they keep turning their heads away. I vow to take the flyer when he hands it to me. It must be awful to stand there all day being rejected. However, he only gives me a cursory glance and then hands a flyer to the person next to me.

I stand there, waiting.

Finally, he shyly says, "Oh," and thrusts one in my hand.

The First Prophets' Church, it says at the top, and there's a long explanation of how Joseph Natto, an Episcopalian minister, had a vision way back in 1998 that his preachings about the church were lacking in something. A list of ten rules suddenly appeared in his mind.

This is a real original story.

I look up, and Tonsure-Head is talking s-l-o-w-l-y to a Spanish woman who is staring at him wide-eyed as if the more she opens her eyes, the more she'll understand English. I've noticed that religious nuts always prey on foreigners. Anyone else would be too smart to fall for their fabrications. I'm tempted to go up and ask the guy why he only talks to people who don't have a good command of English. Lately, my life has been about saying exactly what's on my mind, particularly to people who need to change. Unfortunately, religious nuts are the one phylum that loves that. When they're challenged, a dreamy smile crosses their faces like a trail of footprints and they give an answer like, "Oh, you have to have faith, and once you accept [insert name of savior here] into your heart, you will understand." Then they'll surely tell you some story about how once, they were just like you, until they had their moment of inspiration and it changed their life forever.

The key to all religions is simply believing whatever they tell you and not allowing a scintilla of rational doubt to enter your mind. None of us was around 2,000 or 5,700 years ago (or 173.5 years if you're a Mormon—sorry, Mormons) to know what really happened, so people decide whose story to choose, and which steadfast principles to select, based upon such important criteria as what their parents forced them to believe growing up and what other relatives forced them to believe growing up. At least Mormons hold off on baptizing their kids until they're eight, but is an eight-year-old going to be any more resistant than a baby?

I keep watching Tonsure-Head speaking mas des-pac-i-o to the Spanish woman and I wait around to see if he'll try to convert me, too. That wouldn't be so bad, if he can give me good answers to my questions about religion. If he does that, I'll give him a chance. That's a big if.

Suddenly, a strange feeling wells up in me that I get once in a while. It feels hollow and icy, and it's right in my gut. It makes me want to warm myself up inside. I look at him and wonder if this religion is all he has. Who am I to make fun of it? Maybe it's something he loves. Maybe he's lonely.

Something else makes me sad, but I can't put my finger on it. Then, the feeling goes away in a few seconds. Good.

I keep waiting for Tonsure-Head to talk to me, but he ignores me. I wonder if he realizes that because he himself is not a minority, he himself would not be one of the people he would have reached out to on the street. How hypocritical.

I give up, take the flyer home, and tape it to the side of my protruding closet. It's got an address for the church on the bottom.

It's an organization, so if I join it, I can fulfill the second goal on Dr. Petrov's list. But if I go to one of their services, my real goal will be to infiltrate this organization and expose it as a cult. I don't want it taking advantage of people. I'll protect the gullible.

Several days later, I finally have the pleasure of bringing my top-ten list to Petrov. Even though it's really a top-eight list.

Before I can discuss it, though, Petrov asks me again if I've made any new friends. I tell him that I haven't, but to please him, I mention my conversation with Douglas P. Winters.

"Sounds like he might have been flirting with you," Petrov says.

"Eh."

"Are you interested?"

"He seemed a little…sex-obsessed."

Petrov sits back. "I know you think that most people are sex-obsessed," he says. "While I have no doubt that it's true in many cases, I would gather that if you were older, and if you had more sexual experience, it wouldn't seem as glaring."

Of course. Petrov thinks I'm a virgin. Everyone assumes that if you think the world is sex-obsessed, you must not have had sex. As if sex is so all-consuming that once you have it, you can completely justify the fact that it's scrolling through everyone's brain twenty-four hours a day. Plus, people think that, in general, if you express perfectly logical criticisms of the way society works, it means you're "uptight" and "need to get laid." As if sex is a cure for everything.

I haven't ever told Petrov about my experiences with Professor Harrison.

I guess it's true that, because of confidentiality rules, he wouldn't be allowed to tell my father, which is a plus. But I don't see why he has to know anyway. At least, not yet. I spent years in college not telling people about Harrison. I'm good at it.

"How do you know I'm not sexually experienced?" I ask.

"Are you?"

"I don't see how it's relevant to a discussion of whether other people are sex-obsessed. I can have opinions regardless of whether I, myself, have had sex."

"True," he says. "But it's hard to comment on what it's like to take a plane if you've never been off the ground. However, if you have had sexual experiences, and you want to discuss them…"

"Nope," I say. I decide that I'd better change the subject quickly—this time, anyway. "I thought about joining an organization last week."

"Really?" he says, interested.

I tell him about Tonsure-Head and the church, and how it might be a cult that should be exposed.

Petrov says, "You would have taken the flyer anyway."

"What do you mean?"

"Even if you didn't want to expose the church as a cult, you would have taken the religious flyer anyway. You would have taken the flyer for the same reason you keep coming to see me even though you say you don't need to."

Oh, won't he please enlighten me about my very own secret motivations for every single thing I do, which I'm sure he has a brilliant theory to explain? "I come here to get my father's money's worth," I say.

Petrov says, "You come here to talk to me. I'm paid to listen. Maybe you're insecure and think other people won't listen to you. But I do. If you really wanted to stop coming here, you'd refuse to. But you come, just like you took the religious flyer. What are you doing?"

"Looking at your clock," I say. "I never noticed it before. You have it strategically placed up on the shelf behind my head, so that when you look at it to see how much time we have left, I'll think you're looking at me. And it's a big clock. I guess you wouldn't want people to go a second over."

"It's not entirely selfish," he says. "If a patient runs over the time, it backs up all my other patients."

"I always kind of wondered what you do if someone's in the middle of a big important story about himself, and his time's up," I say. "Do you suddenly say, 'Hold that suicidal thought until next week?'"

"I try not to get into anything too heavy in the last few minutes of the session."

"Oh, well, that's cheating. If only forty minutes of a forty-five-minute session can be dedicated to serious talk, you're gypping people out of five minutes."

"Carrie," Petrov says, "we're here to talk about you."

"Well, if I talk about you, it brings me out of my shell."

"Ah," Petrov says. "It does?"

"No. I just figured you'd like that. Some self-analysis. Deflecting things to you helps me. I thought you'd like the hypothesis."

Petrov sighs. "Did you bring your list of ten things you love?"

I pull it out and hand it to him. "Yes, but it's a top-eight list."

"You always have to be the contrarian."

"No, I don't. Ha ha. Get it?"

1. Cherry soda
2. Street sounds
3. My bed
4. The green-blue hue of an indoor pool
5. Starfish
6. The Victorians
7. Rainbow sprinkles
8. Rain during the day (makes it easier to sleep)

"Tell me," he says. "When's the last time you had a cherry soda?"

I think. "Not since I was little."

"What about rainbow sprinkles? When was the last time you had them?"

By the shore, maybe. Dad and I used to get vanilla soft-serve ice cream in those airy flat-bottomed beige cones. "Not since I was a kid, again."

"But they're in your top eight favorite things."

"I guess I just haven't made them a priority."

"I think," Petrov says, "that part of the reason for your depression is that you deny yourself things, or you don't seek out the things that make you truly happy. Not everything has to have analysis behind it. Why not just enjoy yourself without thinking sometimes?"

"So when did we decide that I was depressed? Neither of us has ever mentioned the term. We've talked about how the world is full of hypocrites, how a lot of people aren't that smart or don't talk about things that actually matter, and last time, you said you understood that I was younger than everyone else in college and that might have made things harder for me. But now all of a sudden I'm depressed. Did your friend Eli Lilly just ship you a free eight ball of Prozac?"

He looks beaten. "I shouldn't be so quick to label. But I think you'd be happier, and more at peace with the world, if you sought out things you enjoyed. Sitting home all the time can't make you too happy. When you were in school, you moved ahead by taking tests and getting good grades, and you certainly could feel yourself progressing that way. But now that you're out of school, I think you're in a bit of a holding pattern. If you did more activities related to things you loved, you probably would meet like-minded people and move forward with meaningful friendships and relationships. That's why I thought it would be good for you to join an organization."

"Should I go find a cherry-soda club?"

"Let's add a Part B to the first part of your assignment," Petrov says. "The first part was to write a list of things you love. Now, for 1B, go out and do some of them. Get an ice-cream cone with rainbow sprinkles. Go to the store and buy cherry soda."

"Okay."

He looks at my list again.

"You also mention sleep, and you mention rain."

"Sleeping in the rain," I say. "I'll get on that right away."

"Good."

He is so oblivious.

When I get home, my hand immediately shoots into my mailbox, which I love almost as much as my bed. I subscribe to fourteen magazines, and just seeing the cavalcade of colors in my box fills me with joy. But what's more, each day brings the potential for new surprises. This is the kind of hope that keeps me going when nothing else does. Maybe the MacArthur Genius Grant notice will come in the mail.

But today there's only something white and thin inside.

It's an actual letter—rare these days, in our e-mail driven society. It's in a fine white wove envelope, and my name and address are typed neatly in 10 pica that looks like it came from a typewriter and not a printer. It's from the dean's office at Harvard. I've finally gotten him to respond to my request, the rogue.

Dear Carrie:

Hope this finds you well and I am sorry it has taken me so long to respond to your letter. As always, I appreciate your concerns. However, as I mentioned during our conversation at your father's function last year, I don't see, as I didn't see then, a need for an honors program at Harvard. Even though you maintained in your letter that it is important to allow "the best of the best" at our school to interact, we believe that every student at Harvard is already the best of the best....

Bull. That's what I had thought before I'd arrived there. I thought everyone would be a genius and wouldn't look at me funny when, for example, I wanted to talk about philosophy or current events at a party or in the dorm lounge. Some of the kids were okay, but some would go "whoosh" and cut their hands above their heads when I said something they deemed too intellectual. I also met people whose test scores were much lower than mine, and some of them had rich alumni parents or played lacrosse or dived really well and that's probably why they got in. There were also plenty of beer-chuggers and bubbleheads and people who talked nonstop about sex, which one would think is odd for a school that everyone had to study like hell to get into, but I guess that's why their gonads exploded as soon as they got fifty miles from home. I thought that by having an honors program, the students at Harvard who were actually smart could be together.

On rare occasions, I did encounter smart people in school. Once in a while, I'd end up at a mixer with the other prodigies, and we'd discuss the difficulties of being fifteen in a sea of twenty-one-year-old drinkers and Lotharios. I felt a kinship with the others, but they soon grew to love seeing how much they could get away with, while I didn't.

That was around the point that Professor Harrison began to express a more-than-academic interest in me.

I fold Dean Nymczik's letter and balance it in the alley between my computer and printer. Dean Nymczik doesn't understand. Few people do. There are a great many people who believe themselves to be smart—in fact, I'd be hard-pressed to find someone who doesn't—but none of them are smart enough.

And this is my father's Big Lie.

The exact lie—let me see if I can remember it correctly—was this: "When you get to college, you'll meet people who are just like you."

He'd say, junior high is tough, high school is tough. In college, they'll be just like you.

Just wait until you get to college.

They were not. And they are not. I went through four years, and now I'm out. On the rare occasions I meet people now, I find that they consider snowboarding a cultural activity and that their main reading material is TV Guide. And I don't know how to respond to that.

So mostly I stay in bed.

Chapter Three

There's a good reason that I don't have any friends in the city. Most people's friends are people they met at college. And most people they became friends with at college are people they met freshman year. And most people they met freshman year, they met during the first few weeks of school.

I did start off with a few friends freshman year. My roommate, Janie, was my friend. But she dropped out of school in November. Another friend I had was a girl named Nora, who was a prodigy, like me. The week before the start of classes, they kept having receptions for prodigies. At one of them, I was standing by the window, staring outside and holding a cup of 7UP, and Nora came over to me. "You look bored," she said. "Do you know anyone here? I don't." Then she dragged me over to other groups of people and we stood next to them until we were included in the conversation. It took Nora only a little while to be the leader of the conversation. Unfortunately, the fact that she was so friendly meant she quickly became friendly with a lot of people. She started organizing all kinds of things, especially during the first few weeks of school. She'd get an idea for something to do, like walk around Boston or head to a movie, and she'd e-mail a bunch of people including me, and we'd meet up and go. But people like that never stay friends with me for long. They're so outgoing and loud and popular that they get swept away by people who are more like them. I shrink in that kind of competition. Nora contacted me less and less. I think she also got a boyfriend. I saw them on campus together. At first, even after we stopped doing things together, when Nora and I would pass each other around Harvard, we would wave to each other. After a while, we just nodded. After another while, we started pretending we didn't see each other. It's weird how once you dip below a certain level with people, you're no longer above the say-hello threshold and you have to pretend not to see them so that it's not awkward. Maybe it happens because it starts getting too risky. You're not sure they'll say hello back, and if they don't, you'll feel embarrassed. I remember that it was also that way with certain professors on campus. Students in a huge lecture class would definitely know the professor, but we wouldn't know if they really knew us. So saying hi to them on campus would put pressure on them to figure out who we were, but if they did recognize us and we didn't say anything, they might think we were being snobby. It was a real quandary.

When I think back to Harvard, I get mixed feelings. I remember the beginning of each semester, when the air would turn cool and I'd look out my dorm window at all the students strolling in their hooded crimson sweatshirts through the fallen leaves. I'd get excited because there were new classes and new possibilities to come. But my hopes would fade quickly as the semester wore on. No one would talk to me in class. I'd eat alone in the dining hall, and I'd spend Saturday night looking out my window at everyone else, just like the previous semester. And it wasn't that I wanted to be doing what they were doing, but that I wanted them to be doing things with me that I wanted to be doing. And what hurt most was that I was on a campus that students around the world would give their eyeteeth to be at, so I should have been absolutely thrilled, but instead, it seemed like it was everyone else's place except mine.

And now I'm in New York, in a hip part of town that people around the world would give their eyeteeth to live in, and I feel exactly the same way.

The only period during which things were different was when I was with Professor Harrison.

I don't remember thinking much of anything the first time I saw him. It was English 203, The Modernists, second semester of sophomore year. There were twelve of us in the class; they'd broken it into two sections. The other section just got a grad student, and mine got a full professor. We were lucky.

Harrison was average height, about forty years old, with brown hair that was starting to gray. He had a tendency to wear soft V-neck sweaters. He told us the first day that he didn't want this to be a typical English class where we just read the novels and competed to give the best deconstruction. He said that, once or twice, he'd ask us to write our own modernist pieces. I was a little nervous because I've never been as good at writing as I am at other things. Most people like writing to be intimate and revealing, and I resent having to tell the most private details of my life in order to interest people. Plus, writing isn't as exact as other subjects. In high school, I would sometimes start a creative writing assignment and feel like I was skating into the middle of the ice with nothing to hold on to. My best subjects were math and science. I was also pretty good in philosophy and literature, but not at writing my own literature.

Harrison went around the room and asked each of us to tell where we were from and what our major was. I found myself wishing that most professors did this, since people in many of my classes didn't really get to know each other. This was my chance. I said that I loved reading and observing human behavior. When I finished, Harrison smiled, nodded and said, "Welcome to the class."

We left that day with a writing assignment: to introduce ourselves and then talk about something we disliked about our personalities. Harrison said that plumbing one's own flaws was a characteristic of modernist writing. I wanted to impress Harrison right away, so I had to do this properly. In my dorm room, I lay on my stomach on my bed, cooled by the chilly air that blew in through a crack in the window. I agonized for an hour over the opening line.

Eventually, I decided on, "Of the three grades I skipped, second grade seemed the most abrupt."

There. I'd put the most salient thing about me first. And it was a little revealing. Surely he'd like that.

I added, "Suddenly, I'd gone from pencil to pen, from printing to script, from oral show-and-tells to oral reports, from running from boys to watching classmates chase them. Skipping fourth and eighth grades was a breeze."

Yes, this was good.

I told some more about myself, but finding something I disliked about myself was hard. I thought of the first quasi-modernist book I'd read, Dostoyevsky's Notes from Underground, when I was nine and my French lesson had been canceled. The protagonist had to, it seemed, try and say every extreme thing that came into his head to see what happened. I didn't have a similar quirk. I thought some more. What could I write about that would make a good modernist essay? I could invent something. Sometimes I feel…like a cockroach. Sometimes I feel like a swing set. Nah. I decided to write about being too studious. It wasn't very intellectual, and it wouldn't incorporate much symbolism. But what the heck. It was just one assignment.

During the second and third classes, Harrison didn't mention the essays we'd turned in. We dissected various modernist authors. One kid in the class, Brian Buchman, was the biggest kiss-up I'd met yet, and at Harvard that was quite an achievement. If he'd been sincere, I would have admired him, but he had a tone that was clearly false. Half of what he was spewing was stuff I'd learned in high school, but he made it seem like he was discovering nuclear energy.

When the third class ended, and everyone was shoving their books into their natty black backpacks, Harrison called me up to his desk.

I stood there while Brian Buchman said goodbye.

"Do you have a few minutes, or are you in a rush?" Harrison asked me. "Do you have time to come to my office?"

"I have time."

We walked down the hall to a pentagonal cul-de-sac with a wooden door in each wall. A few of the doors had yellowing newspaper cartoons taped to them. Harrison's door was blank except for his name. We entered his office and he sat at a rusty metal desk. He had a few newspaper clippings taped to the painted-white cinderblock walls, and there were papers piled high on a broken chair. I'd heard before that academics got no respect, and the size of Harrison's office proved it. He was a well-regarded professor, and this was what he had to work in.

Harrison leaned back. "I found your introduction very interesting."

"Thanks." I noticed there were no photographs on his desk.

"You said in your essay that you study too hard."

"Well, maybe there isn't such a thing," I said, trying not to be nervous. "But some people say that."

I remember noticing that he had a maroon sweater on and suddenly thinking it looked good on him. He had slightly wavy hair and intense brown eyes. He said, "Starting college at fifteen doesn't sound easy."

"Well, it's not so hard academically. But…"

"Socially, it could be hard."

I nodded.

"You sure you don't have somewhere to be right now?"

"No," I said. "I mean, yes. This is my last class on Thursdays."

"You the oldest in your family?"

"I'm an only child."

"Mmm," he said. "I had a younger brother. It created some tension when I got so much more attention in school."

"Did you skip grades?"

"I only skipped one grade. But I found it hard. For you to have skipped three…that must have been quite an adjustment."

I nodded again.

"How are you finding school?"

He looked straight at me. I hadn't found anyone that interested in me since back when I had interviewed for college in the first place.

We ended up talking for more than an hour. We got to things I hadn't told anyone. I told him about sitting in my dorm room freshman year, after my roommate had moved out, feeling miserable even though everyone kept saying how lucky I was to have the room to myself; I talked about the earliest smart things I'd said to adults that had made their eyes widen, like going up to a woman in the library when I was seven and pointing to her copy of Call It Sleep and saying, "That's a good book." I talked about figuring out how to play "Für Elise" on the inside of the piano when I was five. I stopped several times for fear I was boring him, but he kept urging me on. At times, he would reciprocate, telling a story about something smart he'd done as a kid, or a time he had felt out of place, and I almost felt as if he thought he needed to impress me. That was strange.

"One day, the boy who lived next door to me was reading a comic book on his stoop," Harrison said. "He wouldn't show it to me, so I stood in front of him and started reading it upside down, out loud. He was amazed, even though it's not so hard to read upside down. He thought I was a genius. Then he ran and got a bunch of his friends, who kept giving me things to read upside down. They made me feel like some sort of superhero."

I told him about something that had happened with a neighbor of mine.

"When I was in first grade," I said, "this sixth-grader who lived on my block came up to me on the playground at school and told me he was doing a report and he needed an example of a case in which the First Amendment wouldn't apply. All the kids used to ask me for help, even the ones who picked on me. I told him that yelling 'Fire' in a crowded theater was an example, even though we have the First Amendment right to free speech. Then, the next day, in the lunchroom, he ran up to me all out of breath and said, 'Carrie! Carrie! You'll never believe this! I looked in the encyclopedia, and they took your example!'"

Professor Harrison threw his head back and laughed. I realized then that the story was funny, and I laughed, too. He laughed some more, and that made me laugh more. The more we laughed, the more it seemed fun just to laugh, even after the joke had gotten stale. It was a good feeling that something that I'd merely considered strange in my childhood was now amusing, an experience to look back at and laugh about with someone. There were plenty of bad things that had happened—oh, if only I could recycle them into amusing stories! And Professor Harrison would understand.

But our time had to come to an end. Harrison looked at me

and said, "Well, I know you have to move on." I said, "Not really, but…" but he just laughed and got up. He shook my hand. His hand felt warm. I said I appreciated the discussion, and then I left.

As I walked back, my mind raced a million ways.

He was smart—no, brilliant.

He liked to hear me talk.

He encouraged me to talk more, and always had a response.

I felt more excited about the conversation than I had from any in years. But I also knew that this was probably the last time we'd spend that kind of time together—probably he was having those sorts of meetings with every student to discuss their essays, and probably they were all as enchanted as I was. And just like with my outgoing friend freshman year, I'd quickly move out of Harrison's scope, overshadowed by people who were louder and more "fun." Besides, surely, Harrison already had a throng of people outside of class that he belonged to. Former students, relatives, colleagues. He was great. How could people not swarm around him?

There was still relatively little I knew of him, but what I knew was terrific. I felt like I wanted to back him into a corner and quiz him for hours. And of course, I also wanted him to ask more things about me. I had been saving things up for years to tell someone who was interested, who cared.

Harrison hadn't made fun of one thing I'd told him. He hadn't said "whoosh." He hadn't barked "SAT word!" when I'd used a big word. He'd agreed with what I'd said and sometimes built on it. The most amazing discovery in the world is someone who understands what you're about without your having to go through your entire life history to explain it.

But my time was over.

During the next class, my feelings were confirmed. I got no wink or knowing smile from Harrison. He didn't single me out in any way. I was disappointed. I still thought I should mean more to him. Hadn't we shared secrets? Weren't we friends now, whereas everyone else was just a student to him? He had told me about feeling alienated and lonely as a boy. Were those things you told everyone? Had he told everyone?

I kept looking at him. He was so handsome, so smart, so steady. I doubted he'd ever been into getting drunk at parties.

The person who got the most attention in class that day was Brian Buchman. Not that Harrison had a choice. Buchman went on and on, and Harrison ate it up—one genius to another. I was filled with jealousy. I wanted to say something equally brilliant, but neither I nor anyone else in the class had a chance to get a word in with motormouth running.

Buchman talked about "The Stranger." He said, "Not that, by the way, the English translation can even come close to the French…" and Harrison nodded in agreement. Buchman called Camus "superb" and made the "okay" symbol with his thumb and forefinger as he said it. I wondered if vomiting would cost me an A. An airheaded girl in our class, Vicki, stared at Brian the whole time, cocking her head to the side like an attentive terrier. Brian wasn't bad-looking. But what a phony.

Harrison didn't look at me once. I felt miserable.

When the class ended, Brian and the professor were still talking. Neither of them glanced up as I went out.

I left in a foul mood.

I walked toward the Square, and it looked like everyone on campus was having fun. Two people in down jackets pitched a Frisbee back and forth. A gaggle of fraternity guys was horsing around with a lumbering Saint Bernard. A girl and her boyfriend were fake-fighting in front of the library.

In my dorm hallway, I smiled when two girls from my floor passed me, but they kept talking and didn't smile back. That was embarrassing. I opened my door, dropped my books on my dresser and climbed into bed.

I lay there for maybe half an hour in a fetal position, racked with malaise. It was almost a month into the semester, and already, everyone had crystallized into groups.

I listened to the end of a branch scrape repeatedly against my dorm-room window.

The phone rang.

"Carrie?" a voice asked. "It's Professor Harrison."

"Hi." I sat up.

"I just was wondering if you'd be up for dinner tonight. I know you probably have plans…"

Something inside me seized. A one-on-one dinner? Would this count as a date, or just a discussion? Would there be other students there? What had inspired this? How should I act? What if I said something stupid? At least I had already read half of the books on the syllabus, so I could hold my own in that respect. Besides, Harrison had enjoyed talking to me that first time, right? I shouldn't be nervous.

"Sure," I said. My voice probably cracked.

"What kind of food do you like?"

"Uh, whatever you want."

He laughed. "You ever eaten Moroccan?"

"No."

"Then we'll do Moroccan."

He seemed to like it when I hadn't tried something. I would soon learn that. He liked being a teacher.

I hung up and thought about what to wear. I didn't know if you were supposed to look good for a man who was asking you to dinner but who was a respected elder and not someone who could potentially have a romantic interest in you. I didn't really know how to look good, anyway. Looking good involves trying to look just like everyone else, and I don't spend a lot of time looking at everyone else. I pulled on a blouse that I'd worn to a formal dinner with my father a year earlier. I did have an adult-type wool coat. I trotted down the stairs, glad to be joining the other people who had somewhere to be. A chilly wind blew. I felt excited and nervous at the same time.

I waited on the lawn. Harrison wasn't there yet. I gazed back at my dorm. It looked like a three-story Colonial house. Several of the lights were on. They represented people who were stuck inside, not about to step into the thrilling unknown.

Professor Harrison's car was so small that I didn't realize it was there for the first few seconds. I guess Harrison didn't notice me at first, either, because he peered in his rearview mirror for a second before realizing I was walking toward him. He got out, came around and opened the door for me. It wasn't necessary, but it was a nice gesture. "Hello," he said.

"Hi."

I climbed inside, and he threw the door closed. It was incredibly warm inside. The heat was blowing full force. He walked around the front of the car, illuminated for a second by his own headlights.

Harrison slid inside. "Any preference?" he asked, playing with the radio dial.

"Whatever you—" I started, and then became aware that maybe I was being too passive. I'd already let him pick the food. "Classical?"

Harrison found a classical station, and I sneaked a peek at his profile. He had a softly curving nose, and a pleasant expression on his face. We talked about composers. He knew a lot about their lives, even more than he knew about their music. I'm always impressed when someone is well-versed in a topic that has nothing to do with their main discipline. It shouldn't be so unusual, but when one keeps meeting person after person who doesn't have any academic passions, to find someone well-versed in three or four really is a miracle. We talked about Edvard Grieg, whom I'd always been a little fascinated with. Harrison noted that he'd entered the conservatory around the same age that I'd entered college. The two of us talked about him for a half hour. Everything I knew, he knew.

We parked in a small lot behind the restaurant. Inside, it was dark but alive with people. When the waiter came up to us, Harrison said, "Back room." The waiter escorted us through a doorway full of burgundy beads. The back room was small, the walls covered in fuzzy red felt. None of the four tables was occupied. "Hope you don't mind," Harrison said to me. "I like privacy."

"Me, too."

"I wouldn't want students to see us and think I'm playing favorites," he said.

"You don't take them *all* out to dinner?"

He winked. "Only the best and brightest."

I looked down at my menu. There was a gold tassel hanging from it.

"It's too bad you're not old enough to drink," he said. "They have this sweet kind of red wine here…"

My eyes glossed over the list of entrées but didn't really take anything in.

"Do you like sweet things?" he asked. I nodded. The waiter filled our water glasses, and David ordered a Coke for me and a glass of red wine for himself.

But when his wine came, he held it out to me. "Try?"

I hesitated, then took a sip. It was sharp and sweet at the same time. "It's good," I said.

David took a sip. He was actually putting his lips where mine had just been, and it was a little exciting. He held the glass out for me again. The waiter returned as I was drinking it, and a look passed between him and David, but neither said anything.

After David took the glass back, he rested his chin on his hands and stared at me for a minute. "It looks good on you," he said.

"What does?"

"The wine. It turned your lips red."

I didn't know what to say to that. I picked the menu up again. It was odd that he could stare at me without feeling embarrassed.

He only stopped staring when the waiter came to take our orders. David asked if I'd decided, and I said I hadn't, and he asked if I minded him ordering for me because he knew some things I should try.

After the waiter left, he said, "So, what do you really think of our class?"

"I like it," I said. "I like the way you incorporated our own writing—"

"No," he said. "Not the curriculum, the students."

"Oh. I guess...they're fine."

"What about Vicki?"

I shrugged. "She seems nice."

"Tell me what you really think."

"Well—"

"Come on. Our secret."

"Well, she's a little..."

"...bit of an airhead?" Harrison said.

I laughed.

"You agree?"

"That's what I was thinking of."

"Between you and me," he said. "We can both keep secrets, right?"

"Right," I said. "Almost everything about me is a secret."

He smiled. "There's something so fresh about you," he said. "As brilliant as you are, you still have this youthful spark. I can't get over it."

I looked at the table and sipped my Coke.

"What about Brian Buchman?" he asked. "Smart kid, right?"

"He is pretty smart."

"Is he not the biggest ass-kisser in the history of academia?"

I laughed with glee. "I thought you loved him!"

He rolled his eyes. "Oh, Camus is *superb.*"

"'I found the *French* version to be *far* superior,'" I mimicked.

"Oui," Harrison said. The waiter came, and I glared at him. His appearance was becoming an annoyance.

For all David said about my having a youthful spark, he seemed to have one, too, even though he was a well-respected academic. Some of his stories indicated that he was still just as insecure as he'd been growing up, which I liked. There was something else that was thrilling to me: We were laughing together about our class, as if they were below us and we were both high above them.

When the food came, David took his fork and pushed a little of everything onto my plate. "Eat up," he said. "Don't hold back. Enjoy yourself." We ate greedily and took turns drinking from the next glass of wine. We giggled until we'd finished it. Then David ordered more.

We ate, we drank, we laughed, and I knew I was acting completely empty-headed and silly, and for the first time, I didn't care. I was with someone brilliant, who could protect me if need be, and I wasn't worried about anything.

As soon as we left, the cold air hit us. "Don't worry," he said. "I'll turn on the heat as soon as we get in the car." He put his hand on my back for a second. A shiver went up my spine. All sorts of feelings darted through me, but they didn't gel into a consistent whole. I was just feeling an amorphous anticipation. I didn't know what to do with it, as it was new to me.

He backed out of the parking lot and I felt the heat come on. Through the windshield, in the dark, a row of pine trees looked like a spiky sine wave. A few stars were out. It seemed like we were a world away from campus.

"You know, you really make me feel at ease," he said, pulling onto the road.

"I'm glad," I said, because I couldn't think of anything else.

"It's true." He smiled.

"Are you usually not at ease?"

"I don't know if any of us is usually at ease." He looked at me for a second. Something made me shiver again.

David put the radio back on and told me how impressed he was with my knowledge of music. I mentioned my four years of piano lessons. I remembered that my father had put up a poster of Uncle Sam that he'd gotten from the local music store, and it read, "I WANT YOU to practice every day." David talked about a recital he'd been to where his cousin had played Beethoven's Fifth, and just as he'd gotten to the last note, a panel in the ceiling fell down, raining white dust on everyone. The way David described his cousin Stevie, in a little navy-blue suit and bow tie, which got powdered up like a jelly donut, I had to laugh. The two of us talked at length about good and bad childhood music experiences, about the odd teachers we'd had in our music classes in school and for after-school lessons, and about other extracurricular activities, and before I realized it we were back at my dorm.

I didn't know what time it was. I'd had a lot of wine. I knew it must still be early, but it felt late. Only two or three windows were lit up. I sat there, feeling the alcohol wash through me. I waited for my eyes to focus.

"Well," David said. "I had a nice time."

"I did, too."

"Got your keys?"

"Hope so." I began digging through my purse.

David reached into my purse and grabbed my left hand. I looked up.

"Do you really want to leave?" he asked me.

He slowly began massaging my palm with his thumb, in a circular pattern. I returned to staring into my pocketbook.

"If you could do anything right now, what would it be?"

I knew he wanted me to be the one to suggest going somewhere else. If it was my idea, it would be less illicit. But I didn't know what to say.

Before I could decide, he leaned over, put his hand behind my head and brougt his lips to mine. He stopped for a second and looked at me uncertainly. I turned to face him, and he kissed me again. I could hear the motor running. Soon he had his hand on the back of my neck.

Then he pulled away. "I told myself right after we had that talk in my office the other day that I wouldn't let myself do this."

He actually had been thinking about this since our talk the week before! And he hadn't been able to resist! I couldn't believe it. It was the first time I'd been wanted that much, and not just to be on someone's spelling bee team.

"Look," he said. "I can let you go, or we can go somewhere."

I paused.

I had no choice. "Let's go."

He had some of the same paintings in his living room that I'd had in my bedroom growing up. Before I had a chance to tell him, he was walking down the hall, calling for me to come on a tour. His apartment felt like the warmest place I'd been since leaving home. There was a fireplace in the living room, thick rugs everywhere, and fat pillows smothering the couches and bed.

We didn't linger in David's bedroom. I followed him back to the kitchen.

"Anything to drink?" he asked, heading around the counter.

"I think we already did that," I said. The wine had smoothed my speech, hammering out the kinks and stumbles.

David laughed, unscrewing the top of something. He poured himself a glass and set it down.

"Do you ever use the fireplace?" I asked, walking over and sitting on a corner of the couch. It was charcoal-gray, with light and dark areas where it had been rubbed.

"I haven't yet this year," he said. "I was waiting for the right inspiration."

How's it going to start, I wondered. Would he use a bunch of tricks that would get me into his bedroom? Or was that not going to happen? I was assuming it would, even if I wasn't sure whether I wanted it to happen. He did know I was inexperienced, right? He had to. He couldn't expect much. Then again, maybe he *liked* inexperience.

"What are you thinking about?" he asked. No one had ever done that before, simply asked me what was in my head. He put his now-empty glass on the kitchen counter and walked toward me. He looked serious and intense. I noticed a slight wobble in his step.

"Your syllabus," I lied.

"Ah," he said, sitting on the other corner of the couch. "That reminds me. I published a paper on *Speech and Phenomena...*" He began telling me about it, and I liked that in the middle of our sitting in the living room, work was still on his mind. It was strange, though, that after we'd been kissing in his car, we were back at the chaste distance we'd been at before.

I wondered if maybe he was going to tell me to sleep on the couch and tuck me in and read me a bedtime story. Despite myself, I feared it.

"You know," he said, "when I say things about you, like that you're brilliant, or that you look beautiful with merlot on your lips, it's because I really think that. I'm not just saying it to flatter you."

I pointed to the empty glass on the counter. "Wow," I said. "That stuff works great."

He laughed. "It's not the alcohol," he said. "You are just so…"

I cocked my head to the side.

"Are you nervous?" he asked.

Without waiting for an answer, he leaned over, put his hand under my chin, lifted my head and kissed me.

He ran his hand down the front of my shirt, then down my slacks until he got to my kneecap, which he held. He wrapped his arms around me, and we kept at it until I was out of breath. After a while, we went into his room.

He was happy with what happened, and I was left unfulfilled. I wasn't so surprised. It was more academic for me. Something I should experience to know what it was about. But after he was asleep, I looked at him, ran my hand over the comforter and felt lucky to be there.

Class held a new excitement after that. David would lecture, pace the room, then stop and look up and down the aisles with a slight smile on his lips, acting as if nothing was going on when we both knew it was. It was our game. Occasionally, when I thought it was safe, I would catch his eye and raise an eyebrow, and once in a very rare while, he'd wink at me quickly. Sometimes, I would just get a surge of excitement watching him walk around in his soft sweaters, knowing that no one else in class had snuggled against them, knowing that later that night, I would. And when Brian Buchman was droning on and on, and Vicki was swooning, I would feel happy instead of miserable because I knew that later, David and I would laugh about it.

One time, David was a few minutes late to class, and everyone started yammering.

"Maybe we can leave if he doesn't show," said a guy named Rob, who only came to class half the time anyway.

"I *like* this class," a girl said.

"I do, too," Brian said.

"He loves *you*," Rob ribbed him.

"Yeah, and he ignores the rest of us," a girl complained.

"He's probably just busy," Vicki said.

"Is he married?"

"I don't think so."

"Maybe he's gay."

"That would be a shame. He's so cute!"

I told David about this later, and we both cracked up.

In my other classes, I daydreamed. I was somehow able to take notes, but my mind was elsewhere. I would return to my dorm room to find a message from him on my machine, either an invitation to come over or just a call to say he missed me. If there was no message, I'd lie in bed on my stomach and gloss over my reading materials until he'd call. That usually didn't take long. Then, he'd pick me up outside the dorm and we'd head out to eat or to his place. On the nights in which he had to get his work done, I stayed in my dorm room and did my own work. I maintained my good grades because when I wasn't with him, studying was all I did. I had no need for anything else. No need to force myself to head out to some club, meeting or coffee bar to feel as if I was making a lame stab at socialization. No need to wander through the Square alone, looking at everyone else having fun and wondering how I could join in. I had one person who cared about me and wanted to hear my thoughts, and that was all I needed.

The winter was a snowy swirl of schoolwork, fireplaces and him.

As for the physical part, I never got the hang of the Main Event, which seemed to be uncomfortable and ended really quickly, but I didn't care because everything else was great. On weekends, we drove all over Massachusetts, through colonial towns and historic villages and country roads, stopping for cider or chowder or pie. We walked along the harbor hand in hand, talking about places we could travel to, about places we'd never been and places we'd dreamed of as kids. At dinner in a waterfront restaurant, I'd watch the reflections of orange lights shimmering in the harbor, and he would reach across the table, dunk his roll in my bisque, and ask me if he should put this or that book on the syllabus for next semester. I couldn't believe I was affecting what his next semester classes would be reading, or that he considered me intelligent enough to offer suggestions. But he always listened closely to what I said and either nodded or gave me a new perspective. It felt wonderful.

Each of us should have the feeling, even if only for once in our life, of having someone so entranced by us that every inconsequential thing about us becomes an object of fascination. Any old piece of debris that's poking around in our soul can be offered up for voracious consumption.

David and I commiserated on the perils of being smart, of thinking too much. One time, we were driving through a small town, the gray-brown branches of naked trees crossed above us like swords, and I told him the story of how, for a few months in seventh grade, I couldn't sneeze.

"It started out of nowhere," I said. "I was in social studies in seventh grade, and I was about to sneeze, and then I thought about it, and I couldn't. The sneeze got all bottled up under the bridge of my nose and wouldn't come out." Every time I had to sneeze after that, I tried not to think about sneezing, but the more I tried not to think about it, the more I *had* to think about it, so I couldn't sneeze. Finally, one night, I confessed everything to my father, and he arranged an emergency meeting with the school psychologist. The psychologist told my father he was concerned that I might have obsessive-compulsive disorder. I had to see him for four weeks in a row. But somehow, I started forgetting to think about sneezing during my sneezes, and the problem disappeared as quickly as it had come on.

David smiled. "If you think a lot about anything, it can ruin it," he said. "If you think about kissing, about the fact that two people press their lips together and move into all sorts of configurations, it seems completely bizarre."

"I'll bet it's worse if you think about it while you're doing it," I said.

"Let's see," he said. And he pulled off the road.

After about a month of my sleeping over regularly, David began telling me a few new things he wanted me to do.

They were only slight variations on the norm, and I considered them a small sacrifice to make. Whatever kept his attention. As long as they didn't go too far.

But soon, he began to tell me some of the things he wanted me to *say*.

They bothered me. They weren't the kind of things I'd ever said before, and I'd probably never say them again, if I could help it. It wasn't just that they were dirty—the words were harsh. I didn't feel I could utter some of what he wanted. But I didn't want to disobey.

"We'll start slowly," he said kindly, one night in his room. "Just like with everything else. I just want you to say this one thing."

I was silent.

"Carrie?"

What's wrong with you, I thought to myself. *It's just words. You know that intellectually. So what?*

But I knew that even if I could say it, it would come out unnatural. And thus, it wouldn't have the effect he was hoping for. I was sure of it.

"Come on," he said, sweat on his brow. "Say it."

"It won't...it won't sound like me."

"Just say it," he whispered. "Say it once." He kissed my lips, then my neck. He ran his hand down my chest and rested it in my crotch, then took his index finger and began circling. "Say it. What do you want me to do to you?"

"'I want... I want you to...'"

"Go ahead."

"I can't."

He sat up. He didn't look so kind anymore. "What's the matter?"

"It won't sound like me. It won't sound right."

"Say it any way you want." He leaned over me and kissed me again. "Come on."

I just looked up at him.

"What's the matter with you?"

"It's not...I can't."

He sat up and looked into the distance.

"David?"

He ignored me.

"Come on. I'm..."

He rolled over on his side and pulled his blanket up. "Forget it. What's the use?"

"Are you mad at me?"

He ignored me again.

I turned over, too, but I couldn't sleep.

I lay there, my back to him, quietly waiting for him to change his mind. I wanted to get up and put on some bedclothes, but I thought that the more silence there was, the more he'd need to break it. I was scared even to breathe. I watched the red numbers on his clock radio change.

Eventually I fell asleep. At some point in the night, I woke up and pulled on a T-shirt. Then I went back to sleep.

In the morning, when I awoke, David was already in the kitchen, heating up coffee. I padded in there, and he gave me a silent nod and went back to the coffee. He also was quiet in the car going back to campus.

I went through my classes upset but trying to concentrate. When I came home, the light on my answering machine wasn't blinking.

I collected my introductory philosophy books and read in bed. An hour passed without a call. I was scared. Why had I been so stupid?

But he would have to give me another chance, right?

I read *Meditations on First Philosophy,* but my eyes just kept rolling over the same words again and again, as if I were highlighting the book in varnish. Nothing stuck. Every few minutes, I looked at my clock. Dinnertime was approaching. I'd have to hike down to the dining hall and sit at the end of a table alone. Doing that always gave me an empty feeling in the pit of my stomach. I didn't want to do it if he was going to call.

I felt hungry. I ignored my stomach and tried again to concentrate on *Meditations,* but I decided maybe I needed something light to read. So I picked up *Thus Spake Zarathustra.*

The phone rang.

I reminded myself, even as I dashed to it, to make my voice sound uninterested.

"Hello."

I wouldn't have admitted it, and it sounds very clichéd, but clichés become clichés because they happen: when I heard his voice, my stomach jumped.

"I went out and got wood for the fireplace," David said. "I could use a little help initiating it."

I wanted to tell him how happy I was that it was him, how scared I'd been, how much I'd missed him and how I would say whatever he wanted. But I didn't. I told him I would meet him outside in ten minutes.

That night, we ate heaping bowls of linguine at an Italian place, then went to David's apartment. Once in the living room, we lay down on the rug in front of the fireplace, a bottle of wine between us. David put his glass down on the brown tiles and lay on his side in an S shape, his knees bent. I rested my head on his jeans and stared into his chest. *Thank God everything's okay,* I thought. It felt so good just to lie there, listening to him breathe. I closed my eyes, and we both lay quietly for a while. Then, I felt his fingers move over my wine-ripened lips. "Come here," he whispered, and he brought my chin to his face. "Let's stay here for a change," he said, and I nodded. Soon he said, "Say it. What I wanted you to say yesterday. Please."

Before he'd called, I had told myself I would, and on the way over, I had told myself I would, but now I couldn't. It didn't seem like the right words. It didn't seem to fit with either me or with us. And why did he want me to say it, when he knew how much it bothered me?

"Say it!"

I started. "'I… I…'"

"Yes?" His eyes were closed.

I couldn't finish.

"Come on," he said. "Go ahead."

"David," I said.

Then I said no more.

He sat up again. "Is this it?"

"I…"

"Is that the best you can do? You're not even going to try?"

I just looked at him.

"One compromise?"

It just didn't fit.

"Didn't I teach you? Didn't I say it over and over? Why can't you learn it?"

I didn't know what to say to that.

"Is it such a hard thing to learn?"

Finally I said, "It's not something I would say."

"But you can *learn*."

"We're not in class."

"Just say it!"

I looked at the rug. "It wouldn't be *me*...."

"Do you always have to be such a goddamn prude?"

Before I could say anything else, he jumped up, stalked into the bathroom and shut the door. I sat still on the rug and suddenly felt very cold.

He came back out in a minute and said he'd drive me home.

We rode to my dorm in silence. He didn't say anything when I got out of the car.

In my room, I curled up in my bed in the dark and stared at the phone, sure he'd call. I rehearsed various speeches in my mind, speeches in which I would tell him that maybe there was a way we could get past this, that maybe there were things he wouldn't say, either, if I asked, that I had already made compromises and that I'd been happy to make them for him, but this was something that bothered me. And if we couldn't get past this, I wanted to say why it was hard for me to yield to his request.

But I never got the chance to say any of it. He didn't call.

The only time the two of us did talk was in class, when all of us were discussing the reading materials. That was it.

The semester eventually drew to a close. He and I never had another personal conversation.

I got an A in the class. I guess David would have been afraid to give me anything less.

By the way, I deserved it anyhow.

For a long time after that, I had trouble seeing couples kissing on campus. Their lives were so normal; why did mine always have to be strange? Did these carefree couples know that for some people, not everything worked out so neatly? Did they appreciate that?

The worst was, I knew a lot of the couples were together just for sex. At least David and I talked about books, music and his work. What did these people who did nothing all day but face-mash actually talk about? Some of the girls on my floor had boyfriends whose biggest accomplishment was making fifth-string lacrosse or flunking astronomy.

The rest of my time at Harvard wasn't much of an improvement. I studied hard, graduated and moved into the apartment my father found for me.

Now that I've just spent some time thinking about the relationship with David, I feel sore and unfulfilled, similar to how I often felt after the encounters themselves.

So I go out to the supermarket to grab some ice cream and rainbow sprinkles.

I wend my way through the murky city air and into the perfume-and-garlic world of D'Agostino. I pluck a frosty pint of Cherry Garcia from the freezer, and as I'm pacing the aisles, I pick up sprinkles and cherry soda, too.

Once I get home, I make an ice-cream soda. The fizz bubbles high above the glass. When I taste it, I immediately realize

I shouldn't have been denying it to myself for so long. The ice cream slides down my throat into my gut. It feels absolutely wonderful. There is nothing better than this.

I pass a mirror on the way back into my room and notice that my lips have turned red.

Chapter Four

In the morning, I'm depressed. I don't know what to do. I have another appointment with Petrov. This probably won't help. But maybe it will.

The sidewalk is soggy, but the sun is out. I keep my eyes on the ground, feeling just as low. When I descend into the subway, there's only one other person in the station. Still, I have to glance up at him.

The way he looks strikes me immediately. He's wearing a gray bowler hat. He appears to be in his early thirties. He's also got on a long raincoat, and he's clean shaven and looks unusually neat. But it's the hat that strikes me. No one wears hats these days, especially a gray bowler hat. He looks like he's out of an old detective movie.

He paces before the complement of full-length Broadway ads: *You're a Good Man, Charlie Brown; Les Mis; Phantom of the Opera*. Occasionally, he starts muttering to himself. Just one of the many people in this city who are on the borderline.

I lean against the wall and stare at the ground, at the oval slabs of gum that have been there so long they've turned black, and at the dirt and stones and wrappers. The Hat Guy is still pacing, still muttering, and I don't want to appear to be staring at him, so I look away. There are so many places where we pick things to stare at in order to avoid looking at strangers. We do it in elevators all the time. But there is hardly anything to stare at on an elevator. I should start a company that manufactures sticky blue dots that read "Stare at this dot to avoid talking to the person next to you." I could make a fortune.

I wonder what people are supposed to talk about in elevators. "Wouldn't it be funny if these Braille 'numbers' were really curse words?" "You know, it has been statistically proven that ninety percent of 'door close' buttons don't really work." "Hey, wanna order pizza from the emergency phone?" "You know, most buildings don't have a thirteenth floor because the builders were superstitious. But *this* building actually used to have a thirteenth floor. It collapsed last year during a storm." Come to think of it, I might use that one.

The light from the subway train comes out of the tunnel, and then the train itself appears. The Hat Guy hops on, and we immediately head to opposite corners of the car like boxers in a ring.

The Hat Guy pulls a long, thin book out of a flat paper bag and again starts muttering. On the train, there's not much to stare at, except ads for community colleges. I think the quality of a college is inverse to how much it has to advertise. You don't see Yale putting ads in the subway. The other ads are about made-for-TV movies on cable. Years ago, you used to be lucky if you could find one decent program out of three networks. Now, through the wonder of cable, the odds have been reduced to one in twenty.

★ ★ ★

I get to Petrov's a few minutes early and the door to his office is closed. I crouch next to the door and put my ear to it.

I hear the guy inside say, "It's in every one. In every sexual fantasy I have, right as we're about to…uh, do it, the phone rings."

Petrov: The phone rings in your fantasies right as you're about to have sex.

Man: Yes.

P: Do you answer it?

M: No. But it completely ruins the mood, and the fantasy's over.

P: So you're getting hot and heavy with a woman, you're about to have sexual intercourse, and the phone rings.

M: Yes.

P: I think you have intimacy issues.

M: What makes you say *that?*

What idiots. Petrov shouldn't even charge me, after having to listen to this dreck all day.

I hear him approaching the door, and I scramble away from it. The guy who comes out is about four foot ten. I wonder how people like him even *have* sex. I'm not trying to be funny. How do people who are so different in height have intercourse? I've seen four-foot-eleven girls with men who look like they're six foot three. When they're in bed, do the girls climb up to kiss them, then lower themselves and have sex, and then, when they're finished, climb back up and kiss them again?

"Hi, Carrie," Dr. Petrov says. "How are you doing?"

"I'm fine." I enter and sit down.

"Is there a 'but'?" he asks, sitting across from me. "You seem hesitant."

"Well," I say, "I sort of have this problem."

"Okay."

"Whenever I'm having a sexual fantasy, the phone rings."

Petrov shifts uncomfortably. "I'd appreciate your not listening in on my sessions."

"I couldn't help it. The door was just flat enough for my ear."

"Let's see what kind of progress you've made on your to-do list."

ZOLOFT®

1. Do things from list of 10 things you love
2. Join an org./club
3. Go on date
4. Tell someone you care
5. Celebrate New Yr's

"I had ice cream," I say. "To fulfill mandate number one."

"That's great," he says. "Did you get rainbow sprinkles?"

"Yes. I made a whole ice-cream soda."

"And how did it make you feel?"

I have to admit it. "Pretty good," I say.

He smiles, as if he's earned a victory. This bugs me, so I add, "I haven't made any progress on getting a date. Or joining an organization."

"What about the guy from legal proofreading who flirts with you?"

"He doesn't flirt with me. And I haven't seen him again yet. I will, though."

"Good. Remember not to back down if he wants to get to know you better. Even if he's not exactly like you, you can still become friends with him."

"Okay."

"Have you found any clubs you might want to join?"

"I'm looking around," I say. "I'm still considering that church."

"You know, you're in New York City. If you pick up the Weekly Beacon, there are lots of events in the listings section."

This reminds me of something. The Weekly Beacon has a very popular personal ad section. It gives you a little more than the usual personal ad websites on the Internet. You can read the *Beacon's* ads in the paper or on the Web, but they also have a feature where you can have a voice mailbox so you can hear the other person's voice and they can hear yours, without having to give out your number at first. So not only can you trade e-mails, but you can trade phone messages, too. That provides me with optimum chance to talk to them and rank their creepiness potential before I have to meet them. A lot of people on the Internet pretend to be different than they are. This is perfect. I should be able to get at least one date and satisfy Petrov's requirement easily, even if this wasn't the method he had in mind.

I can place an ad and tell all about myself. What's more, I can mention in the ad that I have morals and that I'm smart. And I can include my restrictions for the people who respond. That way, I might actually meet someone who has standards and intellectual interests.

I'm definitely going to do that.

Petrov asks, "Are you okay? You seem a little down today."

We go into how my week went, how my father is, and about New York in general, but I don't mention Professor Harrison. I tell Petrov I'm going to rent classic movies after the session. That's how I've been occupying several evenings lately, since I've read a lot of classic literature but haven't seen enough classic films. The movies come from a top-100 movie list recently released by the Association of American Film Reviewers. They actually released a whole bevy of lists, including 100 best movies, 100 best movie scores, 100 best leading men, 100 best leading women, and 100 best movie characters. If I had to do my own film characters list, number 1 would be C. F. Kane, 2 would be Nurse Ratched, 3 would be Dr. Strangelove, and 4 through 21 would be Sybil. There are some great characters in movies—greater than in real life.

When I leave Petrov's office, I figure I'll walk home instead of taking the scumway, so that I can pick up a DVD on the way. It's not that long a walk. Maybe this is good practice for staying out on New Year's Eve.

A few blocks out of Petrov's office, I see someone familiar. It's Hat Guy again. He disappears around a corner. Is he following me? It's awfully odd to see someone twice in one day whom you've never seen before.

I wonder if my father is having him tail me to check up on me. I decide I'll follow him a bit. I run up the block and around the corner. He disappears again. I try to catch up, but I lose him.

Maybe I'm imagining it.

When I get back to my apartment building, Bobby is outside, bending over a cellar window that's caked with mud and damp leaves. He notices me from between his own legs. "Hey, beautiful," he says. I quickly turn and don't say anything. I push the front door open and jog up the stairs, which have been trampled for so many years that the black rubber matting beneath the carpeting has bled through on the edge of each step, and the color of the rug has turned from yellow to sallow.

When I reach the top, I stop. I stand there and feel a hole in my stomach. All Bobby did was say, "Hey, beautiful." And he's old; maybe saying it brought him joy. Why was I so mean? What if he really *does* think I'm beautiful? What if, as far as he was concerned, he was just being nice?

No one else consistently tells me I'm beautiful.

I stand there and feel sickness wash over myself.

Then, the feeling goes away, like it usually does.

★ ★ ★

That night, I get called for legal proofreading. It turns out to be even more monotonous than the last assignment. I sit with three other proofers in a room that's almost completely barren. The desks look like they were swiped from an elementary school: manila tops, metal green insides. The floor is white and dusty. It's freezing in there. It must be the room they don't let their clients see.

The other proofers are much older than me. I look at them, but unfortunately, none of them look like they'd make a good date. I will have to keep looking, and I'll have to place that ad soon.

The four of us sit like bored students in study hall, waiting for work. The other proofers discuss a variety of topics: whether Walt Disney is really frozen, trying to name all of the ingredients in a V8, leaving a dog out and forgetting you left it out, kids drinking chocolate milk with their school lunch every day, Japanese cartoon characters that look American, bad television shows. A man and woman talk about their belief that today's television is much worse than when they were kids. People always say that, but I guess they don't realize that TV is always going to seem worse now than it did when you were twelve. Anyway, I happen to like TV. I've met people who will self-righteously declare that they don't own a TV set, as if it makes them morally superior to everyone else, as if they are declaring they have never told a lie or broken the law. There is absolutely nothing immoral about television. It's not even unhealthy. Vapid and stultifying, maybe. But we all need it sometimes. I know I do. My mind worked so hard for the first eighteen years of my life that it needs—and deserves—a virtual brain pillow to rest in.

Around 3:00 a.m., the room is silent. Everyone is reading newspapers. I'm starving. At least, that's what I tell myself. Probably, I'm more bored than hungry. I get up, go to the kitchen, drop some coins into the snack machine and grab a bag of pretzels. I return to my seat and start eating. A few people turn around. I can't help it. Pretzels crunch.

I start to feel like everyone is looking at me. I put the bag aside and sit quietly. But I see the pretzels there, their tiny knobs calling out to me. My mouth waters. I know it will water until every last pretzel is gone. The psychology behind that is interesting. When I can take it no more, I grab the bag, head into the kitchen and scarf down the pretzels. I hate peer pressure.

When I return to my seat, I decide I'll write a draft of my personal ad for the *Beacon*.

I take out a pen and print:

PRODIGY SEEKS GENIUS—I'm 19, very smart, seeking nonsmoking nondrugdoing very very smart SM 18-25 to talk about philosophy and life. No hypocrites, religious freaks, macho men or psychos.

I can't wait to see the responses I get. I pull out my pocket calendar and write on it, on a date next week, "E-mail personal ad to *Beacon*." I'm giving myself a week to find a less-desperate way of meeting people. But if nothing else works out, I can place this ad and answer other people's.

The next night, I'm scheduled to return to the firm where Douglas P. Winters works. I'm excited. I tell myself that I must dig in my heels and ignore his salacious comments, as he may be my only prospect for a date by New Year's. But I hope that he doesn't drop me before it happens because he realizes, as David did in college, that I still have morals.

David left me wondering for a long time if all men would be like him, making me do things that felt wrong, then immediately shutting me down coldly if I didn't. And I hated the women who routinely gave in and made it easy for them to be that way. Nowadays, I don't think every man is evil, but the good ones can also get a good-looking woman, so a woman who isn't good-looking just has to lower and lower her standards until they're down around her ankles. It's not fair; it's just life. I sometimes think that women are the most hypocritical beings around. They complain from nine to five about how men are pigs, and then they give them what they want from five to nine. But I can't say they're doing it out of any malice; it just comes from neediness. I've heard feminists say that women shouldn't "need a man," but it's not that women need a man. It's that most people need *someone,* and if they're women and they happen to be heterosexual, their choice is limited to men. And if they're not beautiful women who can pick and choose, their choice can be limited to self-centered men. All right, maybe it's not so bleak, but it'd be less bleak if people actually had standards and tried to hold out, like I did by refusing David's requests.

At night, when I push open the glass doors of Pankow, Hewitt and So & So, Douglas P. Winters looks happy. "I've got pistachios!" he announces, then breaks into an evil laugh. I tell him I can't wait for him to give me one. Then I wend my way through clusters of desks to the supervisor and pick up a small document. All I have to do is make sure that the typist correctly inputted the proofreader's corrections. Oldie is in a different cubicle, so I don't have to deal with him.

As I read through the document, I gradually realize that it's somewhat intriguing. It's stamped *Confidential.* It's about two major banks that are going to merge. I wonder if I can sell this information.

I finish it and turn it in. The supervisor says there's no more work right now. So I head out to Doug.

Doug's bangs are wet with sweat. He motions to a seat.

"Hot in here?" I ask.

"I have a cold," Doug says.

"Didn't you have a cold last time I saw you?"

"I'm allergic to work."

"Go home."

"I'm allergic to starving."

"I just read a document about a bank mega-merger," I tell him.

"Sounds like a page-turner."

"I was wondering if the information's worth anything."

"Probably," Doug says, "but that would be insider proofreading. A lotta guys went to jail in the eighties for that. Did you sign a confidentiality oath when you came to work here?"

"Yeah."

"Did you sign it in your real name?"

"Yes."

"Bad move."

"I wanted my real name to be on the checks."

"That's true," Doug says. "Well, I didn't sign any agreement. You could slip me the documents."

If I want to work on getting him to ask me out on a date, I could throatily add, "Well, *you* could slip *me* something, too." But I'm not that desperate yet. There's still the personals—placing one and responding to other people's.

I laugh at my "slip me something" thought, and Doug asks, "What?"

"Nothing."

"Come *on*."

"No."

I've been laughing at my own secret jokes my whole life. Why stop now? I understand them better than anyone else.

"Come on," he goads.

I have to lie because I know that Doug is one of those people who won't give up. I say, "I was laughing because I just remembered a joke I heard two kids tell each other in the subway yesterday."

"I'm waiting," Doug says.

"Uh… Knock-knock."

"Who's there?"

"Interrupting cow."

"Interrupting co—"

"MOOOO!"

He laughs. "Not bad. It's hard to find good jokes that are clean."

"True."

"I have a joke," Doug says.

"Is it clean?"

"No. But there aren't any bad words in it."

"Okay."

"What did Little Red Ridinghood say as she sat on Pinocchio's face?"

"What?"

"Tell a lie! Tell a lie! Tell the truth! Tell the truth!"

The supervisor comes out. "Carrie? I have a job for you."

The assignment takes an hour, and then things are quiet. I reach for the pile of magazines that apparently have already been ravaged by the full-time staff (the staff that has time to lambaste their sons-in-law and, judging from a gift that has been left on the desk, to create a little dog out of an eraser and five pushpins), and lying flat on top is a magazine article about Human Papillomavirus. I read about how the majority of women have it, how it's spread by sexual contact, how it might be the cause of cervical cancer, and how even condoms can't prevent it. I guess that's God's little joke—people actually started protecting themselves from AIDS, so now there's something that's spread by sex no matter what. I bet someday there'll actually be a disease that can kill you just from having sex, and that people will decide to keep having sex anyway. Maybe there will have to be a ten-year sex moratorium in the country in order to eradicate it.

When it's time for "lunch break" at 2:00 a.m., Doug invites me to eat in the kitchen with him. He looks tired—he keeps tugging at his shirtsleeves, and his short hair is a mess. The artificial fluorescent lights shine brightly above. Doug doesn't eat, but he drinks coffee. It's amazing how many people are addicted to coffee and won't admit it. Some people are as obsessed with coffee as sex. But I guess an obsession doesn't count as an obsession if everyone's doing it. I guess it's perfectly normal to say, "Oh, I just can't put on my underwear until I've had my first cup of coffee."

It's funny—we all look down on China's past addiction to opium, as if we're above all that, but most of modern America has to be doped up on caffeine in the morning and plied with alcohol at night. I don't know that we're any better than the Chinese. Perhaps we need both substances to get through life. But if everyone needs these medications just to cope, isn't something wrong?

Anyway, I'm ignoring the matter at hand: proving that I can go on a date. I keep sneaking looks at Doug in order to figure out if I could ever kiss him. He does have nice tufts of hair and a cute craggy chin. But I still don't know him well enough to be attracted to him. Then again, it's early. If it was just a first date, I wouldn't have to kiss him right away.

I mention the papilloma article to Doug. "Can you imagine what it would be like," I say, "if there was a disease that could kill everyone unless they stopped having sex?"

"Forget it," Doug says. "I'd fucking *die*."

"Or the converse."

He sips his coffee. "Can men give each other the papilloma thing?"

"I guess."

"Damn. Just when I was ready to accept condoms."

Does that mean he's gay?

I look at him. Yeah, come to think of it, he is. I feel stupid.

"Maybe that's how the world ended the first time," Doug says. "Maybe our civilization was as advanced as it is now, and then sex killed everyone. We can control nukes better than our sex drives…"

He keeps chattering and I pretend I'm listening, but I'm really just trying to take in the fact that he's gay. I have to think of things like that over and over until the shock value wears off. There are a great many things that shock me even though they shouldn't. Obviously someone being gay should not shock me. I wonder if I can go out to eat with him and still count it as a date. Can having dinner with a gay man count as a date? What makes a date a date? I guess there has to be a possibility of something romantic happening. So what's it called if you have dinner with a gay man? A gayte.

Well, I can send in my personal ad next week.

At 4:00 a.m., my shift is over. The firm calls for a car service to drive me home. I wonder what would happen if I asked the driver to take me to Chicago. I wonder how far I could get him to go without his calling his supervisor. Maybe I'll try each time from now on to get the driver to go a little farther. It would be worth being banned from temping. Maybe Atlantic City is the limit. Although the last place I want to go is somewhere where a bunch of seventy-year-olds make love to three slot machines at a time and shriek at you if you get too close.

One of the world's greatest pleasures is sitting in the back of a hired car at night. From where I'm sitting, the city looks like a sleeping villain. The heat is blowing full force. The wheels coast evenly over the smooth road. There is no music on, owing, I think, to some old Giuliani Rule. Right now the world exists just for me and the few other people in the city who are up. It's too early for even the delivery trucks and the most anxious commuters.

When I get back to my apartment and undress in my room, I notice that the light is on in the apartment of that couple across the street. Their window is big and boxy, revealing a table, stove, drapes and hanging plants. But I don't see the couple. I guess they're in another room. For just a second, I feel a connection to them. They are up at this odd hour, and so am I. I want them to come to the window, wave and smile, intrigued by the fact that we have something in common. We share a secret, a quiet time of the night.

I strip down to my underpants because I've left the heat on too high. My throat is dry, and I drink a cup of seltzer. Then, I crawl into bed and fall asleep. When I wake up hours later, the light in the couple's apartment is off.

At nine o'clock, I'm too tired to get out of bed. I roll onto my back and pull my covers up to my chin. Beams of blue daylight stream in overhead. I decide that, for a while, I will simply lie here, listening carefully to the street sounds and seeing where my thoughts transport me. I've done this once or twice before, just lain here and listened to see what comes to mind. It's amazing how many far-off sounds and unusual noises you can isolate if you concentrate.

Lately, vague stimuli have been provoking obscure childhood flashbacks. I think maybe the reason that so many of my recent memories have come from early childhood is that I'm at an age where I can't be considered a kid anymore, yet I don't have kids of my own, so the only way to experience childlike enthusiasm is to fantasize and remember. I'm sure Petrov would have an explanation.

I relax as much as possible and close my eyes. All is silent.

Then, I start to hear birds chirping. There are two of them, exchanging their high-pitched staccato reports. It reminds me of when I was three and my grandfather and grandmother walked me around the shady grounds of their apartment in London, and we came upon a cracked robin's egg lying among the tufts of grass and knotted roots. It was such a pale and beautiful shade of blue that I almost cried. They encouraged me to lift it up. Inside, there was nothing except whiteness, the purest white I'd ever seen. Each time I visited them after that, I looked for more eggs, but couldn't find any.

I was fascinated at that age with so many things: revolving doors, mirrors, clocks, trains, fans, elevators, hydrants. I soon wanted to know how all of these worked—same with eggs and animals—and this led to a house full of science books that I devoured and spat out like so much gum. To balance that were all of the novels—I don't even remember reading kids' books when I was two, like my father tells me I did, but I must have quickly graduated to more advanced stuff.

The air outside is still, save for the distant rumbles of buses. Now I hear glass breaking. Someone must be setting down a trash bag full of recyclables. The sound reminds me of the wind chimes one of our neighbors had on her back porch when I was younger, and how, one day when there was a hurricane, they whirled around fiercely the entire day, jingling and spinning like a carousel out of control. I was glued that afternoon to the TV. I lay on my stomach charting the storm, using the wind direction and velocity to figure out when it would hit land and how long it would stay. In the evening, the power went out, and my father lit a candle and we sat in the kitchen for an hour and talked in the darkness. The rain pummeled the windows and the wind blasted the roof, but we were safe inside. I talked about school starting up again; Dad talked about what it was like when *he* was in school. We talked about the first apartment we lived in in New York when I was two and a half, right after we moved out of London. I think it was the longest talk I had with my father, and one of the few I've had with anyone. I haven't thought about that day in a long time.

I lie back, my eyes still closed. The next sound I hear is a fire truck, well in the distance. When I was little, every year, Santa Claus used to come squealing down my street on a fire engine. I used to gaze out at all the kids running after him with a mixture of pity and disgust. I never believed in Santa Claus, not even when I was two and a half. That was when my father tried to tell me about him and I gave him a dozen reasons why it was impossible. My father has since told me that that's when he knew I was smart. But I wonder if it would have been more fun if I hadn't been smart. It might have been nice to believe in Santa for a little while. If only I could have given up a few IQ points for some ignorant bliss. But I guess I don't really want that. Not yet.

Outside, all is quiet again. The street is mine. Everyone else is at work.

People who don't do this, just lie still and allow their thoughts to transport them to different places, are missing life. I can't imagine that most people who go to work each day do it. They would never have the time.

But ultimately, is there a point to all of this thinking? I've always thought that my thoughts would someday serve a great purpose in the world, but the more days that pass, the more unlikely it seems. I've considered starting a log of my thoughts and ideas, but I fear if I do, I'll feel obligated to run to the log and write down every thought I have, and it will become an obsession. Maybe I can limit it to ten brilliant thoughts per day.

I'm not ready to get up yet. I stare at the ceiling. There's an ornate decoration in the middle, around a naked lightbulb. It's a few concentric circles with rose petals, and a fleur-de-lis at the north and south ends. It looks regal. I wonder who it was that lived in my apartment 100 years ago. That would make a great book, researching everyone who lived in your Manhattan apartment before you did. You could tell the complete story of some socialite in the twenties and then go on to a soldier in the forties and eventually get to the twenty-something editorial assistant, messenger boy or all-around slacker who preceded you. Maybe that's my calling, to write that book. I wonder what the best way would be to figure out who lived here before me. I do know there must have been a group of foreigners at some point, because when I moved in, there was a stack of old records on a high shelf in my closet, and they were mostly polkas. Maybe the former residents were Polish.

Wait a second—*are* polkas Polish, or do I just think that because they both start with "Pol"? I must go to my dictionary and look this up.

This is ironclad evidence that it is important to have time to oneself during the day, as I do. If I was at some mind-numbing job for eight hours, I would not have the energy to be blazing paths in etymology as I am right now.

The dictionary describes its origin this way—and I'm not joking—"Polka, Polish woman, fem. of Polak." Polak? My father told me—after we went to the Arts High School to see *A Streetcar Named Desire* and we were talking about Stanley Kowalski—that "Polak" was a slur people used to use before the world got more politically correct. So it's funny that polka might be the feminine of a slur.

Now that I've looked up polka, I should look up polka *dot*. I can't imagine where that one came from.

It says "one of a number of regularly spaced dots or round

spots forming a pattern on cloth." It doesn't give an etymology, which is a real gyp, as far as I'm concerned. Oh, wait, we're not supposed to say gyp anymore, because it's short for Gypsy. It's considered offensive, like so many things.

I wonder where the term "gypsy moth" comes from. Now I have to look that up, too. I admit I have a problem.

It's defined as, "a moth having hairy caterpillars that eat foliage and are very destructive to trees." That is so flattering! If I were a Gypsy, I wouldn't be as concerned about gyp as I was about gypsy moth.

I really must put this dictionary away. It's got so many treasures inside that I can't stop plucking them out. Saying I'm just going to look up one word is like saying I'm going to eat just one potato chip, or that I'm going to open up the NPR Christmas catalogue and order just one leatherbound listeners' diary and pen set.

Suddenly my phone rings. I hope against hope it'll be someone I know. Usually it's a telemarketer or a wrong number.

I don't recognize the number but I might as well see who it is. I wait until the third ring to pick it up. There is such a thing as being fashionably late with phone calls. One ring is desperate; two rings is too soon; and four rings is risky. I wonder if *Cosmo* has written about this.

"Hello, ma'am. Is the head of the household in?"

"No," I say. "Big Bruno is out at the construction site. But little old me might be able to help." Sexists!

"Well, ma'am, my name is John B. Robertson, and I'm calling to give you a great offer. Because of your excellent credit rating, you are invited to a free luncheon during which you can choose to take home either a new Sony video camera or a weekend vacation for two. All you have to do is answer a few questions and then attend the three-hour session. Can I have your name?"

"Mary Jane."

He laughs. "Could I have your real name?"

"Mary Jane is my real name. Jane is my last name."

"Oh," he says. "I'm sorry, ma'am. It's just that we get a lot of wise guys. Could you please tell me where you live?"

"Down the drain."

"I should have known you weren't telling the truth."

"If it's any consolation, I wasn't lying. I was *joking.*"

"I see. Do you think that you can tell me your real name?"

"I think so."

"Okay."

"Anne Sexton."

"Thank you." I guess he's writing this down. "Address?"

I give him the address of the coffee bar where Ronald the Rice-Haired Milquetoast works. He could use the fan mail.

"Now I need to ask you where your income falls. We're asking you to select from two choices. Would you say it's A, less than $30,000 a year, or B, $30,000 or more?"

"A trillion dollars."

"Okay, so that would be B, $30,000 or more. When you go away on vacation, do you go A, within a half hour, B, within two hours, C, within eight hours, or D, more than eight hours away?"

"The question is worded improperly because if the correct answer is A, then the correct answers are also B and C. If your vacation is within a half hour, that also means that it's within two hours and eight hours. And A is a dumb answer, anyway, because no one takes a vacation to a half hour away. Especially in the 212 area code to which you are dialing. At rush hour, it can take a half hour to go from Christopher Street to Canal Street. Has anyone ever taken choice A, a half hour away?"

"Not too often."

"Then eliminate it."

"That's a good idea, ma'am. I'll pass that on to my supervisor."

"I appreciate that, John," I say. "Hey, John, tell me something. Where are you calling from?"

"Out in Arizona."

"Yeah, most telemarketers usually call from out West. It's gotten cold here already. Is it nice out there?"

"It's not too bad."

"What kind of salary do they pay you?"

"Um…"

"Do you have any kids?"

"I don't—"

"How do you feel about organized religion?"

There's a click. He's hung up.

I think I'm the first person in telecommunications history to make a telemarketer hang up on her. That alone should clinch me the MacArthur prize.

I actually kind of wish John hadn't hung up, though. For a telemarketer, he wasn't so bad. Maybe he hung up by accident. Maybe he'll call again.

A minute later, the phone does ring. But it turns out it's my father.

"How are you?" I ask.

"I'm fine," he says. "I'm in Luxembourg City. How are you?"

"Pretty good," I say. "I'm at home, in a tiny village in the States, sometimes referred to as 'The Village.'"

"It sounds charming."

"It is, sometimes."

"And how are the other village dwellers?" Dad asks. "Have you met anyone new…socially?"

My father has never come right out and asked about romantic relationships, and I've never told him anything. I certainly never told him about Professor Harrison.

I wonder what it's like to be a father of a daughter and know that eventually, she is going to be defiled in some way. It may take thirteen years, or seventeen years, or thirty-one, but sooner or later, your princess is going to have a prince's jewels in her silk pillow. I guess you either have to not think about it or pretend it doesn't exist. Like headcheese.

"No one special," I say.

"But you're going to try to make new friends, aren't you?"

"Sure," I say. "Hey, when are you coming for Thanksgiving?"

He hesitates.

Uh-oh.

"Well, honey, there's been a change of plans," he says. "I have to be traveling that entire week. They don't have Thanksgiving in Europe. I absolutely promise I'll come for Christmas."

I'm disappointed. There were also two years during which I stayed at college for Thanksgiving instead of coming home to the city because Dad was abroad. He works for an investment bank, analyzing foreign companies, and he travels a lot of the time. Staying at school over break wasn't so bad; I actually met some nice people from my dorm who also were there over break, mostly students from out West who didn't want to go home for just four days. But I can't complain because usually my dad tries his best with holidays. He knows I don't see many relatives and that holidays are one of the things that are important to me.

"You have my word on Christmas," Dad says. "No matter what. I'd never let you down on Christmas."

"I know."

"But I don't want you to be alone on Thanksgiving. I have some friends who'd be happy to have you over."

"I don't want to be someone's charity case."

"Come on. I'll make a call."

"I'm actually excited about planning the whole day alone," I say. I do still have a few weeks until Thanksgiving to work that out.

"Are you sure?"

"Yes. It'll be nice to have the break." Not different. Just nice.

"All right."

As I hang up, I wonder whether my father is distant because he feels guilty about promises not kept. Like the Big Lie. But maybe I can figure it out over Christmas.

As for Thanksgiving, it will be strange that day watching out the window as carloads of people's relatives arrive and take off. I suppose I'll try to cook a decent meal. Maybe I'll pick up a rotisserie chicken at the supermarket.

Hat Guy is wearing his gray hat again, but not the raincoat. It's too sunny for him to get away with the raincoat, I suppose. He's sitting in the window of the coffee shop where Ronald the Rice-Haired Milquetoast works when I pass by. He couldn't have known I was coming. Could he?

Two can play at that game.

I double back, head into the shop and order cranberry tea. Ronald is on the job. He smiles as he hands it to me. "How's it going?" he asks. I'm too busy to talk to him, so I mumble something and grab a table by the window with my back to Hat Guy. Now, instead of him following me, I'm following him.

But I guess he's not, because he finishes whatever he's drinking, crushes his cup and gets up to leave. I briefly catch a glimpse of the books he's toting.

At the top of each, it says, "Piano/guitar/vocals." They're Broadway songbooks. The day I saw him in the subway station muttering, he must have been running lines or singing to himself.

I get up to get napkins, but really to listen to Ronald and Hat Guy's conversation.

Ronald asks him, "How's the new pad?"

"Good," Hat Guy says. "It's good." He shuffles his songbooks to avoid dropping them.

"See you." Ronald nods, and Hat Guy walks out the door.

I finish my tea and hand the mug to Ronald.

"That was Cy," Ronald says. "He lives around the corner." I don't say anything, so he continues. "Cy just moved here. Just got an acting job off-Broadway. He used to have to come in all the way from South Jersey for auditions." When I still don't say anything, Ronald adds, "It's really funny."

Hey, pal, if I need to be told, then it isn't.

In the evening, it's quiet in my apartment, and I feel alone. I know it's my fault. I have to push myself more.

There must be something or someone out there to challenge me.

I heave open my window and stick my head out to breathe fresh air. I notice an elderly man walking by in an old-fashioned suit and cap. He reminds me of this kid in my elementary school, Jimmy Miller, who came in one year for Halloween dressed up as the principal, in a ratty suit and cap. He got sent home. I think that we always remember kids from elementary school best by something bad they did or something bad that happened to them. Even though I was concentrating on being the kid who got straight A's and who could recite every major presidential speech and who was the only one to know all four verses of the "Star-Spangled Banner," I also remember other students by their titles: David Rosner, the boy who threw up in gym; Sandi Anthony, the girl who had to go to the hospital after a projector fell on her head; Ken Meltzer, the boy who wet his pants two days in a row. No one ever forgets the kids who threw up or wet their pants in school. Someday I'm going to see one of them in the *New York Times* wedding section, and I'm going to wonder if their new husband or wife knows the story, and whether I should write and tell them. I wonder what it's like to know something about someone that their spouse doesn't know, like what they were like in first grade.

I take a last whiff of air. It feels cool, crisp and inexplicably tentative, like there's a subtle harshness creeping in. It feels almost as if it's trying to transform into a solid.

Chapter Five

The next evening, the newscasters say we are in for a major snow-storm.

The reports get more and more dire. On the radio, the jazz station DJ says in his soothing voice that we should expect four to six inches. On the six o'clock news, they say six to eight. At eleven, they say a foot. This excites me somehow.

Before I go to bed, I gaze up at the streetlight. It's not snowing yet, but it will. I curl up and drift into a confident sleep. I am excited to see what the world will look like when I wake up.

In the morning, everything is quiet except the sounds of motors in the distance. A sheer white light streams in through my window, and I know what there is to know: Everything's canceled.

I look out at the naked trees, thin fortresses of snow built up on each branch. I have to admit, it's beautiful. Just enjoying the view would be another Petrov-pleasing activity. I climb onto my windowsill, which I outfitted with soft black throw-pillows some time ago, and hug my knees. I rest my back against the side of the sill. I can barely make out the apartment across the street, as the snow is still falling, the flakes small but darting fast in zig-zag patterns. Even though I can't see my neighbors across the way, I think about how lucky they are to be huddling inside, listening to music, drinking hot cider or reading on the couch. I think of David and his fireplace, even though I don't want to. I wonder what he's doing now, if he ever thinks, at least once, of me and the things we did together. I wonder if I should call him sometime, just in case. But whenever I passed him on campus after the relationship ended, he wouldn't look at me. For a second, I wonder if, now that I'm older, I could say the things to him that he wanted me to say. But I still don't think I can. They're the kind of things someone else would say, someone different than I. And it's a matter of principle, anyway. If I gave in and did something that made me uncomfortable just because I was pressured to, I'd just be as bad as everyone else.

Besides, if that's what he wanted most out of a relationship, I'm sure he found it in someone else by now. Or maybe not. After all, he was still single into his early forties.

I suppose I also should not admit that I miss him. Or more, the way I felt at the time.

I read in the window for some of the morning, and in the afternoon, when I turn on the TV, it's snowing on *General Hospital*. It's amazing how soap opera producers have such prognostic abilities. I wonder if they have their own forecasters.

On the screen, the characters hash out their affairs and illegitimate babies and amnesiac former lovers above typed white letters that scroll slowly:

****A winter storm warning is in effect until 8 p.m. this evening***...Stay tuned to this channel for further developments...

Then, the "Special Report" art flashes. A newscaster blathers about the "blizzard," and behind him there's footage of people waiting in line at supermarkets. I can't remember any snowstorm in my nineteen years of life that stopped enough milk and eggs from getting through or prevented people from reaching the nearest store, yet, they act like they have to stockpile a month's worth of food. I think maybe what happened was that once there was a snowstorm in the 1930s that was so bad that people couldn't get groceries for days, so now, every time we might get a little precipitation, they act like Armageddon is coming. It's sort of like the old people who hide all their money under the mattress because they grew up in the Depression when the banks blew their life savings. But I think the more likely reason is that people enjoy pretending there's a crisis just to show off how prepared they are. Hey! Look at me! The boards on my windows are bigger'n yours! In my driveway, I got a four-by-four, and in my pantry, *canned yams!*

I decide I'm going to enjoy the rest of the storm, trite as that may be. The Inaccuweather forecast says the snow could keep up into the night. I'll take full advantage. I'll make cocoa, swirling with cream; I'll curl up under mountains of comforters, light a couple of candles, keep the television on and hide away from the destruction.

During the 5 p.m., 5:30 p.m., 6 p.m., and 6:30 p.m. newscasts (molest me if I'm wrong, but aren't there too many newscasts?), the mayor can't seem to keep away from the microphones. "We are advising anyone who doesn't have to be out, not to go out," he says. "The roads are icy and slippery, and there have already been serious accidents." He is wearing the Politician State of Emergency Rolling up My Sleeves Outfit. For those unfamiliar with the getup, the Politician State of Emergency Rolling up My Sleeves Outfit (PSERMSO) is anything informal that is designed to show viewers just how cool a politician is in a crisis, how difficult this problem is for him, and how willing he is to roll up his sleeves and work with the rank and file. In the Northeast, the standard PSERMSO is a baseball cap bearing the name of the local favorite team, plus jeans and a tucked-in shirt. In the South, the shirts are polo. And we see the PSERMSOs not just during blizzards, but "hurrikins," as they call them in Looosiana.

The phone rings.

I hope it's someone I know. I want to talk to someone during the storm. I wait, then pick up the phone on the third ring.

"Hello," the caller asks, "are you Carrie Palby?"

"What might I have won," I say tiredly.

"Actually, I'm calling from Lerman Temporaries. We're trying to set up some temps for the next few weeks because our clients are really busy. Do you have either Wednesday or Friday night free for an assignment?"

Oops! "I guess either one," I say quickly. My feet are cold, so I pull them up, under the comforter. I get scheduled for Wednesday.

On *World News Tonight,* the anchor mentions the blizzard. Sometimes I worry that national news is too Northeast-centric. I'd like to do a study to see if a storm in Connecticut and an equivalent storm in Georgia get equal coverage. There are a great many things I would do a study on if I had the time, materials and funding. It bothers me that I can't. I wonder if others are irked by this, this incessant drive to plumb a million things and the inability to delve adequately into any one of them.

★ ★ ★

When the excitement has calmed down some, I decide I've put off placing my personal ad long enough. There's a *Weekly Beacon* box around the corner. I pull a coat over my sweat clothes and head out.

Outside, it's frosty. For a few seconds, I stop. I stand in the middle of the street, surrounded by plowed-up white stuff. The city is as quiet as it ever gets. When flakes pass in front of the streetlight, they light up in yellow for a second. I look into different people's windows, at their soft lighting and blue flashes of TV. These people are my neighbors and I know not one of them. Why?

I try to make out what people are watching on TV. It's too hard to tell. I notice that the lights are off in the apartment of the couple across the street.

Once I'm back home, I slip under my comforter and open the *Beacon* to the back. There are all sorts of ads for female escort services, photos of big-busted women who pretend they really enjoy posing in front of a camera. How men can get turned on by something that's so obviously fake, I'll never know. And there are a ton of these ads, so there are literally hundreds of men who want to pay for this kind of cheap, meaningless thrill. They could even be men I went to school with or stand in line next to at the supermarket. There's simply no way to tell. It's depressing, but I suppose it only proves that men really are from another planet. I never wanted to believe that. But there are some things that just aren't fair, or as they should be in life, as much as you want them to be. Like that thing about there being one right person in the world for everyone. I believed that when I was little, but it's not scientific, and even though I have maybe fifteen or twenty more years ahead of me to find out for sure, I did go through four years at college and found no one. It makes more sense, mathematically, that there are negative-four people in the world who are right for someone like me, and about six who are right for a busty twenty-two-year-old girl who's beautiful and sprightly and outgoing, so it averages to one for each person. But it really isn't.

The most concrete evidence for men being from another planet is the difference between the personal ads from women and men. As I wander through the "Women Seeking Men," I notice that the women list the following qualities to describe themselves: smart, sensitive, love animals, love long walks on the beach, love museums, love books. They sound like kind, interesting people. The men don't list their hobbies; they stick more to specifying what they want, which is someone "sexy" and "vivacious." What's funny is, the men don't care to hide their *own* visual inadequacies. Two of them say they "look like Anthony Edwards," which just means they're bald. They're lucky that a bald guy got on TV and got famous so they can convey this in some oblique way. I see there is one guy who wants a woman who is "Rubenesque." Thank God for variety.

I look at the different categories. There's a category for married men. I don't know why a newspaper would condone that. But I guess there's a market for it, and they're the only one to fill it. Still, that doesn't make it right.

I scan all the ads more closely. There's something else that strikes me as strange.

It's the very high number of people who declare that they "enjoy working out."

Huh?

I can see enjoying playing a sport, or enjoying movies or enjoying traveling, but there is—and I'm not being funny here— absolutely not one thing that could possibly be enjoyable about working out. I'm not even talking about a difference of opinion or taste or an activity preference. I'm saying that working out is something that you do to tone muscles. It doesn't feel pleasurable; it doesn't involve competition. It involves repetition. There is nothing at all interesting about it. The joy may come when you're all done, because you know that you've done something good for yourself. Or, the joy may come weeks later when you flex your abs in the mirror and fantasize about members of the opposite sex scrambling to you at the beach. But there is nothing enjoyable about the actual process of doing exercises. Writing that you enjoy working out is like writing "enjoy taking vitamins" or "enjoy annual physical exam" or "enjoy colonoscopy."

I've also noticed that people talk about working out constantly these days, whether it's where they work out, how much they work out, or, most important, how guilty they are that they haven't been working out and how they're going to work out tomorrow. Maybe when it shows up in someone's personal ad, it's a sneaky way for the person to tell you how in shape they are. Or maybe it's a clue that they're *not*.

There's a whole code to these ads.

I skim more of them. I learn all about guys seeking women who are vivacious, guys seeking women who are sexy, guys who like sports, guys who like music (who doesn't?) and guys who like "hanging out." Not all the ads are irritating, but some are just so bland that they seem the same. How am I supposed to differentiate?

Then something catches my eye.

There's an ad that says, "SWM, 26, engaged—but looking for more. I've met my best friend for life; now I want to fool around."

How terrible!

The poor girl. She is so sure she's getting this prince of a guy. And what of him? Why is he marrying her if he's not attracted to her? Is someone holding a gun to his head?

I move on, trying to find anyone in the ads who sounds interesting. I'm not very successful. When I finish up, I want to throw the paper away. But I just can't get the "engaged" ad out of my mind.

It makes me angrier and angrier.

And I can do something about it.

What?

I envision a scene in which I bring the ad to the couple's wedding. When the minister asks for objections, I wave the paper in the air and say, "He's advertising to cheat!" Of course, I don't think they really ask that anymore. Probably because today, there's so much cheating and lying going on that everyone would have an objection.

What they should do is advertise weddings in advance in the newspaper, like those legal ads that note that the state will seize this or that property if someone doesn't come forward.

I'm going to get on the Internet and find that ad. I'm going to pretend I'm engaged, and I'm going to meet this guy. I can't change all men—or women, for that matter (I wonder if there actually *are* other women who will answer this ad, and why)— but I can change this guy, who is the biggest jerk I've encountered, and I haven't even encountered him yet!

There was a phone icon next to the ad, which means you can actually call to hear the person's voice. Good idea.

I pick up the phone and dial the 900 number for the personals.

"Welcome to the *Weekly Beacon* personals. You must be eighteen or over to use this service. If you are under eighteen, please hang up now."

Whew—just made it. I haven't felt this great since I got into the Westinghouse Science Project semifinals.

"At the sound of the beep, you will begin being charged for this call. *Beep.* Please listen carefully to these instructions before making a selection."

Oh no. This is costing me $2.50 a minute and they want me to sit through instructions. What a rip.

"To answer a specific ad, press 1."

I do.

"I'm sorry. That character is not recognized."

I press 1 again.

"Welcome to the *Weekly Beacon* personals."

Look how they extort money. I don't know what to do about this. But it seems like if I tried to set right everything I saw that was wrong in the world, I would never have time to do anything else. I assume someone else will complain about this rip-off, but I guess that's what everyone assumes and why nothing ever gets done.

I wonder what it is that makes someone the kind of person who does try to change things. Maybe I should be that rare person. That would be a positive step. Petrov hasn't put it on my list, but I know that looking for ways to make the world a better place could help me become more a part of it.

Perhaps setting this engaged guy straight is a start.

I stay on the phone, wade through two minutes of instructions, and press 1. It asks for a box number, and I tap it in.

"Hi," says a friendly sounding voice. "My name's Matt. I'm twenty-six, and as I wrote in the ad, I'm about to marry a great girl."

He actually sounds normal. I have to prevent myself from being lulled. I have to remind myself that he's a pig.

"I guess I'm happy, but I'm also too young to stop having a good time. Maybe you're in a similar situation. Obviously we'd have to be discreet. If you want to talk more, leave a message on my phone, or send me an e-mail via the Web site."

Beep.

I think for a second. I made the call. I might as well do this. Maybe I can even sound seductive.

"Hi, Matt," I say. "You sound *really* cute. I sympathize fully with your situation. I'm dating a great guy, but there's just no chemistry. I want to see if it's right. When I saw your ad, I thought this might be a…well, a discreet way to do it, like you said. Give me a call sometime and we can talk."

I leave my phone number so he can call and we can get this over with. I say my name is Heather. That's a good all-around name. I'll bet no one named Heather has ever not had her call returned.

I don't mind that Matt will have my real number because if he creates a problem later on, I'll say that Heather was my roommate and she moved to Namibia.

I have one more call to make this evening—to Petrov. I'm supposed to have an appointment tomorrow. But it's certainly still going to be far too blizzardous for therapy. I call his answering machine and say, "Hi, it's Carrie Pilby, I'm just calling to make sure tomorrow's appointment is canceled because of the storm, and I'll assume I don't have to go unless you call me by nine tonight. Bye."

Hey, I'm giving him a whole hour. Otherwise I have to make other plans. Maybe Matt from the personals, who in high school was probably the president of Future Adulterers of America, will call and arrange to meet for breakfast, since his fiancée, future president of Wives Who Look the Other Way, will think he's at work.

Before I go to bed, I review my own written personal ad.

PRODIGY SEEKS GENIUS—I'm 19, very smart, seeking nonsmoking nondrugdoing very very smart SM 18-25 to talk about philosophy and life. No hypocrites, religious freaks, macho men.

I decide to take out "or psychos" because that will only give the psychos a warning to disguise themselves. I put this in an envelope, which I will drop in the mail in the morning. I bet I'll get some promising responses. And then I'll meet some really great people. I feel good about this as I drift off to sleep.

The trucks have been out all night, and the streets are clear by morning. Petrov calls me and apologizes for not having gotten back to me the night before. He says that our appointment is definitely on. Curses.

The subways are running regularly. I wonder what Petrov did last night during the storm. He's divorced. He has two adult daughters. I've seen their pictures on his desk. I wonder if he was alone, or if he has a girlfriend or something. Hey, maybe he has no girlfriend and secretly, he's attracted to me. Maybe that's why he's always so interested in my love life. Imagine if it turned out that he became my date, and he was the one I ended up spending New Year's with. Wouldn't that be a scorcher of an ending?

Of course, he knows my dad, so that's a real turnoff. Or maybe it's some sort of kinky turn-on for him. Maybe we'll make out on December 31 at the top of the Empire State Building, far above the 1,336 red, white and blue lights, and then head to his place to talk Gestaltism till dawn.

"Your childhood memories are interesting," Petrov tells me during our appointment.

"Thank you. That's because I'm so interesting."

"You *are*," Petrov says. "But the *kinds* of memories you've been having are interesting. They're very feeling-oriented and sensory. I think it once again shows that you're hurting yourself by not doing the things that you enjoy. Things that deep down appeal to your senses, not only to your mind. The things that make you truly happy."

"Hmm."

"Look at what was on your list," he says. "Cherry soda. Taste. Starfish. Orange, bumpy things. Look at what you remember. Blue robin's eggs. Red fire engines. You need to satisfy your senses just as much as your mind."

"Maybe."

"Which brings me to our goals list. Do you have it with you?"

"Yeah."

ZOLOFT®

1. Do things from list of 10 things you love
2. Join an org./club
3. Go on date
4. Tell someone you care
5. Celebrate New Yr's

"How are you doing with your goals?"

"I've made preliminary advances on getting a date," I say. I think of my personal ad and my message for Matt the Cheater. "I have to work on joining an organization."

"Okay. So what are you doing about getting a date?"

I don't think he would like me placing personal ads. Nor would he like me responding to ads from engaged men who want to cheat. My dad would not like this, either. "I don't have to tell you," I say. "A date is a date."

"Okay," Petrov says. "So, what else have you been up to? What did you do during last night's storm?"

"You first."

He sighs. "I had a friend over and we watched a movie."

"A *friend?* Female or male?"

"Uh…female."

"Was this a girlfriend?"

"Let's talk about you."

"What movie?"

He doesn't say.

"Was it porn?"

"Carrie. Look. You have to know that there are limits. I am not asking you anything very personal, but I do need to make progress and find out how to help you to meet people and get out there and find some happiness. This isn't about me. It's about you. You would feel better about opening up to people if you could open up to *me,* but you won't even talk to me, and you're *paying* me."

"My father. My father is paying you. I don't need to tell you how I spent last night's snowstorm, last October's nor'easter, the Blizzard of '96, or Hurricane Andrew."

"I realize it's personal."

"It's not that," I say. "You're only asking because you hope I'll say I spent last night alone, so that you can give me your sophisticated Psych 101 explanation. You actually revel in my problems. If I'm miserable, then it means that the rules and moral codes I stick to aren't true. And that makes you feel better about your own life, and about all the things you do, like having spent last night with what's-her-name. So maybe I did spend the storm alone, but if I spent it alone, I chose to. Just like you chose *not* to."

"But what's interesting is, I didn't even ask you whether you spent it with a person," he says. "I asked how."

"But that's what you were getting at."

He doesn't say anything, just sits in his armchair. His hair is damp with snow. He must have gotten into the office right before our appointment.

"Well, here's the truth," I say. "You and everyone else in the city spent last night snuggling under the sheets with someone, talking about ski trips and Christmases past and intertwining your cocoa-singed tongues, and I was just alone with my blankets. Is that what you want to hear?"

Petrov sighs. "Believe it or not, Carrie, I *would* like to see you happy," he says. "I *would* like you to come in here one day and say, 'Hi, Dr. Petrov, life is going great. And I'll tell you all about it.' If you were happy, I'm sure we'd still have things to talk about—not necessarily to work on, but things you might want to tell me about your life, because despite what you think, it's only human to want to talk to someone, whether things are going great or they're going terribly. But with you, I *don't* get the sense things are going great. And you could potentially be a great person and have a major impact on the world, but first you deserve to figure out early in life how to pull yourself out of misery. Analyzing everything to the hilt without focusing on your emotional side isn't going to do it. Do you really want to look back when you're thirty-five and say, why the hell did I spend all those years miserable?"

"But I'm *not* miserable."

"You'd be more convincing if you could even look at me when you say that." He looks at me when he says that. "You know what? Not only do I *not* like seeing you upset, but I don't even think that you *think* I do. I think you're putting up your last defenses."

I look at him. I can't figure out whether his eyes are gray or blue.

"One of these days, you should decide you are going to let someone get to know you," he says. "You can start by trusting me. You and I don't have to be adversaries. Nothing you say goes beyond these walls. I tell your father nothing. I tell your neighbors nothing, I tell my friends nothing, I tell my colleagues nothing. If you like, you can spend a session railing off, even cursing *me* out, and I will sit here and not pass judgment. I'm here to be used. Take advantage of me. Do it because I ask you to."

"What if I'd committed a crime? You would have to tell my father then."

"I would have to tell someone if it was serious," Petrov says. "Yes. That's true."

"So then, what I tell you is not 100 percent confidential."

"A fine point. But I'll make a deal. All noncriminal activities, I won't report to your father or anyone else. So open up to me."

"Fine."

"Tell me something about yourself that you've never told anyone."

"I slept with my English professor."

He stops.

Guess he wasn't expecting anything good.

He's waiting for me to say more, but I don't. Let him squirm.

"You once slept with your English professor?"

"No, not once," I say. "I guess…well, there are seven days in a week, but we used to take a day or two off…."

"We don't need to get that specific."

Ha ha, you bastard.

"Now," he says, "is this actually sleeping, or…"

I give him a look.

"Okay, you had intercourse."

Brilliant.

"And how do you feel about that?"

"Fine."

He looks at me.

Interesting how he naturally assumes it wouldn't have been fine. Interesting how he naturally assumes I couldn't have handled it. It's so condescending.

He asks, "Have you had other…sexual relationships?"

"That guy who has the session right before me, the really short guy, I looked him up after his last session with you," I say. "The two of us went to South Street Seaport together and made out by the docks. In that little area behind the mall."

"Come on."

"I'm sorry, but we did."

"Why?"

"Because if you go to the front of the mall, the view isn't as good. Behind the mall, you have the bridge and all the ships..."

"Carrie..."

"Okay, so I'm kidding about the seaport, but I did look him up. I figured he was lonely, like me. I kept finding excuses to pass his apartment, and eventually, I bumped into him and talked to him. And we went out. And then we went back to his apartment. And then, I might add, into his bedroom."

"I hope you're joking."

"I'm not."

"And you slept with him?"

"Well, we were about to, but the phone rang."

"Ugh." Petrov wipes his eyes.

Then he smiles.

"All right," I say. "So I'm kidding. But not about my professor."

"Okay. Well, I'll ask again. Is he the only person you've been with?"

"Yes."

"Good."

"And Rudy Giuliani."

"Stop that."

"Okay. He was."

"And...why do you think you haven't been with anyone else since? Did he hurt you?"

"See what you focus on? The negative. I was happy when I was with him. It ended. Most people aren't as smart and well-read as he was. That's it."

"Was this guy married?"

"No."

"Do you think—and I'm just asking because I want to find out how this relationship affected you—do you think you're withdrawn because of your relationship with him?"

"I think I had my relationship with him because I was withdrawn."

He nods and writes something down.

"Where is he now?"

"Still at school, I guess."

"Why did the relationship end?"

I don't know if I want to tell him this.

"Because…like the rest of the world…he wanted me to be someone I wasn't."

"Well, he knew who you were to begin with, didn't he?"

"He liked me at first. He said I was fresh, and young. He liked that I was innocent. But then he wanted me to be not-so-innocent. Everyone wants to have their cake and eat it, too. It's like people who wish and wish that someone nonpolitical would run for office. But as soon as the person does, then they're not nonpolitical."

"I see what you're saying. But you did have intercourse with him."

"To see what it was like. So that people couldn't tell me I was complaining about things I knew nothing about. People like you, who assume I've never done anything. Just because I have morals doesn't mean I haven't done anything."

"True."

Something odd is happening. His body seems a little straighter.

And it seems like he's talking to me as if I'm an adult instead of a kid. It's astounding, but actually I think he respects me now. And why? Because I've had sex?

Amazing how having had sex makes someone respect you more. Like you know their secrets; you've sampled their universe; you've shared an experience, and there's nothing more they need to know about you. It really is ridiculous. I think having gone to war or having overcome child abuse or even having witnessed a car accident gives you more knowledge of the human condition.

I stir around at home for a while, annoyed because I have a legal proofreading assignment for tonight. Night jobs are lousy because you spend the whole day thinking about them, and then you have to *go* to them. It's like working the whole day *and* night.

The subway is quiet. Sitting across from me on the train is a tired-looking woman with a head of black, curly hair and a huge, bulging pocketbook. The size of a woman's pocketbook is inversely related to her wealth. The poorer a woman is, the bigger her pocketbook, and the wealthier she is, the smaller her pocketbook. You'd think it would be the opposite, but money doesn't take up a lot of room: one's clothes, papers and life's accumulations do.

The woman gets off a stop before me and I lean back against the hard seat, feeling the rumble of the train as it takes off again.

I emerge from the bowels of the city several blocks from my assignment, in a seedy area near the waterfront. I walk past an empty, fenced-in lot, and then I see an old brick building that says on it *First Prophets' Church, Joseph Natto, Pastor.*

I remember the yellow flyer that I took from Tonsure-Head. I want to peek into the church, but the windows are too high.

Still, I look down and notice a gray ridged outcropping at the base of the building where I can get some footing.

I step onto it and peer in through a small window with bars. The gauzy pink curtains are mostly closed, but I can make out a minifridge with magnets all over it. One is holding a flyer that says, "Sermon, Sundays, 10:30."

I decide I'll go to the church soon. I'll sit in the back row and keep an eye on things. I should be appointed Religious Fraud Commissioner of the Borough of Manhattan. They might as well have one. It's no stranger a job title than Public Advocate.

As I get closer to the middle of town, a shimmering marble building comes into view. The law firm takes up all nine floors. Now, that's money. I recognize the name of one of the partners as being a former city councilman.

I step off the empty elevator on the sixth floor, and there's a reception area with no one in it. There's a plate of fruit and cookies on a coffee table. I imagine the food is left over from a meeting. I want to grab a cookie, but I'm worried they'll say they're not for me. I wait a minute. No one comes in. I tap my fingers on the counter. I wait another minute. I reach for a cookie.

"Hello?" a woman says, coming into the room. I jump. "Sorry," she says.

A supervisor tells me there's no work yet, and walks me to a small windowless room with a white rug and just two desks.

I've brought a backpack full of magazines and mail. I sit down at a desk that's facing a wall, and I look behind me at the other desk. That desk is a mess, with documents scattered everywhere. Some are pinched in black Acco clips large enough to choke a ferret, and some are snug in serrated brown folders. Even the wastebasket is a mess.

I sift through my junk mail and get to a red postcard that says, "Harvard Club young alumni mixer." The Harvard Club:

Something I haven't thought about joining and probably should. They have a clubhouse in midtown Manhattan. Maybe I should have joined as soon as I graduated, instead of looking everywhere and anywhere for intelligent people. If there are any to be found, they'd surely be at the Harvard Club. Right? And joining an organization is on my list. This organization might be better suited to me than Joseph Natto's church.

I pull Petrov's goals list out of my bag and peruse it.

1. Do things from list of 10 things you love
2. Join an org./club
3. Go on date
4. Tell someone you care
5. Celebrate New Yr's

At least my personal ad will be in the *Beacon* this week. I have to get at least one decent response. As for *in*decent responses, I still haven't heard back yet from Matt the Cheater. But I have a feeling I will.

Suddenly someone appears in the doorway. She looks about my age. She has long, sleek hair, a kind smile and bright eyes. I feel disarmed and somehow, instantly calmed.

"Hi," she says. "Are you temping?"

"Supposed to be."

She leans against the door. "I work down the hall. I was bored."

I say, "Are you temping, too?"

"Well, I am a temp," she says, "but I'm here every day. I've been 'temping' for four months. They don't want to hire me full-time because they'd have to pay the agency $6,000."

"It's actually not $6,000," I say, "but it's close. It's based on the rate of pay times the 300 work hours the firm says it loses by giving you up. It's like $5,850."

"*Like* $5,850," she says. "As if you haven't done the math."

"I guess I have." I don't know why I feel so nervous.

"I'm Kara," she says. She shakes my hand. Her fingers are long and sleek, like her hair. She looks down at my desk. "What's that?"

"A list," I say, and I turn it over quickly.

"Looks interesting."

"Just personal."

"Maybe you'll tell me eventually."

"Maybe."

There's a silence.

"They called three of us in for word processing tonight," Kara says, "even though there's practically no work for us to do."

"Why do they do that?"

"They don't want to send us home early because if something comes in and no one's here to work on it, the fit hits the shan." She looks at the empty swivel chair near the other desk. "Mind if I sit?"

"No."

She pulls the chair next to my desk and sits. "Why they called in extra proofreaders, I don't know. But more money for you."

"Mo' money, mo' better."

She laughs, and her hair falls in front of her shoulders. I can tell she's one of those people whom everyone likes to be around because she's always laughing. She's also tall and pretty and probably quite popular with the opposite sex.

"So what's your name?" she asks.

"Carrie. Pilby."

"Ah," she says. "Do you live around here?"

"The Village."

She seems excited by this. "My ex-boyfriend lives there. On Jones Street. He has a new girlfriend, but she's sooo not his type."

I don't know what to say to this, but it's certainly more inter-esting than my mail. "Do you ever see him?"

"Unfortunately, no, but he's playing CBGB this weekend," she says. I'm amazed that she considers me worthwhile enough to tell details of her life to. "I'm trying to get someone to go with me, but my friends are sick of hearing about him. I'll go alone if I have to. I'm going to spend two hours tomorrow in the gym and two hours Friday."

Poor girl. She really thinks this will help. Even if the com-bined four hours in the gym would make her lose an ounce or make her look better in any way, which they won't, they still wouldn't make a difference as to whether her boyfriend wants her back. Even though I know next to nothing about men, I know that whether they're attracted to you doesn't change based on a weight loss of five pounds.

"What's his name?"

"Mark," she says. When she says it, her lips part in a neat way. "He is soooo…amazing." She leans closer. "You know how when you're so into someone, there's absolutely nothing they can do in bed that's wrong?"

I assume it's a rhetorical question.

"Well, I wouldn't have cared what he did, but he knew what he was doing. But I don't care. Women know my body a lot bet-ter than men do."

So not only has she just told me about her ex-boyfriend's bedroom habits, but that she's bisexual, too. I wonder what she'll tell me next—maybe that her uterus is backward.

"You have a boyfriend?"

"No," I say.

She looks at me for an explanation. As if I have to apologize for it.

"I…I know this is weird, but I only like…"

I want to say *guys who are smart,* but I can't say the word *guys.* It's a word that makes people sound stupid and teenager-ish. Even though, technically, I *am* a teenager. On the other hand, I can't say "men," either. That makes me sound forty.

"I only like men…who are smart," I finish. "It's just a weird thing."

"That's probably because *you're* smart," she says.

I shrug.

"I like smart guys, too," she says. "Mark is smart. He's not book-smart, but he's street-smart. Bands don't just end up at CBGB. But maybe I won't go. He's self-centered, like all musicians."

"Are you going to get in trouble for being in here?"

"Nah. They know I'm around if they need me. Besides, it's clear we need to work together on finding you a smart boyfriend. Or girlfriend. I don't mean to assume you're straight."

"I am," I say, "But I really haven't…well, dated anyone… since my English professor."

I've never told anyone about it, and now I've told two people in one day. But I know it'll impress her. Maybe even put me on even ground, which nothing else would.

"All right!" she says, and holds out her hand. I give it a hesitant slap. "Are you in school?"

"I graduated last year."

"You look so young," she says. She keeps staring at me.

It makes me uneasy, so I look away. "I graduated early for my age."

She smiles. "You're smart. That's why you like smart guys. Where'd you go?"

"Harvard. For real."

She laughs. "Do people think you're lying when you tell them?"

"Sometimes they think I'm joking."

"That's because they don't have brains. A lot of people haven't heard of my school, even though it's famous."

"Where'd you go?"

"Smith?"

I nod.

"I don't know what I was thinking, going somewhere with all girls. It would have been better to have some variety."

"Yeah."

"My mom went there, so I went. But I only went for two years. Then I left. I wasn't dumb or anything...I was bored. I just had other things to learn about, not for credit. What's that list you have?"

I shrug. "Nothing."

"You didn't think I was going to give up, did you?" Her eyes really are dark. "I'm not easily eluded. Quick—what's on the list?"

"Nothing."

She teases me by suddenly pretending to reach for it. I get up to try to pull it out of the way, and for a second, her arm grazes my breast. She sits back.

"Well," she says, "in the time we've spent blabbing, we've both just earned five dollars. Isn't that amazing?"

I like the way she thinks. I wonder if I should share with her my theories about work. Then maybe some of my other theories. Maybe I'd lose her as a friend if she knew about my moral crusades. Maybe I should keep thoughts like that to myself. But isn't that like lying? Why should I wait to share things that are an important part of me?

Petrov says I should just find moderation. I'll stick with this one: "I think everyone cheats in their job," I say. "It's so much a part of the system that it's expected. I haven't seen a workplace yet where people didn't spend as much time as possible getting coffee and reading the *Post*."

"No kidding," Kara says. "It's like a fucking job requirement to not do your job. Especially around here."

She puts her elbows on my desk and leans over. She's practically in my face. "Okay, so tell me what I really want to know. How was Mr. Professor? Tell me every single detail, beginning to end. I want the *whole* story."

I wonder if she would have felt it worthwhile to talk to me if I *hadn't* had that experience.

I tell her the story from beginning to end. I even apologize for the fact that I did this with my *English* professor—I've come to realize how trite it was, since no one ever has an affair with their math professor. I guess the things math professors say in class aren't very seductive. Except when they talk about how line AB slides gracefully past the Y intercept.

I slow down a little when I get to the reason David and I broke up.

"I just felt like it wouldn't be me if I said that," I say.

"So too bad," Kara says. "Screw him. There's a movie where someone's asked if sex is dirty, and he says, 'Only if you do it right.' Well, there's really nothing that's dirty unless you're being forced to do it. There shouldn't be any rules for sex except the rule that you should feel comfortable with what you're doing. If you don't, it doesn't matter what anyone else does. If you're not a person who feels comfortable saying 'boo,' then you shouldn't have to say boo."

I nod.

"Although I'm sure it hurt to break up with him," she says. "College gets lonely if you don't have a boyfriend. Or girlfriend."

"True."

"Have you ever kissed a girl?"

"Uh…no."

"I have a female friend who kissed a girl and then kept swearing over and over that it only happened because she was drunk. But ninety-nine percent of the time, alcohol is just an excuse to do what you really wanted to do anyway."

"People are always like that," I say. "They do things simply because they feel like it, and then they come up with an excuse. Some of the stuff they do is really hypocritical. I've seen people do things they didn't believe in until two seconds ago, and then they come up with a rationalization for it. It drives me crazy."

"People can be hypocritical as hell," Kara says.

"Yes."

"And that's what makes life wonderful."

"Huh?"

She leans closer. "You never know what's going to happen," she says. "You can feel one way one day and then feel completely differently the next day. You can make mistakes. You can realize you were wrong. You can do things simply because they're indulgent or decadent. We can change our minds, try everything and then settle down when we choose to. We don't know how things will affect us until we're in different situations. It's wonderful."

Her face is really close to mine. I would debate her on this, but I want to keep her talking.

She's silent, though.

I say, "I think that if you declare something is wrong or dangerous, and you know it's wrong or dangerous, you flat out shouldn't do it. And if there *is* a good reason to do it, and if it hurts no one, then it's not wrong. Simple as that. I'm not saying that decadent is always bad. 'Wrong' and 'decadent' do not mean the same thing. No one is stopping you from eating a hot-fudge sundae. But if you believe, and you declare, that stealing is wrong, and you see a little kid with a hot-fudge sundae, you shouldn't steal his and then say it's okay because you *had* to have it. That's what I'm saying."

"I'll give you that," Kara says. "But tell me, do you believe in absolute truth?"

"Yes."

"Do you believe abortion is absolutely wrong, or absolutely right?"

"There are conditions where it's more right than not," I say. "Like if a woman was raped and traumatized and doesn't want to have the rapist's baby."

"Aren't you still killing an innocent baby?"

"Maybe," I say. "I guess you have a point. To modify what I said before, I do think there are objective truths, but I don't know for sure what they are. I haven't made a decision about unborn babies. I don't know exactly where life begins. But maybe there is an answer and I'm not a highly evolved enough life form to know it. There is one."

She considers this.

I add, "I don't know if every single thing is right or wrong. I'm still trying to figure it all out. But what I won't do is decide simply based on what I *feel* like doing. And if I do, I'll admit to it. If it's something unhealthy, hurtful or stupid, I'll try my best not to do it. If it's wrong or dangerous and hurts other people, or even if it hurts me, I'll stop. It seems like no one can pick something and stick to it. There are things that are immoral, and things that are dangerous, and things that are both, and even if the former is worse than the latter, the point is that it makes all the sense in the world not to do them. But as soon as it gets a little bit difficult, people change their reasoning. I've heard people who keep Kosher say it's okay to eat pork if it's in Chinese food. I knew a guy in college who was against people stealing software, but he stole music all the time. Half the people sitting in church are there because they just did something wrong and want absolution. If you're against something, be strong enough to commit to your beliefs."

"It seems there should be a disparity between dangerous and immoral," Kara says. "Do you really think doing things that hurt only yourself are immoral?"

"They're not as bad as hurting other people," I say, "but in the end, they can, in different ways. But that's not even my point. My point is that you should decide what to do based on logic, and then stick to it, not based on what you feel like doing at this particular moment."

"Wow," she says. "I like this discussion. I feel…challenged." She puts her head on the desk. "I don't get much intellectual stimulation most of the time."

"What do you do during the day?" I lay my head on my desk, too.

"I'm an actress," she says. "But I only get a commercial now and then. I'm trying out for indie films."

It almost seems as if she's trying to impress me. It's a strange feeling.

"Indie films are okay," I respond, "but lately I've spent a lot of time watching old movies."

"Have you seen *It Happened One Night?* That's the best."

"If it's not on the '100 best of all time' list, I probably won't get to it," I say.

"And you believe in this list?"

"It's as good a place to start as any. The reviewers were all professors and film scholars."

"What kinds of movies do you like?"

"Movies with a plot," I say. "Not today's movies, where a couple meets and the next scene is them in bed together."

"But that's realistic."

"Not in my life."

She laughs. "I'll take care of that. I'll bring you to CBGB and initiate you into my seedy underworld."

"Not likely," I say, although I wonder if I should let her do this. For research purposes, of course. For Petrov's five-point plan.

"You know, I've been thinking about the problem with you and your English professor," she says, picking her head up. "The problem is, you were young. We all make mistakes in our first relationships. One of the things we don't learn until later is how to say no and still keep men interested. It takes as much skill as saying yes. You can find a way to do it so that they can't get around it, and so that they don't blame you for it."

"Okay...."

"Here's an example. How do you get out of giving a guy oral sex?"

I shrug. "Eat peanut butter?"

She shakes her head. "Guess again."

"Say no?"

"You can't say no. If you say no to that, you've lost them for good. You need a reason." She points to her nose.

"Your nose is too long?"

"No," she says. "Say, 'I've got a deviated septum.' A deviated septum can block your nose so you can only breathe through your mouth. Therefore, you can't have something in your mouth, because you'd suffocate. It works, trust me. I have a friend who really is a mouth-breather. It's hard when she goes to the dentist because they have all those tools in her mouth. They could smother her."

"Oh."

"Deviated septum. Lesson number one for tonight."

From then on, I will always think of Kara as Deviated Septum.

An older woman with short hair and tiny round glasses peeks into the office. "Do you have work to do?" she asks me.

"Not...uh, right now."

"I have an assignment for you."

I hate that she sounds accusing. It's not like there was work and I ran away from it.

Kara goes back to her desk.

As I work, I can't concentrate well. My attention span is worse than usual. I feel all sorts of good things, although I can't classify them.

The assignment takes about an hour, and then I'm bored. I grab a red pencil and try to write out the periodic table from memory. But I only get up to molybdenum. Darn. I'm slowing down.

Before long, Kara pops her head back in. "I don't think we'll get in trouble if I only stay for a few minutes."

"I hope not."

"Witchy Woman's on break. I'm not interrupting your work, am I?"

"No."

She sits down. "So what's the list?"

"You don't give up."

"I'll leave in a second if you give me a hint."

Might as well level with her. "I see a therapist once in a while." Okay, this isn't exactly leveling, since I see him fifty-two times per year. "And he made up a list to help me socialize better."

I tell her all about Petrov and his silly list. "The organization, I can do," I say. "But it's hard to find a date if you're not into clubs."

"I'll find a date for you," Kara says. "Give me your phone number."

"Okay."

That night, I sleep more soundly than I have in months. In the morning, I wake up and feel happy. I'm not sure why, but I think that, for a change, something good is coming my way.

Chapter Six

I don't hear from Kara on Thursday or Friday. Saturday, the night that she mentioned she and friends were going to CBGB, I figure she'll call and ask me if I want to come along. But the hours pass and she doesn't. I should have acted more eager about it. I have to stop being so passive.

But maybe she really didn't think too highly of me. Maybe she has more exciting friends. She's like Nora, my freshman year friend at Harvard. Kara is a vibrant, funny person whom people like to be around. How stupid I was to think I'd be one of them.

I can't keep putting off this go-on-a-date thing to wait for a miracle to happen.

I put on my shoes and run to the corner to get the *Beacon*. My ad is the fourth one under "Women Seeking Men."

PRODIGY SEEKS GENIUS—I'm 19, very smart, seeking nonsmoking nondrugdoing very very smart SM 18-25 to talk about philosophy and life. No hypocrites, religious freaks, macho men.

I sit in my window and call the 900 number to record an introduction. "Hi," I say. "I'm Heather. I guess if you're listening to this, then you read my ad. Please leave your name and tell me about yourself. Also please leave your Stanford-Binet IQ score. You may leave your SATs if no Stanford-Binet is on file. Thank you." I decide that even if all the responses are from Neanderthals, I'll go on one date. That will satisfy my requirement.

When I finish, I notice that the couple in the apartment across the way is in the kitchen eating. They're sitting across from each other, talking and gnawing on something. There's a bottle of wine on their table. I wish I was in their shoes right now: sawing off a slice of some meat or other, washing it down with a glass of red, chatting and feeling the warmth. The couple can't be that much older than I am. Why aren't we friends? Why don't they ever invite their neighbors over?

I decide to ask them. But I need their names so I can find out their phone number.

Getting neighbors' phone numbers is not hard. I have a system. I pull on my coat and boots to run across the street to check their mailbox.

I stamp in the couple's vestibule, leaving stars of snow on their dirty black mat. Their mailbox says, *Guarino*. I wonder if the male half of the couple cheats on the female half. Like Matt from the personals.

I used to be romantic like everyone else when I was little, and I figured that marriage was something that happened because it was "meant to be." But lately I've been wondering if it's just a necessary social convention. Maybe we've stuck with it because if you don't have at least one person in this rotten world who is bound contractually to back you up when everyone else wants to roll you over with a cement truck, you'll end up wanting to kill yourself. So you sign this contract with someone saying you're going to care about them and support them and not stab them in the back, no matter what happens in life and no matter how old and wrinkly and ugly you both get, and they're supposed to do the same. If we didn't have large numbers of people doing this, the world would get too confusing and probably more lonely than it already is.

I go back to my own pad, hang up my coat, and look up Guarino on the Internet. There are a Thomas and Jocelyn Guarino at that address. I turn off the lights in my room and rest my head on the windowsill, my body on the bed, so they can't see me. I pick up the phone. I first put in *67 so my call can't be traced.

I watch Tom get up from the table and disappear. Jocelyn is looking after him.

Tom picks up. "Hello?"

His voice is deeper than I expected. I guess that when you see someone, you automatically assume many things about them, like what they'd sound like.

"Why don't you have a dinner party someday and invite your neighbors?" I ask.

"Who is this?"

"Does it matter?"

There's a silence at the other end.

Then I hang up. I haven't thought this through. I need a more detailed plan.

About ten minutes later, my phone rings.

Maybe it's Kara. Maybe she's inviting me to CBGB after all. I know it's too late at night for telemarketers. It must be personal. Please don't let it be a wrong number, I think. Don't let it be my father this time, either. Okay, I'll admit it, God. I feel lonely right now. So yes, I need friends *once* in a while. Are you happy?

It's a male voice. "Hi...is Heather there?"

For a second I think it *is* a wrong number. But then I remember that I left my number for Matt, the "wants to fool around" guy.

"This is she," I say.

"Oh, hi. I'm Matt." He sounds a little nervous. It's almost cute. I have to stop myself. If I'm that easily led, then I'm as bad as everyone else. But just because Matt met his fiancée in high school or college, does that mean none of us will ever deserve to spend time with him?

What am I doing? Making an argument *for* cheating?

"You called me," Matt says. "From the, uh..."

"Oh, the *Beacon,*" I say. "Right. I guess I just wanted to see what was...I don't know."

"I guess it's awkward," Matt says. "Well, you read the ad. What's *your* situation?"

"I have a boyfriend."

"Right, right. You said."

"I don't know," I say. "I guess you sounded like an interesting guy, and along the way, I've had thoughts like yours—should I never get to have fun again?"

"Right!" Matt says. "What if you want both? What if you've met the person you want to marry, but you still occasionally want the right to secretly see someone else you're attracted to? If both people in the marriage know about it, it can get uncomfortable. But if it's done discreetly, it won't hurt anyone. In fact, it might even help the marriage. With everyone getting divorced these days..."

"Exactly," I say. "You only live once. Better to have a good marriage and sometimes do things on the side than to ruin your marriage, or to never get married in the first place."

"Yes!" Matt says. "Most people are reluctant to talk about this. But lots of people cheat. They'll probably all tell you it's wrong. Except for themselves. Or in *their* particular situation."

So Matt's not a hypocrite, and he even dislikes hypocrites. But he's not exactly honest, either. He's saying he believes in marriage, but he doesn't believe in sharing his *real* view of marriage with his fiancée.

"But what if your future wife wanted to do the same thing?" I ask.

"Well…" he says.

Ha! Right away he's trying to come up with a rationalization for why it's okay for him but not her. I've already caught him in his own web of dishonesty.

But then I realize I should back off. The purpose of this is to meet him and then tell his girlfriend on him, right? *She* can be the one to put him in his place. It doesn't always have to be me.

"I wouldn't want to know about it," Matt says.

"But you think it's wrong," I say, unable to help myself. "Yet, you want to cheat before you even get married."

"Yes, but *I'm* going to be discreet."

"You're right," I say. What I really want to say is, if you trust your wife so little, if you think you can cheat responsibly and *she* wouldn't, then why are you marrying her at all? If she's not the kind of person who would be careful, maybe you don't have as much in common as you think.

Besides, even if he claims he's going to handle his cheating responsibly, why does he get to be the one to decide everything? Maybe he will allow a lapse in judgment one day, get a disease and give it to his wife. He's already cheating and they're not even married. In five years, he may decide that other taboos should be broken. Then five years later, a few more. As soon as you cross a line you've set, it's that much easier to cross again and again, until there's no line anymore.

But I remind myself that an argument will scare him off, and then I won't meet him. This is all about the possibility that his girlfriend thinks he's perfect. She should know about his real views of marriage. She has a right to. Doesn't she?

Matt and I talk about boy-and girlfriends and commitments and love and divorce and parents, and then he asks if I want to meet him "for coffee" and talk further. I wonder why people always want to meet for coffee. Matt also manages to ask what I look like, ostensibly so he'll know how to recognize me. But he asks a whole lot of questions about my looks. I guess if he's going to cheat, it might as well be with someone hot.

My phone beeps. Believe it or not, I've got two calls at once! Matt and I agree to meet for dinner at the Mexican place near Times Square the next night. Then I switch to my other line.

"Hello, Carrie?"

I'm pretty excited to hear the voice. "Yes?"

"It's me, Kara. From Dickson, Monroe?"

"Yes. Hi!"

"I was wondering if you have plans for Friday."

"This Friday? No. I don't think so."

"I'm making plans to go out with a friend, kind of a girls' night, if you want to come along. My friend flakes out a lot, but if no one ends up doing it, I'll go anyway."

"I'll come along."

Wow! Now I've got plans with Matt for tomorrow, and plans with Kara for Friday.

I get the details on where to meet, and actually feel I'm going to make progress. Real progress! I knew this couldn't be so hard.

The next morning, I have a strange mix of emotions when I wake up, but the strongest is dread. I actually am not looking forward to meeting Matt tonight. It's a responsibility. I am kind of looking forward to seeing Kara. Maybe because that doesn't involve having dinner with an engaged man just to rat him out to his fiancée. But if I don't take on these responsibilities, who will?

I kneel on my bed, part my drapes and peer across the street. The sunlight is blinding. The apartments are reflecting in each other's windows.

Lowering my gaze, I see that on the sidewalk, a punky guy with cropped dark hair and tight clothes is waiting for a girl who's farther up the block. She has flaming-red, close-cut dyed hair, and skinny pants with horizontal pink and orange stripes. I've often wondered about girls who look like her. Most women work hard to look like supermodels these days, but then you have, at the other end of the spectrum, girls who go for the Olympic gold in trying to look bizarre, and *they* always seem to have boyfriends, too, even more often than the supermodels. It is true that their boyfriends always look as strange as they do, but you'd think that just because a man sticks pins in his lips, it doesn't mean he's attracted to a girl who does. I wonder how we're supposed to figure out what anyone wants. I guess the idea is to be ourselves, even though it sure doesn't seem that way sometimes.

I keep watching. My punk rocker friends have disappeared, and I see two guys with a pretty girl. The guys are wearing those thick "nerd" glasses that are popular among Village types. It's unfair to those of us who were bona fide nerds throughout grade school and got picked on for it that once we got out, the popular people went so far as to actually swipe the trappings of our look, turning something we suffered from for years into something they flash like cosmetic dentistry. How come it's only cool to be nerdy *after* it doesn't matter anymore? I always hear famous people talking about how back when they were in school, they were the ugly duckling. If everyone claiming to have been unpopular in school really had been, there wouldn't have been such a thing.

A few yards behind the nerd-glassed guys is a woman walking a Bernese mountain dog. The dog looks too big to possibly enjoy living in a New York apartment, and might be better off—oh, I don't know—on a Bernese mountain. Next I see three people emerge from a building a few doors down, a building with a terrific revolving door. One of the people is a woman with a stroller, and there's also a young woman and her boyfriend. The young woman is in a jogging getup and has her hair in a ponytail, and it's swinging back and forth. A lot of the women on my block look like her.

Suddenly someone catches my eye. The Hat Guy, aka Cy, is walking directly below. Ronald *did* mention that Cy lives around here. He's carrying a cup of coffee. He's walking really slowly. It looks like he's in sweat clothes. Some weird urge overtakes me. I want to run down and hug him. He must have been up all night rehearsing or something.

But I'm not dressed. By the time I could make myself look half attractive, he'd be gone.

This spurs me to get dressed anyway. I don't see Cy in the subway when I head out.

Petrov looks disturbed today. He opens the office door for me, but then goes to his desk to sift through some books with a barely mumbled hello.

I sit in my usual chair.

He keeps sifting through the books.

"Are you mad at me?" I ask.

"No," he says. "I'm sorry. I'll be with you in a second."

I look at Petrov's clock, then at my watch. His clock is three minutes ahead as it is. That means he'll end the session three minutes early. That works out to about six dollars he's gypping my Dad out of. Excuse me, I can't say gypping. But it's such a good word. Gyp, gyp, gyp. It works so well in haiku.

Gyp gyp, gyp gyp gyp.
Gyp gyp gyp gyp gyp gyp gyp
Gyp, gyp, gyp, gyp, gyp

"Sorry about that, Carrie," Petrov says, turning around. "I'll give you the extra two minutes." He sits down.

"You also have to set your clock back three minutes," I say. "It's ahead."

"Ahead of what?"

"My watch."

"And your watch is set to the national clock in Washington, D.C.?"

"No. I guess you're right." I know that conceding a point will startle him.

"Well," Petrov says, "I set mine by 1010 WINS, and it's pretty reliable. None of my other patients have complained."

I just shrug, studying the carpet. It has a million colors in it. The main one is a pale yellow.

"You do understand?" Petrov says.

"Now it's six minutes."

"What's six minutes?"

"You just wasted an extra minute on a silly argument that I put up no argument about. You were two minutes late, plus, your clock is three minutes ahead, and you just wasted a minute. That adds up to six."

"But if you conceded the point, it's really three minutes."

"Now it's seven."

"Seven?"

"We'll end at fifty minutes after. Let's get started."

He just stares, his face twitching in a netherworld between continuing the battle and deciding it's not worth it.

"Eight," I say.

"Oh, for God's sake."

"I felt bitter when I woke up this morning," I tell him, in the interest of moving things along.

"And why were you bitter this morning?"

"Because you weren't next to me."

He looks startled.

"Just kidding. I was bitter because I have an obligation tonight, a...party I have to go to." I'm not going to tell him that I have dinner plans with Matt. "And I don't really want to talk about the party. A vague acquaintance from college is having it."

"If you don't want to go, why are you going?"

"Because it's part of your whole socialization plan to prove that I can. But that doesn't mean I'm going to have any fun."

"Hopefully, you'll have a better time than you think. And if you don't, at least you'll know you tried."

"I just wish I could have woken up today happy instead of miserable."

"Well, you don't have a lot of things you enjoy on a daily basis," Petrov says, "so when the only thing you have on the horizon is something you're dreading—"

"Exactly. Dread. I felt dread. A nameless dread."

"You need more things to look forward to, to combat the dread," he says. "You know, I read a book recently"—he looks toward his desk—"I don't think I have it here, but it's a self-help book, and it says that we should all have at least five things we're looking forward to at any given time. They can be a meal, a trip, a celebration, a date... It says if you don't have them, you should schedule some so that they're on your mind to cheer you up. That's a reason you have your top-ten list. To remind you there are things in life to get genuinely excited about. Not just intellectual things."

"But some of the things on my list are hard," I say. "I can't sit around eating ice cream all day. That would make me feel fat and lumpy. And then I'd feel more miserable."

"There are few pleasures without drawbacks."

Love is one, I think. But you can't buy it on the corner of Seventy-eighth and Lex.

"So, what if you can't have your pleasures all the time?" I ask.

"Well," Petrov says, "there are probably small pleasures you might enjoy that aren't on your list. For example, yesterday morning, I took a shower, and I went into my room and put on a new pair of socks that my…friend had given me."

"Girlfriend," I say.

"My girlfriend. And it felt good to put them on. They fit well, they matched my outfit. And I thought to myself, You know, this is strange. It feels so good to put on a new pair of socks, yet I hardly ever buy them. I keep wearing the same old worn pairs. Why don't I buy more socks? I can afford them. They're not so expensive. But each day I rummage through my sock drawer scrounging for a pair of old faded socks that barely match. I could easily go to the store and buy twenty pairs of socks. No one in America buys twenty pairs of socks. We buy a bag of three pairs, and then we spend each morning pondering why we have a bouquet of socks with no matches, rather than just saying, 'I'll buy so many pairs that I'll have a pair every morning, and then some.'"

Not that I'm one to talk, but this is a guy who's giving *me* advice on how to have fun?

"The problem is, we psych ourselves out of happiness," he says. "We don't pay attention to the little things that make us happy. When's the last time you bought a new outfit?"

I shrug. "Standing in a fitting room getting into and out of clothes all day gives me a headache."

"But don't you like wearing something new?"

"Yes. But it's such an ordeal."

"What about socks?"

"I haven't bought socks in a long time."

"Buy socks."

"Okay."

"Can you afford it?"

"Yes."

"Good."

"Underwear," I add. "It feels even better to have new underwear."

For a second, Petrov gives me a look I've never gotten from him before. It looks almost hungry. Is he wondering what kind of underwear I'm wearing?

"Right now I'm wearing black silky underpants, and they feel great. I bought them because they were on the table in a pile, so I knew I could grab them and run out. I don't like to spend a lot of time looking at underwear because there are little kids walking around with their parents, and they stare at you. You could pick up this gauzy negligee with big, soft, full areas for your breasts, and lace all around it, and it's kind of see-through, but what you see through it is little Timmy looking up at you."

Petrov looks disturbed. I guess ever since I told him about Professor Harrison, he's had to accept me as an adult, and now I've told him what kind of underwear I'm wearing. Even though I wouldn't claim to be a supermodel, enough people, particularly older men, have liked the way I look. I've been told I look younger than I am, and I'm pretty young already.

I wear glasses, but I don't have any weird features: no big nose, no pointy ears. My hair is dark and long, and I'm thin, and about five foot four. My only deformity is my desire for truth and justice.

"Carrie," Petrov says, putting down his pen. "Is there a reason for the sudden detour into titillation during today's session?"

"No," I say. "It must be the late hour."

"Okay," he says. "Well, let's go back to your goals list. How are you doing with it?"

"I'm about ready to join an organization and go on a genuine date," I say. "Then I can move on to telling someone I care about them, and New Year's."

"The caring can't be sarcastic," Petrov reminds me.

"I remember."

On the way home, I stop into the coffee shop. Ronald the Rice-Haired Milquetoast is doing something at the counter. On further inspection, I see that he's stacking metal tumblers on top of each other, to see how high they can go.

"Hello," he says, looking up. Then he smiles.

"Afraid I was someone else?" I ask.

"My boss," he says.

"That's a pretty high stack."

"I went a level higher Thursday," Ronald says. "I can't seem to do it today."

"It could be the ambient temperature. Maybe some item that was in the tumblers. Maybe they were washed in cold water and they expanded."

"Nah, my fingers are just slippery." He dries his hands. "Hey, look who's here!"

Behind me, it's Hat Guy, aka Cy.

We both speak at once.

"I've seen—" I start.

"You—" Cy says.

"Carrie lives around here," Ronald tells Cy.

"I live around the corner," Cy tells me.

"I've heard."

We talk, and I find out we're three brownstones down from each other. I can't help but admire how clean he looks, in every way. His hair is neatly combed back. His eyes are a sparkling blue. They're so deep that there must be a lot behind them. "You ever go out on your fire escape?" he asks.

"Not often. No one ever inspects fire escapes. I'm afraid if I stood out there it might collapse, and then what would I escape on?"

Ronald laughs. "And what if a fire started on it?" he says. "You'd need a fire escape escape."

Ronald is a little slow. I bet I could meet the date requirement with him. But he's just not that interesting.

"How would you throw out a garbage can?" I ask Ronald.

He laughs. "You'd need a can can."

"What if your phone stopped working?" Cy asks Ronald. "How would you call the phone company?"

Ronald smiles. "From here."

A real customer comes, so I bid the two of them farewell. But the minute I get outside, I feel stupid. Why didn't I stay and talk to them? Because I was so scared about looking dumb that I quit while I was ahead. Stupid, stupid, stupid. This is how I thwart myself.

Petrov is right: I do need practice being social. I was actually at the center of two men's attention, and I couldn't handle it.

I did like that Cy was able to talk to Ronald without appearing condescending. He actually seems sincere and sweet.

I turn to the window and look in. Ronald is talking to Cy, and Cy's nodding pleasantly, a smile on his face.

Maybe I can think of an excuse to go back and talk to them more. I turn around again with my back to the window, and think.

I know. I'll say I left something. A pen. I'll say I left a pen.

I round the corner and walk back into the store. As I enter, Cy is picking something up, off the floor.

"Is this yours?" he asks, holding a pen.

Aack! That is freaky.

I stare at Cy, shocked, and he stares back at me, trying to figure out my shock. No way am I going to tell him.

"Where did you get that?" I ask.

Ronald says, "It was on the floor."

"Well," I say, taking the pen. "Thanks."

Now I've really run out of excuses. Darn. Why did there have to be a pen there? What are the odds?

"Cy knows my cousin," Ronald tells me.

"Yeah," Cy says. "I used to volunteer in a kids' theater program, and it turns out his cousin went to it."

"Does the cousin look like Ronald?" I ask.

"No such luck," Cy says, and Ronald laughs.

"Yeah, he wishes he looked like me," Ronald says.

Another customer comes, and I bid them farewell again, since I have to go home to prepare to meet Matt for dinner. I admire how Cy is able to make Ronald laugh. A genuinely cheerful guy.

When it's time, I take the subway uptown and arrive in the Port Authority, then emerge and wander up Eighth Avenue, where I haven't been in a while. As I pass 42nd Street, I'm reminded that they've replaced the porn shops with the largest movie theater, Mexican restaurant and Disney Store ever. The Mexican place is where I am to meet Matt, but I still have fifteen minutes to kill. I walk on and pass the guys who stand on boxes and preach some sort of African-American Jewishness that passers-by never make a good attempt to understand. Every time I have passed them, some tourist has been arguing with them, unaware that about 100 other tourists per day have stopped to do the same thing. I think the street preachers are probably a better tourist attraction than the Empire State Building, because all of these tourists think they're so smart and brave to stop and debate them, and then they can run back to Shaker Heights, Ohio (home to three members of my freshman dorm), and boast to their friends, "Biff argued with these black guys in New York about religion." Maybe the street preachers like being argued with, too, but I guess I already mentioned that religious folks often do.

I see a billboard that says, in black, "To be a supportive parent, you have to work," and then under it, in white, it says, "To be a supportive parent, you have to stay home." There's a toll-free number in small print under it, too small for me to read. I suppose it's the Parental Catch-22 Hotline. It would be more helpful if it was large enough for people to read.

Now I pass a troupe of guys playing "Soul Man" on over-turned pots, pans and trash cans. Some of the street musicians here are so talented that I'm surprised they can't make money doing it professionally. Maybe they actually make more money in the street. I wonder if there's ever been a homeless person who's declared money he made on the street on his taxes. That would take quite an honest person. A saint. I wonder if there is someone out there who is that honest. It's interesting to think about a world in which there are some things that are so honest you can't imagine someone doing them. Even though I some-times think the world is tough for me because I choose certain beliefs and stick by them, there are some levels of honesty that even I don't reach. For instance, if I baby-sat, I probably wouldn't put that on my taxes. I imagine that it would be hard to be honest in every single way possible. I wonder if it could actually be proved that there are cases where flat-out dishonesty is the right thing. That should not be possible, by definition, but is it? One could say that telling a dying woman she looks good is dishonest but necessary. Or saying someone's too-short haircut looks nice. Or saying your mother-in-law's borscht is delicious.

What about the lies that parents tell? There are all those parents who tell their kids about Santa Claus. Aren't they lying and, in fact, committing a sin? And doesn't that make ninety-nine percent of Christians sinners?

It *is* lying. It's bearing false witness.

So Christian parents are sinners from the get-go.

I have to take a break from this. But I do want to come up with the most honest thing a person could do. I would say that listing change you found on the street on your taxes might be the most honest thing. Can you imagine someone doing that?

I can work that into a routine.

She is so honest.

How honest is she?

She is so honest that she reports change she finds on the sidewalk on her taxes. [Applause.]

I wonder if this is how Johnny Carson used to do it.

I double back and head toward the Mexican restaurant to meet Matt. I'm still a few minutes early. Killing time is hard, unless you're avoiding work, in which case you can think of an infinite number of things you need to do. But maybe he'll be early, too. I see that in front of the restaurant there are two women and a guy waiting for people. The guy has a soft black briefcase slung around his shoulder. He's fairly short, but handsome. He's got straight, dark hair. He looks my way, and I smile uncertainly, and he smiles back. He walks toward me, asking, "Heather?"

I almost want to say, *You're no one special. You don't look like any stud. Why don't you just stick with your girlfriend?* But despite myself, I do think he's good-looking. And pleasant, right away. It's not fair.

"I'm Matt," he says, and he shakes my hand. His eyes crinkle a bit. "You hungry?"

"Yes."

We head inside. "Where do you work?" he asks, looking me over. A scraggly-haired waiter who doesn't look a bit Mexican leads us to a table.

We sit down and look at each other. He *is* good-looking. But not in an intimidating kind of way.

"I'm a legal proofreader," I tell him.

"Did you go to law school?"

"No." I'm pleased he thinks I could be that old. "I proofread lawyers' documents, but all I have to know is English, not legal terms."

"I'm sure you're good at it. You look like you're good with words." I accept the compliment silently. Our waiter comes, and Matt asks if I want a drink, and I say I'll stick with water.

"Not to be a spoilsport," I say.

"No," Matt says. "Actually, I don't drink. I'm one of the few."

"Really?"

Matt shrugs. "Never saw the point of it."

"Wow. There's so much pressure to do it in college."

"I know," he says. "I've been called things over it. I have better things to do than get sloshed."

It's funny that some people really just do not care about peer pressure. They're the ones who've been well-adjusted since age five. I'm sure not one of them.

The waiter sets down our waters and disappears.

"So you work in legal proofreading," he says. "Where did you go to college?"

"Near Boston," I say.

"Boston…College?"

"Harvard."

"Oh." Matt nods. "I went to Cornell."

Figures he'd be smart. "Good school," I say.

"Yeah, as opposed to Harvard," Matt laughs. "I'm surprised someone from Harvard would read the *Beacon* personals."

"Why? Because all of us should be out trying to solve Fermat's Theorem?"

"Fermat's was solved in 1993," he says.

I laugh. "Usually, I can get away with stuff like that."

"Me, too," Matt says. "Do you have trouble meeting smart people?"

"Yeah. You?"

"Definitely, at times."

"What about—" I stop myself.

"My fiancée? Shauna's smart."

I can't believe he says her name when he's on a date with someone else.

"She's smart," he says again. "She went to SUNY Binghamton and all. But I don't feel challenged usually. I'm smarter than she is. Most of my friends are her friends, too. I need more…outside interests."

"So you said."

Matt laughs and looks embarrassed. An odd emotion for someone who placed an ad saying he wants to fool around.

I think about how each Sunday, he probably wakes up next to Shauna, pulls on a plaid shirt, dons a baseball cap and heads out with her to the local diner for brunch. As they sit across from each other next to the window, the sunlight spills over their table and they kid around and rearrange the containers of syrup. Over eggs, juice and toast, they talk about the future, and later they hop into Matt's car and drive to the country to see her parents.

"How did you meet her, if she went to Binghamton?"

"High school," Matt says.

"Wow," I say. "You didn't meet anyone else in college?"

"Cornell can be alienating. Shauna visited me there a lot. It really helped. It can be a pretty cold place."

"I see."

"You ever been up there?" he asks me.

"No. I've heard the campus is beautiful."

"It is," Matt says. "Maybe we'll go up someday."

The waiter appears, startling me. "You ready?"

Matt half nods, then stops himself. "You?" he asks me.

"I'll have…two tacos."

"Beef or chicken?"

"Beef."

"I'll have quesadillas con chor-i-zo," Matt says, pronouncing it slowly.

"Coming up."

Matt turns to me. "Shauna hates Mexican. She won't ever touch it."

"Why?"

"Just doesn't like it. Therefore, I *never* get to eat it. And it's like my favorite food."

"Does she drink?"

"Nah. Well, actually, sometimes the both of us have a little wine on holidays. At Thanksgiving."

"The pressure to drink in society is amazing," I say. "Even from families."

"It really is," Matt says. "And people don't acknowledge it as a form of pressure. The odd thing is, they act like *you're* the one out of place because you're not doing what they want you to do, even though you haven't put any pressure on *them*."

"Yes!" I say. "That's true!" I admire him for noticing that.

"It's funny, though," Matt says, flicking a piece of wrapping from the straw off the table, "everyone is addicted to something. Some people have happy families, and they're addicted to their spouses and children."

"Makes sense. What are *you* addicted to?"

Matt smiles. "I guess, challenge."

"That's not bad."

"It can be good," he says. He keeps looking at me. I suppose this is a good sign.

Now a group of noisy teenagers, high-school aged, sits down at the next table. Matt shoots me a look.

"We should have gotten a booth," he says.

"That's what I was thinking."

"Was it just me," Matt says, "or did you find nearly everyone in high school stultifying?"

"Yes," I say. "In fact, they were so stultifying that if you'd used the word 'stultifying' in front of them, they would have shouted, 'SAT word!'"

Matt laughs. "'SAT word!' I remember that. The teachers were lousy, too. Well, some were okay. Two of mine are coming to my wedding."

I ignore this disturbingly wonderful detail. "I'll bet your teachers loved you."

Matt looks sheepish. "Well," he says. "They didn't hate me."

"Were you first in the class?"

Matt nods. "How about you?"

"First."

One of the teenagers at the other table calls the other one a "biter," whatever that is, and I shoot Matt a confused look.

"Got *me*," Matt says. "We said 'dork.'"

"We had a kid whose last *name* was Dork. It didn't hurt him, though, because he was good-looking. He was lucky."

"He was also lucky his first name wasn't Dick or something," Matt says.

"It was."

"Right."

"Really."

Matt smiles. "I'm going to have to go to your apartment and check your yearbook to make sure."

Why is this so easy with someone who is taken? Is that the only time I'll have an advantage—when I'm number two?

"In high school," Matt says, "did you have to pick a quote to go under your yearbook picture?"

"Oh, you mean, favorite quotes? No. We didn't have that."

"We did. My classmates all put in song excerpts. I was the only one who quoted a philosopher. The girl on the left of me quoted from 'Don't Worry Be Happy,' and the girl on the right quoted 'Paradise By the Dashboard Light.'"

We plow through our food. It's alternately salty and spicy, but I barely taste it. I'm too nervous and excited.

Suddenly Matt looks at me and asks, "What's your favorite word?"

What a great question. No one's ever asked me that.

"It's…well, it's not a word, but a phrase," I say. "'Check-kiting.'"

"Check-kiting?" His eyes narrow, but I can tell he's intrigued.

"Yeah. It sounds like what it is. It's a terrific metaphor."

He says, "I should know, but what is it, exactly?"

"Oh. It's like, when you pay one check with another, and then you pay *that* check with another, and you pay *that* check with another, and you keep the money moving and never really have any. The checks are soaring but they're really just worthless pieces of paper, like flying a kite. It's cool."

"That *is* cool," Matt says.

"What's *your* favorite word?" I ask him.

"Doozy," he says. "That's a fun word."

"Where does it come from?"

He thinks. "I don't know. I should look it up."

You can bet *I* will.

He orders us a dessert to share—ice cream with hot fudge and fried banana slices. Matt says he can't ever get dessert when he's with Shauna because she's afraid of getting fat. "She's nutty like that," he says.

"Apparently not nutty enough."

"Nutty enough for what?"

"For…you to leave her."

He looks at me. "There are always going to be things about another person that bother you. You have to decide which are unimportant enough to overlook, and which aren't."

"Oh."

"Besides, it's probably good that she tries to stay thin. I mean, I'm not gonna complain."

I don't know if he's joking or not.

"Don't you worry that maybe you'll meet someone you love more?" I ask. "You *are* still young."

"I have met people here and there," Matt says. "I've loved none of them more. And it's not as simple as that. Maybe I do bitch and moan, but don't get me wrong, I do love Shauna. She's sweet. She's amazing in the way she cares about people. If a homeless guy came up to us on the street and asked us for money, she would either give it to him or explain for ten minutes why she couldn't."

Remaining on our plate is one small hill of vanilla ice cream with fudge strands fading into it, and neither of us wants to be the one to eat the last bite.

"I know you didn't want to hear any of that," Matt says. "Good things about Shauna."

"No," I say. "I just want to understand it. So I don't do anything wrong someday, if I meet someone. I want to know how you know she's the one you're going to marry. Especially if you're still capable of having feelings for other people."

"Well, I know whenever I picture myself twenty years from now, I picture *us,*" he says.

"What if you meet someone you fall madly, madly in love with next year?" I ask. "After you get married?"

"What if I don't?" he says. "She's not going to wait for me forever, and there are things I want. I could wait until I'm forty and lose her and never have a family. I've always wanted that. And I've always thought she and I would have one together. But that doesn't mean I won't have needs."

Needs. I have them, too. So what if Matt and I do get together from time to time? But if I like him, I'm going to want to talk to him, tell him my problems and hear his. And he's already telling them to Miss Sensitive every day. So he won't need anyone else for that. All he'll need someone else for is, well, "needs."

Maybe I can convince him that he'd be better off with me. I can talk to homeless people, right? I can go outside and find one right now.

"What does she do?" I ask, taking half of the remaining scoop.

"Advertising, graphic design," Matt says. "She worked for an ad agency for five years, and now she's going freelance. I'm really proud of her. She's finding it tough, though. It's hard to get that first client. Her parents are helping her out with loans."

"But you'll take care of her."

He grins. "Yup."

After Matt pays and I pay the tip, he says, "So, can we get together again sometime? I know it's a weird situation, but I would like to get to know you better, if you're okay with the parameters. I mean, I'd really like to."

"Sure," I say. He gives me his business card. I know that, with his last name, I can track him and his girlfriend down.

But I don't know if I want to rat him out right away. Is it possible that someone who cheats on his fiancée might not be a horrible person? What if it's true that what she doesn't know won't hurt her? Maybe it's not bad if I keep this from her. I certainly would not be the last person Matt is going to do this with. Maybe only the first in a long line. If he's going to do this now, he surely will ten years from now. He'll move through different relationships in his life, just like any guy who dates. And even if it's hard, he'll always find women to do it. They'll be like me—knowing that someone as smart and attentive as Matt can be hard to find, accepting that of course he met some girl early on and was not going to hold out for us, so we can only be second in his life.

If I *did* tell Shauna about what he's doing, the two of them would probably fight and then patch things up. I wonder if that would include a promise by him never to do that again. I don't know that Matt could make such a promise. Maybe he'd be honest. Maybe she'd call it off. Still, either way, he'd never talk to me again.

Why does that bother me? Okay, I admit that I liked being with him tonight. He's bright and friendly, and I didn't feel nervous or awkward with him. Plus, he seemed to like me. The practice can't hurt. I'm not ready to lose contact with him yet.

But did I have *too* good a time? I don't want to be lured so easily into doing something wrong. He is dishonest. Even if he's charming, he should pay for what he's doing.

I walk home lost in thought, and barely reconnect with my surroundings until I emerge from the subway near my house and the cold air hits me.

When I get inside, there's a message from Matt saying he wanted to just tell me again that he had a really nice time and he'll call me soon. He must have called from his cell phone, right after I left him. Even David never called me right after a date to tell me he had a good time. Why didn't I meet someone like that in college? I can accept not having met someone like that in high school. Even though Shauna did.

I definitely have to go to that Harvard Club mixer. There must be *some* interesting young people who can get my mind off relationships with impossible parameters.

I also am still supposed to meet up with Kara on Friday, and I should have some responses to my personal ad by then. Hopefully at least one will be worthwhile.

No more sitting on my buttocks. I am going to get out there and be someone's Shauna before I miss out and end up forever just being someone's me.

Chapter Seven

Friday afternoon, six hours before I'm supposed to meet Kara at the club, I call the 900 number to get the responses to my ad.

I sit at my desk with a notebook to record the information.

"You have five messages," the automated voice reports. That's pretty good. As long as they're real.

"Hey, whut's up?" the first one says.

Oh, no. I know I said I'd go on a date with any of these people, but already, I can tell I can't.

"My name's Jimmy and I'm five-ten, 185, brown and brown. I'm looking for someone nice, good-looking, warm—" he pronounces it "wom" "—who likes dancing, music, and having a good time. If that sounds good, you can give me a call at 718—"

I press the button to skip to the next charmer.

"Hi. I'm Michael. I don't usually answer these."

That's encouraging.

"But your ad caught my eye. What can I tell you. I live in Queens, I'm in sales—"

Probably Dunkin' Donuts.

"I come from a big family, I like playing tennis, and I drink a lot of coffee."

Figures.

"My hobbies are going to the movies and just having a good time. Anyway, you sound nice. So maybe we can talk more. Give me a call. 718—"

I write his number down. Even though we don't have much in common, he sounds normal. That's a sad standard: He doesn't sound like a psycho, so I'll go out with him. But Michael is bachelor number one.

I forward to the next one.

"H-hi, my name's A-Adam, and, uh, I think I m-meet your requirements. I went t-to T-Tufts University, that's near B-Boston, and I don't know my IQ, but I got 1280 on my SATs, that's p-pretty good, right? I'm twenty-two and I j-just moved t-to the city."

I want to hang up. And I hate myself for it. This guy is smart, so what's my problem? Obviously, I'm just as superficial as everyone else. He's a stutterer who sounds like he spits when he talks. I want to bypass him just like people bypass me because I'm not a partier or because I have morals. Is that fair?

No.

But why does dating have to be fair? I'm tired of feeling like a misfit, and if the first person I start dating is equally socially inept, it will make me more of a misfit. Don't I deserve, for a change, to win?

Nonetheless, I owe it to A-Adam to give him a chance. I am going to stick by my moral codes. Not judging people on superficial standards is a big one.

"I-uh-I know you didn't ask about looks, which is probably why I liked your ad so much—"

Okay, Adam's not superficial, and he actually read the ad. Points.

"But in c-case you're wondering, I'm five-nine and I have dark wavy hair. My m-mother thinks I'm good-looking."

Points for humor.

"My interests include movies, d-dining out, not really into the c-club scene, and I like just having nice talks. I really hope to hear from you. Oh, I don't know if I said, but my name is Adam. Anyway…so, uh, yeah. I'm better in person, if you meet me. I'm at 212—"

Okay. Out of these two guys, I'm bound to get a date. They sound desperate enough. What was I worried about? And there are still two to go.

I press the button to skip to the next one.

"Hi, H-Heather. M-my name's A-Adam. I just l-left a m-message but I think it might have been too l-long, it cut me off and I don't know if you got it. Anyway, I'm usually not this spastic. Heh, heh. W-what I said l-last time was, I'm nice and I like movies, and I really liked your ad, so I hope to meet you…"

I skip to the last ad.

"Hi, I know you might find this unusual, you didn't state an age range in your ad, but maybe we can at least be friends. My name's Don, and I'm forty-six, and I own a coupla computer stoahs in the city. I don't remember back to my test scores, but I do pretty well when I watch *Wheel of Fortune*. I'm basically looking for a lady to take around, show her a good time. I like opera and the finer things, and I'd like to spend money on a classy lady like you. So give me a cawl."

I hang up. Something about "lady" bothers me. I know that it's considered un-P.C. to say "girl" these days, but "woman" makes me think of the full-figured diagrams that used to be in the pamphlets we got in elementary school sex ed entitled "Your Body and You." And "lady" is worse. There should be age ranges. "Girl" goes from one to thirty. "Woman" goes from thirty-one to a hundred. "Lady" goes from forty to a hundred, but she has to work in a casino.

I believe I've done some good work today. I have the urge to put the phone numbers away until later.

But I think of Matt. He seemed better than all of them. I admit that I'd sort of like to see him.

I go to the dictionary to look up his favorite word, "doozy." It says that it may have come from Duesenbergs, which were luxury cars in the 1930s. I've heard them mentioned in old movies. That's really cool. I'd like to tell Matt about it. But I know I shouldn't call him.

Maybe Michael or A–Adam from the personals will be just as interesting. It's worth giving them a shot. So I press *67 on my phone to protect my confidentiality, then return phone calls from both of them. But of course, neither is home because it's during the workday. I don't leave messages. I'll try again later.

At night, I'm not sure what to wear to meet Kara at the club. I'm not going to wear what girls who go to clubs wear: clothes so flimsy they freeze. They spend the evening walking bent over with their arms crossed in front of themselves. I'll be warm and unsexy.

When I get to the club, it's dark and crowded. I feel nervous, but then I see Kara, aka Deviated Septum, rounding the corner. "Traci blew me off," she says. "She's a flake. I'm so tired of people who are like that. Let's go upstairs."

We have to walk single file because it's so crowded, and I fear losing Kara, but she continually looks back at me. It's nice. Everyone seems tall, and lots of people are wearing black. The second level is quieter, and there's a strange blue light hanging over everything, cigarette smoke wafting into it. The tables are lit with round red candles. At one, a man is clasping a woman's

hands in the middle and staring at her. Neither of them is saying anything. They're either madly in love, or extremely drunk.
If there's a difference.

Kara sits down, opens a matchbook and strikes a match. A tall
black waiter with a shaved head arrives and bends over. "What'll
you ladies have?"

Kara looks at me. "I'll have a Cosmo," she says. I don't say
anything, so she adds, "Sex on the Beach."

"What's in that?" I ask.

"You'll like it." She waves the match out and takes a drag on
her cigarette. "I guess you can get it without alcohol, but what's
a virgin Sex on the Beach?"

I shrug. "How's Dickson, Monroe?"

"One big party," Kara says, and then she laughs.

"I shouldn't have asked."

"Hey, I admire your optimism." She looks around. "No cute
guys here tonight. Or girls."

"I met one yesterday."

"Girl? Or guy?"

"A guy. We had dinner together. I'm not sure about him.
He's...stuck on an old girlfriend."

"Forget it," Kara says. "You'll never measure up. And don't
believe it if he says he wants to stay friends with her, either."

The waiter delivers our drinks. "The guy I had dinner with
doesn't drink at all," I say.

"What a weirdo," Kara says. She accidentally tips over her
drink, then picks it up. "As you can see," she says, "I've already
been drinking."

I look back at the couple who've been staring at each other.
Suddenly I notice that one of them is wearing a ring. Is it a wed-
ding ring? The guy notices me staring, so I look away. I ask
Kara, "What do you think of people who cheat on each other?"

She shakes her head. "I think that's so low, cheating."

"You don't approve?"

She stubs her cigarette in a clear brown ashtray. "I do not. I'm pretty liberal, as you know, but cheaters are the lowest of the low. I mean, how do you justify that?"

I just shrug.

"You're going to cheat, don't get married. Don't have a boyfriend. No one's putting a gun to your head. People who complain about their significant others make me sick. No one forces you to commit to a relationship."

This amazes me. Even people like Kara, who seem to advocate doing almost anything, will still come up with rules to stick to and to judge others on. I guess their sticking to *some* moral code makes them feel like they're good, even though they flout so many others.

"You know how you can find out if someone's having an affair with someone?" Kara asks.

"No."

"Ask her if she knows his middle name."

"Oh."

"It always works. When people are in love with someone, they always want to know their middle name. Women especially. Men don't do it as much. Women will always want to know the middle names of men they like so they can use them to tease them. What was your English professor's middle name?"

"Lance."

"See?"

I smile. "I guess you're right."

"Did you ask him?"

"What his middle name was? I guess I did."

She laughs. "Once I was dating this guy and I found out his middle name was Seymour. I couldn't be attracted to him after that. I don't ask anymore."

She stands two matchbooks up like tepees. It's funny the

things people will do with paper when they have nothing else to do.

"This guy you met yesterday," Kara says, "did you sleep with him?"

"No," I say.

"Do you want to?"

"I…I don't know."

"Remember," Kara says, pointing to her nose. "Deviated septum."

"Got it."

"But you never rush in, right?" she says. "You haven't been with anyone since professor…what's-his-name?"

"David. Harrison."

"How can you stand it? That was years ago."

I shrug. "I'm asexual, I guess. I'm just not obsessed with it."

"You haven't met anyone in the meantime who you'd just want to throw off your clothes and jump on top of?"

"No. And way too many people do that. If you just do it to do it, why does it mean anything?"

"Why does it have to?"

"Because…it should."

Kara waits for more.

"Because you can get diseases. Because you're reducing it to nothing. And people can still get pregnant because of it. It's immoral for a reason. Not just something in the Bible, and I'm not a religious person, anyway."

A guy bumps into my chair, then keeps walking. The music downstairs ebbs a bit.

Kara shrugs. "You've said you're asexual. But then, if you don't have urges to do things, how do you know that you're really moral?"

"If I had them, I'd try to control them."

Kara shakes her head. "Everything in the world is based on

feelings, or level of feelings. If you had a greater sex drive, you might not think people were sex-obsessed."

"Maybe. Maybe not."

"Well, consider this," she says. "It does make sense to do everything based on logic, but no one in the world does. *No* one. It doesn't matter what they say. If we thought everything out and acted according to our conclusions, there would be no murder. Why does a guy kill or steal or rape? His urge to do it, or desire to do it, overcomes him. He doesn't think it's right. Okay, maybe in some cases he does think it's right, but usually he knows inside that it's wrong. There are basic things we do that make no sense. Next time you have an urge to do something, even something small, like put on the radio, stop yourself. See how it feels. Maybe you can stop yourself for a few seconds. But if you really, really want to hear the radio, you won't be able to stop yourself for very long. Now, there are some things we are lucky enough to have built up a moral aversion to, and then our thoughts become part of our feelings. We find killing someone for no reason not only cruel and immoral, but repugnant. If I tell you I'm going to step on a baby, you have a visceral reaction. You don't have to compute it mathematically and tell me it's bad. Do you?"

"No."

"Where does this come from? Socialization? Maybe. But maybe it's a part of us. We are all made with different kinds of urges. Some of us love to cook. Some of us love to swim. Our differences keep the world running. Some of us have monster sex drives. Some of us can get along without it. Some of us are attracted to both men and women. Some are only turned on by young boys."

"Are you saying that's right?"

"Not at all," she says. "Because it's not fair to the kids. But for a second, think about someone who is only turned on by young boys. What if that really is the *only* thing that turns him on sexually in his entire life? Think about someone who has to go eighty years without fulfilling any sort of desire toward something that turns him on. And believe me, being turned on, and actually fulfilling that feeling, is the most amazing rocketship ride in the world. But what if, because of the way you are, the only thing that can bring you to that height of all heights is forbidden? What do you do?"

I don't know what to say to that.

"Get counseling? Maybe. If the only thing that turns you on is something that can hurt another person, yes. But we think that a kiddie sex abuser, in our society, is the lowest form of human imaginable. The kind that not a soul has sympathy for."

"And you do."

She shakes her head. "No."

"So...I don't get the point."

"The point is, there are cases where urges can hurt innocent people, and we have to be careful about them, but there is middle ground, and there are times when moral laws can't govern everything. Like the antiquated wait-until-you're-married-for-sex deal. How can you blame people for wanting to feel good?"

The bar has framed covers of New York tabloids on the wall. There's one of the Yankees winning a pennant. There's one of men landing on the moon. There's a cover of a Spanish newspaper with a picture of Joey Buttafuoco above the words, "Me acuesto con Amy."

"I don't know," I say.

"Tell me," she says. "Tell me *one* thing that really turns you on."

I'm tired of people wanting me to tell them my sexual secrets. As if I owe them.

"It doesn't have to be sexual," Kara says. "I mean anything. Why do you get up in the morning?"

I think about it.

"I don't," I say.

A smile crosses her lips.

She leans in toward me. She has a pert nose. Pert is the only way to describe it.

"Wouldn't you like to open your eyes in the morning," she whispers, "and have a reason to lift your head off the pillow?"

The music from downstairs gets louder. "Like what?"

"Like some raging, monster drive you can't control."

She stares at me for a second, then sucks in her lips. "Tell me what I asked before. What are some things that turn you on? Nonsexually. Just things you like."

I think of my top-ten list for Petrov. "Starfish. Cherry sodas."

"Okay," she says. "What if I said, you can never see a starfish, you can never drink a cherry soda. What if, suddenly, they became immoral?"

"You're acting as if I said people can't have sex," I say. "If you're careful about it, and you're not hurting someone, or cheating on them, then I'm not condemning that. If you're lousing up your body, which we'll all pay for later, or you're peer-pressuring other people to do what you do, and bringing down the standards for everyone, then there's a problem."

"But you say that people are too sex-obsessed," she says. "Well, do you think we're also food-obsessed? Or sleep-obsessed?"

"Sleep obsession doesn't hurt anyone," I say.

"Sex does?"

I know there's an answer to this, but I can't think of it.

"It doesn't," Kara says. "If it's between consenting adults, it doesn't."

"If you give someone a disease…"

"Then it does. Other than that, it doesn't. You shouldn't do anything that hurts other human beings, I agree with you. But you should feel good during your eighty years of life, even if it offends people who cling to some Victorian standard that arose a hundred years ago because people falsely believed masturbation gave you hairy palms and that God didn't want you to knock boots. You're not a religious person. If you were, then we'd have to argue differently because you could say you believe in the Bible and that temptation comes from Satan. But you don't believe in Satan. You believe in reality."

"Satan?" some guy turns around and says. He gives us the pinkie-and-index-finger-up sign, then smiles and goes back to his food.

Kara rolls her eyes. "You want to go somewhere else? I mean, I know I've totally offended you...."

"No, I'm glad we're talking about this."

"I do hear some of what you're saying," she says. "I don't agree with it all, but I respect that you're willing to talk about it with me. I just think you have to live a little, stop setting such rigid boundaries. You'll feel better."

Kara gets up, pays the waiter even though I offer, and I pull on my coat. I wrap my scarf around my neck. Kara looks at it.

"That's a nice scarf," she says.

"Thanks."

"It looks expensive."

"My father got it for me."

We make our way down the stairs and outside. "Do you get along with him okay?" Kara asks.

"He's all right," I say. "I don't see him much. He's in Europe right now." I don't want to go through my whole family history. "Do you talk to your parents?"

"No," she says. "Not to be...well, I'm not trying to play on your sympathy, but I haven't talked to either of them since college. They kept using me against each other, and I finally decided they deserved each other more than either of them deserved me. They wouldn't even pay for college after a certain point. I don't talk to them. It's hardest on holidays, but in some ways, it's easier."

"I've been parentless on holidays, too," I say.

She smiles. "Well, maybe on the next one we'll put together a celebration and round up some of us orphan-types."

It's cold outside, but there's no breeze. A lot of people are staggering in the street, and a few are yelling.

"Sometimes, when I'm getting ready for bed," I say, "I hear all the people outside going to the bars, and I know they're around my age, they all sound so jubilant and gleeful that I feel guilty being inside."

"Don't."

A guy with a hooded gray sweatshirt walks past us and nearly trips over himself. He must be sloshed. Or stoned.

I ask Kara, "Have you ever done drugs?"

She shakes her head. "Just pot."

I take it as a given that she assumes I naturally agree that pot doesn't count.

"You?" she asks me.

I shake my head vigorously.

Kara laughs. "I should have known. Even pot?"

I shrug. "That's a drug."

"I guess," she says. "But it's not addictive. If you only do it once in a while, it's like taking a trip somewhere."

"No, it's not. It must be illegal for a reason."

"Because of people who abuse it, and because of all the illegal activities surrounding it," she says. "There's absolutely nothing wrong with it if you're responsible about it, which the government naturally assumes we won't be. It's like gambling. Or prostitution. It really has nothing to do with morality. As usual."

"Well, we all pay for the health problems that smoking or drugs can cause," I say.

"Maybe," she says.

Her block is quiet, with a lot of trees springing up from small round planted panels on the sidewalk. There are several hand-painted signs reading "No Dogs."

"You want to see my apartment?" she says. "It's nothing much, but we can talk there. The only noise is when Pat and Stephen are singing."

"Pat and Stephen?"

"Yeah. They live next door. Stephen's this totally talented pianist, and the two of them have people over once a week and do sing-alongs. It's so much fun. But the best part is, after everyone leaves except the two of them, it goes dead silent, and you know something's going on next door because you can't hear anything. It's so romantic. You know they were waiting the whole time for everyone to leave so they could get their hands all over each other."

I make a face.

"Oh, come on." She brushes my cheek with her hand. "Admit you find that sweet."

"Yeah, it's sweet."

"It is. Here's my stoop." She gets out her outdoor door key and indoor door key and walks up the stairs and turns the upper lock key and the lower lock key. "This is the place."

Each room is painted with light pastel colors, and on the walls, there are murals of the moon and stars. The bedroom is the biggest room. It's got a queen-sized bed, a television, and a round table in front of a bay window that overlooks the street. Kara has left the window open slightly, and the pale curtains billow in front of it. "You want something to drink?"

"Uh…"

"I'll get us tiny wineys."

"Tiny wineys?"

She nods and leaps up. I gaze at the decor. The lights are off, and I can see more outside her room than inside.

Kara comes back with two miniature bottles of wine and two glasses. "Ah, living alone," she says. "Can't live with it, can't live without it." She sets the wine bottles down on the table that's tucked into the bay window.

"They come in packs of four," she says. "Wine for one." I open mine and pour. She does the same. Waves of vino bounce off the sides of the glass. Suddenly I feel jubilant. I haven't had much alcohol since my incidents with David. I screw the top back on. Kara lights little candles and puts them on the windowsill. "I love candles," she says. "They really warm things up."

"Yup."

We hear a door creak next door. "Oh, Pat and Steve must be home," she says. She lights a cigarette. It makes her face glow for a second. Despite all of her drinking and smoking, her lipstick is still on perfect. I don't know how women do that. It must be one of those things they all taught each other in eighth grade that I missed because I skipped it.

I lift my glass and take a gulp of wine.

"So, do you really think people are sex-obsessed?" she asks.

"I don't know," I say. "It just seems like it's such a priority."

"Well, it is a driving force, that's true," she says. "I know you probably think I'm sex-obsessed because I bring it up all the time. But I swear, there are also times when I'd rather sit in bed and read a book. In fact, after my last breakup, I was honestly thrilled to stay home, plow through some Chinese, eat a pint of Ben & Jerry's and watch old movies. But then I'd pick up some old romance flick, and I'd be watching it alone, and it would be really steamy, it would get me all wistful."

She pauses. "Carrie?"

"Sorry," I say. "I was getting all wistful."

"See?"

"No, for Ben & Jerry's. I love Cherry Garcia."

She laughs. "You are hysterical."

She leans across the table. Her nose really is perfect. I've never seen a nose like that. I wonder if it's sculpted. "I bet you want to kiss me," she says.

"How much do you think I've had to drink?"

"I bet you want to anyway."

"I want to go hang out with Pat and Stephen."

"I'll bet David was okay, but I'll bet there are things he really didn't know how to do."

"He was...over forty. He must have known what he was doing."

"He may have *thought* he knew. Obviously he didn't, if he wasn't pleasing you. Some people, especially if they haven't been in a long-term relationship, only rise to the level of their sexual mediocrity."

"David told me he was supposed to get married right after college," I say. "It fell through."

"He didn't know anything," Kara says. "You were with him all winter and he never figured out how to get you to enjoy him."

"I enjoyed talking with him."

"Do you enjoy talking with *me?*"

"Yes."

She fixes a gaze on me.

"Talking," I add.

She takes her index finger and runs it in a circle around my lips. It tickles. "The wine is getting your lips red."

"David used to say that."

"Did he do this?" She runs her finger down my neck, then around one of my breasts, concentrically. Then she leans in and kisses me.

I stop her and wipe my mouth. "He never got lipstick on me."

"This isn't supposed to wear off," she says.

"I think I should go," I say. "Obviously we've had too much to drink."

"Excuses."

I stand up. "It was good to talk to you again."

"It's late. You sure it's safe to go out?"

"I'm going to take a cab." I step backward and knock over a stack of papers and magazines. "The *New York Review of Books?*"

"My ex-boyfriend used to get it."

"He must have been smart," I say. "Do you have his number?"

"You're denying your sexual orientation again."

"I'm not gay."

"Maybe not. But you're at least a tenth bisexual. Maybe twenty percent."

"I'm going to get a cab. Thanks for everything." I leave and run down the stairs. I want to forget about this by morning.

Chapter Eight

I wake up feeling considerably better than a few days ago, but strange, of course. But it's an interesting kind of strange. Not much happened, at least. I left lines uncrossed.

There must be something I can do to avoid analyzing last night. I have made up my mind to visit Natto's church tomorrow. But not today.

Maybe today I'll buy a journal and use it to help figure out what happened. I've been wanting to get a journal for a long time. The nice thing about living in the Village is that it means you're close to New York University, and NYU has the best stationery shops in the world, I suppose because of the writers and film students. You can find forty-two colors of paper clips; twenty-three sizes of envelopes; seventy-six kinds of pens; markers with gold ink, silver ink, chartreuse ink, invisible ink, disappearing ink, peppermint ink, glittering ink, pink ink, scented ink and glue ink. It's been too long since I've been stationery shopping. The problem is, I suddenly need everything I see. Take those long pink erasers. All of my pencils have their own erasers, so there's no need for me to buy a pink eraser, but they just look so clean and nubile that I have to caress them. Forget what Nabokov said: the real pleasure in life is fondling office supplies. I could bite those pink erasers.

Petrov will be proud of me if I buy new office supplies. I'll be giving in to an urge to do what makes me happy. While I'm out, I also could pick up some new socks. It does feel good to have warm, clean socks in the morning. Heck, might as well go on a simple pleasure spree.

I'll also stop at one of those stores like Balducci's that have groceries for the wealthy and buy some things, even if a quarter pound of lunch meat is six dollars. Who cares? I have the money.

Yes, I know—there is something laughable about a person who thinks she's getting wild because she's going to buy office supplies. Well, you have your fun. You can watch your pornos and smoke your pot and climb onto your rooftop with a bottle of hooch and howl at the moon, but I will RUN MY FINGERS OVER MY NUBILE PINK ERASER AND GASP IN ECSTASY. And I won't wake up with a hangover or unsightly teeth marks on my neck.

After I get dressed, I stroll outside and feel jubilant. It's unseasonably warm. I smile at an Asian girl who's walking past, her mittened hands half-shoved in her coat, and she smiles back, then looks away shyly. Wow, a smile between strangers. I wonder how many I can get today. I head in the direction of Avenue of the Americas and smile at a lot of other people, who also smile back. It's strange how my moods can change. There are reasons for my good and bad moods on some days, but other days, there aren't. I wonder if most people feel as good as I do today *all* the time. If so, should I find out what they're doing, and do it? If it's drugs, should I get some? Is it some chemical they have that I'm missing? Is it something that's possible for me to obtain?

Garlicky fumes shoot out of the glass door of a gourmet grocery store and curl under my nose. This one isn't Balducci's, but they're all pretty much the same—tantalizing mixtures for twenty dollars a pound, lots of ritzy women filling the aisles. One of the best things about New York is the rich old ladies who still think they're glamorous. They wear the same caked-on makeup that they did when they were twenty-five; they get their hair done once a week; they hold their dainty pocketbooks in their hands rather than over their shoulders; they wear coats with furry sleeves and carry themselves like they're floats in the Macy's parade. Their hair is gray and thin; their wrinkles cause the makeup to crumble, and their sunglasses can't hide their crinkly dark eyes, but there's something beautiful about them. They are New York.

"Is this thirteen dollars a pound?" one woman is asking another in front of a glass display, and I notice some sort of red pâté that you can sample. It's in a small metal cup next to a leaning tower of teabags. "In Gristede's," the woman tells her friend, "they have the same thing, but it's darker." Her friend's nose twitches. "If it's darker, it can't be the same, Lucille."

I am tempted to leave without buying anything. I am sorry to leave the two old ladies. I love old people. I love listening to the warble in their raspy voices. I think this has to do with the fact that I hardly ever got to see my grandparents. My father and I moved out of London when I was two and a half, and we rarely went back to visit, although we did once in a while. We moved to the States that year, not long after my mother died. I guess I love my mother, but I don't know if you can honestly love someone you never knew. Sometimes we feel the need to say we love people just because we're supposed to, but we don't feel love deep inside. When I see a picture of her, of course I feel love—I have a picture of her at my parents' wedding reception next to Dr. Petrov and his wife, and both of the women look beautiful. I also love hearing stories about her. I respect her and care about her, and I guess she's part of me. But can I say I honestly love her? I used to send Christmas cards to my grandparents once a year, and I signed them "love," but I barely knew them. I guess *love* is a word you're entitled to use any way you want.

I've finally managed to get that sad story out of the way quickly. Cry for a few seconds and get over it.

The rest of my day is fine. The journal expedition leaves me fitted with a handsome beige leather-bound notebook with a white map of the world embedded on its cover. I also purchase four pairs of socks and three pairs of underwear. I don't bump into any baseball-capped boys when I'm poking at the panties.

When I get near my block, I'm surprised to bump into Dr. Petrov!

"Hey!" I say.

"Hey!" he says, looking startled. I don't blame him. You're not supposed to bump into your doctors outside of their offices. It's in the Talmud.

"What brings you to my neighborhood?" I ask. "Spying on me?"

Petrov laughs. "Is this where you live?"

"Right on this block."

"Ah," he says. "Well, no. I have a friend in this area who I haven't seen in a while. And you? You've got a lot of packages."

"It's…Christmas presents," I say, trying to hide the bags behind my back. No way am I going to tell him it's underwear and socks.

"Good!" Petrov says. "I'll see you next week."

"Yup," I say. I run up to my apartment and lay my office supplies and clothes out on the rug.

The next morning, when I wake up, I must give Petrov credit. I am quite excited to pull on my toasty navy blue socks and milky-white underwear. Otherwise, I do dress sternly, as church is no laughing matter.

By ten, a bunch of us are packed into an auditorium and I can hear seats clacking as people get up and sit back down. There is some murmuring. I guess every weekend they get new recruits. I am in the next-to-last row beside a man in his forties who looks skinny and has big eyes. A short man in a faded suit walks on stage.

"Good morning," the man says. "I'd like to welcome you to the First Prophets' Church. We are, as you know, an unconventional church. We believe in one God, we believe in Jesus Christ, but we also believe that in each lifetime, there is someone who must interpret the word. We know that some people interpret God's word to fit their liking. The president uses it. Southern preachers use it. This lobby uses it, that lobby uses it. Joe Natto, whom I'll introduce next, had a vision one day, which you can read about in the pamphlets on the back table or in his forthcoming book. Why should you trust Joe Natto? After listening to him today, you'll see he gains nothing from the interpretations he gives or the wisdom he shares. People have come up to me after his sermons time and time again and said to me, 'Eppie, he's real. Joe Natto is real. You can feel it.'"

Eppie clenches his hands and continues.

"When he talks, he's talking to you. When he prays, he's praying for you. And *with* you. We are a church that believes every member is integral to spreading the word of God. And the *work* of God. Joseph Natto was a teacher. He taught in the inner city. He reached hundreds of children. He left to lead a

church, where he will now affect hundreds of children and their
parents and their neighbors and all of us with fund-raising that
will someday build community centers and spur community
programs. Joe believes not just in talking, but in doing. Now,
here he is, Joseph Natto."

With that kind of buildup, you'd expect music. But it's very
quiet as Joe takes his first steps onto the stage. Then, there's clapping. It builds. He bows. He's of average height. He has dark
hair, swept to one side. He's in his early forties. Most people in
the room seem older. More than half are women, and they look
fat and saggy. I feel bad, like this is a church for people who have
nothing else. Maybe that's the way it is with all churches. I'll stay
just long enough to make sure these people aren't being taken
advantage of.

"Welcome back, to those who are back," Natto says.

"Welcome," say the people in the audience, a few nodding.

"Welcome to newcomers."

"Welcome."

"So it's warmer outside than usual," he says. "So we don't
have to care about the homeless, right?"

No one speaks.

"It's winter. We're inside, in a warm place. They're not. We're
among friends. They're not. When we walk past them as we
leave here today, let's give them our spare change so they can feel
the warmth we feel right now."

There's clapping. I notice that there is a man a few rows ahead
of me who probably *is* homeless. A thin bumpy scar extends
from his forehead down his eyelid, and he has a ripped plastic
bag at his side.

"We have to stop making excuses," Natto says. He begins
strutting across the stage, then reverses direction and heads back
to the microphone. "That person looks okay. This guy's fat, so
he's not starving. That person's a drunk. I'll just keep these dol-

lar bills to myself, let them burn a hole in my wallet. Maybe I'll go buy a pound of gizzard loaf at Gristede's."

Now I feel guilty. That guy who did the warm-up was right. It *does* feel as if Natto is talking to me.

Suddenly he stops. Freezes. Then just as suddenly, he grabs the microphone.

"*You* are not *like that!*" he says.

Everyone sits in rapt attention.

"How do I know?"

He stands there.

"How do I know? In the front row, how do I know?"

The woman, who has some sort of box on her lap, moves her head slowly from side to side. She's transfixed.

"Because you're here," he says. "A lot of people make excuses not to come to church. 'It's Sunday. I work all week. I'm tired.'"

Natto's mouth droops.

"'I don't want to miss the McLaughlin Group. I have eczema, so I need people to pray for *me*. I'm wearing a saggy diaper that leaks. My feet hurt. My son has a birthday party to go to.' Do you remember when we were kids, nothing was open on Sunday?"

A few people in the audience nod.

"I do. There were no excuses then. Now you can build an entire house with a swimming pool and a cabana on Sunday. Your kids have soccer. Your book group meets at three. You can't go to church!"

He looks around the room. I think he eyes me for a second, but just as quickly, he moves on. I definitely feel like a minority. Not just racially, although in this room I am a racial minority. But I feel like a minority because I'm nearly the youngest person in the room. I do see a skinny Latino kid who looks sixteen or seventeen; he's sitting beside a fat woman.

"But you came here. So you don't make excuses. You care. You're giving an hour or two of your time. God respects you."

Natto pauses.

"God! Respects! YOU!"

Someone sneezes.

"God bless you. He respects you and you and you." Natto points to a few people. "And when you go out there and give out my flyers, you'll get more people in here, more talking about the word of God, and more doing instead of just talking. And when they're asked to donate to the church, to keep it going, so it can spread God's word and help other people right here in our communities, once we get some momentum up— they won't make excuses to avoid church. They'll be proud to come. They'll be proud to give. They'll be proud to do whatever part they can. And the Lord will *respect them.*"

One person starts clapping, and a few others join in, and then the applause is thunderous. I catch Eppie, the warm-up act, smacking his hands together on some steps to the left of the auditorium, and I know quicker than rain that he was the one who started the applause.

"I love all of you," Natto said. "You gave up something to be here. Just as God gives his love. You gave your time and your heart to come here. As you leave today, there will be opportunities to donate to the church, and also to take flyers to bring in other worshipers like yourselves. We work through faith, but also toward concrete results. This isn't one of those churches where you sit in your seat for an hour and pray to God to help the poor and then run home and eat cake. This is a church about learning and doing things in accordance with God's way. And so for being here, I respect you!"

Eppie starts the applause again—I have my eye on him now— and it gets louder and louder. Natto gets onto a more specific topic. Today's is poverty. But after all that, he leaves with an appeal for a donation. It's so sad that someone can't start a church for altruistic reasons. There are forms on the tables behind us for Natto's forthcoming book. It's $12.95. Eppie and some other guys are collecting forms and money.

There is also a stack of membership forms encouraging us to open our wallets again: it's twenty-five dollars for a trial church membership. You can go to church for free, but if you join and pay the dues, you can be a part of their Bible study group, youth group, singles group or discussion group.

Joe Natto has disappeared. At the back of the room, I come face-to-face with Tonsure-Head, the guy who first gave me the yellow flyer that morning. He's alone; I can tell that. He didn't bring a girlfriend or son with him. He folds a dollar bill and slips it into the slot. Then he leaves. I want to know this man's story. It's odd. Two months ago, I thought I was the only one in this city alone. But the more I get out, the more I see that there are other people alone. The thing is, though, they don't seem to be normal. They all have some sort of problem. I seem like the only normal person who's alone. Why is that?

I figure that I shouldn't just walk out of the church. I do have a purpose here, don't I? I want to expose Natto. I want to stand up and shout, *You're only here to hawk your book! Go on Letterman!* I want to tell people just to give their money directly to a boy in the ghetto. But what if this really does make these people feel good, believing in Joseph Natto?

Look at me, wimping out again. Trying to think of a reason not to bust Natto. I keep doing that. I haven't made one move toward telling Matt's girlfriend on him, and now I'm wavering on the church, too. Things I thought were wrong a month ago now don't seem as bad. Am I becoming like everyone else? Just doing what's easy, and then rationalizing it? Maybe I *should* keep going to this church to protect the people who come here from being ripped off.

I could use the religious education, anyway. I could say the reason that I never go to church in general is because it's all bunk. I could say that it's for idiots. But the truth is, the reason I never go to church is that waking up at nine o'clock on Sunday morning is a goddamn pain in the ass.

"Carrie!"

I whirl around, and some woman is running to a man with a cane. "Harry! Hurry up, we're in a hurry!"

My hearing must be going.

Back home, the sun is shining in and making square patterns on my rug. I hang up my coat and lie down and curl up in the spot. It's warm there. I used to do this all the time when I was four, find a sunny spot and curl up in it. I had a cat that liked to do that, too. It liked to come and lie in the sun next to me. It was black, and its name was Midnight. We were supposed to take care of it for a month for friends, but the friends ended up being gone three months, so I started considering it *my* cat. But then one day I came home from school and it was gone. Its owners had picked it up. I felt lonely being the only one in the sun spot.

After I regroup on the rug, I go to the video store. I haven't made progress on the classic film list lately. I stroll around, and eventually I come upon *Network*. But it has taken me a half hour to find something I want to see. I worry that they won't keep making movies quickly enough to keep up with my lonely nights.

I also manage to find *Out of Africa*. I take them home, lie in bed on my stomach and watch them back to back.

When *Africa*'s over, I'm groggy. It's dark. I look out the window and something startles me.

There are Christmas lights around the Guarinos' window across the street! We haven't even hit Thanksgiving yet, and they've already started to hang Christmas decorations. But what's nice about it is it's an unselfish gesture. The lights are meant for Tom and Jocelyn's neighbors, not for themselves. They're telling the rest of us Merry Christmas without a sound.

Maybe the season will put me in a good mood for a change, instead of a stagnant, bland one. Maybe Tom and Jocelyn will have a party for their neighbors and I'll get to know the people around me.

I'm glad the holidays are coming. I don't know what I'll do for Christmas, except see my father, but that in itself will be nice. Holidays are a chance to be kiddish again.

My visit to the Harvard Club the next evening leads me back through Times Square. The street preachers are out in full force again, pointing and sparring with the tourists. I round the corner to 44th Street and see several Ivy League banners billowing above the awnings to their clubs. The Harvard flag is crimson with a large *H* on it. The face of the club is brick, not the usual harsh pockmarked red brick but a softer pink variety, with borders of beige stone. It pleases me. Perhaps such a moment of happiness, even if it's fleeting, bodes well. I love old buildings. I love them inside, too. I live for ripped tears of wallpaper and long windows and crystal doorknobs and interior columns. This building has all the indications of possessing such.

I walk up to the front door and a man opens it for me. I feel guilty. I haven't even joined the club and already they're waiting on me.

Inside, there's a fellow at a gold-colored podium. He's bald, in full crimson garb, and he asks, "Can I help you?"

"I'm here for the reception."

He breaks into a smile and directs me to my left. What did he think—I was going to break in?

The walls are a sort of red that seems more ruby than crimson, and there are framed black-and-white pictures of old men in suits. I pass a small reading room that holds copies of the campus newspaper. It reminds me that once, when I was a senior, I wrote the paper a letter. They had run an interview with a philosophy professor about situational ethics, and he'd made an argument that I could disprove fairly easily. The letter I wrote was clear, and I told them they should run a correction, but they never got back to me. So I called the editor, and he said that they don't run corrections unless something is out-and-out wrong—but it was. He said it was a complex point. I guess the staff thought it was easier just to leave something that was flat-out untrue in the paper. Sometimes it seems that even the people who act like they want to get to the truth only want to get to a certain point of the truth, and after that, they just want to make nice.

I return to the hallway and continue toward the room with the mixer. As I near it, the bass pounds my ears, and a loud symphony of voices emanates. Inside, it's wall-to-wall people in dark suits with drinks in their hands, all talking at once. I can't make out an audible sentence.

I look around and feel underdressed. I guess all of these people came straight from work. Some have briefcases slung around their shoulders. How old are they, twenty-three?

Even though I thought, or hoped, some people would come to this event alone, everyone seems to have a group. Some are standing in a circle, some are crowding around the bar, some are sitting on the red couches.

If I can get to a corner, the traditional refuge of the shy, I can take stock of the situation. I move to the wall and edge along it. I make it to a corner, near where a group of people is pushing two couches next to a table. "Tell me about your new job!" a long-haired girl says to a guy. Within the same group of friends, another pair is hugging. It occurs to me that for all I know, the eight people on these couches were my year at school, and I knew not one of them. I guess there were thousands of people at Harvard whom I didn't meet. My father once asked me if I thought I would have been happier at a small school. Honestly, I don't know which is better: being at a campus with thousands of people and not getting the chance to feel close to any of them, or being at an intimate college with only 400 people and still not meeting anyone you have things in common with because all the people you might have had things in common with were among the thousands who went elsewhere.

I hang back and watch. The lights are dim. The room is smoky and full of perfume. There's entirely too much perfume in New York. It even gets into the newspapers and magazines.

The group of people closest to me is focused on one girl who keeps talking and making everyone laugh. The majority of the group is men, and I'm impressed that this one girl can hold four men's attention at once. I'd be too nervous. I'd probably spill my drink or trip over my shoes. I step closer to hear what she's saying. "So then I said to them, well, I'm not going to stand here and watch the two of you throw away the best thing you have in your life. Give *me* the fucking ceramic Garfield." Laughter explodes. I don't know what she's talking about, but I can laugh, too, so I step closer, near the outside of the circle. That's what Nora was good at in college: blending into a circle. One guy across from me keeps giving me strange looks, but no one opens up. I decide I'll count to ten. If no one talks to me by ten, I'll leave. Any longer would be humiliating.

No one does.

I retreat to my corner. I look up. No one is approaching me. I burrow through my pocketbook, find an ATM receipt and crumple it for later disposal. I look up again. Still, no one is approaching me.

I survey the room. It's dark and full of chatter. Even nerdy guys with thick glasses and bad posture have their groups. Even among losers, I'm an outcast. I see a Harvard Club application on the floor, a dirty footprint emblazoned across it, so I pick it up.

I finish reading and peer over it. One would think, with all the guys in the world who complain they can't get a girlfriend, they'd take advantage of someone standing in a corner alone. Maybe they're just not trying.

The music gets even louder. The smoke hurts my eyes. The bass fills my ears. It's so loud in this room that I'm not sure how any of these people can have a meaningful discussion. And they certainly can't meet new people. How could they? Everyone looks similar; why would anyone come over to me or to anyone else here? How would you pick? How can you tell who you'd have anything in common with? This is supposed to be a mixer, but it's really only about hanging out with people you already know.

I make my way to the bar. There are several people standing against it already, and they motion with their hands to get the bartender's attention. I get jostled and ignored. I have to stick my elbow over the bar to keep my place. Finally a bartender asks me what I'll have. Normally I try to order a seltzer in order to avoid paying outrageous bar prices. But I'm irritated so I permit myself red wine, even if it's eight dollars. After I've got the glass in my hand, I feel a little better. The reason I'm not talking to anyone else is that I'm *drinking*. That's it.

I put the wine to my lips and look around. I notice that every once in a while, someone disappears down some stairs. After the fourth person heads down, I decide I should see what's down there.

I make my way through the clusters of suits and trot on down. It's a comfortable carpeted alcove with two bathrooms. There are five women in line outside the women's room, and only one guy outside of the men's. Typical. I get in the women's line. I think about the times I sat in the bathroom in elementary school to get out of uncomfortable social situations. I always hated when teachers asked us to pick partners, teams, anything. Kids would cluster together immediately like it was a chemical reaction, and I would be left alone. So I'd ask to go to the bathroom, and then I'd sit on the toilet for a while.

Now I am at the Harvard Club, socialization having failed again.

But I notice that the guy standing outside of the men's room doesn't go in.

He keeps standing against the wall with his arms folded, staring at the floor. He looks down-to-earth. Short, with light wavy hair and a puggish nose. I could see girls overlooking him because of the shortness. Maybe he's down here for the same reason I am: to hide from the crowds.

The girl at the front of my line goes in. Pretty soon I'll be in. I have to figure out something to say to the guy quickly. I look over and smile.

A brief smile crosses his lips. Then he looks away. It's probably shyness more than snobbery. I certainly have been accused of the latter when the problem was the former.

"Less crowded down here," I say to him.

He nods. "It is."

"Hiding out?" I ask.

"For now."

We're both silent for a second.

"Have you been to other Harvard Club things?" I ask.

He shakes his head. "This is my first."

"Seems okay so far," I say. I smile.

"Yeah," he says.

He smiles back.

"Beats staying home, I guess," I say.

Then a girl emerges from the rest room. She says to the guy, "Ready?" and he nods. "See ya," he says to me, and they disappear up the stairs.

I feel like such an idiot. I enter the bathroom not a moment too soon and lock myself in a stall. I sit on the toilet and stare at the nicks and scratches in the beige stall door. I stare until they fade into a molten manila blur.

Why should I have been foolish enough to think that anyone in the world besides me is alone?

I did say earlier that I'd met a lot of people who were alone lately, but they're all people who are strange in some way: my lecherous landlord, a meek old bald guy, Ronald the Rice-Haired Milquetoast. No one normal. Then again, maybe I'm not normal. Maybe there's something wrong with me, and I don't know it. If I were crazy, I surely wouldn't know it, right? By definition, I wouldn't. People who are insane can't know it, or they'd change their behavior. They think they're fine, and that everyone else has problems. Just like I think I'm fine, and that everyone else has problems.

The Unabomber, who happened to be a Harvard graduate by the way, was awfully smart, and he thought he had all the answers. He really did think he was doing the right thing by sending explosives through the mail. He was sure that no one else understood the importance of what he was doing, and that he had to do it.

Am I insane? What if I am? What should I do?

Now I'm scaring myself. Maybe my sitting on the toilet, thinking these thoughts, is more evidence that I'm mentally ill.

But I'm questioning my sanity, and maybe that means I'm sane. Only a sane person would do that. I doubt, therefore I am.

The Unabomber probably never believed he was anything less than sane. If he'd put his actions to logic, they wouldn't have held up. Nothing I do hurts people. But how do I know that

that's the logic system I should go by? It's not written anywhere. I just decided on it. Well, wouldn't Petrov know if I was insane? I'm not even on medication. Yes, I'm okay. Calm down.

I am going to pick myself up and walk out of this bathroom with my head held high. So what if the automatons here don't want to know me? It only proves I was right to spend so much time inside my apartment in the first place.

I ascend, and I dance through assailing elbows until I'm out the door.

Times Square is awash in lights of every color imaginable: purple, orange, blue. I wonder what it's like to work there, with pink or green light constantly splashing all over your desk. I descend into the subway and return to my apartment. It feels good to be away from the crowds and noise and smoke.

I climb outside onto the fire escape, taking my journal. The air smells like burning leaves. I inhale deeply.

I sit down on the frozen metal. The moon is out. I have always liked my view from the back. It's only a view of the rear ends of other apartment buildings, but it doesn't matter. Here, nothing is spruced up or renovated—it's tangled jungles of metal and concrete and brick and stone, just like a hundred years ago. A lot of the fire escapes have painted-over placards saying there's a fine for putting anything there that obstructs mobility. I would like to know if this has ever been enforced.

A rich tomato smell wafts under my nose. Someone must be downstairs stirring sauce. I take a good whiff. I wonder if I can find this person and knock on her door. I wonder if she'd invite me in to eat. Wouldn't that be nice? Maybe I would find out she was my long-lost aunt and we would gab for hours, making up for years of lost time.

I could write about this proposition in my journal. I could even make up a short story about it. I've never written a complete short story, even in college. But my fingers are too cold to write. I park my journal between my feet and decide to sit and think.

The Harvard party was supposed to be my avenue to meet smart people. I feel like a failure. But the difference is all one person. If there had been one person at Harvard who'd thought I was great for four years, I would have been okay. We would have been two happy, comfortable people and then drawn others to us by extension. If I'd known one person at this party who'd been committed to staying by me the whole night, we could have joined other groups easily.

But I didn't know one person.

The episode with the guy in the bathroom reminds me of a similar embarrassment during my freshman year. There was a study break at one of the lounges. I walked across campus to attend. The room was very Ivy Leagueish, with dark wooden faux columns in the walls and long windows with longer white drapes. Some people were sitting at tables, and the rest were milling about or hanging out by the snack table. It seemed as if not one person was at the event alone. I didn't see anyone who looked familiar. I decided that I would plant myself at a small empty table that was not far from where the food was. That way, maybe someone would sit down next to me.

I sat at my table looking out at people, my chin in my hands, purposely trying to appear ready to talk. There was a table about forty-five degrees to my elbow that had three guys and a girl at it. I noticed out of the corner of my eye that once in a while, the guy sitting closest to me would look at me instead of listening to his friends. I pretended I didn't notice and kept looking straight ahead, but I was aware of him.

He looked at me again. I kept my eyes on the buffet table.

He looked again.

I thought about how I should act. I moved my hair from

behind my ear, because my hair looks better when it's not tucked back. I made sure my feet were under the table, since I was wearing ratty old shoes (I won't walk blocks in high heels. I'm sorry).

I kept my eyes on the buffet table.

Finally the guy tapped me on the shoulder.

"Hey," he said.

I smiled.

"Can we steal your chair?"

He took a chair from the table I was at and dragged it over so some girl could sit down.

I felt miserable.

I wondered: When am I going to be the one whom someone steals a chair for? Will I always be the donor of the chair?

I still wonder this, today.

I can't possibly be the only one in this city who feels like this, can I?

Everyone has to start somewhere. There must be people who move to New York and know no one. How do they meet people? Or maybe everyone else knows the secret to making new friends. They must have learned it in one of those grades I skipped.

Maybe I'm just not doing this enough, going out. Maybe Petrov's right. Maybe I have to keep forcing myself to attend social events for practice, which I hardly ever did in college. Okay, so this party attracted all Yuppie types, but perhaps the next one will bring out people who are shy and alone like me. I can't give up this easily. There will be more parties, more events. And all it takes is striking up a conversation with one friendly person who might lead to more.

But the very thought of doing this again makes my blood freeze.

Why does the idea of going to more of these events scare me? It has nothing to do with my moral issues. I do find a lot of people morally weak, but that's not the reason I have trouble meeting them in the first place.

Maybe I fear going to parties because it's risky.

That's it, isn't it? I have no advantage in these situations. In school, teachers liked me. I always felt the most comfortable in the presence of adults. They found me smart. They got to know me through the work I was assigned. All I had to do was sit home at a desk and work hard on my homework to gain their affection. I had *control* over it.

Maybe that's why I act like grades and test scores are so important. They were. They help me make progress.

Now no one cares. In a bar or at a mixer, I am just me. And no one gets to know me unless they talk to me. And I don't know how to make that happen.

Maybe I should start listening to Petrov. He has ideas.

I don't have to admit to him that his ideas are right. I just have to use them in my own life.

It's so hard to push myself, though. And what if my worst fears are true—what if I'm *never* able to connect with anyone?

But then, sitting on the frozen fire escape, a buoyancy overtakes me. Because I think of something.

I did talk to the guy by the bathroom.

So okay, he had a girlfriend, and it turned out to be humiliating. But I *am* capable of talking to strangers.

I will do that more. I will talk to people. It's got to work out sooner or later.

I stand up. It's cold out. I look around for Cy. He seemed like a nice guy—with a certain sweetness rather than speciousness. He's not out on his fire escape tonight. But I have a feeling I will see him eventually.

There's no rhyme or reason to this belief, but I've still got it. I guess if you don't do drugs, and you don't gorge yourself constantly, and you're not in love, the one thing that's left is hope. Hope that something more is out there. If you don't have hope, that's when the antidepressants come in.

★ ★ ★

That night, I get a call from Matt and we make a date for dinner the next night. I'm excited as heck. I want to dance around the room. But why? I can't have a relationship with him. Obviously, it would be wrong. I am taking his attention away from Shauna, on whom he should be focusing it.

I should do what I said I would in the first place—find Shauna and tell her what Matt's doing. Or at the very least, I should meet with Matt again just to tell him off. But I admit that I like him a little. I had a good time with him. Why should I be the one to give up a good time? Nobody else does. Why should it be *my* responsibility to change people like him?

Maybe I *should* cheat. Shauna is the lucky one. She won't ever have to go to a party and stand in the corner contemplating her ATM receipt. She won't ever have psychologists writing up lists of ways for her to socialize. She won't sit home alone on Thanksgiving because her family only consists of one person, and that person's in Luxembourg. Because she happened to go to the right high school, she has a normal life. All of the pieces fell into place. She won the great vacation, the new car and the fabulous prizes. I have nothing. I can't help it. I was good for nineteen years and it didn't work out. Sorry.

That's stupid, though. I have at least ten years before I have to worry about these things. Why am I giving up already? Because the most normal guy who was in the *Beacon* personal ads is engaged.

Well, I will figure out the right thing to do. I have a little time, I guess.

Just to see if there's an alternative to Matt, I pull out the phone numbers for Michael and Adam, the guys who answered my personal ad, again. I call both of them, but neither is home. This time, I leave messages on their answering machines.

★ ★ ★

Around eleven that night, I get a call to do legal proofreading at a firm I've never been to. Because it's late, they send me a car. At the firm, they put me and an older woman at a table in the middle of a silent, well-heated law library. For two hours, we stare across the table at each other and listen to the distant hum of some refrigerator or copy machine. I do a twenty-minute assignment and they send us both home.

In the back of another hired car, at two in the morning, I gaze up at the lights on in the apartments. Again, I am part of the small and secret community of people who are up at this hour. I don't see the actual people, though, just their lights. Some of the windows have potted plants on their sills; some have tiny gates; some have decorations or cleaning products; but they all have the same silent somnolent glow.

I think that this is a beautiful world. You just have to find the small things in it to love.

Matt looks nervous as he comes into Pellerico's at seven. He doesn't see me waiting at a table. He stands at the front, near the register, then looks at himself in the metal panel on the wall and pushes his hair back. Suddenly he notices me. He looks sheepish.

After we both get our menus, he says to me, "I know I don't drink, but are you sure you don't want anything?"

"I guess I could go for a glass of wine," I say.

"White wine," he says to the waiter and I can tell he actually knows less about alcohol than I do, which is definitely strange. "So," he says. "How was work today?"

"Kind of slow." He doesn't know how true that is.

"No one making mistakes?" Matt smiles. "Is that considered bad for you, when no one makes mistakes? Do you get nervous?"

"Yeah," I say. "It's terrible to admit, but I do feel happy when I catch a mistake. If there aren't any, I get nervous that I'm doing a bad proofreading job."

"I hear ya," he says. I hate it when people say, "I hear ya." They only say it if they have zip to add, or when they didn't get a joke. Then, Matt begins pronouncing the dishes on the menu to himself. How irritating. Maybe it's best that I don't have a boyfriend. How can you stand to spend so much time with another person when everyone has so many little things that drive you crazy? Maybe I have less tolerance than other people.

"What're you getting?" Matt asks me.

I hate when people base their order on what the other person's getting. "What are *you* getting?"

"You first."

"You."

"You."

"You."

"You."

"You."

He puts his hands over his ears and says, "You you you you you!" and I laugh, and I like him again.

The waiter appears. "Need more time?"

"No, he's ready," I say. "Go ahead, darling." I smile at him sweetly.

"Ah, you go," he says. "I insist."

"I'm going to decide after *him,*" I say.

Matt sighs, beaten. "I'll have the…peenie a la vodka. Is it real strong vodka?"

Oh brother. One of the nice things growing up with a traveling father did for me was enable me to eat out a lot. Matt apparently missed all of that.

"You can't taste it much," the waiter says. "It's in the sauce."

"Fine."

"I'll have the portobello-mozzarella sandwich," I say.

"Mooosssarel," Matt says, imitating me.

"I can't help if I can pronounce Italian," I say, as the waiter leaves. "And it's not peenie, it's penne."

"Guess my mind's in the gutter," Matt says.

"Maybe that's where it should be," I say.

"At least, in about an hour," he says.

I'm kind of frozen. His eyes are gleaming. The waiter brings us a basket of bread, and we both reach for it. I think we're nervous, because we go through a loaf and a half before our meals arrive. We also use up two little white porcelain cups of a spread that's not quite butter but not quite cream cheese.

"Would you like another glass of wine?" the waiter asks me, as he sets down our dinners.

"Yes, sure," I say.

"I'm practically full already," Matt says, looking at his plate.

"I'll help."

"You'll eat my peenie for me?"

"You should drink," I say. "Then you'd have an excuse to say dumb things like that."

"I don't need an excuse," he says, and he reaches under the table and squeezes my knee. I look around to see if anyone notices, but all of them are busy with their own discussions or lustful thoughts or whatever they're doing.

Then I realize something. I just told him he should drink. There's something wrong with me. I'm becoming the peer pressurer instead of the conscientious objector. I am doing, at nineteen, just what everyone else at college did when *they* were nineteen. Maybe my problem all along was just that I hadn't gotten to the age at which I became a moron yet. Maybe at twelve, you develop breasts, at thirteen, you get your period, and at nineteen, your mind turns to mush and doesn't recover until you're thirty-one. That can't be. I am right. I mean, I was right. Before

I came to dinner tonight. I miss the old me. I can't betray the old me. No one else was good to her. She must stay true and defy the corrupting forces all around. But why do I have to be the only one in this world who suffers? Being the old me hasn't gotten me anywhere. The only exciting times I've had in the past three years have been doing risky things: with my professor, with Kara, and now Matt. Yes, I do like safe activities like reading and looking through the dictionary and philosophizing and sleeping. Especially sleeping. But Matt is interesting. Am I going to give up spending time with him? He's not even married yet. This is not a departure from anything.

I will drink some more and stick with Matt right now because, for one thing, I owe it to myself to be with someone like him whom I feel happy with. The fact that he's not married means this isn't really so bad—Shauna probably doesn't appreciate him at all, and probably thinks it's easy to get a boyfriend and that people like me who don't have one are losers, and for another thing, if he *does* deserve for her to find out, then I should hang around him long enough to carry this plan to its completion. Maybe I can tip her off anonymously.

When I finish my wine, a waiter sets a new glass on the table. Its clear meniscus seesaws, then settles. I see the dwindling twilight from outside reflect in it. Matt fills his fork with his penne, but some of it falls off. "I'm an incompetent pasta eater," he says.

"It's okay," I say. "I'll bet you're really good at other things." He raises and lowers his eyebrows.

The two of us work through our meals silently. I like portobello mushrooms and I like mozzarella, but I don't think they complement each other, so I push them off the soggy sandwich and eat them separately. Matt looks as if he wants to question this, but he doesn't. He was too full to eat a second ago, but now he's packing it away. What an appetite.

As if he's reading my thoughts, he looks up and smiles, then resumes eating.

Maybe after he's spent enough time with me, he'll leave Shauna. But am I just as stupid as any woman who believes this? Is it a trap we all fall into? If he wanted to leave her, he would have done it a long time ago. He really has met lots of people, I'm sure. But they were people who wouldn't have accepted just being his hobby. That's the only reason I got him. The only reason I met him. It was under the condition that I'd never be first.

Forget it. I deserve fun. In the name of greater good, once again.

"Dessert?" Matt says, a mischievous grin on his face.

"You were full a little while ago," I say. Half his entree is left.

"We could split."

I look down the menu, then ask him, "Do you like tiramisu?"

He shrugs. "I've heard of it, but what is it?"

"It's like wet, rummy cake."

"Wet is good."

I guess he thinks he's being charming. We order it, and they bring it out, swimming in a white creme sauce dotted with flecks of chocolate. There are two long, thin spoons on the side. They get an A for appearance.

Matt takes his spoon, poises it above the soft beige square and slices off a spongy corner. "Hey," he says. "This is good."

"See?" Wow. I'm actually the one with more experience, for a change.

"I must say," Matt says, "first vodka, now rum. I think you're corrupting me."

"I'm usually the one to be corrupted," I say. "I'm pretty innocent."

"Are you, now?"

"Yes."

I feel a little wobbly. But ebullient, too.

Matt finishes his side and bangs the end of his spoon once on the table. "We did a good job here," he says. "That's teamwork."

When the bill comes, Matt fumbles with his credit card. He says, "Want to see my high-school yearbook, with all the dumb quotes?"

As contrived as our whole meeting is, having come from the personal ads and all, he still has to think of an excuse to get me to come to his apartment. "Where's your yearbook?"

"Back at my place."

"Don't you live with…"

"Shauna," Matt says. "She's not coming home tonight. She's in Jersey because her sister's in a play."

So that's it. The only reason Matt called me to meet him tonight was because he knew Shauna would be out of town; we got dessert because he can't get it when he's with Shauna; and last time, we ate Mexican because Shauna doesn't like it. I'm just her understudy.

Matt's apartment building is brick and old. In the hallway, the air smells musty but the green carpet is clean, and the people living on the first floor have a fuzzy mat decorated with holly along with the word *Joy*. Matt leads me up the stairs to the second floor.

The apartment is tasteful. The living room is black and white, with a coffee table, a full entertainment center (either a gift from someone's parents or a sign that people in their twenties make way too much money) and pictures of Matt and Shauna together all over the place. Them at their prom, looking earnest and young; them at high-school graduation in their caps; them sitting on the beach in winter in hooded sweatshirts.

I look at Shauna and think, *You know exactly who you will be with on holidays. You will get him on his birthday and wake up next to him every morning and go to sleep next to him every night. You will dance with him on your 50th anniversary. When he becomes wealthy through his computer consulting company, you will beam at his side. You know all his secrets. You remember what he was like as a boy. You will have him your whole life, until you both die. Your whole life. That's a long time.* Should I begrudge them?

"My yearbook's in here," Matt says, and I follow him into his room. There's a double bed with a crocheted bedspread, a large TV and piles of books. Matt sits on his bed and opens the yearbook in his lap. The bed sinks. I sit down next to him. "Keep in mind I'm from Jersey," he says. He points to different girls' hair.

"This one looks like a wig," I say.

"You think she's bad, look here," he says, and turns the page. I laugh. Matt adds, "Look at her quote. 'Don't worry, be happy.'"

I like the way his fingers move across the page, quickly yet deliberately.

"It's good that girl searched hard for something profound," I say. Next he comes upon a girl who's blond on one side and dark on the other. "Now, *that's* interesting hair," I say.

"That was our salutatorian," Matt says.

"Come on."

"I told you," he says. "It's New Jersey." He looks at me. "I really like *your* hair."

"It's just hair," I say.

"It's really natural," he says. He takes a strand between his thumb and forefinger and winds it around them. "I like sleek hair." Then he takes another. I lean closer. Pretty soon, we're engaged in a fair amount of face-mashing.

Eventually I look at one of the myriad pictures of Matt with the girl next door, this one poised precariously on top of his laser printer, and I sit up. "I should go," I say.

"Come on," he says, lying on his back. "The night is young."

"Yeah, but I have to work tomorrow."

"So do I. So what? We won't get many chances."

"Just because you're on Shauna's schedule doesn't mean I am."

He sits up. "I know it's not fair," he says. "But you knew the rules going in. And you said you were in the same situation."

"Well, I broke up with my boyfriend. Because I knew that if I'm capable of having feelings for someone else, then I'm not where I should be."

Matt's quiet for a second. "You're young," he says. "You'll learn when you get older that it's not so black-and-white."

"Well, maybe it should be."

"It'd be nice," Matt says.

"That's bleak," I say. "For you to give up on marriage."

"I'm not giving up on anything. That's what this is all about."

The thing is, I don't really want to leave. I want him to convince me to stay. I do like him, and I like exploring the idea of whether you can actually do something like this without hurting someone. Can it really be okay?

"You mad at me?" Matt asks. He reaches out and holds the ends of my fingers.

"I don't have a right to be," I say. And it's true. I don't have a right to anything.

"Come here," he says, and we manage to get back into it. The hints of stubble around his lips tickle me.

He moves his hands up my arms, to my shoulders, then holds my chin.

But I have to stop. I pull myself away before anything major happens. He says he'll call me next week.

Unfortunately, I leave wanting to see him again as soon as I can.

When I'm back on my block, I pass the Guarinos, the couple across the street. I recognize them from their kitchen window.

Nearly on impulse, I say, "Hi!" Both of them look bewildered, and Tom mumbles, "Hi." When I'm up the street, I look back to see if I can catch them looking back at me to figure out who I am. They are. I laugh. They look befuddled, then annoyed that I caught them. I triumphantly keep walking. I said hi to my neighbors; that should signify progress. I guess at this point, if I don't force myself on people, I'll never meet anyone. In fact, I feel like every social thing I do is something I'm forcing. Hopefully someday, I'll find enough people I like and things to do that I won't have to force myself to meet anyone else. But maybe most people are already at that place, and that's why they don't meet *me:* because they found enough friends early on, and now they're comfortable.

It's true, isn't it? Isn't that why no one met me at the Harvard mixer? Because they got into their groups early and gave up? Isn't that why Matt is engaged to Shauna? Because he doesn't want to spend any more time looking for a potential wife? Isn't that why all of my neighbors keep to themselves rather than organizing a block party?

Maybe everyone ought to see Petrov. Everyone is socially lazy. It's not just me. And at least when I am, it's for a good reason: I don't want to deal with hypocrisy, lying and cheating all around. In fact, look at what Petrov's list has done for me so far. Because of it, I've kissed a guy who's engaged and become engaged in kissing a girl who's a girl. Should I stay alone and stop forcing myself out, or force myself out and give up my standards like everyone else?

Once inside my apartment, I take out my new journal and flop onto my bed. Maybe it will help if I sort out my moral dilemmas on paper.

"Acceptable behavior," I write on one side of the page, and on the other, "Unacceptable."

But is there a use? What if I just get an overwhelming urge next year, or five years from now, to do something in the second column? What's the point? Third-graders who learn in school that alcohol and smoking are unhealthy and dangerous will say that it's wrong to do them or pressure others to do them. But over a period of time, they become less and less averse. By high school, they're taking part in it without a second thought. When we're little, we don't think, "Someday, I'm going to grow up and cheat on my spouse." We know it's a bad idea. Why do we know what's moral and wise when we're seven, but not when we're twenty-seven? We theoretically should be getting smarter, not dumber, as we age. But maybe we also get weaker.

But we're not, are we? I mean, we're definitely not physically weaker. So it must be something else at work. Maybe it really *is* Satan. Isn't it funny that that's the answer that makes the most sense?

My God. The religious nuts are right. Everything bad is caused by Satan.

That's silly, of course. There are plenty of things we can resist doing: murder, stealing. But those things are extreme enough that they don't become harder to resist as time goes on.

Well, I can always say this: I'm only human. Besides…

The devil made me do it.

Alcohol made me do it.

I couldn't help it.

It was my time of the month.

I was created to spread my seed.

I was brought up that way.

I'm Italian.

I'm Jewish.

I'm Catholic.

Temporary insanity.

I'm having a bad day.

My parents made me feel worthless.

I was under a lot of stress.

It's just one of those things.
I have ADD.
They do this all the time in Europe.

This should go to some music…

I'm only human.
The devil made me do it.
Alcohol made me do it.
I couldn't help it.
It was my time of the month.
I was created to spread my seed.
I was brought up that way.
I'm Italian.
I'm Jewish.
I'm Catholic.
Temporary insanity.
I'm having a bad day.
My parents made me feel worthless.
I was under a lot of stress.
It's just one of those things.
I have ADD.
They do this all the time in Europe.
Step right up, get your excuses here. Excuuuses. Get your excuuuses!

And they say *baseball* is the national pastime.

Chapter Nine

The evening after my date with Matt, I decide I'll try calling Michael, who answered my personal ad, one more time, even though he never returned the message I eventually left. I flop onto my bed with my phone and dial. This time, he picks up on the third ring. He's fashionably late like me. Something we have in common already.

"Is this Michael?" I ask.

"This is him," he says.

Poor grammar skills. Strike one.

"This is Heather," I say. "You called me…through the *Beacon*."

"Right," he says. "From the personals."

Strike two. He admits it readily, rather than being hesitant about it, like any normal person should be.

"So," he says, "what's up?"

That question's a little broad. "Considering you don't know

me," I say, "I'll spare you the rundown of how Fluffy is doing since her operation."

"Oh, wow," he says. "You have a cat?"

"That's a joke."

"Oh. Sorry."

"Anyway, I guess these things are a little awkward. You said you've never answered an ad before?"

"Not too many of them," he says. "You just seemed different."

"Well, I did put an emphasis on smartness. That's different."

He sounds like he's been lying down and is now getting up, because I hear things creak. "Well, I read a lot, so I figured," he says.

"What do you read?"

"Well, I mean, I don't read all the time," he says. "But sometimes I do."

"Is there anyone in particular you like?"

"Well, I guess science fiction people."

"Anyone in particular?"

"Asimov?" he says.

"I've read *Foundation*."

"You're kidding! That's awesome!"

"It was pretty good."

"That's cool. Girls don't usually like science fiction."

At least he didn't call me a "lady."

As we talk, he slides in and out of my good graces. He seems fairly normal, but not very bright. I wonder if I'm supposed to be the person to hint that we meet. I guess so, since I placed the ad. But I'm not in the habit.

"Well," I say. "We could talk more sometime."

"Uh…yeah."

"I guess we could meet somewhere."

"Wanna meet for coffee?" he asks.

There it is again. Why does it always have to be coffee? Why is it that no one ever says, "Do you want to get carrot juice sometime?" Or, "I know this great peach nectar place." Those things are a heck of a lot healthier than coffee, and better tasting. If I ever meet someone who asks me to meet up for some fruit juice, I'll marry him.

"Well," I say. "There's a Barnes & Noble near my neighborhood. Since you like books."

"Sounds good," he says. "I'll be away next weekend, but how about the weekend after that?"

"Well, Saturday's fine, during the day," I say. "Maybe for lunch. They have sandwiches there."

"Sounds cool."

The particular Barnes & Noble I have in mind is actually close to the police station, which is why I picked it. I think about the girl who met a grad student on the Internet in New York a few years ago, and she went to his apartment, and he allegedly bound and gagged her and held her against her will for hours. He was a smart, quiet guy, and look what happened. You just never know.

Now that I've hung up with Michael, my room is silent again. Very silent. I can barely even hear the hum inside my wall.

I guess it's back to normal for me.

I wonder why I never heard back from A-Adam. Maybe he chickened out. I pick up the phone and call the 900 number to see if there are any new responses to my ad, and the recording tells me that there's one. It's just a few seconds of silence, then a hang-up.

I think about how if I died in my apartment on the day after my appointment with Petrov, no one would notice for a week. My father might call and not get me, and try again, but it could take a few days for him to realize anything's really wrong. I'll bet there are people in the world who couldn't go a few hours without someone noticing they're missing. And there are people who could die on Friday after work, and no one would notice until Monday. But for me, it could take an entire week. Perhaps that is a way to gauge how much you are loved in the world—how long it would take people to notice that you're missing. Right now, I would not fare well.

Soon, Thanksgiving Eve arrives. That afternoon, the streets start to get crowded. People have gotten off work early, I guess. I walk a few blocks to the local supermarket. I figure I'll nab a rotisserie chicken and have a makeshift Thanksgiving dinner tomorrow. I expect the counter where the rotisserie chickens are to be empty, but there's a line that winds back through the frozen foods. I wonder why all these people are planning to eat supermarket-prepared chickens on Thanksgiving instead of the standard turkey. It seems almost sacrilegious. At least I have an excuse. Could it be that there really *are* other people alone?

When I look at them, I doubt it. They're largely well-dressed, impatient and sometimes beside a significant other. Maybe they just don't like turkey, or maybe they're eating the chicken tonight so that they don't have to cook. But who would eat chicken the night before a virtual turkeython?

All of them look anxious. I know that some are ready to shed their business clothes and their pinching high heels and hop into their cars to head out of town. I think about how when I was little, people used to bring their kids from the suburbs to the cities to visit their grandparents on holidays, and how now, people in their twenties and early thirties *live* in the cities, so they take their kids back to the suburbs, where they grew up, to see the kids' grandparents. I guess the trend will keep going back and forth until the suburbs are so citified and the cities are so suburbified that you won't recognize the difference.

I trot through the aisles, collecting cranberry sauce, ginger ale, wine (might as well go all-out), creamed corn, marshmallows, yams and a pouch of frozen buttered peas and carrots. I am not recreating the first Thanksgiving meal consumed by the Pilgrims (who, contrary to popular American belief, were English Separatists and not regular Puritans, a fact that's apropos of nothing except that it's irksome when they teach misinformation in schools), but I *am* recreating the first Thanksgiving my father and I celebrated together. We didn't celebrate it until I was about five because my father had never had it when he lived in England, and I never paid attention to it until we started doing projects related to it in America in kindergarten. That year, we traced our hands and turned them into turkeys; we wrote essays on giant green lined paper about all the things we were thankful for; we learned about the Pilgrims (we didn't learn that they were Separatists) and the Indians (who started being called Native Americans when I was in third grade) and about what they ate, which probably did not include poultry containing a pop-up thermometer. When, during kindergarten, I told my father that I wanted to celebrate, he called around and managed to come up with a hearty list of fixings that turned into a bountiful meal. Except for a few years during college, he has done so ever since.

On the way home, I pick up a few slices of pizza to prevent my mouth from watering thinking about tomorrow's cornucopia.

It's quiet when I wake up the next morning.

I hear a few car doors opening and closing. I hear someone yell, "Hiiii!" But the rumbles of the buses, and the horns of the taxis, are absent. I look outside, and the street is so empty that the faint frosty dusting that coats it on cold mornings has barely been disturbed.

I check the time. Eight-thirty. Too early to eat. Too early to do anything.

I don't know what I'll do this morning. I can't watch TV. The only programs that will be on are sports and the Macy's parade. The parade is a tradition I'm not fond of. It's hard to enjoy: "There's the Snoopy float. Look at it go. It took five men to inflate. It is five stories tall. The circumference of its snout is two pi feet. Its inner temperature is 280 Kelvin." They ought to do parades sponsored by the most downscale of Main Street's urban clothiers, with floats like "Polly Esther" and "Rippy Longstocking." They should run them through the snootiest suburbs in the country.

Such fantasies do not divert my attention from my boredom, or my aloneness. My stomach is empty. I can hear it rumble.

It's too early for my Thanksgiving meal. But I have a hankering for my juicy, succulent, spicy, warm cooked bird.

I decide I'll scrub my kitchen shelves, which I haven't done in a while. I stand up on a stool and rub them down, picking the stickiness off the ketchup and syrup bottles. But doing this only spurs more thoughts about food.

Then, I think, *I'm alone. Why not?*

I don't have to wait for anyone else to eat.

The thought of eating dinner at nine in the morning might make some of us ill, but there's nothing at all unhealthy about it. It just shows what a psychological hold our culture has on us, the fact that something that is in no way wrong or unhealthy seems disgusting.

It's not like I'm going to do it every day.

I quickly pull the chicken out of the refrigerator, where it has oozed some nameless but not wholly off-putting gel, and I place it onto a broiler pan. I set merrily to opening the cans of corn and yams. I position plastic bowls and dishes on the table. I bring a portable radio into the kitchen and turn on my classical music station. The DJ is talking in his soothing voice about Thanksgiving, and it makes me happy. He's alone, too. We're two of a kind.

For a second, I remember that Kara said something about all of us orphans getting together. I wonder what she's doing today. But I'm already set for the idea of eating alone. When I get into a settled mood, it takes a lot to edge me out of it. I do feel a small pang of guilt, but I feel a greater degree of happiness that I forgot to call Kara, because I'd really rather be by myself today. Maybe next year I'll get us orphans together.

I fire up the yams and marshmallows and get the water boiling for the stuffing. I fold my napkin and place it next to my plate. The seasoning for the stuffing smells delicious.

And this, my friends, is the beauty, the wonder, the joy—the reward for being alone! I don't have to sit in the living room inhaling four hours of turkey fumes waiting for someone to stick a charred mitt into the oven and pull out The Bird. I don't have to stare at the parade or some sports event pretending I'm not thinking about tender, juicy white meat. The Bird is mine! The Bird is all for me!

I can pick it apart all day. I can eat chicken for breakfast, lunch and dinner. This is my Bird.

The tinkling of the piano keys on the radio complements the clinking of my wineglass and cutlery as I eat and drink. I'm seated at the black wooden dining table that's from the apartment I grew up in—in fact, much of our old furniture is in my apartment. (The rest we sold or gave away.) I have a pink tablecloth on top, but for a second, I peel it back to look for nicks and scratches on the table, to revel in the fact that each of them was made during some Thanksgiving celebration or dinner party in my youth, which was pretty much the only time we used the dining room table. We had a small circular table in the kitchen for eating that we've since tossed out. This was the fancy one. Each nick must have been made at a different age, at a different stage of life, in the same apartment with the same person. I run my index finger over them.

The chicken tastes wonderful—tender and tasty, much better than I could have cooked. My father has said that my mother was a good cook, and it's quite possible that I might have inherited this talent, but I haven't made many attempts to find out. Even if talents are innate, they require *some* inspiration. I don't need to cook shrimp cacciatore with fennel for just myself. I don't even know what fennel is.

I plow through the corn, cranberries, stuffing and potatoes. When I'm finished, and when the dishes are done, I flop down on my living room couch like a satisfied pooch. On some occasions, there's nothing better than an empty head and a full stomach.

At noon, my father calls.

He wishes me a happy Thanksgiving. He asks again whether he should call some friends in the city so I can go visit them. I decline.

He asks what I'm going to eat.

"Uh, I think I'm going to have this rotisserie chicken I bought," I say, "and some corn and cranberry sauce, and probably potatoes and stuffing."

"Sounds like you've picked up on our tradition," he says. "I wish I was there."

I know he's not just saying that. But I also wonder sometimes if he stays away because it's just easier for him.

"Maybe you can get them to have Thanksgiving in Luxembourg," I say.

"Sounds like a battle I wouldn't choose," he says, "but I am thankful today. I'm thankful I have you."

★ ★ ★

When I hang up, it's completely quiet. More so than usual because there's no reason to expect the phone to ring again. Even telemarketers won't be calling today. Matt sure won't. I'm sure he's sitting around a lively table right now, not thinking of me.

All I've got right now are books, a few DVDs and leftovers.

I read for a little while, then clean my bathtub and organize the top shelves of my closet where I found the polka records when I moved in.

I realize that I need to hear something. This level of silence is too high even for me. I can't go the rest of the day without hearing a sound.

So I stand up on a chair. I say, low, "Aaahhh."

Then, I say louder, "Aaaaah."

Then, I yell, "Aaaaaah!"

Nothing answers back.

I remember something similar I did when I was little. When I was nine, I realized that perhaps every single thing we did in life, even sitting down or humming, was predestined. As soon as I thought of this, I jerked my arm so that I could do something sudden and gum up the works, maybe throw the rest of my life off that predestined course. But after I did that, I wondered if it was even predestined that I would jerk my arm. So I did a quick yell. But then I realized that maybe the yell was predetermined, too. So I suddenly turned my head. I realized that that also might have been predestined. So I pounded the table. But I realized that that could be predestined as well. So I had to give up.

I decide that I should call Kara after all. She probably is home, right?

I go to the kitchen table. After more deliberation, I dial her number. There's no answer. Of course, she found somewhere to go. Who wouldn't?

I guess I could have, too. I could have visited my father's friends. But I'd still have been lonely. Being lonely isn't about wanting to be with other people—it's about wanting to be with people who really care about you.

Out of ideas, I sit on my couch.

I use the time to think about a lot of things.

I think about why most people would find it appalling to ask a stranger for a dime but they're perfectly willing to ask for a cigarette.

I think about the big Thanksgiving conundrum: What exactly is the difference between a sweet potato and a yam?

This one I need to know. I get up and look through the dictionary.

The dictionary says a sweet potato is "a tropical American vine cultivated for its fleshy, tuberous orange-colored root." It reports that a yam is "the starchy edible root of a tropical vine." Maybe the sweet potato is the vine *and* the edible part, while the yam is just the edible part—but it notes that a sweet potato is American, and a yam is tropical. Oh, so many mysteries.

As I doze off at night, I think again about holidays, and family, and Matt, and Kara, and the comics, and yams, and kindergarten assignments, and Separatists, and chicken, and turkey, and that ingredient in turkey that's supposed to make you tired, and then I try to remember its chemical composition, but I'm not wholly successful in calling it up.

On Saturday, I get a call to go in to Dickson, Monroe. I instantly recognize it as Kara's firm. "I've been there before," I quickly tell the legal proofreading assignment person, just to seal the deal in case she suddenly decides to change her mind about my worthiness. I don't know whether Kara will be there, and my heart races. I make sure to look extra neat. I don't know why.

Maybe I just like the challenge of impressing her. Maybe I like the idea that she doesn't look at me and instantly know I'm a misfit. It's like I've pulled something off.

When I get there, I'm thrilled to see that Kara is there. So are two other proofers: a heavyset guy in his twenties, and a short-haired girl who's about five feet tall. Kara gives me a big smile. "Carrie!" she says. She's apparently already been regaling the guy and girl with tales of the daily grind at Dickson, Monroe, and she says to them, "This is Carrie. She rules."

The guy asks if I'm an actress, and I say no, and he and the girl both say, "Good." It seems that the guy, whose name is Billy, is an actor who's trying to get into stand-up comedy. The woman, Tina, is an actress and hand model.

Our supervisor comes out. "What we thought we were going to have you do isn't ready yet," he tells us. "We do have something less challenging, if you're willing to do it. We have these spiral-bound booklets and we want to make sure there aren't any sections missing. So all you have to do is flip through each page just to make sure they're all there. I know that you guys are proofreaders, so if you think the work is beneath you, you don't have to do it. But if you stay, you *will* get full proofreading pay."

"I'm in," says Billy.

"I'm in," says Tina.

"I'm in," I say.

"Good." The guy sets up a desk with piles of boxes, and he steps out. Kara stands across the table from me, where I can see her; she looks lively and sharp today, in ultrahip cat glasses. Billy stands next to me.

"What was his name again?" Tina asks after our supervisor has left.

"Eric," Kara says.

"Eric the bee?" Billy pipes up.

"Eric the half bee," Kara says. "He had an accident."

Oh no. I can already tell that this is some comedy skit I've never heard of, and that neither Kara nor Billy will explain it. People are never willing to tell you what they're reciting when you ask. You have to ask like three times, and then you sound like an idiot. That's what they want. But then again, I kind of understand, since it ruins a joke if you have to cite sources.

Tina asks, "What's that from?"

True to form, Kara and Billy ignore the question.

"Can you sing the song?" Kara asks Billy.

"Of course," Billy says.

"Wait," Tina says. "Stop. Hold on. You cannot sing 'the song' unless you tell us what 'the song' is from."

"Monty Python," Billy says wearily.

Damn! It's always Monty Python. I have to go rent some Monty Python movies. Everyone recites those damn things and I'm left standing there silently like an idiot.

The two of them sing the song. I'm jealous of their rapport.

Eric, the supervisor, returns and gives us the rest of what we need.

He leaves, and we set to work.

"Carrie, how much money have we made already?" Kara asks me.

"Seven-fifty," I say.

Billy and Tina instantly crack up.

"She didn't even look at her watch!" Tina laughs.

"I had just looked at it right before she asked," I say.

"Yeah, Carrie's great," Kara says. "Hey, how much have we made in this discussion alone?"

"About twenty-five cents more."

"All right! Now how much?"

"Another two cents."

"There are worse ways to make money," Kara says.

"I know," Tina says. "I just did Shakespeare in Detroit."

"Ugh," Billy says. "That's awful."

"I prefer Shakespeare in de park," Kara says.

"Now, *that's* awful."

"You know what's impossible?" Billy says. "Mercutio."

"Oh, I know," Kara says. "I never would memorize that."

"My friend does it for auditions."

"That's like running your first marathon with encyclopedias strapped to your ankles."

"Sounds kinky."

"Ha!"

"Hey, do you know anyone who does good headshots?"

"Speaking of kinky."

"No, seriously."

They talk actor talk for a while. I watch Kara, who manages to look lively no matter what the topic.

Suddenly she smiles at me.

"What?" I ask.

"What are we up to?"

"Fifteen dollars."

"All right!"

She slaps me five.

"I had the worst acting teachers in college," Billy says.

"Oh, I made sure I got good ones," Kara says, "especially since I had to pay for it myself."

"You paid for college yourself?"

"Well, I mostly got grants," she says. "My parents were out of the picture at a certain point, so I had to pay the rest."

"Did you have to get yourself declared an 'emaciated minor'?" Tina asks.

Billy and Kara instantly crack up. "Emaciated minor!" Billy says, falling over the table. "Yeah. She had Abraham Lincoln sign her Emaciation Proclamation."

"I meant '*eman*-ci-ated,' or whatever it is," Tina says.

I'm surprised that Kara and Billy laughed, seeing as I had to train myself for years not to laugh at people who use the wrong word.

"I didn't have to get myself declared," Kara says seriously. "I just explained the situation to financial aid. My parents were both fighting, and neither of them wanted to pay. They deserved each other."

"Too bad," Tina says solemnly.

Suddenly Kara says, "Oh my God! I forgot to feed my tarantula!"

"What?"

"My ex-boyfriend gave me this tarantula last week. He was talking to me on the phone, and he mentioned he had this tarantula and couldn't keep it. And I was kind of pissed at him in general, but then I thought, hey, free tarantula."

From her, this stuff comes out of nowhere. I smile.

"I'm getting back together with *my* ex-boyfriend," Tina says.

"I would have talked you out of it a couple of months ago," Kara says. "But now I know what being alone's like. It's boring not having anyone to shave your legs for."

Billy rolls his eyes.

"What?" Kara asks.

"That was more than I needed to know."

"That women shave their legs? You get into a serious relationship someday, and you'll have to watch."

"Great," Billy says.

We talk more and more about our own lives, and Kara discloses more and more.

"My therapist says that I talk too much," Kara says.

"Yeah, well, maybe you pay your therapist too much," Billy says.

"That was one of the things that struck me as so weird when

I first came to New York," Tina says, "that everyone freely admits they see therapists."

"That's because there's probably something wrong with you if you *don't*," Kara says.

"I don't," Billy says.

"I don't," Tina says. "But I probably should."

"Why?" Kara says. "What's your therapy problem?"

"Every time I get down my stairs, I have to run back up at least twice to make sure I locked my front door."

"Where do you live?" Kara asks.

"Avenue C."

"Well, *duh*." Kara says. "Move! That'll be fifty dollars. Next!" She looks at Billy. "What's *your* therapy problem?"

"Well, whenever I see a cop, I fantasize about taking his gun."

"Get your hands amputated," Kara says. "That'll be a hundred dollars." She looks at me. "What's *your* therapy problem?"

"I have too many to name," I say.

"You win," Kara says. "There's no hope for you. You're in the club like me." She comes over and gives me a big hug, then goes back to her side of the table. I can't help but feel happy. Even though I'm not as loud or quick as Billy, I've still won.

The whole time we're saying all of this, we're still flipping through our booklets.

"I'm barely even looking at these now," Tina says of them.

"I haven't even read an actual word in a half hour," Billy laughs.

"Oh my God," Tina says. "Which of these are the done ones and which are the undone ones?"

We all stop.

"This pile…" I say.

"I've been putting my checked ones there," Billy says.

"Those are my unchecked ones, I thought," I say.

"You've been checking my checked ones."

"I was checking those," Tina says.

"You're checking her checked ones," Billy says.

"Oh, no," Kara says.

We all look at each other. For a split second, I'm sure, we all contemplate just making an educated guess as to which ones are checked and putting them aside. But we all have at least a shred of a conscience. We have to start over. We're being paid for our time, anyway.

Billy sighs, and we push them across the table to start again.

We stay a total of six hours. Kara and Billy do improv. Then they mangle Shakespeare. I briefly wonder if they're going to go out at some point, but Billy has a fiancée. Tina seems a little out of the loop, but she smiles a lot.

When Billy, Tina and I are ready to leave, Eric asks Kara to stay another two hours. I'm a little disappointed. I was secretly hoping to go eat with her—I have no other plans. I don't know what it is, but she's just funny. And she says anything that comes into her head. I could never be like that, even if I wanted to. I'm not that brave. I guess being close to her is a way to experience that vicariously.

When I leave, she says she'll call me.

As I head home, I feel confused. About the kiss, and about everything. I could talk to Petrov about it, but I sure am not going to tell him about that night in her apartment. In fact, I haven't wanted to even think about it. It's not bad or anything— it's not immoral, and it certainly doesn't hurt anyone—but it's just not something I'm used to. And it's something that makes me feel different from everyone again.

Next time I see Petrov, I choose to skip all mentions of the kiss, but I do tell him about Kara in general and that she strikes me as an interesting person. I also tell him about my day of legal proofreading.

"What you just described," Petrov says, "sounds like an afternoon of fitting in."

"Huh?"

"From how you're telling it, you didn't seem to feel out of place at all," he says. "You didn't feel like the people around you were beneath you or above you. All of you had a great time."

"I guess," I say. "But you see, that proves my point. We were in a situation where all we could do was talk. And it was a situation where the people, because they were proofreaders, had to be smarter than normal. So it shows that if I do feel like I fit in somewhere, it might have to be an unusual situation."

"Possibly," Petrov says. "But it also might be a start for you. The one girl, who didn't know the difference between 'emaciate' and 'emancipate,' you didn't seem to mind that she was there."

"No. She wasn't bad."

"The more you get used to people, the more you will accept different kinds of people," Petrov says. "You have to realize that even in those who are different from you, there are things to admire."

Heading home, I think maybe part of the attraction surrounding Kara is an attraction to a situation in which *I* feel good about myself.

In fact, everyone I've kissed has been someone who told me I'm smart. But usually, they only say that because that matters to them, which means they share my priorities.

Sunday morning, at First Prophets' Church, the sermon is about Christmas and Christmas gifts. It's good. Natto doesn't carp about the materialism of the holidays, like some people do; he finds ways in which materialism can be converted into a spiritual deed, like buying extra gifts and giving them to a homeless shelter. Or picking one of our gifts and donating it to someone who needs it. Natto doesn't mention his book at all.

But I'm still not sure the "religion" isn't a cult. I can continue my research better if I come to church more consistently. Plus, then I can finally meet that goal of joining an organization. It would be nice to officially get one goal over with. I'm not sure my dates with Matt count as real dates, because he's taken, so that goal hasn't conclusively been met yet; when I see Michael from the personals at Barnes & Noble in a few days, it will count. But it's time to join a group.

I amble over to a long table in the back and fill out the membership form. It asks if I'm interested in receiving information about a youth group, a singles group and a Bible discussion group. I check off the middle one and the last one.

I hand in the form, along with a twenty-five-dollar check. With a few strokes of my NYU stationery store plastic purple pneumatic pen, I've officially joined a club.

"This is Eppie Bronson, from the First Prophets' Church? You filled out a form expressing interest in the singles and Bible studies group?"

"Yes."

"Well," says the voice on the phone, "I noticed you're rather young, and we've been thinking of starting sort of a middle group between teenagers and singles because a lot of our singles are in their forties and fifties. We want to sort of start a young leadership group, which would be people, not necessarily all singles, but they can be singles, in their twenties and early thirties. Do you think you might be interested?"

"Possibly," I say.

"What is it you do for a living?"

"Proofreading. And I'm a sort of philosopher."

"Aren't we all," Eppie says, and he laughs. He has a high-pitched laugh. "You know, we need someone to lead a new twenties-thirties group. We really don't have too many young people in our church, and Joe's hoping to attract more. Would you have an interest in discussing the possibility?"

"Maybe," I say. "I do want to learn more about your philosophies. I mean, I don't…"

"I know," Eppie says. "It's a new church, and you don't want to get taken in by something you may not agree with. Joe loves converting cynics. And honestly, we don't want you to take everything we say as gospel. Put it through the wringer. Challenge it. That's what First Prophets' is about. We're not brainwashers. We need new voices. Like yours."

"Well, I could think about it," I say.

"We can set up a time for you to meet with Joe Natto if you'd like."

This seems rather quick. They must be desperate. Or just new. If I meet Natto, will he see through my cover? "That sounds interesting," I say.

"We'd definitely like to bring more young people into the church," Eppie says. "There are a lot of young people who've just moved to the city and feel guilty that they haven't been going to church. This gives them a way to be a part of something new and exciting."

I don't want to be taken in, but he's saying the right things. I set up an appointment.

After I hang up, it's quiet again. I hear a car puttering past.

I look at the TV pullout I've saved from my paper. Just soaps and talk shows.

The phone rings.

I hope it's Matt. Then I chastise myself for hoping it's Matt. Maybe it's A-Adam. Maybe Kara. At least now I've got people who it could be.

I wait until the third ring.

"Is…Carrie Pilby there?"

The woman pronounced my name right. Maybe for a change it's not a sales call. Maybe this is the call that will change my life.

"Yes?"

"I'm calling to let you know you've won a free month of *Women's Week*."

A letdown, as usual.

"After your free month, if you're interested in getting the next forty-six issues, which would be the full year of issues, you can order them for only $14.95."

"If you're giving me a free month, that's four issues," I say. "If I can buy another forty-six and that's considered a year's worth, that's fifty. The magazine is called *Women's Week,* and there are fifty-two weeks in a year."

"We have double issues at Thanksgiving and Christmas," she says.

"But what if something happens with women during the weeks you're not publishing?" I ask. "What if women land on the moon? What if a band of angry Pygmy women holds up the White House?"

"Would you like to try the free offer?"

Suddenly I feel bad for her. The only people who do these jobs are people who really need the money. Otherwise they would get a job that pays better or doesn't require you to get hung up on for half the day. Why should I act superior? I'm not.

"Okay, I'll do it," I say. I'll just write "cancel" across the bill when I get it. I know this woman will get a commission if I accept this. All it's going to cost me is a few seconds of my life.

"Really?" she says. "I mean, thank you. Let me get the rest of your information, ma'am."

"You're welcome."

For a change, I feel like I did something good. When I hang up, I don't feel as bad about myself as usual.

I return to bed. I still feel alone, though. Maybe I'll meet Michael Saturday, we'll hit it off, and then I won't ever feel this way again.

I wonder what Matt is doing right now. I was better off when I didn't know what I was missing.

If I were Matt's girlfriend, I'd call him at work right now and say hi. I would ask how his day was going.

I think of Shauna. What if she is a nice person? She probably is. Am I horrible because I want Matt's attention, too? If Shauna isn't going to be enough to keep him happy, maybe it's better he find that out now. And maybe he'll realize there *is* one person who can keep him happy forever, happy enough to never want or need to cheat—it's just not Shauna.

I lie in bed a little longer. The silence is unnerving.

I decide to listen to the 78s that I found when I moved in here. I haven't done that in a while. I put one on, and it's a polka. It's scratchy and I love it.

The choppy sounds fill the room. They bring me to life. I whirl through the bedroom, living room, kitchen, bathroom. I touch the medicine cabinet, skip out past the painted-over window in the wall, head back to my room. The music spikes and drops. I leap into the air as if I am in a giant flowing skirt. I hop onto my bed and off. Someone on the record claps three times, and I do the same.

I'm having a Pilby Party: a party for one. I love Pilby Parties. I'm the only guest, and I always fit in.

The phone rings. I lower the music and pick it up.

"What are you doing?" Matt asks. "Having Oktoberfest in December?"

I laugh, happy to hear from him. "It's the old records I found when I moved in here."

"You have a record player?"

"Yeah."

"Why?"

"I like old things."

"Do you have a CD player?"

"No."

There's an odd silence.

"I was half expecting your voice mail. You off today?"

I think quickly. "Night shift tonight," I say.

"Oh." He's quiet for a second. "All right, I'll level with you. I was calling because I'm having trouble not thinking about you. I'd really like to see you."

Whatever I did, I did right. And he was thinking about me when I wasn't there! Just like Harrison used to do.

"Are you able to meet up for lunch this week?" Matt asks. "Tomorrow?"

"Tomorrow's a little busy," I lie. I lie because I wonder if Shauna's out of town tomorrow and that's the only reason he's asking me.

"Thursday or Friday are okay, too," he says, "if they're okay with you."

All right. He's being flexible. "You know, I just realized, tomorrow's okay," I say.

"That's great."

"Will you get in trouble at work?" I ask.

"They don't really pay much attention to how long our lunch goes at my job," he says. "I'm a consultant anyway, and I move around. It's not like I'm at one desk all day. And I'm there till six some nights, or I'm in by eight in the morning. They know I do my work."

Matt's office is near the Harrigan's in Union Square, which is one of those family-style bar-restaurants whose menu spans everything from Southwestern to Cajun to finger food to fifty flavors of margaritas. I meet him in front of the roped-off entrance, and a woman says, "Smoking?" and we both shake our heads. It's packed.

"Work crowd," Matt says. "Don't worry, I'm paying. The prices here are double what they would be in a normal city."

We slide into a booth. Matt is smiling. He seems genuinely happy. Very light. I wonder if he's changing his mind about Shauna, now that he sees there's more out there. I'm both guilty and hopeful at once. It's not like I'm in love with him or anything, but I do like him, and it'd be easier to feel good about this if I knew he wasn't about to take his vows and spend ten days in Hawaii with someone.

Harrigan's is decorated with tin signs and corporate logos. There's a red Reading Railroad sign, a giant metal Pepsi thermometer, a circular blue Morton's salt ad, and a Maxwell House sign.

"Teddy Roosevelt used to eat there," Matt says, sitting down. There's a mirror on the side, and I see us both in it, him in a white dress shirt and tie, me in a red sweater. We don't look half-bad together.

"Teddy Roosevelt used to eat *where?*" I ask.

"Maxwell House. Maxwell House coffee was invented in the Maxwell House hotel in Tennessee, where all the rich and famous used to hang out after the turn of the century. Supposedly, Teddy Roosevelt was eating there one day, and he even said he enjoyed it to the 'last drop' and that became one of their slogans."

"Why did it happen to be Teddy Roosevelt who said it?" I ask. "Why wasn't it, like, Ernie the Bellhop?"

Matt laughs. "I guess you're right."

The waitress appears. "Welcome to Harrigan's. We have several specials, as you can see in front of you, as well as a new tutti-fruiti margarita."

"Tutti-fruiti? We'll have to do that," Matt says.

"Two?" the waitress asks.

"Yes," Matt leaps in, before I can say anything.

When she leaves, I say, "I thought you didn't drink."

"Yes, but since we're in Harrigan's, and since you can get margaritas in kids' flavors, and since we're celebrating our first workday lunch together, it's acceptable."

"I was hoping for bubble gum flavored."

"I was hoping for wild cherry or creamsicle," he says. "So, how've you been doing?"

It's sweet of him to ask. "I've been fine," I say. "How are you? How's work?"

Matt shrugs. "It's pretty good, except there's this new guy there who's annoying as hell. His name's Tad. Whoever heard of someone named Tad?"

"Abe Lincoln's son," I say.

"Figures you'd have heard of someone named Tad."

"We did a play on him in elementary school."

"On Tad Lincoln? Must have been boring."

"On *Abe* Lincoln."

"I wouldn't want to be named *Abraham,* either," Matt says.

"You know what was weird?" I say. "My teachers in school always said Abe Lincoln was considered ugly in his day. But no one in my class ever thought so. My teachers said maybe that's because we're used to looking at him. Have you ever thought of Abe Lincoln as ugly?"

"I don't know," Matt said. "I want to see a picture of him now, to see."

"I'd give you one, but I don't carry around pictures of Abe Lincoln."

"I do." Matt pulls out his wallet and takes out a five-dollar bill. "Yeah, he ain't bad."

I have to admit that Matt's pretty clever. I think if I were around him, I'd be continually surprised.

Someone a few tables away is delivered a birthday cake, and we wait for it to pass. Matt says, "I hope no one ever does that to me."

"Me either. I hate surprise parties."

"So do I. Anyone who knows me knows I don't like them. My parents threw me one once, and when everyone yelled 'Surprise,' I cried."

He looks cute when he says this. "Aww. How old were you?"

"I don't know. Five?"

We both order, and I notice a metal Esso sign. "Do you know how Esso got its name?" I ask.

"No. Only that it became Exxon eventually."

"Right. But back when they broke up Standard Oil in 1911, Standard Oil became a bunch of different companies, like Standard Oil of New Jersey, for instance. Eventually they got all cutesy and abbreviated it to Esso—S.O., get it?"

"Wow," Matt says. "That's cool."

"Another branch was Socony, Standard Oil Company of New York. That became Mobil."

"Happy motoring," Matt says, raising his margarita glass.

I clink glasses. "Happy motoring."

I think of how I haven't seen "Happy motoring" written on a gas station since I was a kid, and how Matt probably shares that, and how it's nice to have childhood pop culture reference points with someone. That was something I never had with Harrison.

"Antitrust theory interests me," Matt says, "because it's so antithetical to the theory of our capitalist system, and yet, so completely in line with it. Our country was founded on the idea, among others, that if you work hard, and you get more and more successful, you get to enjoy the fruits of it. You can over-come whatever situation or class you were born into with sweat and determination and ideas. But there's this nondelineated point at which if you will become *so* successful, you will get punished for it. And this is necessary because if you have a monopoly, you can do things that a regular market wouldn't allow, so there is a need for trust-busting. But the idea of the government knocking you off because you've done *too* well in America—that's strange, isn't it?"

"Yes," I say, and I take a sip. "I confess that among disciplines, economics isn't the one I'm most well-versed in, although I've always wanted to learn more."

"Economics bores me," Matt says, "and yet, I play the market all the time. There's psychology involved, too, not just numbers. I don't buy powerful stocks—I buy little ones that I think might rally."

"Are you good?"

Matt suddenly looks bashful. He shrugs.

I get the feeling it's a hidden talent of his, that he's wildly suc-cessful at it.

The waitress puts down our food. I drain my margarita, while Matt has a tiny bit left.

"More drinks?" the waitress asks.

Matt winks. "For her," he says.

When the waitress leaves, Matt raises his glass. "Here's to… to…"

"To good friends?" I ask.

"You know what?" he says. "Millard Fillmore came up with that."

"I think it was John Quincy Adams who first said, 'What'll it be?'"

"You've hardly eaten your food," Matt says.

"I'm too excited to eat," I say. "I want to tell you about Sanka."

"What? James Buchanan invented it?"

"No," I say. "This is serious. What it stands for. It stands for *sans* caffeine."

"No shit."

"Really," I say. "And Chicklets are chicle pellets."

"I never thought about that."

I can't seem to stop babbling. "'Brillo' is Spanish for 'I shine.'"

"You're just a fountain of knowledge."

"3M stands for...guess what?"

"I'm going to get this one. It stands for Mmm... mmm... good."

"No, that's soup, silly. It stands for Minnesota Mining and Manufacturing."

"Hmm."

"Necco is short for New England Confectionery Company."

I'm delivered my second margarita and I take a big sip. I put the glass down. "I read all kinds of wacky things all the time. Right now I'm going through this phase where I rent the top 100 movies..."

"Oh, the AAFR list? Yeah, I keep meaning to rent some of those. Half the time I go into the video store and have no idea what to rent."

"Me, too, so anyway, the list inspired me to take out this book on the origins of Hollywood. It said that Samuel Goldwyn, the Goldwyn of Metro Goldwyn Mayer, that wasn't his name. His name was Goldfish. But he had this partner named Selwyn. And the two of them combined their names to make a company, Goldwyn. And I was wondering why they decided to do it in that order, like, why didn't Mr. Selwyn's name get to be first, followed by Goldfish? And then I realized that if they did that, the company would have been Sel-Fish."

Matt laughs. "So this is what goes through your head all day."

"Nah," I say. "Only during first period."

"Come on. Don't tell me you order your days like school."

"Sure. I keep seven alarm clocks in my room, each set for a different period."

"You're lying."

"Trivia, gym, lunch, nap time—my favorite—art and music. I was in music when you called."

"Bullshit."

I'm actually making him smile. He gets me. The job interview guy never got me. "Okay, I made that up." I finish my second margarita. This stuff is good. I lick the salt that's encrusted on the glass. "Are you going to be late getting back to work?"

"I can be late."

I saw into my fajita. I have to be careful not to make a mess with the sour cream, salsa and guacamole. I've had so much to drink that the spiciness of the food is blunted.

"What are your parents like?" Matt asks.

He must really like me if he asks a serious question like that. "My mother died when I was two," I say.

"Oh, I'm sorry."

"It's okay. She had cancer. I don't remember her, really. My father tells me about her sometimes. It's hard for him to talk about."

"Well, if you ever want to talk to me about it."

"That's nice of you."

"Well, I like you."

I look at him. He's smiling. "Thanks."

"How did they meet? Your parents."

I think about it. "They worked at the same company."

"What does your dad do?"

"Investment banking stuff. He travels a lot."

"You must be very self-reliant."

I shrug. "I try."

He looks at me sympathetically. "It's impressive."

"Grows you right up." To negate this, I put a bit of guacamole on my spoon and pretend I'm about to fling it. He laughs. "I was born in London," I say. "We only moved to New York when I was two."

"No way," Matt says. "I was born in Paris."

"Really?"

"My mom was getting a doctorate in French studies. My parents are both college professors."

It always seems like people who are interesting had interesting parents. But then again, sometimes they had really awful parents. In any case, Matt obviously got a lot of support growing up. "Did you go to public schools?"

"Yeah," Matt says. "My parents are big public school fans. But they also taught me outside of school. Every night they discussed current events with me and my sister at the dinner table. And my mom started teaching us French before we were ten. She was one of those people who believed you have to learn a language when you're young."

"Really?" I say. "I hate to say this, but say something in French."

"*Sans* caffeine," he says.

"*Très bien,*" I say. "Unfortunately, that is about all I remember of my seventh-grade French."

"That's because you didn't start learning it before you turned ten."

"I did."

"Ha."

"I took Spanish, too," I say.

"Say something in Spanish," Matt demands.

"Eat-o your burrito, gringo."

He laughs.

"Fun fact," I say, unable to resist. "Gringo comes from 'Griego,' which is the Spanish word for 'Greek.' Because 'Greek' can be used as a word to mean something foreign, as in, 'It's all Greek to me.' So they took Griego and it mutated to 'Gringo.'"

"That's pretty interesting," Matt says.

"So is this margarita." I polish off the very end.

"I hope you're not driving today," Matt says.

"I'm out of Essolene."

"Put a tiger in your tank."

"Martin Van Buren invented that."

The waitress comes by. "How is everything going?"

"Fine!" we both bark at her. She looks like she just got hit in the face. "Take your time," she says, and walks off.

"She wants to get rid of us," Matt says.

I shrug. "What kind of issues did you debate at the dinner table?"

"Mostly our discussions were about Ronald Reagan. My dad's a political science and history professor. He actually teaches the theories, not presidencies or elections. He complains that students today only want to learn about campaigns. They want to read Ted White's *The Making of the President,* and he wants to teach Michael Harrington's *The Other America.*"

"Ah," I nod, although I haven't heard of either of those. But the fact that he believes I do, and that he doesn't need to stop and explain them to me, is flattering. And I will just keep listening to him, and I will learn. Professor Harrison was like that, too—he would talk to me about things I hadn't heard of as if it was a given that I had. Like I was his colleague. I loved it. I felt like after every conversation with him, I'd learned at least three new things. And I had also impressed him by revealing my knowledge of three others. It was a challenge, a fantastic give-and-take.

"I don't agree with my father on everything," Matt says. "He's kind of a leftie, and I'm pretty much in the middle. But he always sat back and let us debate. He'd ask my sister and me questions rather than just give us answers. Like, 'Well, I can see why you'd say that, but what if X and Y happened?' It was great."

I can imagine meeting Matt's parents. I'd sit at the table with his family at Christmas, passing the mashed potatoes, hashing out the tenets of Marxism, then ladling out the gravy and interventions.

"So, you want dessert?" Matt asks. "I think I'll skip it."

"Nah," I say.

"Another margarita?" He grins in mock-sinister fashion because I've clearly had enough. "Another," I say, "and I won't make it past 14th Street."

"I'll get you home," he says. He orders me another and watches me guzzle it down.

Even though I offer to pay for my share, he insists. I wobble out of the booth. When we're both in the vestibule, he suddenly puts his hands around my waist and kisses me.

"Sorry," he says. "I couldn't wait. I've never had this much fun on a workday."

I smile. "Thanks."

"I need to get back to work, but I wish I didn't have to."

"I can try to squeeze into your briefcase."

"That makes me sound so old," Matt says.

"I can try to squeeze into your bookbag."

"That's better."

Outside, the sun has broken through. A cold breeze blows.

"You are so cute," Matt says. "I mean it. You look so young. Just like, a girl. I mean, I don't mean that in any offensive way."

"I don't get offended by 'girl.'"

"And then you say these really sharp things. It's great."

"Thanks."

"You want to stop by my place for a little bit?"

I don't even question the wisdom of this. "Okay."

He takes my hand. Obviously, neither of us is being responsible, since Shauna could see us.

As if reading my mind, Matt says, "Shauna's away today. She's got a meeting in White Plains with some guy her dad works with to talk about PR. He's a Kraft executive. He might throw her some work."

Great. "How's that going?"

"She should land an account soon. I'm not so worried." He looks off at the sky. "We don't need the money much, but she feels better when she's working. I don't think she just wants to sit around the house waiting for me."

My hand feels cold in his. He's still talking about "we." But maybe it's just because he's used to it.

Matt starts swinging my hand, like we're two kids on the playground, and I let him. This is funny. I start to feel good again.

It seems like it takes forever to get to his place. "Are you sure you won't get in trouble?" I ask.

"No."

He leads me upstairs. As soon as he closes the front door, he pulls my blouse out of where it's tucked in, kneels and kisses my belly button. "I'm sorry," he says. "I'm just so turned on right now."

For a second, I feel like I'm someone in some movie, that I'm over by the wall watching this happen. Then the feeling goes away.

"Come on," Matt says. "In here."

I enter his room and he pushes the door shut. He takes me in his arms and pulls me onto the bed. Then he gives me a long deep kiss. "I learned this in France," he whispers.

"You mean, when you were a baby?"

"I had an ambitious nanny."

He slides his hand down and unbuttons my pants.

It's been years since I've been naked in front of anyone. But I'm not that self-conscious right now. I step out of my pants and then we end up back on the bed.

I look at the pictures of Shauna.

Ignore it, I think. *Why does everyone else get to have fun?*

Matt firmly puts each of his hands on my shoulders, pinning me. He crawls on top of me and suddenly feels very strong. I like it.

After we've kissed a bit more, he gets up and undresses himself. I guess he's figured out that I won't do it for him. I've never undressed anyone. I'm not *that* unselfconscious.

But I start thinking about how I need more to keep him interested in me and to get his mind off Shauna. I should save one thing for next time. It's hard, but I whisper, "We better stop."

He looks up. "Why?"

"I just think we should wait until next time." It's also true that I'm not completely sure about this. I don't want to do this and then feel awful afterward, like I have about everything lately.

"I want to see you as soon as I can," Matt says. "Any chance I get. I mean it."

"Good."

I pick my clothes off the floor, and Matt sits on the bed, watching me. When I bend down to get my shoes, I notice something among the tangled computer wires under his desk, and I can't help reading it—a dusty yellow Post-it that fell there. Written in pen is: *M—This is my reminder to you to call about the cable thing. I love you to.—S*

This depresses me. Something about the misspelling of *too.* It makes Shauna seem—I don't know—sweet, or real, or something.

I put my shoes on, and I feel sad. She does love this guy, and trusts him.

But then, I'll bet she doesn't feel bad for *me*. I'll bet she never even thinks about the people who can't share their daily responsibilities and struggles with someone else—the people who will always have to call about the Cable Thing themselves.

When I get home, there's a message on my answering machine. It's Matt, saying he had a good time and that he wants to see me as soon as he can.

Part of me can't wait to see Matt again. And part of me feels bad. I know this is wrong, at least partially wrong, no matter what rationalization I put on it. Rationalizations are for other people. I'm supposed to be a person who doesn't allow herself to dupe herself. Isn't that what I've prided myself on? I can't just talk myself out of things, push them to the back of my consciousness. I should instead work through them.

Am I really hurting other people by seeing Matt? That should be my standard. Hurting myself—that may be stupid, but at least the odds are that it only affects me. Health issues, like smoking or drinking, are things people do mostly to themselves, so maybe they're not quite as bad as the moral issues. At least, not until people start pressuring others to do them, which they often do, or until they start hurting others because of them. But what I'm doing with Matt, fooling around, could directly hurt others.

Matt and Shauna are engaged. By my seeing him whenever he decides we can, I may be letting him believe in some uncommitted, unrealistic fantasy. It may hurt his relationship with Shauna. It may take his attention off appreciating her and doing things for her as much as he should. They spent all these years together.

I don't know what's right anymore.

I have no one to talk to about my confusion. Kara hates adulterers. I don't have any other female friends. I have my date with Michael from the personals soon, but I don't think we'll become best buds. I also can't tell my father about it, nor Ronald the Rice-Haired Milquetoast, who acts as if he wants to know me but sometimes seems a little slow on the uptake.

There's Petrov.

He is confidential, right? He is there to listen, right?

I don't have to tell him about Matt, exactly, but I do want to bounce off him all the moral quandaries that are clanging around in my head. He's really supposed to be there to listen to problems, not to help me analyze the world, but so what? For what we're paying him, he should do whatever I want. He should take a course in reflexology and spend each session kneading my wounded tootsies.

The next afternoon, Kara calls.

She invites me to a holiday party at her friend's on Saturday. I want to see her, but I have to figure out how to properly relate to her. I worry that I might say the wrong thing and then she'll realize that I'm not cool enough to fit in with her and her friends. I quickly tell her I have a date.

I don't know why I lied. It was a split-second decision, and one I instantly regret.

"Who's the date with?" Kara asks. "That guy from last time? Did you sleep with him?"

"Not him," I lie. "Someone new."

"You are on a roll! How'd you meet this one?"

"Uh…through friends."

Her phone clicks. "Oh, I have to take this call!" she says. "I'll call you back and maybe we can get together a different time."

"Okay—bye."

I hang up. I wonder why I was so incredibly stupid. I do want to hang out with her again.

What if she doesn't really call? What's wrong with me?

I climb onto my window loft. I decide to hold off on calling Kara back. I'll do it if I don't hear from her soon.

I sit there, watching the cars roll past. Cars look more appealing when it's raining. Especially black ones with square headlights and tiny beads collecting on their hoods. So *film noir.* I wonder if I should save up for a car. But having a car in New York is like having a baby. They start crying in the middle of the night. You constantly have to worry about where they are. You have to mop up their leaks.

This would be the perfect afternoon for an old movie. But that means I'd have to go out to get the movie. That's the problem with rain—by the time you realize how nice it would be to stay in and watch a movie, you have to temporarily *not* stay in in order to get the movie.

I put on my raincoat and pull a hat over my head. I grab my umbrella and trot down the stairs.

The sidewalk is full of puddles. I splash in some as I walk. I do that all the way up the street. If puddles are inevitable, might as well enjoy them.

When I get around the corner of my block, I see someone familiar walking across the street.

I duck behind a parked car so he can't see me.

The person is wearing an overcoat and a scarf, but I'm pretty sure I know who he is. He pulls his umbrella lower and his head disappears.

I slip into an alleyway to watch. Dr. Petrov climbs some steps to the stoop of a building on the corner. He stands there in order to fold his umbrella and shake it off.

The front door opens and a tall, ponytailed young woman

steps out. The two of them kiss romantically. Petrov hugs her tightly. Then they disappear inside.

I stand there, dumbfounded. Last time I bumped into Petrov around here, he said he had a friend in the area. Is this his girlfriend?

I look up. The light comes on in a second-floor window. For a second, I see the two of them together in the window, but then they disappear.

This girl seems rather young.

I wait for a car to pass, then run across the street and step into the vestibule. I pull my usual technique of looking on the mailboxes.

There's only one apartment listed for the second floor: S. Rubin/D. Leshko. I think I may have seen this girl around the neighborhood before. But I think I've seen her with a guy. I can't be sure. A lot of the girls in my neighborhood look alike.

When I come back out, I head back across the street and look up at the window. I see them in there again for a second.

Only one thing to do.

I run home and thumb through the Manhattan white pages for a number. There are lots of Rubins, but none at that address. There is, however, a Leshko at the address, a Daniel Leshko.

I punch in *67 to stop my number from being traced, and then I dial.

It rings a few times. Gee, I hope I'm not interrupting anything.

A woman answers. "Hello?"

"Is Daniel Leshko there?" I ask.

"He's away on business," the woman says. "This is Sheryl. Can I take a message?"

"Actually, I'm doing a quick two-second phone survey for *Women's Week* magazine," I say, "and I know you're busy, but I just want to ask you two questions, and it would really help me out a lot in completing my quota."

The woman sighs. "I don't want my name used."

"No problem."

"Okay."

"We're calling 500 people in preparation for our next issue," I say. "All I want to know is, do you live alone, with a roommate, with your significant other, with your spouse, or none of the above?"

"Uh, with a husband," she says. "With a spouse."

"Okay," I say. "Well, thank you."

"What about the second question?" she asks.

I hadn't even thought of one. "Uh...to win a free ten-year subscription to *Women's Week,* please answer the following. What is the most commonly used phrase in the English language?"

"Uh...I don't know..."

"I'm sorry, that's the second most common. Have a nice day." I hang up.

This woman is fooling around with Petrov while her husband's away! I can ask him leading questions at my next appointment to be sure. He's divorced, so he's not cheating on anyone, but *she* sure is.

Perhaps she was the one who was at his place during the blizzard. Maybe she's the one who's always buying him new socks. Maybe she's whom Petrov thinks of when he wakes up in the morning.

That's why I saw Petrov on my block that day.

Now I can come up with a goals list for Petrov: Don't fool around with a woman in her twenties who's married. Don't do it in the same neighborhood as one of your patients.

I seem to know a lot of cheaters lately. Matt. Sheryl. Maybe I'm just paying too much attention. But that doesn't mean everyone's like that. Kara, for instance, says she'd never cheat.

Maybe I should have faith. Just because a lot of people are doing something doesn't mean everyone is doing it. Why am I forgetting that? I remembered it well enough at Harvard, when people were beer-guzzling and having one-night stands. I want to stay true to the old me. The old me knew where she stood.

The new me is watching the rules get fuzzy. I don't like that. How can you make decisions without guidelines? How can you have guidelines if you keep changing them?

I do have one guide: Petrov's list. And I'm going to do everything on it no matter what, and after that, I'll have the experience to decide how to live. Yes, that's a good format to follow. For now, stick to the list.

The thing about the list is that it's stuff most people do without thinking. Dating. Joining clubs. But I don't do these things. And maybe the reason I don't do them is that the people who do them *aren't* thinking. And maybe my problem is I think too much. So Petrov's list is things that normal people, less-smart people, do without thinking, and I have to do them so that they become part of *my* thinking, because the only way I'll do them is if they *are* part of a thought-out list.

From what I glimpsed of the girl, she's pretty—tall, with long hair. Poor Petrov. A gray, bespectacled professional, having gotten divorced and raised two kids, trying to keep the attention of this black-haired, dark-eyed Barbie. He's like that anchorman in *Network* who's so impressed when the young vixen actually wants him.

Why am I listening to Petrov's advice, anyway? Is he really happy? Maybe he's only happy when this girl's husband's away and he can get some of her attention.

In the morning, the sun is out, but the puddles remain to prove that the day before was brutal. I wonder what's happening in the Rubin/Leshko/Petrov household. Probably, they're all at work.

I hope Sheryl isn't one of his patients. That would be disturbing.

Maybe she has it all. She gets a doting father figure at noon and a dutiful young husband at night. Should I want what she has?

Around nine, I get a call to do legal proofreading at a firm I haven't ever been to. It's in the daytime, for a change. I fill a backpack with magazines, playing cards, my journal and *A Brief History of Time.* That should cover at least half the shift.

It feels strange to be sitting in an office while the sun's out. Everyone is in suits. I do get a few assignments, but mostly, I'm bored. During the course of the day, I manage to: read four months' worth of the *Atlantic Monthly;* play solitaire; make a graph of the last ten movies I've watched and how they rated on a scale of one to ten; fantasize about beating up the woman two desks over who records her voice mail message fifteen times before she's satisfied (and it's just, "Hi, this is Trudy"); create a flip cartoon on the pages of the firm's directory; create a flip cartoon on the pages of *Black's Law Dictionary;* create a flip cartoon in the pages of the regular dictionary; and check my answering machine six times.

To kill more time, I decide to dial David Harrison's number in Boston. I've wanted to do that for a while.

I make sure no one is looking, then slide the phone slightly off its black base and tap the push buttons. I still remember his number, but I'm great at remembering numbers, always. Each one has some relation to some other important number. I can't ever play the lottery because I would think of too many combinations to pick.

The phone rings, and I hear a woman's voice on an answering machine. "Hi," she says. "We're not home. Please leave a message." It beeps. It didn't say who "we" is. I don't know if it's still David's number. I have to accept that it might be. I guess I always had sort of hoped, or perhaps assumed, that he'd never find anyone he cared about more than he cared about me. I know that's unrealistic. But I suppose when you stop having contact with someone, they're frozen in time in your mind. Well, he wasn't right for me, anyway. Only for the first few weeks. And anyone can seem right for the first few weeks.

Since I'm thinking about checking people's answering machines, I have another flash of brilliance. I call the phone number for Petrov's girlfriend, Sheryl. I want to see who's on her answering machine.

The machine picks up and says, "Hi, you've reached Dan and Sheryl. Please leave a message and we'll get back to you soon."

More confirmation of the cuckolded couplehood.

I think for a while about people in normal relationships, who don't have to play games with phones, who don't have to worry who's on the answering machine. What is it like to feel that confident and fulfilled? Or are there other problems? I think there are people in the world who would have us believe that there is no such thing as a problem-free relationship, that people simply cannot fall into a mutual, compatible love that is infinite and wonderful and rational and true. It's a bleak view. I hope the naysayers are wrong, but maybe that's the way it really is, just like how men are from another planet.

I still have time to find out.

The day comes for my date with Michael from the personals. I head to Barnes & Noble early to grab a table at the café. Someone has left a little stack of magazines on top, and I pick up one called *Rope* and begin thumbing through it. It's actually all about rope. That's just bizarre. I see that two tables away, there's an old man reading *Puppies*. I don't even want to ask.

Every time someone new comes through the front doors, I hope it's not Michael, because each person looks stranger than the last. First there's a guy with a beard down to his waist. Then a guy with sunglasses and a cigar. Then a crew-cutted ten-year-old. I realize that since I didn't say anything about looks in my ad, I really *could* get a guy with a beard down to his waist, or green hair, or fluorescent spandex pants. There are a million things that could be odd about someone you meet through the personals, especially if you try not to be superficial and you don't mention looks. Okay, I guess we all care about looks, it's just that different things bother each of us. We can't help it. Someone might specify that she wants someone blond and blue-eyed. I might specify that I don't want anyone with a Mohawk haircut. Does that make me any less superficial?

Finally a guy in his late twenties comes in. He has a high fore-head and dark hair, with long sideburns. He's got a black leather jacket on—not punkish or anything—but it is leather. He looks my way, and I don't look away. Then he smiles and comes toward me. He had bragged on the phone about how tall he was, but he's actually fairly short.

I wonder why it's so hard for people to just be honest.

"Heather?" he asks.

"Yes," I say. "Nice to meet you."

"Nice to meet you." He smiles and gives me a once-over. So obvious. Ugh. We sit down.

"Now, let me remember," he says. "Yours was the one with all the smart stuff."

"And you," I say, "were the one who said he never answers ads."

He laughs. "Well, until this issue. I figured, if I was spending the money to call the 900 number, I might as well listen to a few others. But yours was the one that made me make the call."

I pick up the magazine on the table. "I was looking at this," I say. "It's a magazine about ropes. What could be the audience for that?"

"I don't know," he says seriously, as if I've asked him to do intense research. I was honestly looking for a laugh. Oh well.

"Do you—" he starts, and I say, "Are you—" at the same time, and we both finish our sentences.

"What?" we both say.

"I—" I start.

"Do you—" he starts, and I give up. "Do you want to get a sandwich?" he asks. "I usually don't eat breakfast."

"Breakfast is an important meal," I say.

"It's all sugar," he says. "Sugar cereal. French toast. Muffins. It's like waking up and eating rock candy." He seems really angry about this.

"So make eggs."

"Fat," he says, then shakes his head and goes up to the counter. I follow. "Turkey and cheese," he says, then looks at me. "What are you going to have?"

"Since I ate breakfast today," I say cattily, "maybe I should just have a Diet Coke."

"A Diet Coke for her," Michael says, and then, to me, "Sure I can't get you a bagel?"

I cannot deal with people who don't understand sarcasm. "Maybe I'll actually have a sandwich, too," I say.

"You don't have to ask my permission," Michael says. "It's *your* money."

If I had any friends, I might actually tell them about this. I lean over the counter and tell the woman that I'll skip the Diet Coke and have a turkey sandwich along with some apple juice. Then Michael and I sit down.

"So," he says. "You didn't say anything about how you looked in the ad, but you're not so bad."

"Thanks."

"Do I look...okay? Is this what you'd like?"

Is he out of his mind? "We could find something more interesting to talk about," I say.

Suffice it to say that the rest of the conversation does not go well. We interrupt each other, don't laugh at each other's jokes (well, I can't really laugh at his, since he doesn't make any), and argue over the fact that he thinks all classic literature is bunk and has no relevance to current society. I point out that a lot of themes and phrases from classic literature come up in conversation every day, even in regular pop culture. "People paraphrase 'Friends, Romans, countrymen,' all the time for comic effect," I say.

But Michael's never heard of that.

So I say, "I guess it's all Greek to you. That's Shakespeare, too, by the way."

He says, "What is?"

I give up.

When we finish eating, I stand up. "Well," I say, "it was nice meeting you."

"Yeah," he says. "I've never seen anyone drink apple juice straight from the jar before."

I don't even know what to say to that. I fold my napkin and try to pick up crumbs with it. He stands and says, "So...can I call you?"

"Sure," I say, but I'm thinking, *If you want to, you've got a pretty low standard for compatibility.*

I walk outside feeling creepy and depressed. I don't want to believe this is what my life has come to.

But a second later, I feel so liberated I want to jump into the air. I don't have to go on another date, ever! That's it! I've proved that they're awful! And now, I can check dates off my list. I can tell Petrov I tried.

Matt didn't really count because he's taken. This was a real date! Now I can go home and do whatever I want. I can have a Pilby Party. I don't have to compromise for anyone else.

When I get home, my message light is blinking. I pray that it's not A-Adam. I decide that if it is, I'll have a conversation with him, and if we have things in common, we can meet. If not, I'm not putting myself through another nightmare. But it's not him. How dare Adam reject me. Who does he think he is? Well, no matter. It's Eppie confirming that I'm supposed to meet with Natto after church tomorrow. I don't have to call back unless I have a change of plans. But I don't. I'm free and clear.

I've made a list of things I love, gone on a real date, and I've joined an organization. That takes care of three things on Petrov's list. I've only got two things left to do: tell someone I care about them and go out for New Year's. Then I can figure out what I've learned.

Maybe, to fulfill number four, I can tell my father I care about him when he visits for Christmas. But it's kind of weird with my dad. I haven't said "I love you" to him since I was ten, and he doesn't say it to me. I'm pretty sure he loves me, but we just don't say it. Maybe I'll say it to someone else. I don't know who.

I think about the date I just went on. I wish that it had been with Matt instead. Matt would have gotten my jokes. He would have made some of his own. Matt at least would recognize basic Shakespeare. But I can't call him. I have to wait for him to call *me*. Whenever that might be.

I decide to dial up the voice mail for my personal ad, and it tells me that there's one new response.

It's the forty-six-year-old who called last time. "I just wanted to cawl back and say, if the reason you didn't get back to me is becausss of the age—" he pronounces "becausss" to rhyme with "boss" "—everyone I know tells me I look a lot younger. So I hope that doesn't bawtha you. Anyway, like I said, if this interests you, give me a cawl."

He still hasn't told me anything about himself. No thanks.

There are a lot of women in their forties in the personals looking for men; yet, this forty-something guy goes hitting on a nineteen-year-old. Not really fair.

In the morning, my father calls. We talk about Christmas plans. He tells me that lately, I've sounded happier. This worries me. Maybe my being bad is doing me good. What if it's really good to be bad? What if you can't be happy without it? Is that why people had to invent religions that make you fear hell? Because it is only fear, not common sense or morality, that will keep us in line?

"Maybe I'm happy because of the season," I tell Dad.

"That's wonderful," he says.

He tells me about his job. He tells me about a guy he met who might have a business report that could use freelance proofreading, so maybe I can get some work from him. We hang up and I decide this calls for some spending of money. I do need to get my father a Christmas gift.

I grab my red umbrella and head outside. The rain has temporarily stopped, and the air, thick with moisture, kisses my cheeks. I open my umbrella, and a guy passing me shouts, "It's not raining!" People in New York can't keep their big mouths shut. If they're not sexually harassing you or ordering you to smile, they're evaluating the use of your umbrella. Then, there's running. Try running really quickly through the streets of New York one day, and see if some guy doesn't yell "Run! Run!" within five seconds. I'll bet my right kidney on it.

The people who call out at you don't realize that, besides the fact that they're making you feel bad about something that you didn't realize you should feel bad about, they're just taking part in this big conspiracy to make you be more like them. What if you're a different kind of person? What if you don't feel like smiling or opening and closing your umbrella every second? Is it their job to change you? Why do strangers have to remind you that you're different? If I'm supposed to learn to accept other people, don't they have to accept me, too—or do the rules of lenience not apply when you're in the minority?

Two final questions on this topic:

1. How easy is it, really, to smile on demand? Isn't it like being ordered to sneeze?

2. Does this ever happen to *men* who don't smile or put up their umbrella, or are these comments only directed at those of us who are expected to respond shyly?

As I leave my block, I pass Petrov's girlfriend Sheryl's apartment. I peek at the windows, but don't see her or her husband anywhere. I certainly don't see Petrov.

I am cheered by the Christmas decorations in the stores. Macy's has dancing Santas, both white ones and black ones—which, if I were Asian, I'd complain about—along with snow globes, teddy bears with rotating heads, and music boxes that gracefully ping their way through all of the songs I sang in church when I was very little and we actually went. To strains of "Hark the Herald Angels Sing," everyone wafts through the perfume section in hats and scarves. I buy my father office stuff, which he always likes—a fancy desk clock and a pen set. Down in the cellar, there's a pyramid of candy boxes wrapped with gold paper and fuzzy red bows that are so pretty I have to pick up at least one. Some of the candies are caramels, which my dad loves, and some are chocolates. I get a box of each. I'm not sure whom I'll give the chocolates to, but hopefully by Christmas there will be someone deserving of this gift.

The Macy's in New York looks decades old on the outside, with various levels and columns and letters saying "R.H. MACY & CO," but the best thing about it is located inside—the wooden escalators. They've got to be at least fifty years old. The steps are all made of wood, and they kind of pass into each other like teeth. Escalators were another of my many fascinations when I was young. The Otis elevator company actually invented the word *escalator*. At first, it was a trademark. The word *escalate* actually came from it. I did a report on them in school. We had to pick an invention. Everyone else did the lightbulb or the phonograph. I bet there isn't a kid in existence who hasn't done a report on Thomas Edison. He's second only to Helen Keller in terms of report topics.

My next stop is a bookstore, where I buy a pair of unabridged dictionaries for me and my father. If I ever get sick and have to stay in my apartment for a week, I can have a field day reading it. What does it mean to have a field day with something? When I get home, I can look that up in my unabridged dictionary.

I continue up the street, and I realize I'm not far from Times Square. I'm hungry. There's a pizza place, a chicken place, a giant microbrewery (even if that's a contradiction in terms), and the Mexican place where I had my first date with Matt. I should go there because it has positive associations for me. Maybe if I eat alone, I'll meet someone. That will definitely be a Petrov-pleasing activity.

I hook a left onto 42nd Street. I feel self-conscious going into a big restaurant alone, but a few of the people at the bar seem like they might also be alone. They stare at their little plates of food or talk to the bartender. I select an empty stool and order quesadillas and a margarita. The bartender asks me for ID. I've gotten away with underage drinking so many times I guess I just take it for granted. I suppose I'm usually with older people, so no one cares. I tell him that I left my ID at home, and he gives me a look that lets me know he knows that I know that he knows I'm lying. I say that come to think of it, I'm in the mood for lemonade. It still does a good job of washing down the quesadillas.

The trickle of patrons gets heavier and heavier. I can see everything that's going on in the mirrored wall behind the bartender. It has odd flecks of brown in it. I watch the people come in. Many of them are in the usual navy blue and black suits. The progeny of sixties sellout parents are millennial sellout twenty-somethings.

Eventually someone catches my eye. It's Matt.

He's with a girl. I think she must be Shauna. The waiter leads them to a booth on the other side of the room.

But Shauna doesn't like Mexican food. And this girl doesn't look like the girl I saw in the pictures. She looks to be in her early thirties. She's in a suit. Her hair is short, straight and bouncy. She and Matt are laughing. Matt doesn't notice me.

She could just be some girl from his job. The more I watch, though, the more they look like they're having a really good time.

I eat my food and keep watching them in the mirror. They laugh. Matt nods. They eat. Matt points out the window. His companion shakes her head.

I finish my food, pay the bill and head over.

The woman's hand is on the table, resting in Matt's.

"Hi, Matt," I say.

Matt looks startled. "Oh, hi," he says. The woman's hand slowly recoils. "Uh, this is Beth."

Beth nods at me. Matt doesn't tell her *my* name.

"You two work together?" I ask.

Beth looks at Matt, as if to decide what to say, and Matt shakes his head. "We met…recently."

"At a party?" I ask sweetly.

Beth looks at Matt again. Matt doesn't say anything. "Through friends," Beth says.

"Friends from college?" I ask.

"Friends, uh, friends," Matt says.

"Well, I hope you two have fun," I say, and I take off. He doesn't come after me. He met her through the ad, obviously. Was I a fool to think I was the only one he would have met through it? And that he wouldn't cheat on me like he was cheating on Shauna? Cheaters cheat. And if you are cheating and get cheated on, you don't have the right to complain. It's like buying cocaine, getting home, finding out it's not real cocaine, and running to the cops to file charges.

I'm angry. I want to yell at Matt. But I can't. I have no official connection to him, no reason for him to care whether I'm mad at him or not, and no reason for him to call. I'm not his fiancée. The only thing I have the right to do is, if he calls and asks me out, say yes or no. That's it. The rest of his time belongs to Shauna or to whomever else he wants to give it. I can't get angry. I'm number two. Or three, four or five.

I honestly can't understand someone who needs to see as many people as he does. But what if he needs to be with many people in the same way that I often need to be alone? Maybe it's like Kara said: Do I have the right to judge, just because I don't have the same drive? I don't know. Somehow, it doesn't seem right. In four or five months, Matt is going to voluntarily stand in a church and take a pledge to be faithful to Shauna. The only thing I've ever taken a pledge to was the flag, in school each morning, and I didn't even really do that because it's fascist to pop up like a Whack-a-mole every day, so I only pretended by moving my lips. Sometimes instead I recited the Twenty-Third Psalm or Sonnet 18 or the Checkers Speech.

When I get home, I lie in bed for a while, depressed. My

stomach feels like it wants to sink through the mattress down to the box spring. Nothing will make me feel better.

Except one thing.

I fish the box of chocolates out of my Macy's bag and eat half the box.

The next morning, I really don't want to go to church. What's the point? Why do anything? The more you learn about someone and the closer you get to them, the harder you fall when they reach out and rip the rug out from under you. Then again, I know it's my fault.

I force myself up, feeling hollow inside, and I walk to the subway.

I don't know how to put it any other way, but Natto's sermon is stirring.

It's about a series of devastating floods and mudslides they had the past week in Venezuela. I've only heard a little about it, and I chide myself because thousands of people died.

"Why would God do that?" Natto asks. "Babies, mothers, sisters, animals, everyone was treated equally by the Venezuelan floods. Some people killed were pure good. Some were so young that they never even had the chance to act on their good intentions. Why were they all killed? Can anyone come up with a good explanation?"

Not really, but I'll bet Natto will!

"There's a passage in the Bible," he says, "Isaiah 55:8–9. 'For my thoughts are not your thoughts, neither are your ways my ways, saith the Lord. For as the heavens are higher than the earth, so are my ways higher than your ways, and my thoughts your thoughts.' What this passage tells us is, there is a reason, but we don't know it yet. God knows. He sees things that we do not. He *knows* things that we do not. We cannot understand God."

Natto pauses.

"Do I believe this?" he asks. "Do I believe God has a reason? To explain thousands of deaths? I'm not sure. Even for a scholar of the Bible, even for someone who tries to believe, it's very hard to see what good could come of such devastation and destruction. Such carnage and carrion."

SAT words!

"So how were these people judged? How will *we* be judged? We get up every morning thinking that if we're good, we'll make it to heaven, and if we're bad, we'll have trouble. But then we see a six-year-old girl die of cancer. We see raging waters and mud swallow innocent people in South America. And we see our neighbor, who cheats on his wife or steals from his boss, become wealthy. We see our cousin, the liar, win the lottery. What sense does this make?"

A few people shake their heads. I want to know, too.

"Got me," Natto says. "Got me. But I'll tell you this. I want to know. I want to find out. And I'll tell you two more things. One is, overall, we have seen a lot of times in life that what comes around goes around, haven't we?"

A few people nod.

"In the case of Venezuela, there's no good explanation. But we see sinners locked up every day, and brave men rewarded. And last night on the news, they showed heroes, people who saved lives in Venezuela. We saw people working together. Rescue workers. Relief workers. And that is God."

He stops pacing.

"That is God," he says again.

He goes back to pacing. He has a strong gait.

"These people do good. And if one of their planes crashed on the way back to wherever they came from? What sense would that make? I don't know. I don't claim to have all the answers. And maybe there are cases where I will never ever understand them. This is something a lot of churches don't want to admit, but I really might never have the answers. And sometimes, this might make me very angry."

I like this.

"But I said there were two more things I'll tell you. One is that we have seen that what comes around goes around. And here's the second thing. We judge within ourselves. Those people in Venezuela, the dying, if they led a good life, they knew it. They died at peace. They knew that they didn't deserve it, that it was just something that happened. But a guy who's been hurting people, who suddenly feels a rumble and the sky caves in, he's lying there, torn apart, and besides the physical pain, he knows in his heart, or he feels in his heart, that he's being punished. He can't lie there and say, *Please God, I don't deserve to die.* Because he knows he did wrong, and he has to apologize and make amends. And so in that way, judgment comes upon him. And we all know in our hearts, whether we're to be judged in the afterworld or not, that while we're on this earth, we judge ourselves."

He's actually making sense.

"No man who has been an awful person can, in good conscience, pray to God to save his dying sister without first apologizing and pledging to live a better life." He pauses and looks out, into the audience. "No man who's worried about something can ask God for help without taking back the bad he's done. Sooner or later, we all own up to the hurtful things we do. That is why all of us, whether we think life is orchestrated or happenstance, must stay true to our knowledge of right and wrong. And that will most likely correspond to God's sense of right and wrong. Ladies and gentlemen, I've read the Bible, and sure, there are some things in it I'd like to understand better, but in many places, it makes a lot of sense. Don't be a good person just because it's in there, or just because Joe Natto told you to, or because you read it in my *own* good book, or because you're afraid you won't get into the pearly gates." He bends down a bit and makes a little funny shape with his hands as he says this. "Be a good person because when you did look at the Bible, or when you did listen to a sermon, you believed that what's in there was right. Not out of fear. Not from rote memorization. Do it because you've thought about it, and you *believe* it. And if you don't believe it, ask me about it. Challenge me. I can be wrong. I want us *all* to understand. I want us to think. I want us to believe."

Clapping starts, probably from Eppie, and then everyone joins in.

"I see more people in this church than last week. Last week, I saw more than the week before. You are all bringing people in, so right away, you are doing a good thing. There should never be a disaster befalling any of us, if what's right is right, but if there is, if that happened to befall us, we'd know it wasn't our fault. We'd know we were good. And we did positive things that we didn't have to. We wouldn't go out of this world blaming ourselves. We must do our best to stay true to ourselves, even in the face of a sometimes-cruel world. We're strong. Can I hear you say, 'We're strong?'"

"We're strong!"

Natto nods decisively. "Let's take a moment and pray silently for the people of Venezuela."

We do, and we finish, and Natto talks some more, and it's over. A few people cluster near the door to buy his book, and I head back through a hallway to Eppie. "Right in here," Eppie says, and I'm taken into a small office with a miniature brown fridge, a bulletin board, and three desks piled high with books, newspapers and magazines.

I wait a few minutes. Then Natto comes in, wiping his brow with a towel. "I tell ya," he says to Eppie, talking now in a worn-out voice, not his sermon voice. "Ah," he says when he sees me. "You're Carrie?"

This rarely happens, but I almost get the impression he's attracted to me. And I'm not someone who thinks that a lot. There are women out there who think every man who walks past them is hitting on them. I think that they have no self-esteem, so they talk about that to build themselves up. But the reaction I get from Natto when he sees me is sudden surprise, as if he was hit in the face with a gust of wind, like when the subway's coming and you feel it in the tunnel a minute before. "I'll take it from here, Ep," Natto says, and Eppie leaves.

"Mr. Bronson called me about the twenties group," I say. I try to figure out how old Natto is. He can't be anywhere near my age, but he doesn't look Petrov's age, either. Maybe he's forty. He has a Roman nose and dark hair, neatly combed to the side.

"Yes," Natto says. "That's a demographic we're not reaching." He sits down. "I'm sorry about all the clutter."

"It's all right. My desk at home looks like this."

"Do you read a lot?"

"Yes." To give him things to like about me in a hurry, I add, "It's one of my favorite things."

"Mine, too. Where'd you go to school?"

"Harvard."

"Not bad." He smiles, leaning back. "How long you been out?"

"Out? A year."

"And what brought you to the church?"

"I got a flyer on the street, and I wanted to find out if you were a cult."

"And?" He leans back. His eyes are twinkling.

"I liked what you said today. Especially when you admitted that you don't have all the answers. I had this one professor freshman year who admitted on the first day of English class that he hated Joseph Conrad, and I thought it was great. I didn't agree with him, but I liked that he had the courage to say that. And the funny thing is, he taught Conrad better than any teacher I'd ever had."

"Was Conrad one of the students?" Natto asks.

"Oh," I start. "No. He—"

"Just kidding," Natto says, and he smiles. "I know who he is. I even read *Lord Jim.*"

"I never read *Lord Jim,*" I say. Now I'm the dumb one.

"Don't read *Lord Jim.* It's the worst one," he says. "What's your favorite literary period?"

"Victorians. And the Modernists."

"That's a ridiculous term, though, isn't it?" Natto says. "*Everyone* is modern. Do you remember the story about the head of the U.S. Patent Office, who supposedly said in 1899 that everything that could possibly be invented had already been invented? Well, the story's apocryphal, from what I've read, but the message is clear—people always think they're as modern as can be. Here we are a hundred years later, saying *we're* the modern ones, as if there will never be anything more advanced. Well, actually, now we're post-modernists. Isn't that the period we're supposed to be in now?"

"Yes."

"How can we be in the 'post-modern' era? That term makes no sense. And what comes after post-modernism?"

"I guess it has to go on forever."

Natto leans forward. "So you came here to make sure we weren't a cult. Where did you get the flyer?"

"From a guy with…he's balding and kind of short. He was giving them to mostly Spanish people, but I hung around."

"How did you know the people were mostly Spanish?"

I laugh. "I mean, he was *mostly* giving the flyers to Spanish people. Sorry. Spanish-speaking. Not from Spain."

"Ah," Natto says. "Well, maybe he was doing that because they're more polite than the Yuppies. People can treat you badly when you start a church, or anything else that's new. The Mormons, they got it the worst. But I won't get into religious history now."

"Mormons are interesting."

"Very interesting. I was a religious studies major. Religion, theology, philosophy. English minor thrown in."

"Where'd you go?"

"City College," he says. "Had a great time there. It really doesn't matter where you go to college as much as what you make of it." I know that he's right. "I was in three different foster homes before I was eighteen, and books were the only constants in my life."

I look around. There are books piled on Natto's desk, on bookshelves, on the floors.

"So, do you think we can get more young people into our church?" Natto asks.

I know he wants to sell his book. I know he claims to have had some sort of vision. But I don't feel like challenging him right now.

Wait. There I go again, wimping out based on feelings. Doing what's easy, like everyone else. I didn't rat Matt out to Shauna. (Yet.) I actually kissed Kara. And Matt, too. And now, I'm becoming transfixed by a cult. Help!

I am warming up to this place. But this is how cults get you.

Then again, maybe I should play along to see what's really going on.

"I think you could get a lot of young people in," I say.

"How?"

"Have your congregants pass out flyers to all people, not just minorities," I say. "Have them go to places like Wall Street and Union Square and Times Square, where the young people work."

"How do we keep them from throwing the flyers away?"

I actually feel like my opinion matters. "Well, you need something to let them know what your church is about, and that it's different from all these other churches. Like the Jews for Jesus, they have the best literature around. Their flyers almost make me want to convert to Judaism just so I can be a Jew for Jesus." It's true. Their literature is strewn with cartoons and jokes and pop culture references. But I guess converting to Judaism just to be a Jew for Jesus would be like having a sex change so that you can be gay. Which actually would not be such a bad idea for some of us. If I had a sex change and became a man, I think the guys I could date would be much more interesting. I wonder if they'd be able to sense that I'd been a woman. What would happen if I dressed as a man, dated a gay man, and got him to fall in love with me? Would that mean that he was suddenly straight? And what if I then revealed I was a woman? Would he suddenly become unattracted to me? Or would he stay attracted and be straight? I should write a movie about this.

"What do you think our flyers should say?" Natto asks. "What would make someone your age pick one up?"

I gaze at what's taped on his walls. Church flyers. An ad for a play at CCNY. Newspaper articles pertaining to churches and church groups. A Domino's pizza coupon. A scroll with a story called "Footprints." "I don't know," I say. "Something like what you said today—'We don't have all the answers.' Or maybe even bolder—'Church is a drag.' Then you open it up, and it says, 'Except at First Prophets'. The hip new church that's attracting young people in droves.' Or something like that. But it's not just the words. You need a really neat design. Someone with advertising or graphics experience would do better than I would."

"Hmm," Natto says. "I wonder who I can get?"

I think.

Shauna.

She's starting her own advertising firm.

She needs clients.

"I know someone," I say. "Sort of. Through friends."

"Great!" Natto says. "Would he be interested?"

"It's a she," I say. "I actually only know *of* her. She's just starting her own firm, so maybe she'll do it for free, if she thinks it'll help her business."

I hate this, but as I talk, I find myself searching Natto's desks and cabinets for a photo of a wife and kids. It seems strange that someone single would start a church. There are certain things it just seems like a person doesn't do unless he's got an immense pool of support behind him. Maybe Eppie Bronson's his lover.

"Your mind's working," Natto says. "That Harvard mind. I can tell." He's amused, and his eyes are turning to slits as he peers at me, like a TV screen the second it turns off.

"I'm thinking," I say. His comment reminds me of David, the way David used to ask what I was thinking about. David Lance Harrison, professor of English literature. I wonder if Natto's reminding me of him is a bad thing.

"Well," Natto says, getting up and clapping his hands. "Got to go talk to my parishioners. I'm going to give you a call, and maybe you can talk to this advertising person."

"I'll try to set up a meeting," I say.

As I leave, I see him walk over to a short, fat woman and shake her hand. She's there with her elderly mother, and he's got his head cocked, giving them his full attention. She talks with her hands and gestures a lot. He's amazing, the way he can listen without a look of condescension or boredom. I think he means it, too. He seems genuinely interested. It's compelling the way people respond to him. That's the kind of person I want to be around. But so, apparently, does everyone else.

I have an advantage in getting his attention because I'm young. I wonder if that's my only advantage. But everyone needs something, and they have to work it. Men can dash across a ball field or bang on a guitar or run for president and win a thousand pairs of adoring eyes. Women can wear a short skirt or talk in a throaty voice and get men to bend. Yes, I'm being very sexist. But sometimes it's true. What it comes down to is that in many cases, we do have differences, different strengths and weaknesses, and they sometimes correspond to our stereotypes. Are they right? No. Some things just are. Just like Venezuela. We don't always have to accept it. But sometimes that's the way it is.

Chapter Ten

A few mornings later, I go to my appointment with Petrov.

"I need the full hour today," I tell him, sitting down. "I mean, I know it's forty-five minutes, a forty-five-minute hour, but whatever. I need all forty-five. I'm not going to argue about it. Let's start now."

"Okay." He smiles. "Is the list working?"

"It's not going too badly." It is true that I met Matt, in a roundabout way, because of the list, which is not necessarily good, but at least it made things interesting. It's true that I joined the church because of the list. Even if what's happening isn't great, it's still happening. If I'd sat inside, nothing would have happened. And if I get out there and go to a party or on a date, even if I dislike it, perhaps it eventually will lead to an invitation to a *better* date or party. I'll call this...the social butterfly effect.

"So, which things have you done? Gone on a date? Joined an organization?"

"Both," I say. "I went on a date with this guy Michael."

"Great! You met him how?"

At this point, I have to lie. "Through legal proofreading," I say. "The date was lousy, but I feel optimistic that someday I'll go on a better one."

That's only because any date I go on couldn't be worse.

"Good," Petrov says. "Do you want to talk about it?"

"Well, we were sitting in the law library," I begin.

All of the inappropriate routes this story could take flash through my mind. I have to resist the urge. This has to be believable.

Petrov leans forward. He's excited.

"And we ended around four a.m. And he lives near me, so we got into the hired car together."

And then, I think, *we stopped in front of a huge mansion, and he said, "I live here. Would you like to skinny-dip in the indoor pool?" So we ripped our clothes off and raced to the water. Under the skylight, we tasted every inch of each other's wet bodies. After we came up, I could see the love in his eyes, as well as the redness from the chlorine.*

"So he started talking to me, and he said he just graduated from college, and we had some things in common, and we agreed to meet up at Barnes & Noble that weekend."

"Great," Petrov says. "So how was that?"

"It was all right. We didn't have much to talk about. And he got weird. He has all these strange food preferences."

"Like what?"

Boy, is he nosy. "He skips breakfast every day, and made me feel guilty about wanting anything with fat in it. And then, at the end of the date, he said, 'I've never seen anyone drink juice from a jar before.'"

Petrov laughs. I think the laughter is partially to encourage me, to make me feel like what I've done is normal.

"Maybe that was a compliment," Petrov says. "Maybe he's hoping...never mind."

Ah, so I am not the only one with my mind in the gutter. But I decide to feign innocence. "What?"

"Nothing. So are you two going to see each other again?"

"No. He's weird."

"But...."

"You said one date. If I have to go on a second, I want time and a half."

Petrov settles back. "Well, so was it a bad experience? Honestly, were you glad you did it?"

I have to think. "It didn't change my life," I say. "But I guess I wouldn't have been doing anything more important at home."

"That's the spirit," Petrov says. "What else are you up to?"

"I went to that church," I say. "It's actually not bad. I'm going to help them get publicity for their church group for people in their twenties. They want to get young professionals in town to start coming back to church."

"Wonderful!"

"At first I thought it was a cult. I don't want to be bought off. But it seems okay."

"Maybe you should trust your instincts," he says. "You might be heading in the right direction."

"I might," I say.

He beams.

"But there's a weightier topic I want to talk about today," I say. "Something's been confusing me."

"Okay," he says.

"Well, I know this guy who cheats on his fiancée. And I know that a lot of people cheat. The whole cheating thing has me confused. You know how I've always said that people are hypocrites and don't stick by anything? Well, I'm sure when people get married, they never intend to cheat. They take an oath. But so many people *do* end up cheating. And I know marriages are long, and they can get dull. But does this make it right?"

Petrov takes a deep breath. "Well," he says, "I guess it's situational. Each person has to decide for him or herself what's right."

"Are you saying there might be cases where cheating is right? Even though the other person doesn't know about it and would feel hurt if they did know? Even though you could be taking risks?"

"That's a bad thing," Petrov says. "Yes, you could be hurting someone."

"So if you have the urge to cheat, if you're very attracted to someone else, should you break up your marriage and date the other person?"

"Sometimes there are things to consider," Petrov says.

I look at the picture of Petrov with his two children. "Your daughter's about twenty-eight, right?"

"Yes," Petrov says. "Samantha, yes."

"If she were dating a guy who was fifty, how would you feel?"

"I…I would feel kind of strange," Petrov says. "I'd want to make sure he wasn't taking advantage of her."

"So you'd never date someone Samantha's age."

He stops. Thinks. "Everything depends," he says. "Some people are at different ages mentally. You, for example. You are nineteen, and in some ways, very very mature."

"That's what Professor Harrison used to tell me."

"I'm sure he did."

"But back to what I'm getting at," I say. "Adultery. Wrong? What if there's no justification, and someone is married and just cheats because he or she is attracted to someone else. No abusive spouse, no bad situation."

"These are questions…Carrie…that I can't…."

"Twenty years ago," I say, "twenty years ago, I bet you would have had the answer. I bet you would have thought cheating was wrong."

"Yes," Petrov says. "I did have a friend who was cheating on his wife back then, and I thought he was a slime for it."

"Well, now," I say, "you've developed, what. Tolerance? Or ignorance?"

"Well…"

"Basically, we change our rules to fit our situations. We have firm beliefs until something affects us and makes us feel different. You believe in something that's right, but then it becomes *inconvenient*. Morality is inconvenient. You have feelings for this girl who lives up the street from me, and suddenly you do something that you found abhorrent in an earlier incarnation."

Petrov looks nervous. His eyes seem moist.

"I can keep a confidence like you can," I say. "You haven't told my dad about Professor Harrison. I won't tell Sheryl Rubin's father about her."

He sits up straight.

"Sheryl Rubin," he says.

"She lives up the street from me."

"And…?"

"I saw you two kissing in the window."

He lets out a breath. He looks at the ground.

"You can tell me," I say. "It's confidential. I promise."

"I have no guarantee of confidentiality. *You* have one. And I'm here to help *you*."

"You said a while back that you hoped one day I could come in and say, 'Everything's great, but I want to talk anyway,'" I say. "You made it seem as if you want me to treat you as a friend. But I can't because of the inequalities. You know everything about me and I know nothing about you. I just want to know your justification. It'll help me. Or have you not even bothered with a justification? I'm not saying this to pass judgment. I just want to understand more about morality, situational ethics. Changing sides, who's a hypocrite and who's not. About having fun, and whether you should live to be eighty never having done some things because they're wrong. Why is it that if you've never smoked pot, you make a great presidential candidate, but if you've smoked it just once, it looks so bad? Why is there such a difference between one and zero? Why is it that if you've never had sex, you're a virgin, but if you've had sex only one time in your life, you're not? Does one act one time put you into a completely different category? If drugs are wrong and dangerous, then we should all die never having smoked pot. But if someone dies having smoked it once, just to have the experience, is that awful? Are there lines we should absolutely never cross, and is crossing once as bad as crossing a thousand times? Can we cross once, decide never to do it again, and be moral? Or should we just never ever cross the lines?"

"You're asking a lot of questions," Petrov says.

"Because of church," I say. "It's making me think."

"Normally, it doesn't."

"You just think that because you're Jewish," I say.

"Lapsed," Petrov says.

"See, you *can* talk about yourself."

With that, he starts laughing. And I know he'll say something.

He thinks for a second. He looks down at his brown shoes, which have tassels on them. Then at his rug. Finally up at me.

"I do part-time consulting for Sheryl's agency," he says slowly. "She works with abused children. We spent a lot of time together."

I nod.

"I invited her for coffee." He shrugs. "We talked. We talked more. We wanted to spend more time together."

"And?"

"You and I really shouldn't talk about this."

"Theoretically, we shouldn't," I say. "But you're a family friend. Besides, there are hardly any people you *can* talk to about it. And I need to. I promise that anything you say today, I'll forget when I leave. In fact, I'll pretend you made it up to help me. Just tell me. Do you feel guilty? I know Sheryl's married to a guy named Leshko."

Petrov doesn't deny it. He just looks down at his shoes.

"Do you condone what you're doing?" I ask. "That's what I need to know. Has it suddenly become okay?"

He's silent for a second. Then he says, softly, "I don't condone it. But if we hadn't done this, I'd be sitting here, thinking about her all the time, not concentrating on my work. I was seized. I had to see her."

"Are you in love with her?"

"Let's move on...."

"It's hard to tell, when it's not a regular situation. If you had her all to yourself rather than a quarter of the time, would it be as exciting? What if you two had a regular routine, and there weren't all these challenges and parameters?"

Petrov keeps looking at the rug. "I don't know," he says. "She could end it tomorrow."

"And," I say seriously, leaning forward and putting my hands together, "how does that make you *feel?*"

He shakes me off like I'm a pitcher. "We have to stop this."

"I'm sorry," I say. "I just have so many questions."

He sighs. "I know. Tell me what you're thinking."

"That people say that it's not a black-and-white world," I say, "but maybe it should be. And even if there have to be shades of gray, then maybe those shades could have borders."

"They could," Petrov says.

"There are things that seem wrong, and then when people do them, they try to justify them and make everyone else do them, too. And that's even *more* wrong."

He nods.

"So I have to know. You once thought cheating was wrong. Now you're doing it. What's your justification for what you're doing?"

He pauses. "All right," he says. "If you must know...my justification for things...well, I used to be a religious person, and even though Jewish people don't have hell and penance and all that, I did try to stick by moral codes. And what I said when I started seeing...her...was that maybe God wouldn't have wanted me to have these feelings if they weren't valid. And I thought about how I met her working with children. That can't be so bad."

"And you believe this?"

"No." He looks at his hands. "I'm probably, like you always say, a hypocrite. I can't deny it. And maybe it's wrong. But it's not so wrong, not so wrong as other things. There are worse things people do. This doesn't meet the standard of hurting someone else right now."

"It might be hurting Sheryl's husband."

"He's away for days at a time..."

"Excuse."

"*He* might be cheating..."

"Excuse."

"But maybe..."

"Excuse."

"I didn't even say any—"

"Excuse."

"I—"

"Excuse."

We both sit there in our chairs, hanging like tired tennis players ready for the next lob.

"Maybe," I say, "she'll leave him."

He's lost in thought.

Maybe he doesn't really want her to leave her husband. Maybe he does and he hates himself for it.

I don't know what he wants. But neither does he. He doesn't know what he wants. Like Natto doesn't know what God wants. Like I don't know what I want.

But don't I have a faint idea?

I want to do what's right.

I also want to be happy.

Is it necessary for these two things to be exclusive?

What if it is? Should I do what Petrov does, keep lowering the bar a bit? But won't I just keep lowering it again and again, for whatever situation I run into? Isn't that what people do in these situations? When people steal, lie, cheat, break the law in some way—don't they at some point lose the feelings of guilt or reluctance because they've crossed the line so many times that their new mentality tells them everything's okay?

Is it true Petrov's actions aren't really hurting anyone? Are there things that hurt people only in theory and not in reality? Is Matt really hurting Shauna if she never finds out about his lovers? Is Sheryl Rubin hurting Daniel Leshko? Is Kara hurting anyone except herself when she smokes? Is the belief that these people are hurting each other based on societal taboos more than reality?

Petrov puts his chin in his hands. "My therapist," he says finally, "is a psychoanalyst. Which, I admit, is a problem right there. But he's a smart man. He keeps trotting out the old line about Sheryl wanting me because I'm a father figure. As if a woman in her late twenties can't be attracted to a man in his fifties. But you liked your professor, right? He was older. Doctors like to shove things into little boxes."

I'm still processing the revelation that Petrov has a therapist.

"Do you think your therapist has a therapist, too?" I ask. "And do you think *he* has a therapist? And does his therapist have a therapist? For all you know, you could be your therapist's therapist's therapist's therapist's therapist's therapist's therapist's therapist's therapist's therapist's therapist's therapist's therapist's therapist's therapist. And the question is not what this daisy chain of doctors means for you, or for any of them; the question is, what does it mean for New York?"

Petrov and I look at each other.

Then, suddenly, he says, "We're out of time."

I look at the clock behind me. It's true. We're five minutes over.

"I won't hold it against you," I say. "I'll just dock five minutes from your next session."

Petrov gets up unsteadily, as if finally climbing out of a train wreck. "This was an interesting session," he says.

"You're telling *me*."

"I suppose I'll see you next week."

"I hope so," I say. "I know you feel weird, but honestly, I learned a lot."

"Sarcasm?"

"No, I'm serious," I say. "I'm sure you learned things, too."

"Yes," he says. "I learned I should close the shades."

Petrov can't tell anyone about our talk. He'll probably benefit from it somehow. Maybe it will get him thinking. Sheryl will benefit, too. Next time she sees him, he'll be rumpled and shaken up. And she'll get to play nurse to him, cooing all over him. Women love that.

On the other hand, I made him feel guilty. Is that good or bad? Is it going to make a difference? Will we, in the end, always follow our urges anyway?

As I head home, I relive the session in my mind, and I don't snap back to reality until I see a fluorescent sign in the coffee shop reading, *Now Open 24 Hours.*

I walk in, and Milquetoast is sleeping sideways on the counter.

"Ronald!" I yell.

He springs up. "Cappuccino?"

"I don't drink 'chinos," I say. "Those are pants. What's with the twenty-four-hour sign?"

His mouth is bumpy and out of whack, like a dog's chops. He wipes his arm across it. "Murray, our manager, it's his new idea. I was thinking of taking that shift. It pays a dollar an hour extra."

I feel bad for him. Or anyone who does something they dislike just because it's a dollar more an hour. Whenever I see a window washer twenty stories in the air, I always hope he's a brave guy, not just a poor guy who needs extra cash. If I were that high up, I'd jump to end my pain quickly.

I want to help Ronald. I feel guilty for what my life is like, sleeping half the day and never having to pay rent. And then I look down on people who have to worry about these things. What is my problem?

I have one of those moments again where there's a sickness in the pit of my stomach, where I feel a bit hazy, where something is wrong, something big. I can wait until it goes away. But maybe it shouldn't. Maybe I should face it and solve it.

Do I know who I am? Can I face the parts I don't like? Am I judging people by black-and-white standards in order to justify my inability to talk to them? Ronald isn't brilliant. So what? I can still make an effort to talk to him.

"Have you seen Cy lately?" I ask Ronald.

"Once or twice," he says. "Have you looked on the fire escape for him?"

"I've looked," I say. "But I haven't seen him."

"He's a nice person," Ronald says. "Cy's really nice. He says hi to everyone in the shop when he comes in, even if he doesn't know them. But he only really has long discussions with me."

I smile. "That sounds nice."

"He keeps strange hours. I'll probably see him more when I work the lobster shift."

"Lobster shift?" I say. "I thought it was called the graveyard shift."

"I think they're the same thing," he says.

"I wonder where those terms came from."

"They don't have a lot to do with each other, lobsters and graveyards." He laughs.

"Swing," I say. "Swing shift. Wasn't that a game show? The twenty-five-thousand or half-a-million dollar pyramid, where they'd give you a list, like lobster, graveyard, swing, and you'd say, 'Words that come before shift'?"

Ronald shrugs. "I don't have cable."

"It's not on cable," I say. "It was thirty years ago."

"I wasn't born yet," he says.

"I wasn't either, but they showed things in syndication when we were little, didn't they?"

"I don't remember," Ronald says.

There's silence for a few seconds. But I'm not going to give up. I owe it to him—and to myself—to try harder with people.

"So, how are you doing in general?" I ask.

He grins. "Good," he says. "I'm good. My parents might help me move to the basement apartment in our building. My own place."

"That's great," I say.

"Hey," he says. "I know you're busy a lot, but do you ever want to…get coffee sometime?"

"Ronald," I say, "this is a coffee shop, and I come in here all the time, and I never order coffee."

"I just thought…" he says. Now I feel mean again.

"What else do you like to do," I ask, "besides drink coffee?"

"Oh, I don't drink it," he says. "I just thought *you* might. I don't like coffee. That's why Murray likes me working here. He knows I won't drink it."

"Sort of like the eunuchs guarding the harems."

"What?"

"Nothing. Do you like movies?"

"Sure, but I don't have cable."

"I'm not talking about cable," I say. "We could go see a movie someday. Or get lunch or dinner."

"That sounds good!" Ronald says. "We could eat before my shift."

I go for days without social contact, and it might be nice to have someone in the neighborhood to eat with. And I *would* like to know more about Ronald than just the basics we exchange when we bump into each other. He could even become, well, a friend.

"I'll visit you on your next lobster shift and we'll make plans," I say.

"Great!" he says.

"Maybe I'll bring lobster," I add.

He laughs. "Not live ones."

"Have you ever seen *Annie Hall?*"

"I don't have cable."

"It's—never mind. Well, I'll see you later."

"Hey, Carrie."

"Yeah?"

"You know, you're a nice person, too."

This stops me. No, I'm not.

"I wish I was."

"You are," he says. "Of course you are. Just like Cy. Like that day you asked me why I was stacking the tumblers, or whenever you see me in the street, you ask me what's new at the coffee shop. You always talk to me. It's nice."

"Well, thanks," I say uncertainly. It is true that I never see anyone besides me or Cy bothering to talk to Ronald. But it seems like the least I can do for a neighbor. "You're a nice person, too."

He grins.

"I'll see you soon," I say.

I go to bed early that night, then wake up at four in the morning. I don't feel tired, so I push myself above my window and look down the street, toward the building where Sheryl and Dan live. I wonder if Petrov is inside her apartment. Maybe he's been avoiding the neighborhood since I caught him. But I still wonder.

I wonder if, across these power lines and pigeon-poop-encrusted cornices and light poles and antennae, Matt is sleeping across Shauna, his head on her body, and she's running her hand over his hair, comfortably believing everything in her life is right where she wants it. I wonder if Kara is curled up with some bartender or waitress, if Stephen and Pat are side by side, if Natto is with anyone. I know I'm not. Maybe for now, that's okay. Being with someone seems awfully confusing.

I get drowsy again and sleep until ten.

It's a week until Christmas. I don't have Matt and Shauna's home number, but I do know his last name, and he just happens to be listed. I call around two in the afternoon, and Shauna answers. "Hello?" she says. She has a sweet voice. Which makes me feel bad all over.

I say I've worked with her former employers, and I tell her that they recommended her for a project I know about in my church. I tell her a little bit about it and give her Joe Natto's number. Then I call him right away. It sounds like he's munching on something.

"It's good to hear from you," Natto says. "I'll be expecting her call. You know, I know you're probably a busy young lady—"

Ugh.

"And if I ever infringe on your free time, please let me know. But I really think you've got a lot of energy to bring to the church. I might be able to pay you for your time. Maybe even a salary. You could be a sort of PR consultant."

A job? A real job? "Well, you don't have to—" I say.

"You're well educated. You have good ideas. You're smart, you read a lot, and you could represent the church well. You deserve pay for your experiences. Do you write? Are you a good editor? You said you do legal proofreading."

"I think I'm okay."

"I'm not trying to buy your loyalty. I know you're a cynic by nature, as all intelligent people should be. But what I'd need is a few hours of freelance work here and there. These sermons, it's hard to think of topics all the time. I mean, I know they're divinely inspired and all, but…"

I laugh. "God isn't giving you ideas fifty-two weeks a year."

"Yes," he says. "I could definitely use someone like you."

I feel accepted and encouraged. I haven't felt that way in a long time.

Natto's line clicks. "Oh," he says. "That's my other line."

"Might be Shauna," I say.

"Probably. I'll give you another call soon and we'll set up a time to go over some things."

"Sounds good."

"Bye," he says. That's a blessing, for those who don't know. *Goodbye* is derived from "God be with ye." Good b'ye. Get it?

I go to my dictionary, just to make sure it's in there, that I haven't been misguided all these years. It is. Then I look up *dictionary*. What it theoretically should say is, "You're in it, stupid." But of course, the constraints of professional etiquette prohibit the authors from being direct. The definition is, and I'm not kidding, "A reference book having an alphabetical list of words, with information given for each word, including meaning, pronunciation, etymology, and often usage guidance." Then, it's got three other definitions that basically say the same thing. I guess it doesn't want to give anyone short shrift in explaining itself. Or the lobster, graveyard or swing shrift.

That reminds me to look up *lobster shift*. But when I try to find it, it's not there.

What a gyp.

I have bought a tiny Christmas tree for my little living room, and it's by the doorway to the kitchen. I have strung bright lights around it, white as popcorn, and piled my father's wrapped gifts underneath. I've even hung two stockings on nails in the wall. I've filled them with candy, and even though I know what's in them, I can't wait to get them Christmas morning.

I've opened the sofa in the living room so that my father can sleep on it. I should probably make sure it's away from the front door so Dad won't wake up at night, wander outside, look into Petrov and Sheryl's window, and catch them playing Strip Dreydl.

I have sprayed fake snow on the Christmas tree, but I confess it smells bad and I knew this and still I did it anyway. I won't get snowed again.

As I'm walking around in a toasty thick green sweater I bought, humming to myself, my father calls. "I have the place decorated," I tell him. "I even bought stockings. I just need to get a comforter for the sofa bed."

"Oh," he says. "I didn't know if you'd want me to stay at your place, or in a hotel."

"You should come and stay here. I want us to have a normal Christmas, like people all across the city. Even the Jews."

"Okay. What time do you want me to come by?"

"Do you want me to make dinner," I ask, "or do you want to order?"

"We could order," he says. "I don't want to put you through the trouble."

"If you show up around five, we can order food and then watch TV or a movie. I want us to wake up Christmas morning and open presents, like when I was little. And stockings."

"Stockings."

"I put your favorite caramels inside. And…well, it's a surprise."

He laughs. "All right. It's great to hear you sounding so happy. I'll see you Friday."

At my pre-Christmas visit to Petrov, I tell him, "My father said I sounded happy when I talked to him."

"Is that bad?"

"No, but I don't like someone else judging my emotions. If I'm *not* happy, then he's making a judgment that doesn't ring true."

"So you're *un*happy?"

"No. I guess not."

"I don't think so," he says. "I think things are going to change for you."

"My beliefs haven't changed."

"No, but I think you realize that you need to talk about them and be willing to consider other ideas. I bet if I ask you something that I've asked before, you'll give me the answer."

"Like what?"

"Tell me what makes you cry."

I think a bit. "Nothing. But there are some things that might make me sad."

"Okay. What makes you sad?"

Before I can answer, Petrov says, "Don't say what you were about to say."

"Why?"

"It was going to be sarcastic."

I shrug. "I—"

"Don't say that one, either," he says.

"How did you know?"

"I was right, wasn't I?"

I guess now I have to come up with a real one.

"The word 'mommy.'"

"The word 'mommy' makes you sad?"

"Yes," I say. "It always has."

"Why?"

"I don't know. It's always said by someone vulnerable. Someone who's needy. A certain kind of needy."

"Hmm," Petrov says. "What about 'daddy'?"

"That's generally said by a princess who's asking for a new car. So yes, that makes me sad, too."

Petrov laughs. "I almost had you. I almost had you talking about your emotions for two consecutive sentences."

"Maybe we'll get to three next time."

Petrov rubs his hands together. "You know," he says, "one day, you might be in danger of letting someone get to know you."

I look at him. I guess he wants to know me. That wouldn't be so bad.

For the two days before Christmas, my phone doesn't ring at all. No legal jobs, no telemarketers.

I decide I'll make one last call to the personals to make sure there are no more responses to my ad. It turns out that there is a lone straggler.

"Hi, I'm John," the voice says. "I'm a thirty-eight-year-old, financially secure, emotionally secure, never-married white male who is looking for a woman to wine and dine, take on vacation, and show a good time. I'm not into head games, emotional baggage, couch potatoes or gold diggers." I can tell he's reading from a script. "I am five foot ten, 170 pounds, with brown hair and brown eyes. I am looking for someone active and attractive, playful and sexy, with no baggage. She should look great both in dresses and slacks, in sneakers and high heels. If this sounds like you—"

I think what he should really be looking for is his own personality.

Someone should call him back and tell him that. It's scary that he's thirty-eight. Have people really been doing him a favor all his life by not telling him?

I write down his number and call him. I get his voicemail.

"Hi, John," I say. "I wanted to let you know that I'm not going to leave you a real response to your answer to my personal ad because you were reading from notes. Also, you have to expand your horizons. You have to look for someone who's a real person with quirks and hobbies and fears and dreams, not just a mannequin in dresses and high heels. By the way, everyone has baggage. What if you find some woman who doesn't have any, and she's beautiful and happy, and the two of you have kids, and one of the kids is disabled. Or what if one of you gets sick. How will you handle it? What will you do? Life isn't perfect, and you better learn how to revel in its imperfections before you finally come upon one and it's too late to learn."

I hang up. I hope I wasn't too harsh. Besides, I was half giving that advice to myself.

After I hang up, the pre-Christmas silence is unnerving.

I use the time to think about a few things.

I think about how the word *loophole* is redundant.

I think about whether *almost* really does count in horseshoes.

I think about how bankruptcy lawyers can ever collect their fees.

I think about whether it would have been more honest for George Washington to just not chop down the damn cherry tree in the first place.

Finally I go rent movies: *The End of the Affair, Affair to Remember, Love Story, Jane Eyre*. I wonder if there's a trend here. I remember reading once that a lot of what we choose to watch or read is meant to make us feel better about our own lives by seeing other people's fumbles and failures and being glad it's them and not us. I suppose films about other people's forbidden affairs provide a sort of solace.

On Christmas Eve Day, I'm nervous. (It's so annoying to have to say Christmas Eve Day, but what better way is there to describe it?) I feel similar to how I used to feel when my father was setting up my birthday parties as a kid. I'd run to the window to see if anyone was arriving, then back to the living room to watch him set up "pin the capital on the foreign country" or "vocabulary piñata." I stopped having parties when I turned eight and was already too young for my classmates. I guess I never really had friends in school after that, but fans—people who needed help with their homework, people whose mothers told them to be nice to me, people who figured that at least I wasn't mean. I never really figured out how to keep friends because I never made them.

I wait at the window and see a sedan come to a stop in front of my house. I run downstairs and catch my first glimpse of my father since summer. He has always been tall, with salt-and-pepper hair and a beard, but now his hair looks much grayer. When did my father get old?

But he smiles at me and I know he's happy. He looks teddybearish. I run outside and hug him.

"You look so mature!" he says. I smile, and Bobby peeks out his window. I don't think Dad's seen him since he rented the place for me. "Hey, Bob!" Dad yells. "How are you doing? Keeping Carrie safe from the Village people?"

Bobby bobs his head nervously. Then he disappears into his lair.

My father's raincoat trails behind him as he heads up the stairs with two suitcases and, hanging off his arm, an insulated bag of Chinese food he picked up on the way over. He puts his bags down and we set up the plates.

When we sit down, he says, "Well, you're going to have to tell me everything about what you've been up to. Phil Petrov can't tell me."

"He keeps an eye on me," I say, smearing plum sauce on a rib.

"I know. I know he does." Dad looks at me. "I need to do a better job of that. I'm going to be in New York most of next year. I've made sure of it. I'll buy dinner for all your friends."

"That should be cheap."

He smiles. "So," he says, "tell me what's going on in your life."

I pick up my chopsticks, and he does the same, even though I've always been better at using them. "Well," I say, "there's this new church I've been looking into. They're trying to lure young professionals who are cynical and stopped going. It's better than I thought it would be. The guy who runs it seems to want people to think for themselves."

"A church that lets you think for yourself?" he says. "That *is* new."

"That's what Dr. Petrov said."

"He's Jewish. He's not supposed to say that. Only we can pick on our own religion." He pulls out a cigarette. "Mind if I smoke in your house?"

"You know you're killing yourself."

"I only do it once in a while."

"It'll save seven seconds of your life if you don't."

He stops. I feel a test coming on. "If I end up living to be seventy," he says, "what fraction of my life have you saved by preventing me from smoking this cigarette?"

He used to give me these tests all the time when I was in elementary school. I loved it. Let's face it; I love challenges. I'm like Matt. Damn.

"You've saved two billionths of your life," I say.

He's flabbergasted. "That's amazing!"

"No it's not. I just made it up." I run to my room and return with a calculator. "Oops. I was off by a billionth. It's really three billionths."

"I'm still impressed that you know how to calculate it on a machine."

"I've always liked math," I say.

"I always wondered why. You read so much, but your best

276

subjects in school turned out to be math, science and philosophy. Not writing and the arts. Why?"

"Math and science are exact," I say.

"But you like philosophy, too, and philosophy isn't exact."

"Philosophy can be a search for the exact," I say.

"How so?"

"There are whole passages on causality. The idea that if I let go of a ball, it'll drop to the ground. We've decided, through science, that gravity is pulling this ball. We've determined there are formulas for how fast it will accelerate, even how many times it will bounce, and how high. But that's science. In philosophy, when studying questions of causality, we ask, 'What if, even though it happened that way in 100 billion trials, it's a coincidence? How do you know that the one-hundred-billion-and-first time, it'll happen that way, too?' Now, science assumes, and we assume, that it will. Everything, or at least lots of things, have an order to them, a formula. But that doesn't satisfy a philosopher. He wants to be even more exact than the scientist. We're talking about a field in which you have people doubting their very existence in order to prove it. A scientist says, I can tell you that the dropped ball will accelerate at the rate of 9.8 meters per second squared, because it always has. But a philosopher says, there's no way to prove it always will. It may have been a coincidence that it happened 100 billion times. Philosophy attempts to be even more exact than science. I love it and I hate it."

He looks impressed and concerned at the same time. "Well," he says, "I suppose that's why ignorance is bliss. We'd all like to believe the sun will rise tomorrow."

"And that the Bible is right, and there is a heaven, and we have to be good to get in," I say. "And that we all know what good means, and what bad means, and that we know the answer to every question of morality and behavior. But then, the lines get blurred, and we're not so sure we want these absolutes after all."

Dad puts down his chopsticks. "I'll never get this," he says.

I hand him a fork.

Dad and I watch the last fifteen minutes of *It's a Wonderful Life* together—the rest is a colossal bore, so each year for the last five years we've purposely just watched the last fifteen minutes—and then he asks if I want to sit in the kitchen and talk. Even though we talked through dinner, I think he has something more serious to discuss. We haven't had a really long talk since the hurricane. He makes cocoa and we sit down.

He rubs his face with his hands.

"About the 'Big Lie,'" he says.

I shake my head. "I—"

"I thought it was true when I said it," he says. "I thought—"

My plan has always been to make him feel guilty about the Big Lie. For some reason, that made me feel better. But now that he starts talking about it, I feel bad. I don't want him to think everything's his fault.

"You had every right to be disappointed," he says, looking down at the table.

"Maybe I took it too literally," I say. "At the time, I thought you meant that people in college would be *exactly* like me. I wanted it to be true *so* badly. I couldn't wait to finally find a place where I'd fit in. I didn't realize there would be such a gulf, that I'd have to work so hard to understand people."

He looks as if he's straining under the weight of raising someone for most of their years and still not knowing the verdict. "In elementary school," he says, "you were so far ahead of your classmates. Your teacher and your principal agreed it was best to move you up. Once we figured out the appropriate grade level, you thrived academically. So yes, I assumed once you got to college, with all those brilliant students, you would thrive socially as well."

"I started off in college only feeling a little bit different," I admit. "But I did expect the people there to have boundless intellectual interests and devotions and a clear set of moral views. As they began to get closer to each other, they changed more and more. The more they changed with no explanation, the more I felt like a freak. And then I wondered, Why am *I* the freak?"

Dad puts his chin in his hands, but he's smiling at me. "You're a good person," he says. "You know that? I didn't know what kind of person you'd turn out to be. But you're a good person. And I'm glad. I don't think you should compromise on the good that's within you." He sits back. "But what I failed to do was teach you how to become friends with kids your age. If you won't compromise your own standards, can you also accept others who aren't just like you, intellectually and morally? Can you accept sinners and not their sins?"

He's right—this is one of the biggest things I have to work on now. But even if I stop expecting people to be just like me, I know that they're still going to push me to be just like them. Why is it that liberal people believe no one has the right to pass judgment on their liberality, but it's perfectly fine for them to censor other people's rigidity?

Dad is looking at me in a strange way. Finally, he says, "You remind me of your mother sometimes. More and more, the older you get. Maybe that's obvious."

He doesn't talk about my mother easily. I don't say anything.

He says, "She and her sister read everything growing up— literature, history, everything. You know that none of the women in her family had gone to college. But your mother decided at the last minute to save money to go to school so she could teach English. She got an administrative job at our firm, and I wouldn't have even paid attention to her, but one night, I was having an argument with some of the men in accounting about British political history. One gentleman kept arguing a point and trying to make me look like an idiot. So your mother came up to us. I thought she was going to ask something about work, but she just said softly, "That's not true." She gave a whole peroration on why my colleague was wrong. The more she talked, the more I fell in love with her. And not just because she was taking my side. Every day, I waited at work for everyone to leave so I could talk to her. At first it was nonsense, but we talked for hours. She was amazing. She'd say whatever she felt to anyone. She would have told off the head of the company if she'd felt it was right. I couldn't hold a candle to her as a person. And God, what a mind."

I look into his cocoa. It's swirling.

"That's all beside the point," he says. "There probably is never a time and place where a brilliant person will fit in completely. A hundred years ago, your morality would be more in line with other people's, but you probably wouldn't feel any more like you fit in than you do now. You'd be dying to burst forth and pour your intellect on the world, and you'd be repressed. Yet today, we live in a society where you can do anything. The consequence is, morality has become relative. And you, with your concerns about what's right and whether you should hew to it, are an anomaly. Is that bad? I loved your mother to death. She was different, too. Yet so was I. We were different from the world, yet similar to each other. I wouldn't have wanted her to change or give up anything that really mattered to her. The same goes for you. Re-evaluate? Maybe sometimes. But don't feel forced to come to any easy conclusions. Some people debate the issues you're considering all their lives."

"I'll be the one," I say, resigned. "I'll be the one who debates them all my life."

He smiles. "You're cursed. Cursed with a mind. Use it. Don't fear it. But don't let all of your thinking destroy you."

That night, my father stretches out on the futon in the living room and I repair to my own room. I climb into my window loft and sit there, hugging one of the square black pillows. Across the street at the Guarino household, the lights are blinking rapidly: red, green, dark yellow, white. It's peaceful. Inspiring.

I turn off the lights in my room and do something I haven't done since I was in the single digits.

I kneel beside my bed and pray.

"God," I say, "I'm not going to lie. I don't know if you exist, or how I should treat you if you do. I want to be a good person. I'm not sure what this entails. It seems less clear to me each day. I went to a new church recently. So in a way, you help, whether you exist or not. And maybe that's the point. You get me thinking about what I can do to be a good person. Well, it's Christmas Eve, so I know you're getting a lot of requests, 'Please help everyone pronounce *in excelsis Deo*,' et cetera. I'd like to pray for the homeless, the old, the sick, and I guess anyone else who's not doing too well. And I'm sorry for when I judge people. I'm also sorry for some of the things I've done lately…it just seems so hard to avoid them. That's no excuse. Is it? I know it's not."

I think of Matt. He hasn't called me since I caught him cheating with Beth. If he had called me again, I would have turned him down, but the scary thing is, it's only because I caught him. That's what it took. It wouldn't have been because he was engaged to Shauna. It took me seeing him with yet a third person to finally stop me. Part of me knows that if I hadn't caught him with Beth that time, I probably would have slept with him. So what is it that changed me into the kind of person who would help someone cheat? If it was that I became more forgiving, or more understanding, is that good, or bad?

"Anyway, God," I continue, "thank you for giving me a good life. I do appreciate it, and I'll keep trying as much as I can to be a better person. Amen."

Add that to the excuse list: I'll try.

I really will be a better person.

Starting after New Year's Eve.

After I finish my list.

Chapter Eleven

What's left is to tell someone I care about them, and to go out for New Year's Eve.

But two days before New Year's, I haven't gotten any invitations to parties.

I need to do *something*. I could spend the night out alone, but that's a cop-out. If I'm going to do this, I should do it right. It's only one night.

I gather my courage and leave a message for Kara. "I know you're busy, but I was wondering if you know of any good New Year's parties...." I sound awful, but it's all for the list.

If she doesn't call back, I'll still go out somehow.

But Kara does call back later. "Carrie!" she says. "Where've you been?"

"Nowhere special," I say.

She says she's going to a "progressive party," in which she and some friends will move from apartment to apartment all night, eating and drinking. The starting point is her place. I tell her I'll be there.

New Year's Eve morning, part of me wishes for my old life. If I had my old life, I could excitedly plan to gather Chinese food and ice cream tonight, rent a movie, and jump into bed. Or I'd just listen to music and dance around. I'd be having a fun, safe Pilby Party. All the things I want, and no chance of disaster. Very tempting. But I've done that already.

If I stay inside today, I won't feel out of place. But if I stay inside until I'm forty, I may venture out and find the world has passed me by. Why are these my options?

I could go to grad school, if they offered a master's in remedial socialization.

I start getting dressed around seven. I stuff my money and ID in my pocket. I leave my journal on my bed so I can report on the party later. Since I've looked at my luscious, comfy bed, it's hard to turn away. It calls to me. It would be so easy to dive in and snuggle up.

I flip the light and walk out.

It's cold.

Very cold.

I want to reconsider. Jack Frost is nipping at my nose, fingers, elbows, toes, ears and firm round buttocks. If I am going to stay out, I should be wearing five sweaters and a scarf. But no one at the progressive party will be wearing five sweaters and a scarf. In fact, some of the women passing me in the street aren't even wearing coats. Trading common sense for fashion, as usual.

I make my way down my front steps. I look back and see through Bobby's window that his TV is on. I guess he's alone on New Year's Eve.

But I won't be. For a change.

There are lots of strange-looking folks outside tonight, people decked out in fluffy pink boas, leopard-skin hats, green hair, chains, collars, leather pants. Why am I repelled by these things? What's wrong with differences? Because they scare me. Because they're risky.

I find myself hoping the people at the party will be normal. But what is normal? If I had the answer to that, I'd have the answer to everything.

I arrive at Kara's not a moment too soon. I've come only ten minutes after the official staging time of the party, figuring I'd be unfashionable for a change, but this crowd doesn't know the word. There's a line to get into the apartment. Next door, I hear the music blasting at top level. That song "Get Off" from the 1970s is playing, and all the guys next door, who I'm sure include Stephen and Pat, are singing, "Aw, aw, aw, aw." I'm glad I wasn't alive in the 1970s. I would have hated it. I would have hated the sixties, too. It's strange to think of how different all of us would have turned out if born in another decade. In the 1950s, Matt and Shauna would have been the Cleavers.

Finally I get inside Kara's place. Her living room is a mishmash of wooden tables with nachos, bowls of dip, pretzels, little cups, and bottles of all shapes, sizes and colors. In a corner, three girls with long, crossed legs are sitting on the floor and smoking, looking drugged-out. Against a wall, a tall, skinny guy in an orange shirt is leaning in and smooching a blond girl. I look closer and realize the girl is Kara. She's dyed her hair. "Carrie!" she says. "You look great!" Then she says to the skinny guy, "What's your name again?" She hiccups.

"Barn," he replies, and she starts laughing.

"Here," she says to me, waving her arms at him. "You need your mouth washed out, for free?"

"No thanks," I say. It's only eight-fifteen, and already she's drunk. This is not a good sign. "How many more houses are there?" I ask.

"What?" she yells over the din.

"How many more apartments?" Leave it to me to ask a logical question in an illogical setting.

"I don't—" hic "—know."

"Seventy-five," says Barn, and he leans in and kisses her more. He's got what look like black woven armbands tattooed on both biceps, and for some strange reason, they look good on him. I'd be afraid to get a tattoo myself, but I'm attracted to this. I don't know why. Scary.

Kara breaks away and calls to me. "I'm not going to the other apartments!" she yells. "Carrie! Stay here. Right?"

"Okay." She's the only one I know, anyway.

"Well, I'm going," says Barn, and he wipes his mouth off.

"Good," Kara says. "Somebody give me a drag."

A few people leave, but more show up. Kara sits down at a table and beckons me to do the same. "I haven't even been smoking," she tells me. "I mean, pot. And I still feel stoned. It's, like, secondhand hooch." Then she laughs.

"I guess it works."

She hiccups. "Do you want something? Have you had a drink yet?"

There's a pitcher of something icy and blue. She pours me a giant plastic cup and I take a gulp. It tastes good. It doesn't even seem like there's alcohol in it, although there must be. "What is this?" I ask.

"I don't know," she says. "Poison. Ouch!" She gets up and throws a bottle cap off the seat, then sits back down. "Someone is fucking trying to kill me."

"I doubt they're trying to kill you with a bottle cap."

"It may *look* like a bottle cap," she says, but she doesn't finish the thought. She reaches her finger out and sticks it in the salsa.

Then she dabs a little on each of her cheeks. "My name is Conchita Rivera de Salsa."

She stands up and claps. "Olé! I need a Latin lover." She turns to me. "Do you want to be my Latin lover?"

"Ix-nay."

"I didn't say pig Latin."

I pick up my glass of Blue Whatever and finish it.

"That's the way," Kara yells. "Go Carrie!" She fills another and hands it to me, then wipes the salsa off her cheeks and steps closer until she's in front of my face. Her nose is almost touching mine. If only her nose's perfectness could transfer. "Come up to the roof with me," she says.

There's a latch on the roof of her closet, and she pulls it down. A stepladder made of natural wood emerges. Nice. Kara climbs it and I follow, careful not to spill my drink. The ladder creaks and must be dusty because it makes me want to sneeze. I think about sneezing and I can't. Drat. I'm regressing and ascending at the same time.

No one follows us, and Kara closes the latch behind her.

Once I'm on the roof, I am hit with a gust of cold air. The stars are all around, a glorious infinite galaxy.

I stand straight up. Below, I can make out the artistically pruned rooftop gardens of New York, which are sometimes greener than in suburbia; in the distance are fireworks and airplanes and red air traffic control lights that appear and disappear.

I feel like the two of us are the tallest people in the world. The sky is spinning around me. Kara stands next to me. I drink my drink. It's still cold out, but I barely feel it.

"Look at the moon," Kara says.

"Ka-*ra,*" someone calls from downstairs. "Where'd you *go?*"

"I don't want to talk to them," she says. She walks over to a folding chair that has a blanket draped over it. "Bring a chair over," she says. I drag one across the roof, and it bumps and stutters. Far below us, there's revelry in the streets: Noisemakers, hollers, laughter, sudden screams.

"New Year's Eve, big fat deal," Kara says, sitting down, as if she wasn't the one who donated her apartment for a party to mark the very occasion. "That's something on a man-made calendar. Not like the equinox or the solstice. That's the cosmos. That's spiritual. We should have parties for *that*." She throws her fist in the air. "Party for the solstice!" Her voice shoots into the New York sky, past the Chrysler Building, through Co-Op City, maybe into Westchester.

Kara pulls the blanket off the chair and lays it on the ground. She crawls onto it and rolls over on her back, staring at the sky. "Come here," she says, stretching her legs. "The view's better."

I get off my chair and crawl over, feeling ready to tip. I lie down on the blanket with my head perpendicular to Kara's. All of a sudden, I think there actually was a lot of alcohol in those blue drinks.

A whole lot.

She looks at me. "I didn't think you'd ever call again," she says. "I want you to be my best best friend in the world."

"Do I have to give you my lunch money?"

"Is that what your friends made you do? That's mean."

"I wasn't popular, like you."

"You're popular here," she says. She grabs my hand and kisses it. Then she stretches out.

"Kara!" a voice screams from downstairs. "Where are you?"

"Oh my God!" she shrieks back. "You guys suck!"

I hear a siren go by. The poor police must be having a terrible time of it.

"Let's sit up," Kara says. "I'm cold." We sit up, and she puts her arms around herself. "I don't like my friends," she says.

"Make new ones," I say.

"Where?"

"In church."

She starts laughing.

"Some of my friends are so immature," she says. "I'm not going to have parties anymore. It attracts the wrong people."

"It attracts people who like parties."

She just looks at me. "You are so smart. You are just so smart. Your lips are blue." I worry that she might try to kiss me again, but instead, she just looks at me and makes a fish face.

The wind is blowing. I stare at the sky.

Kara looks up. "What do you want to do?" she asks.

"Sit."

"No, with your life?"

"What makes you think the answer's different?"

She laughs. "What did you major in?"

"Philosophy."

"Oh, then I guess your answer was accurate. They should, like, combine that major with something you can support yourself on. Like philosophy of deep fat frying."

I lean back and look at the stars. The roof feels cold against my back. "What job would you *least* like to do?"

"The person who sings the national anthem at golf. Can you imagine, the world's most boring sport, and you have to sing the world's most boring song?"

"The la-a-a-nd of the free!" I yell.

"And the home of the…"

"Braaaaave!" we sing together.

"Now you're cookin'!" she says. "You're a grand! Old! Flag!"

"You're a high-flying flag!"

I have a bad voice. Awful. But now, as we sing together, there's nothing I'd rather be doing. I realize why so many people want some sort of musical hobby, whether it be a band, a chorus, or play. When someone joins you in song, you are never out of place.

When we've gone through the few songs that we both know all the words to, including "Yankee Doodle" and its successor, "Great Green Gobs of Greasy Grimy Gopher Guts," Kara asks me, "What are your resolutions?"

I have an idea of why she's popular. She brings up good discussion topics. "To make new friends and to be less judgmental."

"Sounds good," Kara says. "I want to get a real steady job. No more of this temping shit." She swats the skinny brown end of a beer bottle, and it spins in a circle. "You know, last weekend they called me to do an emergency typing shift at another law firm. And the next day, my boss called me and said, 'We can't ever send you back to that firm.'"

"Why?"

"Some supervisor claimed I went into someone's office and was listening to music. And I was like, I don't even know what you're talking about." She turns to face me. "I swear I don't have any idea."

"I believe you," I say.

"So I told her that. She said, 'They're sure it was you.'" Kara's voice breaks. "She didn't believe me. No matter how long I worked there. And I was doing well with them…" She trails off.

I've never seen her so unhappy. I guess alcohol can make you go both ways.

"What if I'm never permanent at *anything?*" she asks.

I hug her. I don't remember hugging anyone other than my father. "Are they going to fire you from Dickson, Monroe?"

"No. But my boss at the temp place is all snotty now. Before, I was the star temp." She wipes her nose. "It's like, you don't really work for anyone. You're just a piece of meat that can type.

And I have to pay my own health insurance. I have friends who temp, and their daddies and mommies pay it all."

She puts her head in my lap. I watch an airplane make its way across the sky, the light in front illuminating bands of clouds.

"Kara!" someone calls.

"Oh, what am I doing?" Kara says. "This is supposed to be a party." She gets up. "You are such a good friend." She gives me a hug. "We're going to have to get together and analyze this when we're not drunk. Let's go downstairs."

As I descend, I feel cold again. In the living room, someone calls Kara over. I follow her to a group of people who are having a conversation.

I stand in the circle and listen, but the topics change so fast that I can't keep up. They're talking about entertainment, but not about personalities as much as styles, and I have never been able to get sure footing in those kinds of discussions. It reminds me of when I was in high school, when the kids would discuss various hallmarks of pop culture, and although I did watch some TV and knew a few of the people whom they were talking about, I never knew the right kind of comments to make or the kinds of judgments that fit in. They'd say, "So-and-so got fat," and "I don't like her haircut," and "Look at who she's dating!" and I had no idea why some things were cool and not others, and why most kids knew exactly the right things to say. I believe that pop-culture literacy can be as important as overall literacy, but I could watch a sitcom a hundred times and not feel comfortable declaring that the main character's new boyfriend was "cute," and I might know that a certain singer was the one who had that big hit on the top forty stations, but I wouldn't know whether her haircut was cool. I understand some of the basics, but I just can't bring myself to care about the criteria—not because I'm trying to be stuck-up, simply because it isn't part of me, just as some of my peers don't share all of *my* interests. The only difference is, there are more of them than me, so I need to be able to talk to them.

Now, at Kara's, I'm in a similar situation. "His sideburns have gotta go," a girl in the circle says. "His girlfriend's a witch," someone else says. "In real life, or on the show?" "Both!" "She should have stuck to movies." "But she got to work with so-and-so." "He's scrawny, though." "I think he's cute." "Doesn't he have his own band?" "Yeah. He's about as good a singer as he is an actor." "He looks like so-and-so." "He's so good-looking, and he does all these movies where he looks like a Neanderthal." Kara comments, "His forehead's too big." She seems engrossed in this. I feel silly standing there, not knowing what to say. I decide I'll pass the time by getting another drink. Maybe by the time I'm done, Kara will be bored with these people. I head into the kitchen.

The kitchen is very narrow. People are standing against both walls as if in a police lineup, facing each other. There's a bottle of wine on the stove top. I pour some into a plastic cup.

A tall guy finishes talking to the girl next to him and watches me pour, then gives me a line about how following hard with soft liquor makes you drunk quicker, or get sicker, or get sicker quicker, or something. I'm amazed at all these drinking rules. When did people learn them? Again, must have been eighth grade.

I settle into a spot along the wall.

"So, who do you know here?" a girl asks me.

"Kara," I say.

The girl looks at the guy questioningly. "Who's Kara?"

"I don't know," the guy says.

"This is her apartment," I say.

"Oh. Right!"

Another guy says, "What do you think she pays for it?"

"I heard someone say eleven hundred."

"I *love* that," the tall guy says. "I love it when someone gets a good deal on an apartment. It's like good sex."

"In New York, it is."

The girl whispers something in the tall guy's ear. He nods. He leans in and tells me, "We're going to go get a hit. Want to come?"

Of course, my first instinct is to say no, and I don't even know what they're going to get a hit *of,* but I also *want* to know. I want to watch them do this, since I've never seen anyone take drugs. I'm not even cool enough to ever have been given the *opportunity* to do drugs. Except in Washington Square Park, where they used to always whisper "Smoke, smoke" in your ear as soon as you walked in, and you were supposed to know that that meant pot. You'd think that the cops could have busted all of them, but I guess saying "smoke, smoke" isn't against the law. Some of these dope dealers are so ingenious you'd think they could put it toward something legal.

"Sure," I say, with more couth than I have.

The tall guy gives me a nod. He's got wavy short hair that's matted against his forehead, and some sort of beaded wooden necklace around his neck. The girl takes his hand and leads him out, and I follow.

We pass the circle of people that includes Kara. I wave to catch her attention. "Leaving?" she asks.

"Yeah," I say. "I might be back."

"Okay!" she yells. "Well, happy new year if you don't. Call me! I mean it!"

I smile. "Happy new year!"

"Call me soon—ow! Get off my fucking foot!"

I grab my coat and head into the hall.

In the hall, I see a few people waiting to get into the apartment next door. Among them is a familiar face.

"Carrie!"

My eyes narrow, and then I remember. "Douglas P. Winters!"

"Oh, it is so great to see you," he says. "Hug!" He hugs me. The guy he's with, who's wearing a black bow tie, looks at us both strangely. "She's really a man," Doug tells him.

"Work it, sister," his friend says, and he slaps me five.

The girl and the guy from Kara's party stop in the hall. "I'll meet up with you," I say.

"Three B," the guy says. "Don't bring any cops." He smiles, and the girl winks.

Doug brings me into Stephen and Pat's apartment. People are dancing, and one guy is sitting on a wooden dresser singing. Doug puts one arm around me and the other around his date, and we join in. It feels good to sing. He shows me around. "This is my girlfriend," he tells someone at one point. The person responds, "Yeah, and I'm Elvis Costello."

It occurs to me that during the day, at work, some of the people at this party have to hide who they are. Now they're among friends, and they can let their guard down and revel in the freedom. There's something appealing in that.

I make my way to the alcohol table and pour myself a glass of something pink. It ain't lemonade. The smoke stings my eyes, and I look around for Doug. But I imagine I'm not the one he's there to see.

A guy comes over and sings with me. I feel surprisingly unselfconscious. In fact, I can barely see the other people. Everything looks a little fuzzy. All I know is there's some guy in front of me, and the music sounds good, and the drinks taste good, and everything's good. I drink more. The room is packed, and it's smoky. And I don't care much, because for the first time in a while, I'm too numb to think about myself.

The guy who was singing with me leaves. I walk around a little more, but I suddenly feel strange. I look around and notice that I'm one of only three girls there. Correction: two. I just noticed the Adam's apple on one.

Oh. Correction, one.

I walk past the front door and hear someone who is entering the room say to someone else, "Well, maybe I'll *keep* my jacket and throw *you* on the bed."

I finally spot Doug. He's busy having his shirt yanked off him. I go over to him and yell goodbye, over the music. He leans over and gives me a kiss on the cheek and tells me to come do some insider proofreading soon. He seems much more loose than he ever did at the firm. What do all of us have at our core that we spend most of our time hiding?

The hall floor is bare, shiny and white. My shoes squeak as I walk across it.

I forget which apartment number that couple said.

I feel funny. I don't want to be around drugs. It doesn't feel like me. I can accept that maybe some things that are dangerous might not be wholly immoral, although they can be stupid and a pointless risk to take, but it doesn't mean I have to do them if I don't feel comfortable. Then again, I can watch. This is the night to see what it's all about.

That feeling comes back: that hollow feeling in my stomach, that funny, kind of sad feeling. I realize that when I get it, it's usually because I don't feel right about something, particularly myself.

I think the couple said 3B.

Against my better judgment, I take the stairs and knock. No answer. I wait, and knock again. Nothing.

Good.

I take the stairs down, finishing a cup of pink liquid. I feel keyed up, too keyed up to head home. I wonder if I should go back up to Kara's party. But what is there to do if I go back? Drink some more?

I feel like dancing through the darkness, jumping off the curbs like in *Singing in the Rain,* which I rented last week. I want to grab someone's hand and spin around. I want to ride the top of a subway car like it's a mechanical bull.

I leave my empty cup on the stairs and take a step out into the cold, loud world.

The streets are packed. Everyone is moving in groups, some in costume, all talking loudly. New Year's Eve is like Halloween meets freshman year.

It's frosty out, but not windy. I float into the middle of a pack and let myself get carried along. Still, I know I am alone. The people I saw upstairs were okay, but I didn't feel close to them. I'm not saying I can't like them, or that I didn't have a good time with them, but there is a difference between friends you have fun with and friends you feel a close connection to. I wouldn't put anyone I was with tonight into the second category yet. In fact, I would hardly put anyone into that category.

I stumble west and head up a small street, passing an elementary school. Upstairs, a soccer ball is wedged in a horizontal push-out window. Downstairs is a taped flyer advertising a hamster that needs a home; there also are bake sales and a play coming up. I feel like I'm in the suburbs for a minute.

I continue west. I suddenly realize where I'm going: Times Square. Just to say I did. That oughta shut Petrov up for good.

As I reach Sixth Avenue, I hear something I have heard many times in my life: backwards bass. Backwards bass is the thumping sound that comes from another person's party, one to which you are not invited. The loud muffled thump is the sound of speakers aimed at other people, people who are part of the group. It fills the air and makes your eardrums throb. People's laughter is wafting over, along with their smoke and the smell of beer.

The alcohol floods me again. I feel good. There was a momentary lapse of liquor. Now I'm ready for whatever the night has in store. I stumble along. In front of me is a girl with magenta hair and pigtails. The freaks are out tonight. Even among freaks, I am a freak. Among normal people, too. What category do I fall into? D.P. Displaced Prodigy.

I hit Sixth Avenue and begin heading north. Some of the blocks have managed to miraculously retain their old-time Village charm, with faux gaslights, brick alleys, iron railings. The brownstones are four stories tall, with stone stoops wide like mothers' laps. The painted garage doors were, I'm sure, stables only a few decades ago. But as the numbered streets pass from the single to double digits, the retail stores encroach and the buildings get taller and taller.

I dig my hands into my pockets, trying not to bump into any-one, which is definitely not easy, and proceed north. The build-ings reflect a hodgepodge of zoning. One contains white columns, pink fire escapes and sea-green paneling; its neighbor has bricks so stained they are nearly black, with a pair of fat gray water towers on top looking like overfed twins in conical Chinese hats; then, sandwiched between these architectural call-ing cards are gaudy video stores with signs lit up in seventies Technicolor, and walls that double as jeans ads. I bristle and con-tinue on, ducking under blue scaffolding branded with *Post No Bills,* past palm readers, jewelry stores, and an electronics dealer who advertises that he fixes VCRs and microwaves, where sure-ly a previous sign referenced radios and TVs. I descry a white mansion-type building with a zillion crevices and alcoves, and I wonder who lives there, but moving in for a closer look, I see it's inhabited by retail. I vacillate between being transported back to a simpler time and smashing headlong into that unbreakable windshield that is the future.

There's something I notice more and more. On the brick

buildings, running down the sides, are faded painted letters telling which businesses used to occupy them. Many are garment businesses, and I can make out some of the letters. Probably because I'm now in the garment district. I begin noticing so many of these old ads, in fact, that I wonder how I missed them growing up here.

I walk slower, getting lightly bumped by people, so that I can read.

On 26th Street is Goldstein Furs & Skins. On 27th Street, Hollander Co., Ladies Underwear. At 28th Street are Brucker Bros. & Aronof / Dresses And Costumes / Furriers / Freedman & Clotzer / Manchurian Furs. Near 29th are Maid Rite Dress Co. / Hoffman & Horwitz Suits & Coats. Farther up are more furs, skins, silks, suppliers and dyers. One building says, in yellow, For Space In This Area Call Berley & Co., Inc., 11 East 36th St., with a phone number. I'm disappointed to see that it's a regular number, not a number that starts with two letters like MU6-5000. I love old phone numbers.

Where are Mr. Aronof and the Brucker Brothers today? Are they appalled by women wearing blue jeans? What ever happened to the old business partners Freedman and Clotzer, and Hoffman and Horwitz? Do their families still speak to each other? Do their grandkids pass the buildings and realize that those are their grandparents' names there? I wonder what types of stories these men could tell, if they were still around.

I also wonder if anyone else ever thinks about these things. I look around and notice that no one else is staring up at the buildings. They're all looking straight ahead.

I get elbowed and I move on. Cabs honk at each other, people curse out of rolled-down windows, dogs yelp. Now I am out of painted-wall territory and into a shopper's Shangri-la. I pass a toy store and several clothing stores. High above 32nd Street, running from the tenth floor of an office building to the

tenth floor of a department store, is a beautiful enclosed verdi-
gris walkway whose origin and purpose are, I suppose, known
to those who work there. I pass a blue bank of freestanding pay-
phones, against which a couple is making out. The third pay-
phone is off the hook. When I first moved back to New York
after college, I used to put the phones back on the hooks all the
time. Then, one time, I put a phone back on the hook and a
guy came out of nowhere shrieking about having someone on
hold. I got a pretty good idea it was drug related, and I apolo-
gized and got the heck out of there. Now, when I see a phone,
I let it hang, and when I see someone putting one back on the
hook, I wonder just where that person is from.

I continue on, marveling at black streetlights, which are M-
shaped like seagulls, their clear bulbs hanging at the ends as if
dripping from wings. I travel through a cloud of perfume that has
some sort of off-pickle undertone that makes me happy and must
remind me of something from my childhood.

I spot the clearest wall-sign on a building yet: Style Undies
Mfg / Children's / Distinctive / Underwear / Gowns / Pajamas
/ Bo-Peep Mfg Co / Brother / & / Sister / Individual &
Companion / Clothes / Play Togs. What is a play tog? I'll have
to look it up. That drives me crazy, a word I don't know. After
my perfect verbal SAT score, there shouldn't be a word I don't
know. I try to figure out if it's supposed to be a *Y* instead of a
G, but someone jostles me. There's no stopping or standing on
New Year's Eve.

I continue north past Walk/Don't Walk signs, office buildings, shoe stores, gyms. Slapped on a light pole is a thin white
square of paper saying *No Parking Sunday, Police Dept.* and under
it, as a kicker, is some marketing genius's fluorescent orange
sticker advertising *24-Hr Towing.*

Around 38th Street is when I see the snake.

There is a multicolored, lit-up quivering serpent running

down the corner of a building. As I get closer, I realize that's what a lit-up wall-sized ad in Times Square looks like from the side.

As I approach the polychromatic creature, I see the other trademarks of Times Square: the orange lit-up scrolling Dow Jones "zipper" that displays the news; mirrored office windows reflecting millions of tiny lights; ESPN Zone, steak places, nut vendors, caricature artists, and incense stands trailing thin caterpillars of smoke that creep into our noses intending to arouse our wallets.

The noise is pollution—a loud, bubbling din accompanied by sirens, signals, shrieks, squeals. The crowd thickens and soon I can barely move.

Everyone seems happy. They're laughing, talking, hugging. I start feeling miserable again. The people are tall, the buildings are taller, and I'm just below them.

Suddenly a voice next to me says, "Are you alone?"

I turn.

"Come with us!"

It's a woman in a black wool coat, talking into her cell phone. "Me and Eddie are meeting at ten. No, it's packed here. I can barely get through. Ow. Someone just bumped me again. Yeah, I better go."

I hate cell phones.

"Hello. Ed? I don't know what got into me. I just invited Jessica. Well, she called and she was kind of *hinting*. I know. Well, you don't have to talk to her. Hey, hold on a minute. Hello? Jess! Yes, on Broadway. Yes, right. All right, well we can't wait to see you! Bye. Hello, Ed? That was her again. So I felt sorry for the girl. What do you want?"

I want to keep listening to her conversation, but the noise-makers drown her out. Can't people be polite when someone is on the phone?

She makes her way into the crowd, and I follow her, deciding to be a people-listener. I will try to isolate other people's conversations, catch their phrases, see if they're talking about anything worthwhile. I manage to hear a few snippets:

"Not only didn't they discipline the dog, they left the cheese out for everyone to eat."

"Urinals? Forget it. I can't ever concentrate if someone's in the next *stall*."

"I had no idea it meant something different in England, and no one talked to me for the rest of the trip."

"Weren't you supposed to use that money for grad school?"

"I think he faked it to get mouth-to-mouth."

"So she, like, bought the clothes in New Jersey, 'cause the tax on clothes is only three percent there, and she wanted to go return them to the Macy's in New York so she could get the eight-and-a-half percent sales tax back, and we were like, first of all, you'd be only gaining like five cents per clothes, and besides, like, Macy's is going to *know*. It's on the receipt. She's, like, a moron."

Petrov thinks I'm negative about people, but look at everyone talking about each other behind their backs! I don't talk much about people behind their backs—so why is being privately irked by them so bad?

I walk swiftly ahead so I can follow Cell Phone Woman into her party. She hasn't managed to get too far ahead of me. She seems to be on the phone an awful lot. "Everyone from the show!" she says. "Even David, and Alcott. You have to go! Yeah, on the sixth floor!" She gives a corner on Broadway. Maybe I can follow her. And meet her "friend" Jessica, who clearly needs better friends. The corner she mentions is nearly in the heart of Times Square. And right now, so are we.

Then, we're completely at a standstill.

There's nowhere to go. People's shoulders are pushing against each other. The lights assault us: red, blue, pink, green. The conversations mix to form one roar. Confetti is raining from everywhere, showering slowly. The ads on the Coke display are exploding. We're in a wonderful phantasmagoric dream kaleidoscope.

"I'm, like, totally stopped," Cell Phone Girl says. "I may have to crawl through someone's legs."

"Tonight!" booms a speaker. The crowd packs tighter, shoulder to shoulder. "We present..." I manage to look around, and still find that not one other person seems alone. Guys are hugging shiny-dress-clad women; burly men are laughing with their friends. Don't people have any guts? Why am I the only one in the world who ever has the courage to do anything alone? Why does Petrov think I'm the one with the problem, when I'm the only one with courage? Is there not one other person in Times Square alone?

I don't know if I can blame anyone, though. It's hard to be alone. What's strange is that one more person is all it takes to make you feel like you fit into the world, even though a couple is only one more than one. Just the mere addition of one person makes your life 800 percent better, and makes you all of a sudden fit into the social structure of society. Why does one plus one equal a quality-of-life increase of 800 percent? Without that one person, you must walk alone, eat alone, travel alone, sleep alone. If I had one person whom I fit in with and who was beholden to me, I wouldn't have to prove anything to the rest of the world. I'm sure there are couples who are both misfits, but they fit in with each other so it doesn't matter.

Suddenly I realize I am flanked by a pair of tall men.

"We're, like, squeezing this girl," one of them says to the other.

"It's okay," I manage to yell.

The first guy says, "Jim, come over this way." Then, to me, "You here alone?"

"I'm meeting friends."

"Here?" the first guy says. "What did you say, 'Meet me in Times Square'? Forget it."

"I guess you're right," I say, trying to sound cheerful. I figure I should leap through the window of opportunity before it closes. "What are *you* two doing?"

"Just waitin' for the ball to drop," Jim says, then sniffs. I see the breath come out of his mouth. He has a chain around his neck. "Is it always this cold here?" He blows into his cupped hands.

"On New Year's Eve," I say. "Where are you from?"

"Fresno," Jim's friend says. "We're visiting college friends. But they dissed us." He proffers his hand. "I'm Rudy, by the way."

"Carrie," I say, shaking it. It's beefy.

"What? Shari?"

"Carrie."

"I'm Jim," Jim says.

"You got a boyfriend?" Rudy asks me.

"Nah," I say. They look at me, and I add, "It can be hard for me to meet people who I can really talk to sometimes."

Jim says, "Well, you know, maybe you shouldn't rule out just having sex."

I laugh.

"No, I'm serious," Jim says.

"Very funny."

He is dead serious. They both are. "It's New Year's Eve," Rudy says. "Why don't you just hook up?"

"You'd just have sex with someone you didn't know?"

Rudy shoots Jim a look, then says to me, "Hell, yeah. If she's cute."

"What if she wasn't, but you liked her personality?"

"How would I get to know her personality?"

"You wouldn't speak to someone unless she was cute?"

Jim and Rudy look at each other and laugh.

I look at them. Rudy weighs about three hundred pounds. Jim is wearing a stained Clifford the Big Red Dog sweatshirt. And they're being picky.

"What about a 4-9-1?" Rudy says to Jim.

"Naaaah," Jim says.

"What's a 4-9-1?" I ask.

Jim leans close enough to my ear that I can feel his hot beer-breath. "It's a girl who looks like a four when you're drinking," he says, "a nine when you're drunk, and a one the next morning."

"Owoooooooohhhh!" Rudy howls. "Don't see any nines yet."

"Keep looking," Jim tells him.

"Or, keep *drinking.*"

They guffaw.

Rudy puts his left hand on my shoulder. "Now, tell me," he slurs. "Would Jim be your type?"

I look at Jim, trying to be open-minded. "Maybe," I say. "If I found out that we had things in common."

"You're just a ray of sunshine, you know that?" Jim says sarcastically. "You have a real good attitude. It's such a shock you don't have a boyfriend."

I don't understand how I earned his scorn. Isn't it interesting that people are fine with judging potential mates based on looks, but if you try to mention a nonphysical criterion instead, suddenly you're the snob?

"Well," I say, "It was nice meeting you. I hope you find what you're looking for." I edge past them. I hear one of them call, "Hey!" but I'm not interested. I'm disheartened, is what I am. Just when I start to believe things aren't as bad as I thought, I meet a pair of numbchucks like those two. Is this what's out there?

If so, why do I want to be here?

I look back, and Jim is giving his friend a what-a-bitch look.

Even when I try to find middle ground, I meet people who are so completely at the opposite end of the planet from me. And that makes me feel creepy.

I try to remember which building Cell Phone Woman's party is in. There is a tall hotel that a crowd of people is disappearing into. I walk behind them. One of them gives me a quick glance, but they're busy with each other and don't seem to care when I follow them in. The bellhop doesn't notice. We all squeeze into an elevator.

They press the fourth floor. Maybe there's a conference room there.

The guy who looked at me before looks again. "What floor?" he asks me.

I look at the numbers. I say the highest one. That way, I can wait until everyone is off, then decide where to stop.

When the elevator doors open on four, the group steps out. It is loud, and I hear someone on a microphone announcing something. There are balloons and streamers in the hall. The doors close. I'm in there alone.

A feeling overtakes me.

I must get higher.

And higher.

High above the world.

As I pass various floors, I either hear music or silence.

I decide to stop at the tenth floor. It's quiet. I walk to the end of the hall. I pass silent rooms, then rooms with TVs on, rooms with low discussion and periodic laughter. Then, I am at some sort of red stairwell door.

I push.

Inside, the stairwell walls are white and badly painted, with a brown stain creeping up one.

I head upstairs. There's another level, and it's got a nondescript gray door with a hole where the knob should be. I push again.

I am hit with a gust of cold wind. I walk out, and it is like I have landed on the moon. It's some sort of subroof full of J-shaped metal pipes and quartz. Beyond that, I see the city, lit up like a forest of Christmas trees. Beyond that, the stars.

I tread on black mesh rubber matting over the rocks to a gaggle of overturned plastic milk crates a few feet from the edge. I wonder if anyone has ever been arrested for illegal possession of a milk crate. There were people at Harvard who made dining room sets out of them.

I see crushed cigarettes and a beer can on the subroof, but it doesn't look like anyone has been here tonight. Do I worry that it is dangerous for me to be up here alone? No. Do I worry I am trespassing? No.

Did I have some weird things to drink?

Yes.

I sit on a blue milk crate, ten stories above Times Square, and hear honking below, and sirens, and cheers and various convergences of the three. Then, noisemakers like the ones at football games. The cold air swirls around me, but it feels good. I am finally high up enough to read one of the Parental Hotline billboards, the ones that say, "To be a supportive parent, you have to work" and "To be a supportive parent, you have to stay home." This time, I can make out the phone number: 1-855-NYC-COPE.

There's a number I could use.

I look around. I see black iron fire escapes. I gaze down at roofs that contain debris, plants, and in one case, a broken table whose legs are flattened and bent around it like a smashed spider; farther down, inside glowing windows, are people's heads, couples dancing, cats, lamps, computers. There is black lighting, blue lighting, red lighting, pale lighting. I see a woman in a window looking out, and then a man handing her a drink.

I realize something.

I love this city. God, I do.

This makes no sense. People who wax poetic about New York have always irritated me. It's like feeling nostalgic over the TB shots you used to get as a kid. It's a city. What's to love about poverty and grime? It's pseudo-artsy to speak of a predilection toward such a place. Woody Allen said in *Manhattan,* which is on one of the AAFR lists, that it's a great city, and that he doesn't care what anyone says. Yeah, maybe it's great if you're a forty-five-year-old man and can have a romance with a teenage girl and you've constantly got "Rhapsody in Blue" tinkling in the background like in that movie, but in real life, you'd more likely have a dozen homeless people tinkling in the background. How can someone love such a place?

But I do.

I step away from the crate, kneel down and lie back on the rubber matting, looking up at the sky. A few small rocks on the matting pinch my back, but aside from that, it's quite comfortable. A white film is now covering the stars, like thin curtains at the end of a performance.

The cold air envelops me. The lights spill over the buildings. Red. Blue. Green. Yellow. I am part of everyone else now. We're all in a giant Lava lamp, together.

Lying here on my back, I'm ready for good things to shower upon me. I want the bulbs to explode and rain brilliant bits of yellow and purple and white. I feel ebullient. I wonder if this is the way other people feel *all* the time.

Maybe I *do* usually suffer from depression. Maybe the way I feel now, everyone else feels most of the time, and that's why they're so much more comfortable with the world than I am. Maybe it's chemical. Maybe Petrov was right. How would I know, if I've never felt any way other than the way I usually am? And this feeling I feel now, what if I can replicate it with antidepressants? Even if they're drugs, so what—if I can feel this good with them, why shouldn't I? Is this what it's all about?

I don't really believe I'm depressed, though. But that whole idea is something to think about, the question of whether we should reject anything that could make us feel better. Even if it's a drug.

But tonight, lying under the stark black sky, I need to think about something more important.

I need to think about how I view the world.

Okay, so I think I'm smarter than other people. Okay, I don't have much patience for them. I've already started confronting that. But why am I like that?

It is true that my great acceptance always came from grades. A smile from a teacher was like an embrace for me. I was able to elicit them routinely, just by doing an extra good job on my homework or on a test. I could do that several times each week. It was within my power. Work hard, get a hug.

There were deadlines, assignments, quizzes, contests. Compliments abounded. Teachers would gush on my report card. Each A was a pat on the back. It happened sometimes in college, too.

But now I am out of school. Whenever I figure out what it is I should be doing, I certainly won't be embraced for it.

Instead, I sit in my room. It has structure and it's safe.

One thing I need to do is accept that the value of people, and myself, has little to do with test scores or what college they went to—if they went. I guess I do know that, inside. I can accept people who are different. This is something I know.

But I also have to acknowledge that what truly excites me is learning and understanding new things. I can't help it. When that bulb snaps on and I can see something in a new way, it's exhilarating. And when someone is excited to share this perspective with me, that is wonderful. That's the way I am. If people want me to accept them, they have to accept me.

I also know that the part of me that needs to analyze everything to death leads to the part of me that needs to understand and feel comfortable with the morality behind what I do. If I have to give up these concerns, I'm not me. If I have to be just like everyone else, something's wrong.

I can compromise *a little*. I can decide not to turn up my nose at those who aren't like me, while still staying true to my own beliefs. I can do this without changing myself. I can be strong and still discourage those who pressure me. I can recognize middle grounds.

Yet, there are some other things I know.

I know, standing out here tonight, that I will never be the person pressed up against the wall at a party getting a teeth cleaning by Barn.

I will never be the one horsing around in Harvard Square with a guy and his Saint Bernard.

I will never be the one holding four guys' attention at an alumni club.

I will never be the one sitting on the floor, smoking pot in apartment 3B.

And that's okay.

I need to believe I'm doing the right thing, and maybe learning something if I'm lucky. If others don't think that's valuable, so be it.

I loved being with Professor Harrison. I never felt like a misfit when I was with him. I guess I still was one, but he was, too, and misfits aren't misfits when they're in each other's company. Anything he said that I knew would be considered out of place in society, that a normal person wouldn't say, only made me like him more. He seemed to think the same of me. When he talked about not feeling at ease growing up, I wanted to hug him. We had a comfortable similarity whose milky depths I never wanted to leave.

People might believe that such a relationship, young woman and older male authority figure, always would be ultimately harmful. Maybe it was. Then again, if I hadn't met David, I probably would have spent all winter in my room, studying and reading and not talking to anyone. I would not have been out meeting other students. I would have been with myself.

But if I do end up with myself sometimes, it's not so horrible. I'm not the be-all and end-all, but I *like* myself.

I sit up. A wind blows. It's cold. The roar of the crowd is getting louder.

I had fun tonight; I would not have admitted that before. I didn't do anything too horrible, and I stayed true to myself.

But I am still alone.

Who would think that a person could sit above a crowd of five hundred thousand people, in a city of eight million, and still feel alone?

I walk back to the stairwell, take the elevator down and make my way through the crowds toward the subway station. It's packed.

Waiting on the platform, I hear a conversation among the din. "Yeah, he never drank in college because his father was an alcoholic, but he didn't tell anyone in the house why he didn't, and they treated him like shit the whole time."

I'm reminded that it doesn't matter if a thousand people around me aren't anything like me. I'd understand that guy, whoever he is, who didn't want to drink and stood by it. I would have accepted him. But the problem is, I don't know that I'll ever meet him.

When the subway car slides over to us, the crowd squeezes in. It's so stuffed it's hard to breathe. Finally I get out at my stop and walk back through the cold air.

I still don't feel ready to sleep. The world is going crazy, and I want to be a part of it. If I don't, I'll still hear it outside my window.

At my building, I see that Bobby's shades are down. He's either asleep or out. I quietly trot upstairs and put my key in the lock. My apartment feels warm.

It's about eleven-thirty. Now what?

I check my answering machine, but there are no messages. I should get caller ID so I can see if anyone called just to hear my voice. Half the people who have it have it for psychological reasons anyway.

I get an idea. I dial 1-855-NYC-COPE.

A man answers. "COPE hotline."

"What are you doing inside on New Year's Eve?" I ask.

He pauses. "Volunteering for the COPE hotline."

"That's nice of you."

"Someone has to."

"What's your name?"

"Bob."

"Bob...?" I say. "I think I love you."

He laughs. "Is there something you'd like to talk about?"

"A lot of things, but I'm dealing with them," I say. "I do want to wish you a happy new year. It's very nice of you to be doing something good tonight."

"Ah, we got a few of us here. We're happy to be here."

"Well, I'm happy you're happy," I say. More people who aren't out depending on drugs and alcohol. And they're actually giving up their party time to do something nice!

"Happy new year, mystery caller," he says.

"Happy new year, Bob."

I hang up.

Now what?

I take my journal and flashlight and climb out onto the fire escape. I don't worry that it hasn't been inspected. I sit on one of the rusty metal stairs. It makes my buttocks cold. There's enough light outside that I don't need the flashlight.

"New year's resolution," I write, "figure out which rules I should stick by. Philosophize."

I need to come up with a better resolution than that.

Suddenly I hear the squeal of a little gear. Someone's screen door is opening. Three fire escapes to my right, the person steps out.

It's Cy, only he's not wearing his hat. He does have suspenders on, and his hair is slick as ever. Man, is he gorgeous. I half expect a high-heeled woman to step out next, and for the two of them to start slow-dancing in the moonlight. But it's just him and one of his music books.

"Hey!" I call.

"Hey!" he yells, noticing me. "I was going to practice here. I figured no one would notice tonight."

Wow, someone at eleven-thirty on New Year's Eve who can talk without hiccuping or slurring. "Have you been out?"

"Not till now," Cy yells. Below us, a fat man in a beret is dancing with a stuffed pig. "This is a little much for me," Cy yells. "I'm from a different decade. Reincarnated." He smiles. His face is so clean shaven. "You know 'Man of La Mancha'?"

"Yes," I say.

He looks at his book, then extends his hand and croons "The Impossible Dream."

I hear sirens go off in the distance.

"See what you did?" I say.

He laughs. "Usually I only break glasses."

I hear something crash.

"You want to come over here?" he asks. "It is New Year's. I mean, I guess normal people don't like to spend it alone. Not that I'm normal."

I have to smile at that. "I know you need to practice your music."

"I practice too much. 4R."

That's an apartment number I won't forget. I crawl back inside, then stare at myself in the mirror. Save for a piece of green-blue confetti in my hair, I look pretty good. A fast beat passes by, obviously from someone's car, and I brush a tiny bit of corn chip from my sweater. I lock the door and run downstairs, outside, then three doors down.

Cy's apartment shouldn't surprise me, but it does, in its taste-fulness. In his kitchen, he's got framed Broadway show posters, a pile of records, a phonograph and a piano keyboard. "I can't believe I'm finally in New York," Cy says. "It feels great."

"It took you a while?" I ask, really fishing for his age.

"Ronald told you, right? I was living down in South Jersey. I shouldn't admit this, but I was in my parents' garage. Which was ridiculous. But I wanted to come to New York on my own terms, as someone who was making a living in the theater, not owing money to my parents or having four roommates. You can't always do that."

"Some people never get to," I say. "You should be proud." His chin is about even with my nose. I want to nuzzle against his shaven face. I don't even worry about whether it's the alcohol. "Did you study theater in college?"

"Yes," he says. "At Mason Gross." He tells me what year, and I put him at twenty-nine or thirty. Eleven years older than me, but Petrov did say I was mature for my age.

He walks through the kitchen. It's expansive, with a clean white floor. "This is the only room in the house with room. Check this out." He drops a 78 on the phonograph. "Was my grandmother's," he says. "That was when I started learning to love this stuff. I was a weird kid."

I can't help but smile at someone so into something that's not alcohol or drugs. He spins around, then stops and holds out his hands for me.

Cy is the most unusual person I've met since moving here, which is a good thing. We dance for a while, slow, and then he sits me on a couch and shows me half a million things. It's as if he's waited ten years to show them to someone. He's got that stack of 78s, an electric piano keyboard, and he's writing a musical. The guy can play any song on the piano you ask for.

I don't detect anything scheming or self-conscious—I get a sense that rather than purposely trying to avoid bad behavior, bad behavior isn't an attraction for him. He makes no excuse for listening to old records or wearing a hat. It's just the way he is. I can't help but be entranced by it.

I don't ask what he got on his SATs. I don't ask if he avoids moral indiscretions or whether he has read Rabelais. Maybe he isn't even real.

"Look," Cy says, and he finds his hat. "I'm wearing this in the revue." He does a little dance. It's haphazard and funny.

"I first saw you in that hat," I say. "You were in the subway muttering to yourself. I thought you were crazy."

"I am," he says, and he steps onto a chair, then onto the coffee table, then onto the kitchen counter. "Did you ever do this when you were a kid, pretend the floor was the ocean, and if you touched it, you'd drown, so you had to see how far you could go without touching the floor?" No wonder he doesn't drink. He doesn't need to.

"I must have," I say. "I know I played runaways-on-a-boat."

"And the bed was the boat?" Cy says. "That worked until you had to walk across the floor to refill your bowl of Cheetos." He jumps down and puts his face next to mine. "You know what it's called when you do that?"

"What?" I ask.

"Cheet-ing."

"Ugh," I say, but of course, I like it.

He kneels in front of me. "I would give you anything if you can tell me a worse joke than that."

The first one that flashes into my head is the Pinocchio one that Douglas P. Winters told me at legal proofreading that night, but I can't do that. I tell him a joke I heard once about an Amish drive-by shooting. He laughs. I had told it to Michael at Barnes & Noble, and he didn't get it.

Cy puts the hat on me. "Looks good," he says.

"It's kind of big on me," I say.

"It's Victor/Victoria." He sits on the couch. "A woman pretending to be a man…"

"Pretending to be a woman, pretending to be a man, pretending to be a woman, pretending to be a man, pretending to be a woman…."

He smiles. "You know it!"

"Well, it's kind of famous."

"You'd be surprised how many people know so little. Did you have musicals in your high school?"

"No. They would hold auditions and start practicing, but they kept falling apart. No one would show up for rehearsals. All the drama people went to the arts high school. They drained all the talent from my school."

"Except for you," he says.

"I'm not talented."

"Yes you are. I can tell."

"Nah."

"Yes." He presses my nose for a second, then lets it go. "What did you do in high school? What were you like?"

"Nerdy and geeky."

"Come on," he says. "You must have been in some after-school activities."

"Math Team, Science Team, College Bowl, Decathlon of Knowledge, Mathletes, Olympics of the Mind, Excellent Exegetists, Harvard Model Congress, Quiz Kids, Varsity Physics, Westinghouse Science Project Semifinals…"

"Nerd nerd nerd," he says.

"Theater geek," I say.

"Nerd nerd."

"Theater geek."

We're in each other's faces.

"Nerd."

"Theater geek."

"That is not the proper term," Cy says. "The proper term at my school was 'stage whore' or 'drama queen.' Also, I was in the band for a while, so I was considered a 'band fag.' Who comes up with these things?"

"I don't know," I say. "You band fag and stage whore."

"I'm only guilty of some of those things," he says, leaning close. He looks even better up close. "And *you* should be everything you are." He puts his right hand in mine, then reaches for the other. "Got a request?" He looks over at the 78s.

"Polka," I say.

"Polka what?" he asks.

"Polka *you.*"

He finds a record. The pile smells musty, but I like it, as it reminds me of my grandparents' place. Cy gingerly drops it onto the record player. After the crackling stops and the music starts, some sonorous notes ring out, long and pretty. We dance from the kitchen through the hall to up on the couch.

He puts his left hand around my waist.

Then he looks at me intently.

A loud bang stops us in our tracks.

"Haaappy new year!" someone shrieks below, and there's screaming, stomping, honking, laughing. I haven't heard this much racket since the Yankees won Game 4.

Cy looks at me again. We're both quiet.

"I was hoping you'd end up here sooner or later," he says.

Then he moves toward my neck. I feel his nose and lips at the same time. He feels warm. "I'll bet you were a great Mathlete."

"Secant squared minus tangent squared equals one," I say.

"Whisper it," Cy says, kissing his way down my shirt.

"Secant squared minus tangent squared equals one."

He rises and again kisses me on the lips. I feel a shiver run from my mouth through my body. "Come with me," he says, and takes my hand.

"What's your name?" I ask him. "What's Cy short for?"

He smiles. "Cyclone. Does that put me ahead of you in the bad joke Olympics? Although you were probably in it in high school."

"They had to get rid of it because all the comedians went to Arts High."

He stops at the door to his room. "What's Carrie short for?"

"Carrie."

"What's your middle name?"

Ooh, he wants to know my middle name. "My name is Carrie Constance Pilby."

"Cute name," he says.

"What's your full name?"

"Cyril George Panatogolous."

"I'll call you Cy."

His room is very dark. The shades are black. Maybe because he's up late at night and sleeps during the day. Hey, he's like me.

He shuts the door until it's pitch-black, and for a second, I'm afraid, but he takes my hands and we start dancing again, slow. It feels like it goes on forever. Cy seems a lot stronger than a half hour ago.

Soon we stop. He kisses me in the dark.

In the end, it turns out that he's much better at everything than Professor What's-His-Name.

About four in the morning, a garbage truck rolls by. I wake up. I'm next to Cy, who's curled like a fetus, asleep, and the sheets are all out of place. I sit up and find that I'm wearing a Godspell T-shirt. How did all of this happen? When will God save the people? Oh, God of mercy, when?

I don't feel bad, but I do feel funny, as this is obviously not standard operating procedure for me.

I stand up. What have I done?

Then, I think of something else.

I've done everything on the list!

Except one thing.

I grope around for my clothes.

"Where you going?" Cy asks into his pillow, reaching around with his left hand.

"I'll be back," I say, and I head downstairs.

There are stragglers stumbling home, but mostly, the only noise is the trucks, churning away the evidence of the night's debauchery. Practically embedded in the street are papers and pieces of foil and stepped-on noisemakers. They're like those gun barrels and pennies and metal objects you see stuck in gravel sometimes. What's the story with that? I head around the corner and see that the coffee shop is open. Even at four o'clock, Milquetoast is inside.

He brightens when he sees me. "Hey, Carrie," he says. He really looks excited. I'm glad. There are four or five tables full of people in there, but no one is uttering a word. They're playing with bits of straw wrappers or staring at each other, obviously hung over. "Hi, Ronald!" I yell.

A guy with spidery hair glares at me.

Ronald smiles.

"It's too bad you have to work on New Year's," I say.

"I don't mind," he says slowly. "It's too noisy out there."

"You know, you're my kind of person. I didn't fully realize that."

He grins and looks at the counter bashfully.

"Well, I was home, and I knew you were here, and I wanted to tell you something. I think you're a great guy, and I really like you. You don't lie about anything. You're true. There aren't many people like that anymore. And I think you should stay that way."

Ronald grins broadly. "I like that, Carrie," he says. "That makes me happy."

"I care about you," I say, and he leans forward, and we hug.

"I like you, too," he says.

"Do you want to get that meal tomorrow?" I ask.

"*Tomorrow* tomorrow," he says, "or tomorrow today?"

"I guess…tomorrow tomorrow," I say.

He grins broadly. "Yeah," he says. "That's good. Yeah, that'd be good."

"Here's my number," I say. I scribble it on a napkin. "Call me tomorrow. *Tomorrow* tomorrow." I hand the number to him.

This time, I don't have that hollow feeling inside. I think he really does like me. He's not faking it.

He looks at me funny as I'm standing there. "You want coffee?"

"No, thanks," I say. "I don't really drink it."

"Hey," he says. "Happy new year."

I smile. "Happy new year." It might be a good year after all.

On the way past my building, I see Bobby peeking out his window in his undershirt, and I wave. Bobby smiles. Pleasantly, not lecherously.

A few buildings down, Cy is sitting on his stoop in a button-down shirt and wrinkled Dockers, circles under his eyes. When he sees me, he stands up and reaches for my hands. That's dedication, to get out of bed at four in the morning to wait for me.

Chapter Twelve

I wake up again at 9:15 a.m., and Cy is sleeping.

Now that the alcohol has worn off, I feel embarrassed. The events of last night seem surreal.

The way the light comes through Cy's drapes feels strange; the way his furniture reflects in his wall mirror feels strange; the way his pile of laundry smells is strange. I don't know how people can routinely wake up in different places. Maybe they get used to it. I don't think I could.

I sit up. Cy's face is bunched up, like he's dreaming hard. It looks cute. I'm going to be late for church.

I can't miss today's sermon. I've faxed Natto a few ideas, and this one's going to be good.

I pull my clothes on quietly. I run home and shower. I'm late to church, and I slip into the back row. There are a lot of people in the pews. Despite the crowd, Natto sees me, smiles and winks. I wonder why it's so crowded on New Year's Day. All these people must feel guilty about something.

I spot someone a few rows up who must feel guilty. It's Matt, and he's sitting beside Shauna. She's got short, blond hair, and looks sweet. She turns to Matt, and I see on her the clothes and face of someone who has never had to fight for male attention, who isn't wearing much makeup and has never even worried about it. She won't ever have to change or adapt unless Matt leaves her. She won't ever have to harden herself or compromise. She's lucky. I suppose.

I hate to say it, but Matt looks quite handsome in his suit. His hair is still wet. Hers isn't. I decide this means they didn't take a shower together. I feel relieved, for some reason. That's stupid. I shouldn't care about him anymore. He's a cheater.

"Situational ethics," Natto says, strutting across the stage. "Are they fair?"

Everyone is listening.

"Can we do something we know is wrong, and make up for it by giving a good excuse, say that, at the time, it wasn't as wrong as it might have been in another situation? Last night was New Year's Eve. How many people in this room did something we are now not proud of?"

Everyone looks around. I slump in my seat so Matt won't see me.

"But it was New Year's, right? You were drunk. So you couldn't help what you did. And this morning, you figure, you can come to church and erase the deed."

No one moves.

"Unlike all of you, most people this morning didn't even get out of bed. I am impressed with this congregation. Truly impressed. But why are you here? To give something, or to *ask* for something?"

He pauses. He knows just when to pause. His silences both

make us think and give us a moment of unease. I'm learning a lot about rhetoric from watching him.

"How many people have actually done something wrong, all the while knowing you were going to ask forgiveness later? How many movies have we seen where someone raises a gun, or a baseball bat, and says, 'Lord, forgive me for what I'm about to do.' Well, if you have to say that, then *don't do it!*"

He straightens.

"Forgiveness is for *honest* mistakes. And yes, we are human. We have needs and feelings that conflict with our conscience, and sometimes we give in. But if we knowingly do something wrong, and we do it anyway, that's reprehensible. If we make a mistake, we can ask forgiveness. But if we willfully hurt some-one, we are doing something a lot worse. You don't get absolved just because you feel like it. Otherwise, we could all just do whatever we wanted, and then run to church each Sunday and atone."

Say it, I think.

"Adultery," Natto says. "Chea-ting."

Chee-ting.

"What are the chances, if you meet a successful man who's been married for thirty years, and he's in his fifties or sixties, what are the chances that his wife's the only one he's ever been with since he met her? It almost seems impossible these days, doesn't it?"

Matt looks stiff.

"So what's wrong with a little cheating? Why is it called cheating? We know our spouse wouldn't like it. We're doing things we shouldn't be. We made a promise no one forced us to make. Maybe we're opening ourselves up to health risks by cheating. Maybe we're spending time or money or affection that should instead go to our spouse, or our kids. You can make excuses. Now, some people will say, hey, at least a little cheating's better than getting divorced."

Shauna looks at Matt, smiling, then back at Natto. I guess she knows he'd never cheat on her. Oh, no.

A thought crosses my mind. I'll bet that Shauna is rabidly against cheating. Most women who are in committed relationships probably are. Why not? It's very easy to be anticheating when you're settled. It's easy to be moral if you have exactly what you want.

"Is that right?" Natto asks. "Cheating to avoid getting divorced? The reason cheating is called cheating is that you're doing something behind someone's back. Something that could hurt someone. By not being honest, you hurt them. In some cases, maybe it hurts a little. In others, maybe a lot."

I think about the movie *Out of Africa,* which was also on the AAFR list. In it, Karen Blixen goes down to Africa to marry a baron, and in part of it, she starts getting sick, and she finds out it's syphilis. She's never been with a man before her husband, so she knows it had to have come from him. And he has to admit that he got it from some woman. The cad.

Natto stops pacing and looks at a guy in a frayed suit. "I'm not here to pass judgment," he says. "I'm not God. Only you can know your own situations. But what about the Golden Rule? You think you can cheat, but you know you'd be upset if your spouse cheated. If you've both agreed to cheat, then you have an open relationship. Which makes me a little queasy…but in many ways, it's more honest than cheating."

I wonder if this is a bad move, sounding like he even remotely advocates this. But it is a good question.

"In cheating, you are doing something to another you would not want done to you."

He wags his finger.

"Do unto others as you would have others do unto you. In

many religions, that is a defining maxim. In Judaism and some of the Eastern religions, it's phrased slightly differently. There, it's, do *not* do to others as you would *not* want done to you. It all boils down to the same thing—treat people with respect. Come up with a code, and don't change your code to fit a certain situation, or a time. And if you do mess up, sure, you are entitled to ask forgiveness. But don't do something you believe deep inside is wrong and then make an excuse."

I see Matt looking at Shauna. He isn't smiling. I'm sure he'll come up with his own rationalization later, so that he can continue to, without guilt, put his power supply in lots of outlets.

Natto winds up. When he's finished, he jumps off the stage and takes a towel from Eppie to wipe his forehead. Eppie's wife is with him today, a short little woman, and for some reason I'm glad that means Eppie's not Natto's lover. Although I guess you still never know.

I see that Shauna and Matt are coming up the aisle. This is my chance to rat Matt out to her.

I consider this for a second. If I do say something, I know it won't be for the right reasons. It won't be to help Shauna. It'll be to satisfy some sick need for revenge. Which makes it half-wrong. Half-wrong because he *is* hurting her, and in some sense, she should know. So telling her might be the right thing for the wrong reason, but I'm not even sure it's totally the right thing—because I don't know that in the end, she'll leave him, or that he'll really change his ways. Maybe she'll be more guarded, which would be a good thing, but it might also be a bad thing. It might only hurt her. Maybe he has to change on his own. I am not really sure what the right thing is to do. It seems like telling her would be right and wrong at the same time.

Is it possible that there *is* no right answer for what I should do? That maybe this actually is a situation where it's not black-and-white?

Wow. Could that be?

I stand there, directly in their line of travel, like I'm toeing the edge of the ocean waiting to get hit by a wave.

When Matt sees me, his eyes look like they're about to jump out of his head.

"Hi, Shauna," I say, shaking her hand.

"Carrie?" she says. Matt's stunned. "This is Matt. Matt, Carrie."

Matt shakes my hand, looking like he's seeing a ghost.

"Shauna and I are going to do great work here," I say.

Matt still doesn't know what to say.

"Are you okay?" I ask him.

"Pre-wedding jitters," Shauna says, smiling. "We're getting married in April."

"That's very exciting," I say.

Matt says, "Hi."

Shauna giggles. "Slow."

"Like the sermon?" I ask him.

"Loved it," he says, without smiling.

"Do you guys go to church a lot?" I ask sweetly.

Shauna smiles and looks at Matt. "We *used* to," she says. "We think we're going to start going back now."

"Well, it's good you got this assignment," I tell Shauna.

"I'm really excited about it," Shauna says.

"I also really like Joe Natto," I say. "He doesn't pretend to have all the answers." I look at Matt. "We have to judge for ourselves."

Natto joins us and meets Matt. Then, Natto, Shauna and I repair to his office and Matt goes off to meet "friends" for lunch. I don't know if the "friends" are another woman, and I don't care. Hopefully Matt will decide what the right thing is to do.

I'm not going to tell Shauna. At least, not for now. Not until I can determine that it's right.

★ ★ ★

Shauna, Joe and I have a pretty good powwow. Shauna is very excited about her first big account. Who can blame her? She's going to be part of something new and potentially huge. She and I are going to *be* the First Prophets' Church. Anyone who sees it will see it through the prism of our marketing. I'll help with the text. We'll lure the greatest number of young, professional New Yorkers of any religious movement in years.

Oh, and I've read Joe's book. He's brilliant. I didn't like him hawking his book at first, but the content actually is more philosophical than spiritual. If this were another era, he'd probably be trying to get his work published as a book of philosophy, but that doesn't count for much these days. As for the "vision" he says he had, he told me it was more a group of conclusions he came to and not something imbued via an apparition. So he's not a loon. At least, not completely. And what's so bad about being a loon?

After Shauna leaves the office, I stay behind. I tell Joe I liked the book, and that I was worried, because generally, when I meet someone I think I might believe in, I have to contend with the fear that the more I learn about them, the more *bad* things I'll learn. It is true.

He laughs. "You are incredibly astute for nineteen," he says. "Sometimes I feel like the younger one, when I'm with you."

"I like making people feel younger," I say.

"I like feeling it," he says. "I haven't felt that way in a while."

I smile.

"I don't want to make you uncomfortable, and you can say no, but it's lunchtime, and I was wondering if you would have lunch with me. Eppie and his wife may join us, if they're still around."

"Sure," I say, selfishly hoping they aren't.

As we leave the church, people keep coming up to Joe, and

he talks to them. He gives a couple some advice and makes them feel happy. I can't believe I'm going to be spending time with someone so charismatic.

At my next meeting with Petrov, I tell him about New Year's, about Cy (although I leave out the more salacious details) and about Natto. I ask him what he did for New Year's. He says he spent it with his daughter and son-in-law and their kids. I'm sure he would have liked to have been with Sheryl. But she was probably with her husband on New Year's.

I guess he can sense what I'm thinking. "She was out..." he starts.

"I know."

He doesn't say anything.

"I don't know what the answer is."

If psychologists don't have the answers, and preachers don't, and I don't, who does?

Certainly not anyone who pretends to. They know least of all.

"Dr. Petrov," I say. "What's Sheryl's middle name?"

He leans back. "It's...Stephanie."

He's got it bad.

Can he help it?

That night, I finally write something extensive in my journal.

I know some things for sure. Others, I do not know. I know that we are responsible for our actions. Sticking to a set of morals doesn't always give us the capacity to sit in judgment of others, but it is important to stand for something. Even if it hurts some-times. There probably are things that are absolutely wrong and absolutely right. We don't always know what they are, and we may make mistakes along the way trying to figure them out. But we have to try.

It's a cop-out to say there are no absolutes. Anyone who says that is proclaiming that that's an absolute, so right away they're wrong. There are things we should follow. Maybe we learn more as we grow about what's important and what's not. But in truth, sometimes we learn less.

And what if sticking by certain beliefs means we will never fit in? What if we can't find one person who agrees with us? I suppose we should check to make sure we're not being too rigid. We also can try to find others who agree with our beliefs, and see if these beliefs stand up to various tests. Beyond that, we have to do our best and try to muddle through.

I put down my pen and pick up my copy of *Mr. Smith Goes to Washington* to return to the video store. I was disappointed in this one. Politicians today cite Jefferson Smith as if he's some great role model, but in truth, all he does is hang around with young boys and beat up reporters. That's just not cool.

When I get outside my apartment, I see Ronald.

"Carrie!" he says.

"Ronald!"

"What kind of food do you want to get tonight?"

"I don't know," I say. "What do you think?"

He shrugs. "Italian? Chinese? Mexican?"

"Not Mexican."

"It's going to be fun," Ronald says.

His unassuming optimism is kind of charming.

"You want to meet me at the coffee shop at six?" I ask.

"Sure. Hey, what movie's that?"

"Oh," I say. I hold it down, at my side. I guess he has forgotten our earlier discussion. "I'm sorry. I just don't like to say what movies I'm renting. It's nothing personal."

"Okay. I'm sorry."

"No, don't be sorry. Lots of people ask me that. I'm just a strange person. It's not your fault."

He grins. "I'm glad you're strange."

"Well, I'll see you soon."

"See you," he says.

I walk to the video store, return the DVD and take out a couple of musicals. My project right now is to make Cy think I'm an expert. I like being the dumb one. It's a nice change. A challenge.

(By the way, I *didn't* have sexual intercourse with him that night, if that was what you were thinking. Yeah, we did a lot of things, but we stopped short of that. See how jaded you are?)

When the cashier hands me the movies, she doesn't offer me a bag, so I have to ask for one. They'll never learn.

When I get home, I write in my journal, "You should never give up on a principle that is logical, sound, important and integral to your constitution, even if the world seems against it." Just as true now as it was three months ago.

I close the journal, pop in the movie, pull on some toasty new socks, and curl up on my bed. The movie's all right, but I fall asleep nevertheless.

ACKNOWLEDGMENTS

I am tremendously grateful to the following people:

Cheryl Pientka, my agent, for her unparalleled wisdom, humor and patience; Farrin Jacobs, for superior editing and wit; Marc Serges, a true literary sage, for insight and persistence; Matthew Greco, Jeff Hauser and Stacie Fine, for their many invaluable suggestions; Dawn Eden, Eileen Budd, Dan Saffer, Jim Damis, Barry Macaluso, Mary Beth Jipping, Julia Hough, Jonathan Blackwell, Michael Malice, Robert Donnell and Jodi Harris, for advice and longtime literary support; Lucha Malato, Dave Unger and Joe Barry, for keeping me clothed and fed; Jennifer Merrick, for artistic ideas; my brother, Todd; my parents; and Al Sullivan.

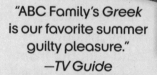

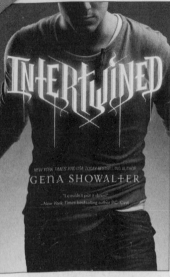
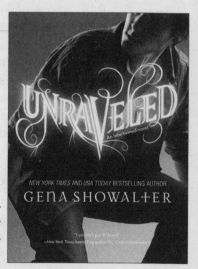